RIDING TRAINS

DANIEL COOK

PAGE PUBLISHING, INC.
Conneaut Lake, PA

First originally published by Page Publishing 2021

ISBN 978-1-6624-0123-7 (pbk)
ISBN 978-1-6624-0124-4 (digital)

Printed in the United States of America

A dysfunctional subculture outside society with different rules to live by.

The adventure of five misunderstood adolescents—Jordan Summers, Shadow Little Hawk, Melissa Wilkens, Jesse Clark, and River Walker—who come from different backgrounds and end up on the same path together, finding their next and safe place to sleep.

A ruthless, deceitful enemy with a purple-tattooed face.

Welcome to the theater of redemption, the thrill of riding the rails, and a world where every Friday night turns into blue Monday.

CHAPTER 1

January 2009

It was a windy day in Tulsa, Oklahoma. The dust in the air made it uncomfortable to breathe and be outside. The visability was questionable. (You wouldn't want to be wearing contacts on a day like this.) However, if you were a traveler and used to living in the elements, this kind of day was a piece of cake compared to spending the night in below-zero temperatures. (Now that was a bitch!)

A man in his midtwenties with a daunting appearance was leaning up against a brick wall in an alley. His purple-tattooed face with jagged scars slashing down each cheek was partially hidden underneath the hood of his soiled black hoodie. The hood was shielding the dust from his eyes. The blowing dust was also a good diversion for anyone that was up to no good.

His name was Bolt, and his evil stare, excentuated by his dark-coal black eyes, vampire-like sharpened teeth, long fingernails, and skinny long face made him very despicable and intimidating for a man who was only five foot eight. (He was almost like someone who was from the undead and should have tried out for a part in the movie *The Hills Have Eyes*.)

He was snearing across the street at a young traveler sitting on the front steps of a two-story apartment building. Bolt despised him because the young punk had crossed him before. Now Bolt had a chance to get some sweet revenge.

Bolt reached into his torn pocket and pulled out his smiley, a common homemade device for street kids. In Bolt's case, it was a padlock tied to the end of a piece of rope. He handed his deadly weapon over to his trusted follower Rat, who did all of Bolt's dirty work.

Besides being a crafty little bastard, Rat was a very good pick-pocket. (He took panhandling to another level.) He could just bump into you and steal your wallet. He got his nickname because of his skinny face that looked like a rodent with a long, pointy nose that twiched, beady eyes, buck teeth, and elephant-size ears. His shadey eyes had the look of a killer.

"Do you remember that prick sitting across the street?" Bolt hissed with a demonic whisper, which was consistent with his dark persona. (Bolt used his illusions from time to time, which he had learned from his freak-show days at the carnival, which we will dive into later.) He had Rat believing that he had magic powers from the dark side.

"Fuck yeah! That was one of the punks that took sides against you."

"He killed my pit bull and stole my fucking girlfriend," Bolt whispered back with hatred in his veins. Bolt wouldn't give hurting another human being anymore thought than ringing a cat's neck. His evil soul would enjoy watching you suffer as he flushed your gold fish down the toilet. He was very abusive to both his dog and his late girlfriend named Shadow. It was odd that he even cared about them with the way he treated them. Bolt was born into a dark shitstorm, which was passed on to him by his daddy, who blistered his back regularly with a belt.

"Well, it's time for some sweet revenge."

"Yeah!" Rat smiled with anticipation.

"I want you to bash his head in. I want to see his blood spilled on the sidewalk."

"I have a better idea." Rat smirked with a wicked smile. He handed Bolt back his smiley and pulled out his knife. "Let's slit his throat. Then you can watch him choke on his own blood."

"I like that idea better." Bolt smiled.

CHAPTER 2

Jordan Summers

JORDAN SUMMERS HAD no idea that his life was in danger. He had just gotten off the phone with his father, Jimmy Summers, and was in great spirits sitting on the steps of his old apartment building for the last time. It was a tearful moment.

Jordan was 24 years old and weighed 165 pounds. He had a rugged, handsome, movie-star face, with a scrawny beard, brown eyes, brown curly hair, a hero's chin, his mom's dark skin, and several tatoos on his arms, knuckles, and back. His only blemish was a paper-thin scar on his left cheek that he got from climbing through a barbwire fence. His body was stout, and his calves were in great shape from all the exercise he got from walking.

He always prefered being by himself. He was very quiet and shy. (You might say he wasn't very good at parties. But not everybody could be like Billy Crystal.) He would be in the back room by himself playing video games while everyone else was gathered around watching the big game.

Jordan was a brooder. The littlest things would send him off to his cave. Not being able to find his favorite shirt would confuse and frustrate him. His behavior could be associated with autism.

But back then when he was a kid, autism wasn't even considered. Attention deficit disorder was the topic of discussion.

Unless it was going out to a movie or to get some fast food, Jordan was content just staying at home. He was born with a great gift. He had an amazing imagination. He could get lost in his room for hours pretending that he was a wizard or a monster. He taught himself how to draw freehand. He was able to sketch detailed drawings of the creatures and characters that he created.

* * *

Jordan had reached the end of his rope. The struggle wasn't worth it anymore. Jordan had been on his own for nine long and sometimes very lonely years. He was fifteen years old when he first ran away. His mother also ran away at that age. However, she didn't put herself through such extremes as her son did. She hitchhiked across the country from Carolina to Los Angeles to be with her mother.

Maybe the biggest curse for Jordan being on the road was how much it drained his ability to trust. Except for a few people, he never really knew what was in a person's heart and what they really wanted from him. If he loved them, they would steal his soul, and if they wanted to kill him, that made him a threat.

He realized the importance of being with his family. He could trust them. Jordan really enjoyed spending time with them over the holidays. Unlike any other visit before, this time it was really hard for him to leave. For the first time in his life, he felt like he belonged there. His family didn't criticize him or pressure him to stay. They just hung out together and had fun playing Monopoly and sharing memories.

The only abnormalty was that his parents, Jimmy and Gina, weren't together anymore. So there wasn't the familiar smell of a fresh-cut Christmas tree in the living room or fresh-baked cookies. Fake trees and catered meals took their place.

* * *

Gina and Jimmy were able to move on with their lives. Gina got remarried to casino owner Sonny Angelini. It was a dream come true. Flirting with him at the school music programs paid off. However, marrying into money wasn't living happily every after. When he was sober, Sonny adored his trophy wife, but on alchohol, he was beligerent and demeaning. So the best course of action for Gina when he was drunk was to stay the fuck away from him.

Jimmy was single after ending a five-year relationship with a woman who was jealous of his ex-wife. The good news was that Jimmy and Gina were able to forgive each other, which made it easier to socialize around the kids.

* * *

After the holidays, Jordan headed back to Tulsa, which wasn't a bad thing. Away from home, it was the most stable his life had ever been. He had a good job as a fry cook at Andy's Grill and had his own apartment that was located across the street from the restaurant. It was small, dark, and a little musty smelling, but it was his. He had money in his pocket every day, and he was starting to feel good about himself. When Jordan was being dropped off at the airport, his dad told him how proud he was of him for having a steady job. Tears came into both of their eyes as they hugged goodbye.

The warm and fuzzy feelings didn't last long when he got back to Tulsa. He had left his cat and apartment in the care of his Native American girlfriend, Shadow Little Hawk. Jordan met Shadow in the early days of his travels. Of course, like a lot of his other choices in life, she was not one of the good ones.

Jordan's mother had given him some money to help pay the rent and buy a few groceries. He found a disaster when he got back to Tulsa. His apartment had been broken into, and his cat was gone. All his video games, TV, and cassette tapes were stolen. Shadow was passed out drunk on the floor, with vomit dried on her chin and clothes.

After a night of hysterics on Shadow's part, with pathetic apologies bounding off the walls, Jordan gave in and forgave her.

Jordan's world got even shittier the next morning, when he found out that he had lost his job. He never understood why he was let go. He had always been dependable and never missed a day of work.

Later that day, Jordan found out from a coworker at the grill that he had been blamed for stealing money out of the till. That really upset him. He was also really disappointed that he never even got a chance to defend himself.

That bothered Jordan a great deal. He took pride in being honest. At the end of the day, all he had was his dignity. And that was taken from him.

Jordan started feeling sorry for himself. He was full of regrets and got really depressed. Shadow's influence didn't help matters. All she was looking for was another chance to get high. All his dreams of success were lost.

"Let's get high, man. Let's get some shit. We can have a good time and forget all about this." Shadow stuck her tongue inside Jordan's mouth.

Jordan caved and listened to Shadow. All the extra cash that he had brought with him was wasted in just a few days on booze and drugs.

* * *

Shadow Little Hawk

Shadow Little Hawk grew up in Stroud, Oklahoma. She had beautiful features. From a distance, she could give Cher a run for her money. She had an alluring, full body with medium-size breasts, long legs, and a stunning round ass that looked exceptional in jeans. A closer view of her exposed the wear and tear of being on the road. She was twenty-eight years old but looked more like she was in her late thirties. She had leather-looking skin from being out in the sun and cold weather. Her teeth were yellowing from not brushing and the hard drugs she was using. Shadow's hair was as dark as the inside of an empty rail car in the middle of the night. She suffered from manic depression and had a mood to match the darkness of her hair. Especially when she was drinking. That was one reason she preferred hard drugs to booze. She wasn't as aggressive and violent. When she was using heroin, she was very laid-back.

She had a younger brother named Charlie. In the early days, her father, George Little Hawk, was well respected within the Sac and Fox Nation. The tribe issued their own vehicle tags and operated several smoke shops and a couple casinos.

But that changed after Shadow's mother was killed in a car accident. Shadow's father never recovered from his wife's tragic death. He started drinking heavily, and eventually his alcoholism did him in, and he became a drunk. Shadow and Charlie were both very young when their mother passed away.

Both kids were pretty much left on their own with no supervision. Shadow was very strong-willed and never listened to any advice from her father. She ended up making bad decisions and getting into trouble. She started off drinking and then added drugs into the mix. She didn't mess around with the light stuff. She went right to meth and then graduated to using heroin.

Early on her father was always there to bail her out. The last straw for him was when she was arrested for selling meth and was sentenced to two years in an Oklahoma prison. After that, her father disowned her. Her brother, Charlie, was the only one who would come and visit at the prison.

Charlie Little Hawk was on the straight and arrow. He did well in school and played high school baseball. He had great control and could throw an eighty-mile-per-hour fastball. There was some interest from several colleges who offered him a scholorship to come play baseball. Charlie opted to stay at the reservation.

After Shadow got out of prison, she found out that she was no longer welcome in her hometown, so she hit the road.

* * *

There was silence, and Jimmy Summers could hear his son weeping on the other end of the phone. He finally broke the silence.

"So, son, do you want to come home?"

"Yeah, Dad. I'm ready to come home."

His dad wasted no time and booked a reservation on Southwest Airlines. Jordan hated flying. Being couped up with a bunch of people in a cramped space with his ears plugged and flying high up in the clouds made him claustrophobic. (When he was younger, he tortured his parents when they flew across the country to visit his mom's relatives. He screamed nonstop when the plane took off until it landed. Several passengers tried their hand at calming him down. But all that did was fuel his stubborn emotions and made him scream louder.)

Jordan preferred the diesel fumes of a Greyhound bus. He felt a lot safer with wheels on the ground. But beggars couldn't be choosers. His dad talked him into flying instead.

Jordan wished he could afford to have a beer on the plane to help smooth out the edges. He also needed cigarettes. Unfortunately he didn't have a pot to piss in. He would have tough it out without his crutches.

In the distance, Jordan could hear the sound of a train horn coming through the canyon. He was amazed how far away the sound could be heard. He had terrific memories riding the rails. He got to see a lot of the country and was proud of the adventures and the chances that he took. It took a lot of guts to hop on a moving train.

Jordan thought about the time he hopped aboard a train outside El Paso. In the boxcar, he was traveling with a family of Hispanics who couldn't speak English. The Sanchez family was very generous and shared their food with Jordan. They were able to get along without speaking. He had fun playing with the two small children that were on the train. Their young, teenage daughter, Juanita, had a crush on Jordan. She was a beautiful girl with dark-brown eyes. They took turns flirting with each other without speaking. They held hands and kissed each other when everyone else was asleep. It was very romantic. Their travels together ended abruptly when they were busted outside Phoenix. The railroad police, or bulls as they were called, arrested Jordan for trespassing and hauled him off to jail. He was later released. He was told to never set foot back in Phoenix again. He was driven to the outside of the city and dropped off.

Jordan wasn't sure what happened to the Sanchez family. He assumed that they were deported back to Mexico. He hoped someday that he would run into them again, especially Juanita. He remembered being hauled off in handcuffs and looking back in the back seat of the police car and seeing her staring back at him with tears in her eyes. That was one of many stories he thought would make a good novel someday.

He couldn't believe it was coming true. He was getting a second chance. He figured in a few minutes that he had better head to the airport. It would take him an hour and half to get there by foot.

Even though Jordan didn't own a suitcase, he was still bringing some baggage back home, including his addiction to alcohol. Jordan was still mentally a young man, with a child in his eyes.

* * *

Across the street, Bolt was waiting for his chance. He was sly and very cautious. He stood back in the shadows watching Jordan's every move.

"So what are you thinking?" Rat asked. He was hungry to get the deed done.

"I wish the fucker would get up and go take a piss in that alley or something," Bolt breathed with an irritating tone. "Look at him. He's just sitting there like a dumb fuck, just spacing out. What the fuck is his problem?"

"I can go take care of it right now. It will just take a second. I will just slide across the street and sneak up behind him. He won't know what hit him."

"Just hold on, dude. You will get your chance," Bolt scoffed. "We have to be careful. We are not out in the middle of some dirt road."

* * *

Jordan was killing time by daydreaming. He wished that he was on a mountaintop somewhere breathing in some of that amazing wilderness air instead of the dust that was swirling around him.

He hoped things would be better this time around. Everything was difficult for him as a kid. In elementary school, he was intimidated by kids his age. None of his classmates would play with him during recess. They would tease him because of his body odor and the stench from wearing the same dirty clothes to school every day. It was like he had the plague or something. The kids made a point to not sit next to him in class. That reputation as the smelly kid haunted him all the way through school.

* * *

Jimmy and Gina Summers' parenting skill on a scale of 1 to 10 was a 2. Young children need a regular routine that they can depend on. Structure gives them security. Jordan never had any of that. He was lucky if he had a bath twice a week. A lot of the time he would be up till midnight, with a babysitter, who was busy talking on the phone to her friends, while his parents were out on the town.

Over time, Jimmy and Gina learned from their mistakes with Jordan's brother and sister. Rose, twelve years old, and an eight-year-old named Tommy were raised differently. Jimmy was making enough money by then so Gina could stay home and take care of the kids. Gina became a very good mother. They had a daily schedule, which included regular meals, taking baths, reading books to her kids, and going to bed at the same time everynight.

* * *

Jimmy and Gina Summers

Jimmy and Gina first met each other at a grocery store. She was working the checkout counter when he was buying a case of beer. At first sight, he fell head over heels for her. Jimmy was a musician who played in a rock band. He was used to having his way around girls.

But Gina was special. She was the most stunning girl that he had every seen.

Gina had a beautiful face with perfect cheekbones and a fabulous smile that lit up the whole room when she laughed. She had brown eyes and matching brown hair with a touch of blond streaks that hung halfway down her back. She was also blessed with a shapely figure.

Every day, Jimmy would stop by the store to see her. No matter how long the lines were at her check stand, Jimmy would just stand there and wait for her to wait on him. For the first time in his life, he was in love with a woman.

Gina always looked forward to seeing Jimmy come through her line. She got a big kick watching him refuse help from the other clerks in the store. She adored his long, curly dirty-blond hair, beard, and shiny blue eyes.

Jimmy told her about his band and invited her to come and watch him play sometime. She told him that she would try. There was a slight roadblock in the way of their romance. Gina was married and pregnant too boot. Oh my!

The day Gina finally told Jimmy the truth about her situation was one of the worst days of his life. They were doing the regular chitchatting as she was sliding his groceries across the label reader.

Jimmy finally got up the nerve to ask her out. "So what are you doing later?"

"I have something I need to tell you," Gina answered nervously.

"Oh no! You have a boyfriend."

"Actually," Gina paused and took a deep breath, "I'm married." She looked down and started bagging up the groceries.

A sharp pain shot through Jimmy's heart.

Then she put the nail in the coffin. "And I am going to have a baby."

Jimmy didn't know what to say.

"I'm really sorry." Gina choked up.

They glanced into each other's eyes and gave each other a tearful exchange. A line of customers started to bunch up behind Jimmy. He kept his cool and congratulated her. He walked out of the store with his groceries and a broken heart.

Jimmy got roaring drunk that night. The next day he woke up lying next to a naked girl that he picked up at a bar. His eyes burned. His head ached from abuse, fatigue, and an upset stomach. Too much rum and Coke will do that to you. He got out of bed and puked in the toilet. He swore that he would never drink again. (Ha-ha, right!)

* * *

A year later, Jimmy ran into Gina at Big Red's Saloon. That was the first time that he had ever seen her not wearing her grocery store uniform. She looked fabulous in her tight jeans. They gave each a big hug. Gina told Jimmy the good news that she was separated and getting a divorce. Her eyes teared up, and she also shared with him the tragic news that she lost the baby.

From then on they were always together. Nothing could keep them apart. One night, Jimmy drove clear across town in a snow-storm with no snow tires to be her. Eventually, they moved into a two-bedroom apartment together. Thank God! Gina had furniture and a television from her marriage. Jimmy didn't have many personal belongings except for his clothes, Fender guitar, amplifier, and a cheap record player.

Their marriage lasted for twelve years. Having three kids put a burden on their relationship. Jimmy worked all the time, and Gina felt lonely. She became tired of having to stay home all the time and only have young childern to have conversation with. She tried to talk to Jimmy about it, but he was too absorbed in his own world. His sales job took its toll on him. He was worn out from smiling and being around people. So when he got home, he just rocked in his rocking chair with one of his kids on his lap watching *Beauty and the Beast* on the VCR for the hundreth time. Gina needed to feel appreciated and have someone to talk to.

The romance in their life disappeared. Their sex life became ordinary. The occasional boquet of roses was a nice attempt but didn't satisfy her need.

Gina started going out to the bars with old girlfriends of hers when Jimmy got home from work. She had no problem finding other men. There was always a guy around to buy her a beer or put a quarter in the jukebox. Most nights she would come strolling home when the magnificent orange mass of the sun had just risen above the horizon.

Jimmy knew his wife was out being unfaithful. It was tearing him apart. He knew that he should have listened to her pleas when she tried to talk to him. But it was too late. He had lost his mojo. He gained a lot of weight and lost his confidence. He hated looking in the mirror and seeing his double chin. And the most painful thing was that Gina wasn't attracted to him anymore.

Jealousy has the power to make people do strange things. Jimmy was relentless, searching for clues to prove Gina was being unfaithful. It was almost like he enjoyed the pain of torturing himself. When she left the house to run errands, he would go through the closets and her belongings. One night she was careless, when she came home drunk and fell asleep. Jimmy went through her purse and found a pager. He went ballistic after he heard the naughty message saying how much she enjoyed having her friend's cock inside her. He stormed upstairs, woke her up, and threw the pager at her. The loud screaming woke the kids up. The two younger ones started crying. Jordan didn't say a word. He had a stunned look on his face.

After that night, they separated and divorced.

* * *

Jordan continued to struggle with school and was not able to keep up with the rest of the class. He was placed in special ed. That further demoralized him and made him even more inadequite and more withdrawn. Things didn't get any better, when Jordan got into high school. He developed pimples and sank even deeper into his dark hole of low self-esteem.

But not everything was lost. Jordan did have some great qualities. He had a great love and a special connection with animals, especially cats, who were quiet and mysterious like he was. Deep down inside they understood and trusted him. It was psychic to watch him interact with them. He had what his dad called fish bowl savvy. He knew how to take care of them and tend to their needs.

Actually, Jordan was very intelligent. He was facinated with history and loved to read. He was just a slow learner in school.

Jordan also had a kind heart. He would give you the shirt off his back if you needed it. A matter a fact, that was how he met Tucker, who was a spoiled little rich kid with a Mohawk, who didn't fit in with the rest of society either. Jordan was standing in line at the school lunch counter wating to pay the cashier. He noticed Tucker sitting by himself in the corner with no food on the table. He walked over with a tray of food and sat down at Tucker's table.

Tucker was more outgoing and started the conversation. "Hey, dude."

"Hey. I like your haircut," Jordan answered back.

"Cool. Most people are freaked out about it."

Jordan laughed. "Yeah. My parents would have a heart attack if I got a Mohawk."

"My name's Tucker."

"I'm Jordan. Nice to meet you. Are you hungry?" He could see Tucker foaming at the mouth, staring at his french fries.

"Can I say that I'm starving." They both cracked up. "My self-centered parents left town and forgot to give me lunch money."

Jordan shared his french fries and gave him half of his tuna sandwich. The way Tucker stuffed the french fries in his mouth made it seem like he hadn't eaten in days.

Jordan told him about his parents' divorce and how humiliating it was for him at Huffacker Elementary School to not have lunch money. Pretty much every day, he was a nervous wreck sitting at his desk waiting for the lunch bell to ring and then having to squirm in line as he inched closer and closer to face once again Ethel, the cashier. A little sympathy for him would have been nice. Instead, Ethel, who was an older, discontended woman, who needed to retire, with a mole on her nose, would roll her eyes and give him an unforgiving, disapproving scowl that made him feel like he was white trash. She would then embarrass him in front of everyone in the cafeteria by bellowing back to the kitchen sarcastically, "Hey, Jordan Summers doesn't have his lunch money again!"

Ethel would then make him stand next to her and wait for a peanut butter sandwich that was given to all the students who didn't have any lunch money. There were a few other students at the school that Ethel made a mockery of. She wouldn't dare mess around with the majority of the kids because they came from upper-crest families in Reno. The old bag finally got her karma when she harrassed one of the school board's kids and was fired.

* * *

Gina tried her best to fit in at the school with the muckety-mucks and the good old boys from the rich part of town. Jimmy was not that concerned about fitting in. The wives were jealous of Gina's beauty and despised their husbands for drooling all over her when she walked into the room at school functions. One of those men was Sonny Angelini, the owner of the Silver Queen Hotel and Casino. He always made a point to flirt with her.

As far as the wives were concerned, the Summers family was not purebred and didn't belong in their circle. Old Reno was run by old Italian blood that owned the land and passed it on to their families. The women were stuck-up bitches that thought their shit didn't stink. It was very hard for outsiders to be accepted, especially the pretty ones like Gina Summers. She wasn't like Midwestern girls, who were fifteen pounds overweight. She was born with the stunning beauty of the South.

* * *

After that day in the lunch room, Jordan and Tucker were inseparable. Jordan was no longer on an island by himself. He had a friend. They forged a close bond together. Tucker was not the best influence. He introduced Jordan to cigarettes, marijuana, alchohol, tatoos, and other kids like him, who were unable to engage with the outside world. The group hung out across the street from the school at Smokers' Row before class.

For the first time in his life, Jordan felt better about himself. He was hanging around a group of kids who didn't judge him and accepted him with all his faults. Even his inflicted stink foot was not a problem. He could spend the night at one of his friends and not be afraid to take his shoes off. The stench from his feet could fill a room in seconds and in some cases could cause dry heaves for some people. He joked that his stink foot could be an interigation tool for the CIA.

His friends got used to the smell, primarily because they all had foul body odor, too, so smelling wasn't a problem for them. It was like living back in the Wild Wild West, where bathing was not an everyday occurence, and that was primarily due to not having indoor plumbing. (In today's world, hygiene is the first thing to go when society breaks down. And these kids were certainly living outside the boundaries of a functional community.)

* * *

At home, Jordan was allowed to come and go as he wanted. His parents were too busy with their own personal issues and raising two other kids.

Jordan's schoolwork continued to suffer, and he started skipping class. The only reason he went to school was because he could be with his friends and all the cigarette butts on the ground at Smokers' Row. More and more, he was fitting to be the model of a highschool dropout.

CHAPTER 3

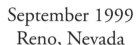

September 1999
Reno, Nevada

It was a beautiful fall day. The sun was shining with blue skies. Jordan Summers, who just turned fifteen, his younger sister, Rose and little brother, Tommy, were hanging out at Virginia Lake. They were sitting at a picnic table eating fast food while their dad was taking a walk around the lake.

Rose, eleven years old, was the spitting image of her mother except for the stunning blue eyes that she got from her father. Rose was the athelete of the family. She had terrific hand-and-eye cordination. Softball was her favorite game. She had a good arm and could hit the ball. Jimmy and Gina loved to watch her play. Unlike her older brother, she enjoyed going to school and was very popular with both the teachers and classmates.

Tommy, who was eight years old, had his dad's light skin and curly brown hair. He was a well-behaved little boy with good manners. Jimmy was very proud of him and loved to show Tommy off when he was out visiting friends or doing errands. He was the perfect eight-year-old.

It was always a special treat for the kids to go to the park, have fast food, and watch the ducks, Canadaian geese, and seagulls battle it out for the bread crumbs.

Virginia Lake was one of the oldest parks in the city. The path that circled the lake was a mile long. The lake had a very European feel to it, with the older Victorian-style homes that overlooked the neighborhood. There were fountains in the middle of the lake squirting water into the air. The lake was surrounded by large oak trees that provided wonderful shade and lots of benches to sit on and take in the quaint beauty of the park. There was a sidewalk that circled the lake that was perfect for running or taking a walk. (You just had to avoid all the goose poop.) Across the street on the east side of the lake was a fenced pasture where several horses ran free and greeted visitors who came over to pet them and give them treats. On the north side of the lake, there was a large picnic area with grass, picnic tables, and a playground. There was a street that ran through the park and separated the picnic area from the lake. The Canadian geese would bring traffic to a halt as they took their sweet time walking back and forth across the street.

Today was one of those special days. Jimmy Summers just got paid and had a little extra cash in his pocket. He treated the kids to McDonald's. Money was tight after the divorce. Usually after paying child support and alimony, there wasn't much left in Jimmy's bank account.

The financial condition wasn't that much better over at their mom's house. Gina had no job and was living off child support. She had gotten the house in the divorce settlement and was a month behind on the mortgage payments. The kids ate a lot of mac and cheese when they stayed with their father in his small two-bedroom apartment. They had better meals at their mom's house because she was a good cook.

Jordan was trying to justify the thoughts that were racing through his mind. "If I were gone," he thought, "then Rose and Tommy would get McDonald's more often. One less mouth to feed."

Of all the kids, Jordan was having the most difficulty adjusting to the new change in their lives. He was already messed up, and the divorce just added to his mental state. As he was sitting there, he noticed an older couple gawking at his new Mohawk haircut. Initially, he didn't like all the attention and wished that he hadn't let Tucker talk him into getting one, but he got used to it and actually got a big kick out of watching people's reactions. Except for his dad, who went ballistic when he first saw Jordan's hair and demanded that he shave it off. After a while, Jimmy got used to it and backed down. However, it did embarrass him to be seen with Jordan out in public. His mom just shook her head and hoped that he would out grow it. For Jordan, it became his sense of idenity.

"Listen up! I've got a secret that I want to share with you." Jordan took a huge bite of his Big Mac. He chewed it and swallowed it quickly. He was a fast eater. He looked around to make sure that his dad was still taking his walk. "I'm going on a big adventure, and I'm leaving soon."

Rose was old enough to realize how disturbed Jordan was. Tommy was too young to understand what was really going on. Her heart was hurting inside, and she remained quiet and listened to what her brother had to say. Tommy was busy trying to finish his meal so he could get back on the swing.

"Rose, I need you to swear that you won't say a thing to Mom or Dad until I leave. Then you can tell them." Jordan paused for a minute. He knew his sister very well and could see the stress in her face. "Pinky swear?"

"I swear," Rose answered. "But I better not get in trouble over this, 'cuz I'll be really upset."

Tommy swore too, with a mouth full of french fries. But it was out of sight, out of mind for him. Tommy spilled some ketchup on his shirt.

"Dad's not going to be happy," Jordan said.

"Will he throw a fit like he did over your haircut?" Rose smarted off.

"You sound like Mom," Jordan joked. Now that she was getting older, he like being able to banter back and forth with her. He loved her wit.

Jordan grabbed a napkin out of a paper bag and tried to clean up the ketchup. He just smeared it even more. He went back to eating his burger. Jordan chose to the keep the details to himself, just in case Rose chickened out or if Tommy accidently blurted it out.

The plan was pretty much laid out. Jordan was leaving with his friend Tucker, who set up a ride with a friend, who would drive them to Truckee. From there they would be on their own and have to hitchhike up I-80 to Berkley. Tucker liked Berkley because he heard that the people there were hippies from the sixties and really cool to be around. Tucker convinced Jordan that California was their destination.

Deep down inside Jordan was scared to death. It was a big decision to runaway and be on his own. He loved his parents, but he felt like he was a burden to them. Jordan knew Tucker felt the same way about his family. It was Tucker who came up with the idea. At first, Jordan couldn't get his mind around it. Whew! It was tormenting for him to think about how he would get food, and where would he sleep? Each day it got easier for him. The idea of having no school, no one to answer to, and no more disappointed parents became more and more appealing to him. He had become one of the many cool, detached youths that were wandering about in a world that wasn't so perfect anymore. (Guess it never was.)

CHAPTER 4

THE DAY THAT would change Jordan's life had arrived. It was dark and cold with rain and possibly snow forcasted up in the mountains. (Not a good time to be traveling over I-80.) He hoped that he wouldn't be freezing his nuts off.

Jordan stuffed his backpack with as many T-shirts, sweatshirts, socks, and underwear as he could. He was able to fit one pair of extra jeans into the bag. Other than that, he had a camouflaged army jacket and the boots that he was wearing.

Earlier in the day, he hid the backpack outside the sliding glass door behind a bush that was located next to his dad's apartment patio. He walked into the living room and told his dad that he was going out for the night and that he would see him later. He asked his dad if he had a few bucks that he could have. Jimmy gave him a twenty-dollar bill.

He walked out the door and sneaked around to the back patio. He slipped his backpack on and headed out. He was emotionally upset as he looked back at the apartment for the last time. It would be a long time before he would see his family again.

Jordan was glad that he never told Rose when he was actually pulling the trigger and taking off. He was relieved though that he told Tommy and her what he was up to. That way, after he was gone, Rose could fill his parents in on what happened and they would at least be relieved that he wasn't killed. He felt guilty inside. He was sad for not being able to tell his parents the truth. But he knew that it had to be done that way.

CHAPTER 5

THE TRANSPORTATION THAT Tucker had arranged was a no-show. That frustrated Jordan. He never handled change and surprises very well. It brought out the dark side in him. He had a quick temper when things got stressful. Internally he wanted to lash out, but there weren't any structures close to him to kick or punch. Back when he was a toddler, he would bang his head on the floor when he got angry.

"I fucking hate this shit," Jordan blurted out.

Tucker could see the anger in Jordan's red face. It started to rain.

"Dude! Don't worry. It's all part of the dream. You and I are going to have to get used this kind of crap," Tucker explained. "The question now is, what do we do next?"

Neither one of them had ever tried to hitchhike before.

Tucker recommended that they take a bus to Sparks and walk to the Cowpoke Truck Stop. There they could try to catch a ride with one of the truckers.

Jordan was not thrilled with the idea but went along with it. The temperature had dropped a few degrees, and the rain continued to pour. The boys could see their breath as they headed toward the closest bus stop. Living outside with no shelter was something that Jordan would have to get used to. His army coat was not rainproof. It was hard to stay warm. Tucker was wearing a ski jacket. He was not under a baptism of fire like Jordan was.

"Dude! Do you still want to go through with this?" Tucker asked.

"Why?"

"Well, I am just curious. I mean, uh, you are losing sleep over this little chicken shit thing that happened to us. You know, this is not a cakewalk." Tucker was putting his sales pitch on Jordan and trying to be tough at the same time. "Talk is talk. Walking the walk takes a lot of guts."

"I gotcha, dude. Well, as I see it, the way things are going, my whole life is shit anyway. I ain't going back to that. How about you?"

"Cool. Me neither, bro." Tucker smiled and put his arm around Jordan. "This is going to be a great ride."

The buses were running slow. It took an hour to catch a bus and to get to east McCarran Boulevard in Sparks. All the bus stops were irritating Jordan.

When they arrived at the Cowpoke, the place was pretty quiet. There were only two rigs in the parking lot. One of the semi trucks had the company logo Wilson Freight on the side of trailer and painted on the doors of the cab. The other truck had a trailer attached to it that was transporting automobiles.

They weren't welcomed with open arms when they walked into the place. Two security guards glared suspiciously at the two boys and immediately approached them.

"Can we help you with something?" an older, heavyset guard with a beer belly as big as a six-pound turkey asked sarcastically. The other guard was in much better shape and was obviously the one who did the heavy lifting, if it was needed. He had a cocky look on his face and had his arms crossed.

"We would like to get something to eat. Is that okay?"

"No! It is not okay. We don't like your type in here. So if I were you two, I would turn around and get your Mohawk, freaky asses out of here."

CHAPTER 6

River Walker

RIVER WALKER, SIXTEEN years old, was alone in the guest bedroom of her neighbor's house. Her mother, Joyce, had just passed away from cancer. She was left all alone with a strange and empty feeling.

She missed her mom. She was her guiding light. But at the same time it was a relief to know that her mom was set free from the agony. Cancer is a very brutal and suffering way to die. It was very painful for River to watch her mom slowly lose the fight. Her mother tried her best to hide the misery of the toxic chemotherapy treatments. However, how hard she tried, she couldn't hide the vomiting, hair loss, and her deteriating body that was melting off her bones.

River's gothic appearance was troubling for most people to get used to. She was Halloweeen 24-7 with heavy white makeup, thick black eyelashes and eye shadow that circled her eyelids, and lipstick. She wore short black hair with white streaks. Despite all the makeup, she had a very pretty face, which made up for her chunky body and big butt. She had a few tattoos strategically placed on her lower back, arms, and legs. She had four piercings on each ear, a piercing on her right nostril, a belly button ring, and a tongue ring to complement the colorful tattoos strategically placed on her body, including a green-and-yellow peace sign on her left arm, a black heart just above her pubic hair, a musical chart with a clef and notes on her lower back, just above her crack, and a coiled green snake with red eyes on her left thigh.

Her wardrobe consisted of all-black attire, including long dresses, jeans, blouses, and long boots. When she was really decked out in her Adams Family costume, she wore spiked leather bracelets on each wrist and a black cape. She was a master with the makeup brush. She could draw different patterns on her face. Her favorite design was to paint three small tears under each eye lid.

* * *

River was always there for her mother. She went to every one of her mom's treatments, from the blood transfusions to the emergency trips to the hospital. She made special trips to the Dairy Queen to bring her mom special treats. Her mom had a sugar tooth and loved Strawberry milkshakes.

She appreciated how nice the Wilkens family was to take her in and let her have a place to stay. The Wilkens, Jeff and Mary, were a respected family in the Mormon community. They had a daughter named Melissa, who was the same age as River.

It was Mary Wilkens's idea to have River move in with them after her mother died. Jeff Wilkens was not pleased but agreed to let her stay at their house until other arrangements could be made.

Mary first met Joyce Walker at a parents' night at the school. They became good friends. When she got sick, Mary would drive River and Joyce to the doctor's office and do the grocery shopping for them.

River didn't quite get the relationship between and Jeff and Mary. They were quite the opposites. Mary was not only a beautiful woman on the outside but also very kind and loving with a big heart. Jeff was all business and very secretive. River guessed that was why he was a successful financial consultant. Whenever she walked into the room, he would stop talking. She assumed that she was the topic of discussion. He also spent a lot of time behind closed doors on his computer in an extra room that was converted into an office.

There was not much affection between Jeff and Mary. They slept in two separate single beds in their bedroom. It reminded River of the *Dick Van Dyke Show*. Her mom loved watching that show on the TV Land channel. River guessed that there weren't a lot of Barry White records being played on the stereo back when they were courting. River did notice that there was more tenderness between Jeff and his daughter, Melissa.

* * *

River got up from her bed, grabbed a Camel Light, and walked outside to have a smoke. She was having one of those missing-her-mom moments. How ironic, she thought. Here she was outside the Wilkens' home dragging on a cigarette. She agreed that wasn't the smartest thing to be doing with cancer in her family blood. She promised her mom that she would stop smoking.

She had some choices to make. She had one more year of high school to go. One option was that she could move back to Pennsylvania, where her mother's brother lived. She could also try to contact her father, whom she hadn't talked to since she was eight years old.

River still considered Albuquerque, New Mexico, to be her home. Her mother never judged or criticized River for who she was. She believed that River would see the light and grow up some day. Her mother knew that buried underneath all her daughter's radical, gothic costumes was a good person.

She was starting to feel like she was becoming a bother to the Wilkens family, especially Jeff Wilkens. Having her in the house seemed to cramp his style. He avoided her as much as he could. Jeff's persona had a very distinguished look that portrayed strong religious and moral values. He liked to dress up in long-sleeve shirts and slacks. He was a tall, thin man in his late forties. He wore Buddy Holly-style dark glasses with short hair and had a long nose and piercing green eyes.

Jeff would never look you straight in the eye when he was addressing you. That raised a red flag for River. Her keen sense knew there was more to him than meets the eye and that made him nervous. He made it very clear that he didn't approve of River's smoking habit and the way she dressed. He was concerned that some of River's behavior might rub off on his daughter, Melissa.

* * *

River was very intelligent and could think fast on her feet. She was equiped with a sharp wit that came in handy anytime she was being bullied or teased.

The preppy Mormon clique found out the hard way. They were a group of girls that ran the school. No one dared to stand up to them. Sally Martin, the ringleader of the group, could make life miserable for you if she didn't like you. She despised the way River dressed and made her the butt of her jokes. Every day Sally would always have something demeaning to say about River.

Normally, River would ignore her or just flip her off. But the day before, she had just gotten the news that her mother's cancer was spreading. River was angry and distraught. That day in the cafeteria, Sally's whiny voice pushed River over the edge. The girls were giggling and pointing at River after Sally made a joke about her big butt.

In front of everyone, River stood up, grabbed her tray of food, and tossed it at the girls. The majority of the ketchup and french fries splattered on Sally. River screamed at them and called them a bunch of hypocrites. She pointed out that they weren't the Goody Two-Shoes that they pretended to be and that the whole school knew that they were sucking the football players' cocks behind the bleachers. She then stormed off with a huge smile on her face. The kids in the cafeteria gave her a standing ovation. No one had ever stood up to the Sally Martin before.

The spoiled brats then marched down to the principals office and told Principal Herman, what she did. Because he was Mormon, he took sides with them. River was suspended from school for two days. But it was worth it. The girls left her alone after that. Her stinging rage had put the fear of God into them.

* * *

River's favorite class was theater. Her teacher, Mr. Dantley, took an interest in her and inspired her to get involved with the drama club. She helped build the sets for the school plays. She was very good with a hammer and had the skill and imagination to build several different set designs. Mr. Dantley spent a lot of time with her and complimented her on her work. Like most theater people, he was a bit odd. He was tall and thin and dressed like a beatnik with long shaggy hair and a scruffy goatee. He liked to wear checkered sweaters with a corduroy sport coat and jeans.

Mr. Dantley was a very touchy and feely man. He was always hugging River and rubbing her neck. She enjoyed the attention. She had never had a man treat her like that before. Over time, she developed a crush on him. She could hardly wait to see him every day. He was always glad to see her too. One day he suggested that she come over to his house after school and practice reading a part for a role that he thought she would be perfect for. She was excited for the opportunity to be an actress. She agreed to come over around 8:00 p.m. As she was leaning against a fence post looking up at the stars, River started thinking about Mr. Dantley and how he deceived her. She thought about that night when she went over to his house expecting to practice for a part in a play. The evening started off innocently enough with them sitting on a couch. Mr. Dantley suggested that they have a glass of wine to take the edge off. River had never had any alcohol before. A couple of glasses later, and she was in Mr. Dantely's bedroom. He told her afterward to not worry about things and that she had the part in the play. He also made her promise to keep their affair a secret. She kept her end of the bargain, but Mr. Dantley didn't follow through on his.

* * *

River was growing restless. She would be turning seventeen in December. She did have another option to consider. She had her own car, an old Honda Accord, a very reliable car, that her mom had bought her. She always wanted to travel and see the country.

River took another puff before putting out the cigarette on the rail of the front porch. She had learned the hard way about trusting men. That was something that was never discussed with her mom.

It still bothered her that she never got the part and Mr. Dantley pretended that nothing had ever happened. He gave her the cold shoulder and moved on to another student. After that, she quit the drama club. It was too awkward being around Mr. Dantley. River felt for the first time what it was like to have a broken heart. She was angry and thought about going to the authorities. But she didn't think that they would take her seriously because Mr. Dantley was so adored and admired at the school.

So here she was wondering what to do next with her life. She had a meeting with her school adviser later in the day to talk about her future. She wasn't so sure that she would hang in there and graduate from high school. She knew that her mother hoped that she would stay in school. That was what kept her going to class. Her world was turned upside down.

Deep inside her, River had a feeling that everything that was happening to her was meant to be and that there was something out there waiting for her.

CHAPTER 7

JORDAN AND TUCKER were pissed off over how they were treated at the Cowpoke. They both knew that this wouldn't be the last time they would have to deal with people who didn't approve of them.

It was still raining. They walked over to the bus stop across the street because it had a waiting area with a roof that sheltered them from the rain. They both lit up another cigarette. It seemed like forever before any of the truckers came outside.

About a half an hour later, two men came outside and walked toward the two trucks. One of them was a huge guy who had a scruffy beard with long hair. The other one was a skinny guy who was wearing a green John Deere hat and a Minnesota Vikings sweatshirt. They seemed to be in good spirits, making jokes and laughing. The man with the John Deere hat looked over at Jordan and Tucker.

Jordan could feel the negative vibe coming from the truckers. This was not a good situation for him. He was not good with conflicts. It was difficult for him to confront anyone if there was a problem. He knew that hitchhiking would be a challenge for him because he didn't like to bother people.

Jordan was lucky that Tucker was the complete opposite of him. He had no problem approaching someone and asking for a favor or to borrow money.

"Come on, dude. Let's go talk to them."

As they got closer, the one with the John Deere cap spoke first. "So you boys are looking to hitch a ride?"

"Yes, sir," Tucker replied with his well-mannered Eddie Haskell pitch.

"Well, here is the deal, boys. My friend Tod here doesn't like to pick up hitchers. He had a bad experience. I, on the other hand, don't like to have more than one person ride with me at a time."

Jordan was disappointed to here that. Tucker saw his chance.

"Well, sir, I completely understand how things are."

"I don't know where you boys are going. I'm heading east."

Tucker looked at Jordan and then answered back, "If you could take my friend Jordan to Winnemucca, I'll try to catch a ride with someone else, and then him and I can hook up later."

"Dude, I don't know if that's a good idea to split up."

It's just a little detour. It's cool. It won't take me long to hitch a ride."

Jordan was still apprehensive about taking off without Tucker.

"Well, have you boys made up your mind?" the trucker with the John Deere hat asked. "I am heading out. Hey, I will see you on the road, Tod."

"All right, Red. You behave yourself and stay out of those whorehouses in Winnemucca."

"Go ahead, Jordan."

The two boys clutched hands. "Peace, brother."

"I will see you in Winnemucca," Tucker said.

Jordan followed Red and got in his semi. He was really nervous. This was a big step for him. He was leaving on his own. It would have been much easier to have Tucker with him. And the other screwy thing was that he was heading in opposite directions of California.

The truck pulled out and headed down the road. Jordan looked in the mirror and could see Tucker waving goodbye.

CHAPTER 8

⸎

Melissa Wilkens

MELISSA WILKENS WAS a beautiful young teenage girl who was hiding a big secret. She had a beautiful face, just like her mother, with perfect features, blond hair, and a slim body. Melissa was very popular at school and very innocent, or so it seemed!

Before River moved in, Melissa never paid much attention to her. She noticed her in the hallway and was intrigued by her outfits. Melissa was a lot like her mother and never judged anyone. Sally Martin tried many times to get Melissa to become part of her group, but she chose not to. She had no problem with Sally or the other girls. They attended the same church, and from time to time, she would go to the mall or movies with them. Melissa preferred to be independent.

Sally took it personally. She was jealous of Melissa's beautiful face. Sally had a huge nose, which was not flattering to look at. She tried to start a rumor about Melissa being gay because she never dated any boys. Sally's malicious scheme backfired on her when the kids in the school supported Melissa.

It was the beginning of Sally's downfall. River's famous cafeteria tantrum put the nail in Sally's coffin. No one feared her after that, and she became the brunt of the jokes. The boys started calling her

Butter Face because she was great from the neck down. ("But her face! Whoa, Nellie!")

Melissa got used to having River around the house. She liked her sense of humor and respected her free spirit. She enjoyed their conversations and listening to River's CD collection. She had never listened to the Clash or the Cure before. It was adventurous and exciting for her. She started to really trust River and considered her to be a good friend.

CHAPTER 9

JORDAN'S FIRST HITCHHIKING experience was not as difficult as he was expecting it to be. Red was a friendly guy who liked to talk a lot. He spent most of the time talking about sports. He asked Jordan whom his favorite NFL team was. Jordan played along and told him he was a Raiders fan. Red wanted to know some of his favorite players. Jordan threw out the name John Madden. He knew his name because of the video game. He told Red that he used to watch the Raiders play with his dad on TV. Red went on and on about what a great coach Madden was.

"So how old are you, boy?" Red asked.

Jordan told a lie and said he was seventeen.

"Well, good! Then you know how to drive?"

Jordan bullshited him again and told him yes.

"So I am sure that you noticed the cars that I am transporting on the back of my rig."

"Sure."

"Well, here's the deal. These cars belong to a dealership in Winnemucca. I will pay you fifty bucks if you help me drop them off."

"Holy shit!" Jordan thought to himself. He had never driven a car before in his life. "Okay. What do I have to do?"

"It's a piece of cake. I will unload them off the rack, and then you just have to drive them across the street into the parking lot."

"Fuck me!" Jordan said underneath his breath to himself. He was a nervous wreck. What the hell had he gotten himself into? He took a deep breath. "Seems easy enough."

Jordan needed the extra cash, but he wasn't sure that he could pull it off. He was scared shitless to think what would happen if he smashed one of the cars into the dealership. He thought about telling Red the truth. That would at least relieve the anxiety that he was feeling. He saw lights up ahead.

"Well, we are coming up on Lovelock."

Jordan was relieved that they weren't in Winnemucca yet.

"Do you have to piss?" Red asked.

"No, I am okay."

Red shook his head as his rig flew by the exit signs.

"I feel sorry for this little town. Ever since the interstate bypassed it, not many people stop by there anymore. It's kinda like the Bates Motel," Red joked. "They used to have a great little whorehouse in town across the tracks. I used to love to stop by there."

Talking about whorehouses made Jordan uncomfortable. He was embarrassed talking about sex with adults. He was still in the wanking offstage.

"It used to cost twenty bucks back then," Red laughed. "They still have a classic courthouse there in the middle of town that is worth seeing. Well, anyway, the next town up the road is Winnemucca. You can take a nap if you want. I will wake you up when we get close."

"Okay." Jordan was pretty sure that he wouldn't be able to fall asleep, but he would give it a try anyway. Surprisingly, he drifted off to sleep.

An hour passed by. Red reached over and nudged Jordan.

"We are almost there, son. Time to clean the cobwebs out of your head. This won't take very long."

The semi pulled into town. There was not a whole lot of things going on in Winnemucca at three in the morning. The streets were deserted. The dealership was located in the middle of town. Red parked the rig across the street in an empty lot. He put his gloves on and stepped out side.

"This will take me a few minutes to unhook the cars and lower them down. Come on, I will show you how easy it is." Red pulled out a key ring full of keys from his glove compartment.

A few minutes later, Red lowered the first car off the trailer. He slapped Jordan on the back and handed him a key for the car.

"Have fun! Be careful driving across the street. We don't need any accidents."

Jordan smiled. He was glad that there weren't any cars driving up and down the street.

"I will get the rest of these unloaded," Red continued. "Just pull in and park the cars to the right of the building there.

The adrenaline was flowing inside Jordan. Even though it was scary, it was kind of exciting at the same time. Jordan stuck the key in the ignition and twisted it to the right. A grinding sound came out of the ignition. Red came over to the car. Jordan rolled down the window.

"I guess you haven't driven in a while, huh?" Red laughed. "Just twist it till it starts."

Jordan tried again, and the car started right up. Red turned around and went back to finish unloading the cars. Jordan looked over at the transmission stick and put it in gear. He stepped on the gas pedal, and the car moved backward. He stomped on the brakes, and the car abruptly stopped.

Red peaked around the corner. "You okay?"

"Yeah, I am fine. You're right, I haven't done this in a while."

It all worked out. Jordan got through the rough spots and figured it all out. By the time it was over, he was having a blast driving the cars. It was a great experience for him. He had overcome the obstacles and taught himself how to drive. He was proud of himself. He thought this running-away business wasn't that bad after all.

An hour later, Red dropped Jordan off at Jenny's Diner at the end of town. It was four in the morning. Jordan thanked Red for the ride. Red wished Jordan good luck and advised him to reconsider his decision to run away.

"Life living under a bridge seems a bit rough to me." Red's final words gave Jordan something to think about.

As Red's semi pulled away, Jordan realized that he was all by himself for the first time. He wondered how long it would take Tucker to hitch a ride and join him in Winnemucca. Jordan was able to nod off and get some rest, but he was starting to get really tired. He was also concerned about how and where he would meet up with Tucker. He was lucky that Winnemucca was a small town. He knew that he should stay close to the interstate where he was dropped off and keep close watch for all the cars that drove by.

Besides being tired, Jordan was starving. He was glad that he had an extra fifty bucks to live off. He decided to go into the diner and get some food.

Jordan took a seat at the counter. He was the only person in the restaurant besides a young, plump waitress with teased blond hair and a pretty face with heavy makeup. He ordered eggs and bacon. The waitress was doing double duty. She was also the cook.

"So I haven't seen you in here before, honey. Are you traveling through town?"

"Yeah, I am waiting for a friend of mine to get here. We got separated on the road."

"Well, my name is Josie. What's your name?"

"Jor...uh... Jordan," he said clumsily.

"Are you okay, honey?"

"Yeah."

"Your kind of shy, huh?"

Jordan nodded his head. He looked away from her. He was embarrassed. His face was turning red.

"Well, shy boy, I need some help taking out the garbage. I will buy you breakfast if you take that can outside and empty it out for me."

"Okay! I can do that."

"Follow me, and I will show you where the garbage is."

Jordan followed her back into the kitchen. She pointed out the large aluminum barrel that was overflowing sitting next to the back door. He lifted the can up and carried it outside without spilling any of the garbage on the ground. He emptied it in the trash bin. He came back in through the kitchen and placed the empty can back where he found it. Jordan could smell the delicious aroma of greasy fried bacon. Now he was really starving.

"Honey, would you like scrambled or fried eggs?"

"Fried please! Over medium."

"Wheat toast okay?"

"Yes, thank you very much."

"Well, thank you for having such good manners. What a good young man you are. You just go on in there and have a seat. I'll have your breakfast out to you in a minute."

Jordan walked back through the double doors of the kitchen into the dining area. He noticed that he wasn't alone. A young sheriff deputy was sitting at the counter. Jordan wasn't sure how old he was. He guessed the officer looked to be in his late twenties. He was a bit overweight but very muscular. He had a double chin and shaved head with a thin beard. (A skinhead in the making. The only thing missing was a Nazi Swastika tatooed on his neck.) He was wearing a wrinkled uniform that looked like he had slept in. He had a gun belt on, and strapped to his side was a cattle prod. (He was definitely way ahead of his time before the Taser became the weapon of choice.)

It had been a long time since Jordan had seen a cattle prod. The first one he saw was when he went with his dad and little sister to a little mom-and-pop hardware store that his dad used to like to go to. His dad hated going to the big box stores. It was hard to find things, and it was always a challenge to get someone to help you. His dad appreciated being able to talk to someone who knew what they were talking about. While his dad was bullshitting with the man behind the counter, Jordan saw the prods hanging off the wall back in the corner of the ranching and farming section. He was fascinated with them. He wasn't sure what they were used for. They looked like belly clubs, except they had a switch on them. He got in big trouble that day when he tried one out on his little sister when his dad wasn't looking. He felt bad about hurting her. She cried out in pain as the electric shock jolted her. He found out later that the ranchers used cattle prods to herd the slower cows along on the cattle drives.

Seeing the prod hanging on the deputy's gun belt made Jordan nervous. He could tell by his look that the deputy was not happy to see him. He took his seat at the counter. Jordan knew that he would have to be cautious. He sensed the deputy's mean spirit.

"Jordan, this is Deputy Burke." Josie poured Frank a cup of coffee. "Would you like something to eat, Frank?"

Burke didn't waste any time. "Maybe." He looked over at Jordan. "So what town do you come from?"

"I just got in from Reno." Jordan could tell that the police officer was disgusted with his punk rock look.

"Well, let me tell you something. We don't like travelers like you bumming around our little town."

"Now, Frank, will you leave this poor boy alone and let him eat his breakfast. He just helped me out and emptied the garbage. He isn't going to cause anybody any trouble. Geez!"

"Girl, you just let me handle this. That's part of my job to keep the vagrants out of town. So how old are you, boy?"

"I'm eighteen, sir." Jordan was trying to be polite and not give Frank any excuse to arrest him. He could see the deputy staring at his Mohawk.

"What's your last name?"

"Summers, sir." Jordan was scared to death.

"Knock off the 'sir' bullshit!"

"Come on, Frank, don't be such a hard ass."

"Girl, for the last time, stay out of my business."

Frank's temper and patience was wearing thin. He gave Josie the stink eye. Josie knew it was the last straw and that she was pushing it and should back off. She excused herself and went through the swinging doors back into the kitchen and started loading the dishwasher.

"All right, Summers, this is how it's going to work. I am going outside to my car and call in your name. That should give you enough time to finish eating. I'll be back in a minute." Frank got up and headed out the door.

Josie stuck her head through the kitchen window. "Sorry about all this. Frank is a hard ass and likes to push people around. He has done that all his life. He was the high school bully. You have to understand, this is a small town, and they don't like strangers hanging around."

Jordan was wondering what his next move should be. He could sneak out the back door or just stay put and take his chances with Deputy Burke.

He wasn't sure what kind of information that Burke would find about him when he pulled his name up. He was pretty sure that it was much too early for him to show up on a missing person's report. There was one fear: he was afraid that Officer Burke would find out that he had been busted for pot back in high school.

Jordan remembered that day sitting at the kitchen table with his dad and the rest of the kids. They had just temporarily moved into a rental. During breakfast, Jordan's dad warned them about drugs being left in the house from the previous renters. He told them to let him know if they found any. Jordan agreed to tell him. The only problem was that it was too late because Jordan had already found a bag of pot out in the garage and had it in his front jeans pocket.

On their way to school, Jordan thought about telling his dad but decided not to. Later on, during first period, he reached in his pocket to see how much money he had. When he took his hand out, the bag of pot came out, too, and landed on the floor right next to his desk. That was very humiliating and embarrassing when he was carted off to the principal's office.

Jordan swung around in his stool and looked outside. Frank was still sitting inside his police car. Jordan was starting to panic. The last thing he wanted to do was to be arrested. He took one more bite of his food and hustled past Josie through the swinging doors and headed toward the back door.

"Hey, don't be stupid. Go back and sit down. You are really going to piss Frank off if you run away."

"I'm sorry, but I have to go. Thanks for the food." Jordan charged out the back door.

Burke came back into the diner. He looked around and saw that Jordan was gone.

"So he is smarter than I thought. I'll have to give the little bastard that."

"Frank Burke, you are such an asshole!"

"Well, anyway, he's not wanted for anything." Frank had a satisfying look on his face. "You and I are getting off work in a couple hours. You know that I could run him in, but that would mean that I would have to fill out some paperwork. And he is lucky that I am really horny for you tonight."

Josie shook her head. "That poor boy out there all by himself. Don't you care about that?"

"Not tonight." Frank rubbed his crouch.

Josie shook head in disgust. "Frank Burke, I must be a crazy woman to put up with your shit."

* * *

Jordan was sprinting as fast as he could. He was a fast runner. He slipped on a rock, twisted his ankle, and tumbled to the ground.

He grabbed his ankle and screamed in pain. "Fucking son of a bitch! Cocksucker!"

He crawled off into the bushes and rested his ankle. He was lucky that it was a minor sprain. It was still sore, but he was able to walk. He looked around to make sure Burke wasn't there. He got up and circled back to the highway. There was a sign on the road that read "Reno, 169 miles away." Jordan's heart was pounding as he limped off. He was now a fugitive on the run.

CHAPTER 10

WHEN RIVER CAME back into the house, Mr. Wilkens was sitting in his favorite chair in the living room. The room was dark except for the lamp lit next to his chair. He was dressed in a robe. It was a weird feeling. She was always used to seeing him in a sweater and slacks.

"Hey, River, can I talk to you a minute?" Mr. Wilkens pointed for her to take a seat on the couch that was in the center of the room.

River sat down on the end of the couch. She wasn't sure what to expect. It was kind of an eerie feeling. She never really talked to Mr. Wilkens.

"I know that this has been a very difficult time for you. Mary and I have been talking, and we have made a decision. If you are open to it, we would like you to stay with us until you graduate."

"Wow! I don't know what to say." A huge load was taken off her shoulders. She was relieved. Her face lit up. "Thank you! Thank you so much."

Except for her mother, River wasn't used to such kindness. She was waiting for the catch. There had to be something on the back end.

Mr. Wilkens got up from his chair and came over and sat next to River. He reached over and put his hand on River's leg.

"Okay then. I am having a hard time sleeping tonight. I am going to into the study and do some reading." He kept his hand on her leg. "Thanks for the talk." Mr. Wilkens then got up and headed toward the study. He turned and stared back at River. "I will see you later."

River shivered. It was very creepy having Mr. Wilkens touch her. It brought back memories of Mr. Dantley. She went back into her room and locked the door. She left her clothes on and crawled into bed. She tossed and turned for several hours trying to get to sleep. She was afraid to drift off. She kept thinking about Mr. Wilkens touching her.

River looked at the alarm clock that was beside her bed. The digital face read 2:00 a.m. As she turned over on her left side, she heard a noise. It was the doorknob. Someone was trying to open the door.

CHAPTER 11

JORDAN WAS RUNNING as fast as he could. His sore ankle wasn't helping matters, and he was out of shape. He kept looking back to see if
a police car was on his tail. He looked ahead and spotted two headlights approaching him. Jordan dodged off to his right and headed
toward a deserted building. The car was coming up fast. It was a few
yards away. Jordan hit the ground. His heart was beating fast. He
shut his eyes and prayed for the car to drive by. He could hear the
car right on top of him. He hugged the ground. The car drove passed
him. He breathed a sigh of relief.

The temperature had dropped down into the twenties. Jordan
knew that he needed a place to stay and sleep until morning. The
empty building was an old mini market that was boarded up.

Two more headlights could be seen coming up in the distance.
Jordan thought about taking a chance and sticking out his thumb
to catch a ride. One lesson that he was learning fast was that he was
going to have to take risks and make quick decisions. As the car was
gettting closer, Jordan decided not to hitch a ride. For one thing, he
was still hoping that somehow Tucker would show up. He walked
back to the abandoned building. He tried to pry one of the two
pieces of plywood off the door. The boards were nailed securely to
the door. He pulled as hard as he could, but there was no give. The
cold weather made it painful when he tried to grab hold. He was
starting to get frustrated and losing his temper.

"Come on, you son of a bitch!" Jordan shouted. He tried again to loosen the boards. It took a lot of strength, but he was able to loosen up one of the boards. He screamed some more profanities from the slivers that he got in his right hand from the old wood. He wished that he had some gloves not only to warm his hands but also to help him when he had some muscle work to do.

It took Jordan another ten minutes to rip the rest of the boards off the door. In the end, it was worth all the slivers that he got. It was still cold inside the drafty building, and he could still see his breath, but it was better than nothing. He found a spot in the corner underneath a counter that had an old cash register on top of it. He tried to get warm by cuddling up. He could barely keep his eyes open. He was very tired.

CHAPTER 12

JIMMY SUMMERS TURNED the television off and peaked in the spare bedroom where the kids were sleeping. He hoped they would have their own rooms someday. He noticed that Rose was still awake.

"Can't sleep, honey?"

Rose sat up in bed. "Daddy, I have to tell you something."

"What's wrong, baby?" Jimmy sat down on the side of the bed and took Rose into his arms.

Tears started flowing like buckets of rain. Rose told her father about Jordan running away. Jimmy held his daughter in his arms and told her everything was going to be all right. He tucked her in and kissed her on the forehead.

Jimmy went back into the living room and sat down. He was upset and stunned to hear the news that his son had ran away. Life was already screwed up enough without this new stress.

Jimmy got on his cell phone and called Gina. As usual, she never answered the phone. Of course it was late, but it still annoyed him that she didn't pick up. His next call was to the police to report that his son was a runaway.

CHAPTER 13

AN HOUR LATER, River Walker made her move. She was pretty sure Jeff Wilkens tried to get into her room. She stuffed her backpack with her clothes. She tried to be as quiet as she could, but the house was an older home and had creaky floors. She decided her best option was the bedroom window. She had trouble opening the lock on the window. With a little extra muscle, she was able to slowly slide the window up. Her next challenge was to remove the screen. She took her time and prodded it loose. She gripped it and softly dropped it on the ground. She paused a second to observe if there was any movement in the house. She grabbed her backpack and purse and climbed out the window. Her backpack banged on the ledge of the window. She stood perfectly still for a minute waiting for things to quiet down. She thought to herself this sneaking-around business was excilerating. She tiptoed slowly around the corner of the house trying to avoid the unraked leaves lying on the lawn. Now she knew what it was like being in a minefield. She opened the backyard gate slowly and slipped outside into the front yard. She ran to her parked car in the driveway.

She was scared shitless that any minute now the front porch light would come on and Mr. Wilkens would be running outside trying to catch her. She dug clumsily in her purse to find the car keys. It was hard to see in the dark, plus her purse was stuffed with makeup—lipstick, a mirror—and a bulky wallet, which made it cumbersome to find her keys. She finally found them. Her hands were fumbling as she tried to unlock the car door. She finally got inside and locked all the doors. She started the car, put it in reverse, and backed out slowly. She then put the pedal to the metal and screeched off down the street. She breathed a moment of relief. She looked in her rear-view mirror. No one was following her. She was on her way and had no destination in mind. She just wanted to get out of town. She had a couple hundred bucks in her pocket.

River knew it was the right thing to do and that Mr. Wilkens had nothing but bad intentions in mind. There was no way that she was going to have another bad experience like the one she had with Mr. Dantley. As she drove off heading west, she saw the sign on side the road that said, "Salt Lake City 602 miles."

CHAPTER 14

IT WAS NOT easy for Jordan to drift off to sleep. It was uncomfortable lying on the cement floor. He finally nodded off and fell into a dream. He was at a Little League game. He was sitting in the dugout at the end of the bench. Jordan never got to play much, and he felt like a failure. Jordan could see his mom and dad sitting in the bleachers waiting for him to get his chance to play. He was ashamed and humiliated for not being a better athlete. He knew that meant the world to his parents. It was a different story with computer games. His eye-and-hand cordination was amazing. On the computer, he was confident and very skilled. He mastered every game he played. There was nobody around to judge him.

Jordan woke up briefly and then fell right back into the same dream. Billy Sharp, whose dad was the coach of the team, started making fun of him in front of the other players. Billy pointed out how dirty Jordan's uniform was and how goofy he looked. Jordan was humiliated. He started twitching in his sleep.

Suddenly, he was jarred awake by a flashlight shining in his face. He was grabbed by two kids and yanked to his feet.

"Well, look who we have here boys, another one of those traveling fucks," said the older kid and leader of the group.

Jordan was scared. He could see that there were four teenage boys that had him surrounded and he could smell the alcohol on their breath.

"We're the welcoming committee here in town. Frank sent us by to say howdy and make sure that you understand that we don't like your kind staying around here. Hold him up straight, boys."

The older kid punched Jordan in the stomach. Jordan slouched over and grimaced in pain. The punch knocked the air out of him. Jordan was struggling, gasping for air. The older kid waited for him to get his breath back and then kicked Jordan in the crouch. Jordan had never been kicked in the balls before. He was paralyzed and sick to his stomach. The boys then picked him up and hauled him out of the building and threw him in the back of their Ford pickup. They drove to the end of town.

Frank Burke was waiting for them in his police car. The boys pulled him out of the back of the truck and dragged him off to the side of the road. Burke got out of his car and walked over to Jordan.

"I hope that you liked our hospitality." Burke smiled. "We believe in five-star customer service. Next time it won't so easy for you." Burke grabbed Jordan by the collar of his coat and looked him straight in the eye. "I don't give a rat's ass what it looks like on the report sheet. If I see you again, I will have no problem putting a bullet between your eyes."

Burke pulled out his cattle prod and bonked Jordan on the top of his head. "Oh, and here is a final reminder for you to remember me by." He then jabbed his prod into Jordan's left leg and pressed the electric shock button. Jordan cried out as the electric shock surged through his body. It caused his muscles to spasm.

Frank had a very satisfying look on his face. He enjoyed torturing Jordan. (He would have been a perfect candidate to work in the dungeons at the Tower of London.)

"All right, Nate, search him and see what he has on him." Nate unzipped Jordan's backpack and dumped his belongings on the ground. One of the other kids went through Jordan's pants and coat pockets. He found the money that Jordan had on him. The kid handed it over to Burke. "Well, what do we have here? Who did you steal this money from, punk?"

Jordan tried to explain how he got the money from his father and helping a truck driver unload some cars.

"Well, that's a pretty good line of bullshit. I don't believe a fucking word of it." Burke kicked Jordan in the side. Jordan grimaced in pain. "I will tell you what. I am going to keep this money and consider it to be a fine for freeloading." Burke stuffed the money into his pocket.

"That will do it for tonight. You boys better get home before your momma comes looking for you." He looked back at Jordan. "And you had better be gone before I come back."

Burke got in his car and drove off.

Jordan stayed on the ground trying to get his bearing. He could hear the boys in the Ford pickup laughing and carrying on as they spun off and left skid marks on the road. He finally got to his feet and limped up the highway. His whole body ached from the punishment. His sore ankle made it difficult to walk, and his left leg was still smarting from the cattle prod.

In the distance, Jordan could hear a car heading toward him. He turned and looked up the road. The car was moving fast and almost upon him. He stuck his thumb out.

He looked up into the sky above. "Please, God. Make this car stop and get me out of this slice of hell."

The car zoomed by. That would be the first and last time Jordan ever prayed for help. Reality was starting to set in. The world was not waiting with open arms to help him. It crossed his mind to call his father to come and get him, but he sure as hell was not going back into town.

Jordan continued walking up the highway. He didn't own a watch, so he didn't know what time it was. He assumed it was somewhere around four o'clock. His current concern was to try, if he could help it, not to freeze to death. He had to hang tough. The battering Nevada zephyr whipped through his clothes. A few more hours and the sun would be rising. It was tormenting for him on how time slowed and the icy pain stretched throughout the body like it crushed prey for extinction. He was in a state of consciousness and numbness. (Wow! Pretty deep thinking for a high school dropout.)

In the pitch-black, Jordan couldn't see much of anything. The lights from the town had disappeared. He was out in the middle of nowhere. He could hear another car coming up behind him. He turned and stuck his thumb out. The car roared by.

At least the adrenaline kept his blood flowing and his mind working. He questioned whether he would ever see Tucker again. He wondered how his dad was doing and if Rose told him what was going on. He was pretty sure that she did because she wasn't very good at hiding her emotions.

He could hear a semi approaching from the opposite side of the divided highway. Jordan hurried across the road and dashed over the median and made it to the other side. (It's funny when you are under stress, how your mind can forget about the pain of a sprained ankle.) He got there just in time to stick his thumb out.

The semi whizzed by. Jordan could see the truck's brake lights in the distance and the rig slowing down. The truck pulled over to the side. Jordan slung his backpack over his shoulder and sprinted to the truck.

The driver unlocked the door on the cab. A round-faced, smiling old man with a long beard and a toothpick hanging out of his mouth greeted Jordan. "Howdy, son. My name is Terry. I am going as far as Elko. Does that work for you?"

"Yes, sir. Thank you so much. I really appreciate the ride."

"No problem, buddy. Hop on in. I do have to stop at the truck stop ahead and get a bite to eat. Can I buy you some breakfast?"

The thought of seeing Deputy Burke's cattle prod again scared Jordan. "No thanks. Do you mind if I just stay in the cab and sleep?"

"Okay. You are sure that you are not hungry?" The truck pulled into the parking lot.

Jordan was starving, but something inside him told him not to take any chances.

"There is usually this pretty little waitress named Josie who works there. Trust me, she is well worth the trip to go inside."

Jordan debated whether he should tell Terry what happened to him. He was afraid, though, that if he did come clean, Terry wouldn't want to have anything to do with him.

"Thanks, but I really need to take a nap."

"All right. I'll be at the counter if you change your mind." The truck driver got out of the truck and went into the diner.

Jordan scrunched down and closed his eyes. He was on his own now. He wasn't sure that California was the place to go anyway. For the time being, he was content being inside the warm cab.

CHAPTER 15

JIMMY SUMMERS GOT off the phone with the police. It was frustrating for him. They weren't much help. He would have to go down to the police station in person and file a missing person's report. Jimmy decided to head into the police station before going into work. He also would try to contact all of Jordan's friends and see if they could tell him anything. He hoped that Jordan was okay. He crawled into bed and tried to get some sleep.

* * *

River was getting drowsy. The last road sign read that she had another hundred miles to get to Elko. She was looking for a safe location where she could pull over and take a little nap. She saw a rest stop up ahead and pulled off onto the exit road. She drove up in front of the restroom facility and parked. She got out and went inside. She was disgusted with the filthy condition of the restroom. River's first thought was, "How could women be such pigs?" There were paper towels sprawled all over the floor. The sinks were caked with dirt, and a poopy diaper was lying on the ground next to the garbage can. And the big bummer! There was no toilet paper. Clearly the restroom hadn't been attended to in quite some time. River figured that budget cuts had something to do with it.

She liked being clean and being able to brush her teeth every-day. That would be an adjustment not being able to take a shower every day. Obviously she realized that this was just the tip of the ice-berg. There would be other obstacles that she would be confronted with. At least the water was working. As she was washing her face, she realized another materialistic fancy that she would have to live without: she was running out of white makeup. That was a biggie! Her gothic look hid her insecurities. She only had so much money to live on, and so far, makeup was not in the budget. Another black hole of humanity forfeited for survival.

River had the whole world ahead of her. She never really trav-eled much from New Mexico—except when she was ten, when her mother flew her to Disneyland. Other than that, she pretty much stayed home. After finishing up in the restroom, she got back in her car and backed up a few feet away and parked under a tree. She locked all the doors and leaned back in her seat to take a nap.

* * *

Jordan finally wandered off to sleep and fell into another one of his recurring dreams that still haunted him. He was in elementary school. His father had just dropped him off at school. There were two kids a grade ahead of him who every day bullied him out on the playground. He could see them waiting for him by the basketball court. Instead of going onto the playground, he tried to open one of the doors to get inside the school. The door was locked. He had no other choice than to go on the playground. The two boys headed toward him. Jordan tried to get away. He couldn't move fast enough. He was running in slow motion. The boys were getting closer. The sudden noise of an automobile woke him up. He took a deep breath. He was glad that it was only a dream.

Out of the corner of his eye, Jordan recognized the Ford pickup.

"Shit!" Jordan ducked down in his seat. He could hear the boys laughing and going into the diner.

A few minutes later a sheriff's car pulled up. Jordan couldn't tell if Frank Burke was inside. The front door of the diner opened, and Jordan could see Josie walk out and get into the police car. Ah! Jordan figured it out. Josie was Frank's girlfriend. The police car pulled out and drove away.

Jordan took a deep breath and closed his eyes. Twenty minutes later, Terry came out and got in his rig. He looked over and saw Jordan sleeping in his chair.

"Well, it's time to get rolling."

Jordan woke up and stretched his arms out and yawned.

"So I see you got a good nap in." Terry smiled. "That's good because one of the rules for riding with me is that you have to keep me company. I can nod off occasionally. Christ, I almost drove off a damn cliff once outside of Santa Cruz. Scared the crap out of me. I guess that's why I don't mind picking up drifters."

Jordan smiled. "That's no problem with me. I appreciate the ride."

"I bet you do. I overheard those assholes in the diner bragging about kicking some punk's ass. So that was you, huh?"

"Yeah."

"I noticed that you were pretty banged up. Here you go." Terry tossed Jordan a paper bag. "I got you an egg sandwich."

"Cool. I'm starving."

Jordan scarfed down the sandwich.

"Holy cow! You are like a wild animal. You should enter one of those hotdog-eating contests." Terry laughed. He dangled his toothpick with his tongue and moved it to the other side of his mouth.

Terry enjoyed paying it forward. Jordan appreciated how kind he was and that he didn't have to talk sports with him because Terry was a CB radio nut and spent most of his time talking to his good buddies. Truck drivers perferred CB radios over cell phones because they could communicate directly and get updated information immediately. Terry's handle was Big Dick.

"Well, let's get going. I am anxious to get home, see my wife, and take a big, long dump on my throne."

They both cracked up. Jordan loved Terry's sense of humor. He needed a good laugh.

CHAPTER 16

RIVER WAS SQIRMING back and forth in her seat trying to get comfortable. She didn't feel safe climbing into the back seat because it made her feel vulnerable. She twisted her head around trying to find a better position to rest. She finally found a spot up against the car window that felt comfortable, but it made her head cold. She grabbed a sweatshirt from her backpack and used it for a pillow. That seemed to work. She closed her eyes.

Suddenly she heard footsteps and the horrific sound of a ferocious, barking dog rushing toward her. She straightened up and looked out the driver's side window. The angry pit bull bashed his head against the door and was trying to get inside the car. She was terrified seeing his foaming, sharp teeth attacking her window.

A voice howled, "Get the fuck back, savage!" The next thing River heard was the animal yelp as he was being kicked. Through the fogged-up window, she saw a frightening face with an evil grin, licking his lips and staring at her. She screamed and tried to start the car. She wasn't able to react fast enough before her side window was smashed in. She raised her hands as a shield to protect her face from the shreds of broken glass.

"Get away from me!" she screeched.

The next thing River heard was a hissing sound followed by a hand reaching in through the broken window, grabbing the back of her neck and bashing her head against the steering wheel. The blow snapped her head back, and blood spurted out of her nose. She was knocked unconscious and slumped over.

CHAPTER 17

TERRY PULLED INTO Elko at six o'clock in the morning. Jordan thanked him for the ride. He drove through Main Street and dropped Jordan off at the edge of town.

"Elko Police are not a whole lot different than the assholes from Winnemucca," Terry said. "The difference is there are more of 'em."

He reached into the back of his cab and gave Jordan a ball cap to wear. He advised Jordan to get rid of the Mohawk. He also handed Jordan a twenty-dollar bill.

Jordan thanked Terry again for the ride and the money. He waved goodbye. The sun was coming up shortly, and he looked forward to watching the sunrise. As he looked ahead, he wondered what was waiting for him down the road.

CHAPTER 18

WHEN RIVER REGAINED consciousness, she found herself lying naked from the waist down on the pavement. Her jeans and underpants were sprawled on ground beside her. Her car and all her belongings were gone. She was pretty sure that she had been sexually assaulted because she felt sticky between her legs. It made her feel dirty and degraded. She was relieved that she was knocked out and didn't have to experience it. She put her pants and underwear back on and went into the restroom. She looked at herself in the mirror and saw dried blood caked on her face from the nosebleed. There were also cuts from the broken glass. She turned on the water from the faucet and washed her face. The warm water made her face feel better. Her body was very sore, especially between her legs. She took a seat on the floor in the corner of the restroom. She vaguely remembered what her attacker looked like before the window was smashed in. It looked like his face was either painted or that he was wearing a mask.

With the flip of a switch, River's great adventure was at a crossroad. She was lucky that she was strong-willed and had the determination to overcome adversity. She never dreamed that she would be in this situation and knew that she was lucky to be alive. Now she had to figure out what to do next, but first she needed to get some rest. Her head was aching and she was confused.

CHAPTER 19

THE BEAUTIFUL SUNRISE was inspiring for Jordan. The spectacular orange sky blanketed by majestic clouds surrounded the mountains in the distance. The brand-new day was very peaceful. He had never paid much attention to sunrises before. He was always sleeping in. The thought of giving up and going home was put on the back burner. He took a swig out of his water bottle. His body still ached from the beating, and the cattle prod left a huge red sore on his leg. It took a lot out of him. He could see now why his dad was so upset when he was messing around and used the cattle prod on his sister. He didn't realize the implications that might have occurred if he had overused it. He was ashamed of himself.

Jordan could see a small gas station up ahead. A good hot cup of coffee and something to snack on sounded good. He could hear crows cawing in the distance and a gentle wind brushing across his face. It wasn't as cold outside with the sun up. The traffic on the highway was starting to pick up.

He kept admiring the beautiful red sky peaking over the mountains. He saw a flock of geese making their way south for the winter. He was amazed at their choreographed formation that was equally spaced and flying in unison. He loved hearing them honk and wondered what they were saying.

Jordan accepted the idea that he probably was not going to hook up with Tucker. He was on his own now. Sometimes it's better to cut the anchor and save yourself. In a way, it was exciting to be in control of his destiny.

CHAPTER 20

JIMMY SUMMERS SAT around the kitchen table, drinking his morning coffee and reading the morning paper. He had to be to work in a few hours. He found his cleanest shirt hanging in the closet and a pair of slacks in the dirty clothes basket. He promised himself that he would do some laundry tonight.

This wasn't the first rodeo that Jordan hadn't come home. The only difference this time was Rose's story and how upset she was.

Today Jimmy needed his ex-wife's help dropping the kids off at school so he could go by the police station. Whenever he really needed her to help out, she always made things difficult for him. He tried her phone and was expecting to get voice mail again.

"Hello."

"Hi, did you get my message?"

"Yeah, I saw that you called, but I didn't listen. I was busy."

Jimmy shook his head. Gina was good at pissing him off. She knew what buttons to push. She could tell by his silence that she had done her job.

"Maybe if you paid your child support on time, I would be more coopertive."

"Money, money, money! That's all you care about."

"Why don't you try following through once in a while," Gina fired back. "So what do you want?"

"Your son has run away."

"What? I don't have time for this shit. He leaves all the time and never comes home. What makes this so special?"

"Rose told me."

"How does she know?"

"He told her."

There was dead silence. Jimmy finally broke the ice and spoke.

"I believe her. Look, he is not home, okay? I need your help today. I have to file a runaway report with the police. Can you take the kids to school and pick them up?"

"No, I have plans."

Jimmy lost his cool.

"Goddamn it! You are a piece of work, you know that?"

"Yeah, well, you're no saint either."

"Don't worry about it then. I will handle it. Oh, and have fun sucking someone's cock today!"

Jimmy slammed the phone down on the receiver. He murmured some more profanities, took a deep breath, and poured the remaining coffee down the sink. He then woke the kids up and jumped in the shower. Jimmy was lucky he had a plan B. He had a friend, Jamie, whom he could count on when he needed a shoulder to lean on or someone to look after his kids. Jamie used a lyric from a Stone's song and told him that there would always be a space in her parking lot for a little coke and sympathy.

Gina was upset, too, and felt guilty. She really didn't have anything to do. She was pissed about Jordan and took her frustration out on Jimmy. She could relate with her son. She did the same thing when she fifteen. Her parents were divorced, and she along with her sister and two brothers lived with her father in Carolina. Her situation was different. There was physical abuse and alcohol that drove her to runaway. Thank God nothing like that was going on here.

CHAPTER 21

JORDAN ARRIVED AT the gas station and noticed a car with a broken window getting gas. There was a strange kid with his face covered up by a hood filling up the gas tank. As he walked by the car, a barking pit bull tried to lunge out the open window. He was caught off guard, and the barking scared the shit of him. The kid smiled at Jordan with dark, black beady eyes and what looked like a tattoo on his face. He could see the fear in Jordan's eyes.

The kid nodded at Jordan as he walked by him. An Indian girl and another punk walked out of the store and headed toward the car. Jordan kept his head down and walked past them. He couldn't help but think about the tattooed face. It was very unsettling. The girl looked back at Jordan.

"Hey, dude, are you looking for a ride?" the girl asked.

"No thanks. I appreciate it, though," Jordan responded back and walked into the store. Jordan watched them get in the Honda Accord and watched the kid with the tatooed face slap the dog across the face. The dog yelped and quieted down. They drove off heading west. He had a creepy feeling about those kids. Jordan had no idea that down the road he would have to contend with that tatooed face again.

CHAPTER 22

RIVER FINALLY DOSED off and was dreaming about sitting on a blanket out in the middle of a field having a picnic. Her mother had prepared fried chicken and homemade potato salad, which was one of River's favorite meals. She could see a man walking toward them. At first, River couldn't tell who it was. She was starting to feel uncomfortable and nervous. When he got closer, she recognized the person. It was Mr. Wilkens.

The nightmare startled her. She breathed in deep and was relieved that it was only a dream. The bad news was that she was immediately snapped back into the reality of being all alone sitting on a restroom floor. Her self-esteem was rattled. Being raped and abused made her feel worthless inside.

River heard a car pull up outside. She got up off the floor and scurried into the farthest stall. She locked the door and climbed up on the toilet stool. Her body was shaking. She hoped that it wasn't the same bunch coming back for more.

The restroom door opened. She held her breath and peaked through the crack of the stall door. She was relieved to see an older woman with gray hair and a little girl by her side.

"Boy, this place is filthy, honey."

"This place is stinky, Grandma," the little girl answered.

"Let Grandma look around and see if we can find a clean potty."

River could hear the old woman open up the first stall. River climbed down from the toilet and opened up the door.

The woman was startled when she saw River.

"Oh my! You scared me too death, dear. Are you okay?" the woman asked. She could see that River was upset.

"No, actually." River broke down and started crying.

"Oh my! You've been hurt." The woman walked over to River and tried to comfort her. She pulled out a tissue from her purse and handed it to River.

"Thank you."

"You poor thing. So you are all alone here. Everything's going to be okay. I will be right back. I have to clean one of the toilet stools for my granddaughter."

The old woman led the little girl to one of the stalls. She took out another tissue and wiped off the toilet. "Okay, Julie, go ahead and go potty. Grandma will be right outside here." The woman then walked back over to River.

River wasted no time. "I was robbed. My, uh, car was—" River was sobbing. She was embarrassed. She didn't like being so weak. She was usually stronger than that. Only her mother had seen her in fragile moments.

"It's okay. I am here for you. Everything is going to be all right now." The old woman cradled River in her arms. "My name's Dorothy. My granddaughter Julie and I are traveling to San Francisco to see my sister and her family. What about you?"

River tearfully explained what had happened to her. She confessed about her running away.

"Well, I'll tell you what. I could use some company while my granddaughter sleeps in the back seat. And maybe we can figure out what you should do next. What do you say about that idea?"

River thought for a moment. She was a bit suspicious. Her experience so far had taught her that there was always a catch to such generosity. At the moment she couldn't refuse a gift horse in the mouth. She had no other options to consider, unless she wanted to stay stuck out here in the middle of nowhere.

"Okay, that's great. Thank you so much for helping me out."

CHAPTER 23

JIMMY PULLED UP in front of the satelite police station that was located off Neil and Peckham. He used to live in a condo right up the street. Nowdays, this part of town was where all the gangs hung out. He had to wait in line a few minutes. There was a woman sitting at the counter filing a robbery complaint. Jimmy noticed Officer Parks, the policewoman on duty, was very thorough, like she actually gave a shit. She made the distressed woman feel important. She treated Jimmy the same way. She was very helpful. Jimmy appreciated her kindness and consideration for what he was going through. She was also very attractive even though the loose-fitting police uniform made her look very masculine. She had shoulder-length blond hair with pretty blue eyes. She looked sort of like Michelle Pfeifer.

She recommended that Jimmy contact all of Jordan's friends to find out if they knew anything. He told her that he had left several messages already to Jordan's friends. She pointed out that runaway cases were not a priority for the department. Jimmy was disappointed to hear that but appreciated her honesty. She gave him her card with her cell phone number on it. She told him to call her if he had any more questions. He noticed that she wrote her first name, Amaya, next to her number. He thanked her and headed off to work.

Jimmy pulled into the employee parking lot at Sears. Before he went into work, he added her number to his address book on his cell phone. He thought about calling her later.

CHAPTER 24

JORDAN FINISHED EATING a bag of chips and a hotdog. He had about ten bucks left. He started stressing about how he was going to get his next meal. But for the time being, his first priority was to get another ride. He walked across the road from the gas station. He was still set on heading east.

Three hours later, Jordan had still not gotten a ride. He was getting tired walking. There was nothing to sit on besides sagebrush and dirt on the side of the road. He would have to walk quite a distance from the road to find a side of a hill and a rock pile to sit on.

Up ahead, Jordan saw a car pulled over to the side of the road. As he got closer, he noticed that it was an older woman and two girls standing outside the car. He crossed the divide and approached them.

"Hi there," the old woman said.

"Hello," Jordan answered.

"I am so glad God answered my prayers."

"Yeah, right!" Jordan thought to himself.

"We have a flat tire. Would you help us change it?" the older woman asked.

Jordan agreed to help them out. Dorothy explained that she and her granddaughter were traveling to California to see her sister and that River was hitchhiking with them. Jordan smiled at River. She shyly looked away.

He pulled the spare tire out of the back of the trunk. He sort of knew what to do. He had helped his father change a flat tire before.

He hooked the jack to the side of the car. As he looked up, he caught River staring at him. She quickly looked away.

The lug nuts were a bitch to loosen up. Jordan was almost ready to give up. He tugged with every bit of strength he had. Finally he was able to loosen the lug nuts and raise the car up with the jack and change the tire.

Dorothy was very appreciative. She handed Jordan a twenty-dollar bill. At first he was too proud to take the money, but she insisted, and he finally gave in. She offered to take Jordan along with them to California. He told her thanks but that he was heading east. He could tell that River was disappointed that he wasn't going with them. Dorothy left River and Jordan alone so they could talk for a few minutes by themselves.

"So this is the first time for you being on the road?" Jordan asked.

"Yeah, what about you?"

"Me too. I was supposed to meet up with a friend, but he never showed up."

"That sucks," River answered. "I can beat that. I had my car and all my shit stolen from me. What a bitch! The fuckers busted my side window while I was sleeping in the car."

River left out the sexual stuff. She was amazed how easy it was to talk to Jordan. Talking to boys before was not her best suit. There was something about him that made her feel at ease and be able to speak openly without being embarrassed. It even crossed her mind to tell him about the rape.

"I think I saw your car up the road at a gas station. It had a broken window. Was it a blue Honda?"

"Yeah, that's it."

"Two punks and an Indian chick got in it and drove away. They were pretty freaky. One of them had his whole face tatooed purple and they had this mean-ass dog too."

"Yeah, that fucking dog scared the shit out of me. He was slobbering all my window and raging like a wild animal. I should report those bastards to the police."

"I am not so sure about the cops around here. I had a run-in with one of them back there in Winnemucca. They frown at run-aways like you and I. They tend to not believe us."

Dorothy rolled down the window of her car. "Honey, it's time to get going. Is your friend coming with us?"

River looked into Jordan's eyes hoping that he had changed his mind, but no such luck.

"No, I am heading east. It was nice meeting you." Jordan waved at Dorothy. He looked at River. "Maybe you and I will see each other again."

"I hope so. Is that a Mohawk that you're hiding underneath your cap?"

Jordan took his cap off and proudly showed it off.

"Very cool." River smiled and got in the front seat of the car. She waved as they drove away.

Jordan was thrilled to get a compliment. As he watched their car disappear over the horizon, Jordan wondered if he had made a mistake not going with them.

CHAPTER 25

It was late in the afternoon when Bolt and his followers sputtered into Truckee on fumes. They were flat-ass broke after spending all the money that they stole from River on gas and fast food. Having a car to travel in was a real luxury for Bolt. Their other choices of transportation were more challenging. Hitchhiking was impossible with Bolt's appearance, and walking on foot took forever. Riding trains was their next best option. The train tracks convenently ran right through the middle of Truckee. So that was a possibility, if they had to abandon the car that was in need of a couple quarts of oil.

Bolt looked back and hissed at Shadow sitting in the back seat. "Well, baby, are you ready to spread your legs for some gas money and some oil?"

"Yeah, I can do that," Shadow Little Hawk answered back. Using her body to make money had become a natural part of survival for her. She started having sex with strangers back when she lived on the reservation in Tulsa. She had the reputation as the tribe whore. Back then she didn't charge any money for sexual favors. All you had to do was get her liquored up and she would cooperate. Even the white boys in town had a taste of her. But like anything else in life, once you do it, you kind of get used to it, and it becomes no big deal.

At least that was how it appeared from the outside. The truth was, if she could go back in time, she would take back all the bad decisions and stayed on the right path like her brother, Charlie.

When they were kids, Charlie and Shadow were always together. They got colds at the same time, and they could always tell what the other one was thinking. It was like their minds were linked together. Their mother believed that they had been given the gift by ancient spirits on how to communicate without speaking. They had an extraordinary system that they used with their eyes and their body language that only they could recognize. It came in very handy when they were playing basketball together. They were able to relay signals to each other and know exactly where the other person was going to be on the court.

They enjoyed venturing out and exploring the country that surrounded the reservation. They mastered the skill of rock slinging. Charlie was an expert. He could hit a target from fifty yards away. Shadow was pretty good too, but her aim was not as good as her brother's. They used a leather strap with a pocket that helped keep the rock in place. You just had to wind up and sling it in the air like lassoing a horse and then fling the rock. The size of the rock was important. The smaller the rock, the more accurate the toss.

Shadow did have some other qualities buried underneath her dark side. She was very intellegent, and before she became an addict, she loved to read books. She had a great memory, and her mind was like a sponge. She knew a little bit about everything, from being a good cook to sowing blankets, to knowing a lot about history. She made two leather bags with a strap, one for Charlie and one for her to carry the small rocks and the slingshot strap. They both carried their bags with them at all times. During her travels, Shadow kept other trinkets in her bag besides rocks, including a small fading picture of her brother, a sharp object for opening cans and beer bottles, and a bandanna for riding trains.

* * *

It was a tough struggle for Shadow being out on the streets after her father kicked her out off the reservation. No one would give her a job, and she had worn out her welcome at the homeless shelters. She had no place to live. She was at the end of her rope. That was the day when she first met Bolt.

Shadow was panhandling on a street corner in downtown Tulsa. Rat was downtown on a pickpocket mission. He approached Shadow and introduced himself. He was a smooth operator and a fabulous liar. He could make a pile of shit sound like a goldmine. He took Shadow to a diner to get some food in her belly. He piled on the bullshit about how great it was traveling and seeing the world. He invited her to come with him back to his camp. His real motive was to fuck her.

After the meal, Rat and Shadow dashed and dined. She got a big thrill out of sneaking out of the restaurant and not paying. It was getting dark outside. Shadow knew that she was taking a risk, but she agreed to go with him.

The campsite was located a few miles out of town. As they got closer, Shadow could see sleeping bags and the flickering flames of the campfire shooting up into the air. There was a young man sitting on a rock with his back to her, a chubby girl sitting across from him, along with a dog laying on the ground. The pit bull got up and started barking at Shadow. She stopped in her tracks.

"Shut the fuck up, Savage." The punk sitting around the fire scowled and then kicked the dog. The dog yelped and sat down.

"So did you find some dumb fool out there to steal some money from?" Bolt asked.

"No, but I brought somebody back with me," Rat answered.

The punk turned around and smiled at Shadow.

At first, Shadow didn't know what to think about the man with the tatooed face. He stood up and introduced himself. He told her to not be afraid of him. Strangely enough, she was attracted to his wild, Apache, warpath appearance. Although when she got a better look, the hissing, long fingernails, and sharp teeth were a bit over the top.

Shelly, the other girl at the campsite, immediately became very jealous of Shadow. She apparently had claims over Bolt. During the evening, Bolt tried to pass Shelly on to Rat, but she wouldn't have anything to do with it. Later that night, he sicked his pit bull on Shelly and chased her out of the camp.

Bolt charmed Shadow into his sleeping bag with lots of cheap whiskey, a soft spellbounding whisper, which he fell in and out of character the drunker he got, and his haunting dark-brown eyes that hypotized her. After screwing her, he introduced her to heroin, and she easily became another one of his followers.

At first, like most pimps, Bolt was very kind and made Shadow believe that he really cared about her. He softened her heart by opening up and telling her all about his childhood and being raised in the carnival business. Shadow loved to listen to his stories.

"Yeah, my dad's job was setting up and tearing down all the rides. And shit, when he was on the job, he would sneak sips of vodka out of a flask." Bolt shook his head. "I don't know how that fuckhead kept it together. I kept waiting for the day when the ferris wheel would collapse and kill a bunch of kids because he didn't tighten up the bolts. It never happened, though. And let me tell you, my dad was a mean-ass drunk. He was very jealous and was always accusing my mom of cheating on him. And if he really got pissed, he would beat the shit out of me with his belt. That belt buckle really hurt." Bolt pulled up his shirt and showed Shadow the scars on his back.

Bolt had a gleam in his eye when he talked about his Gypsy mother, who was as beautiful as Sophia Loren. She ran the games of chance and was a very good con artist. He loved watching his mother play hide the marble under the thimble. She was so deceptive as she moved the three thimbles nimbly around with her fingers. She would bat her long eyelashes to sidetrack all the men crowded around the table. At the same time, she was able to hide the marble in her hand and put it under a different thimble without any of them noticing. They were too busy foaming at the mouth trying to get her attention.

* * *

Things changed after Shadow became addicted to heroin. She was his slave now, and she was at his beck and call. Her mind was consumed with getting her next fix, which made her world pretty for a minute, and then poof, it all went away till the next time.

Bolt had Shadow believing that pulling tricks was just a job to help put food on the table. He assured her that he was not jealous like his dad. Shadow remembered hearing the story about his dad catching his mom screwing the owner of the carnival and killing them both with a knife.

There were a few distorted details with Bolt's story. First, his parents never worked at a carnival. His dad worked in a lumberyard, and his mom was a coctail waitress at a strip club. Bolt was the one that ran away and joined the carnival.

All the beatings he talked about were all true, but it was the pharmacist at the drug store that his dad caught screwing his mom. Oh! And he was not born with a scar on his face. The scars came after he got his face tatooed by an inexperienced artist so he could be the main attraction at the freak show exhibit. He was billed as the Demon from the Undead.

At first it was fun scaring people with all the magic tricks that he had learned from Henric Ustanich, who created the freak show. Henric was born in Eastern Europe and grew up around all the superstitions and folklore. He created Bolt's character. He taught him how to change his voice and whisper with a hiss when he talked. Bolt's original voice was whiny and nasal, which sounded very wimpy. He made Bolt a set of false teeth that was sharp and long, like a vampire or wild animal. He rubbed special potions on Bolt's hands that made his fingernails grow long.

After Henric died of a heart attack, the freak show was closed down, and Bolt was left to survive on his own. At first he wasn't sure what to do. He traveled from town to town staying out of sight because he couldn't walk down the street without being gawked at. There was no way that he could live a normal life in society. He lingered around hiding in alleys until the sun went down. It was easier for him to walk around in the dark and dig through the garbage cans for food.

On the streets of New Orleans, he was known as the Dark Demon. The people living in cardboard boxes feared him and left him alone. It was there, roaming the streets at night among the homeless and mentally ill, that Bolt realized that there was a place for him. It would be easy for him to control them and find followers to do his bidding.

* * *

Shadow took her bra off and changed into a loose-hanging blouse. She looked over at Bolt. She was waiting for the day when he would grow tired of her and have Savage run her off just like the other girl.

"Let's hope we can find a horny bastard at that broken-down gas station up ahead." Bolt smiled and hissed.

CHAPTER 26

FRANK BURKE WAS on his computer looking at a missing person's report. He recognized one of the kids in the report.

Frank filled out the report on Jordan Summers and emailed the information to the Reno Police Department. Later that same day, Jimmy Summers was informed that his son was last seen in Winnemucca.

The only information that he had received previously was from one of Jordan's friends, Tucker, who admitted running away with Jordan but changed his mind and went home instead. Tucker told the story to Jimmy about Jordan hitching a ride with a trucker.

Jimmy called the Winnemucca Sherrif's Department and talked to Officer Burke. He was very snotty. Jimmy finally got the information out of Burke that he saw his son heading outside Winnemucca toward Elko. Jimmy asked him if Jordan was traveling alone, and Burke confirmed that he was by himself.

He thanked Burke for his time and gave him his phone number in case he ran into Jordan again. He called Gina and told her what he found out. Their conversation ended up with Gina blaming Jimmy for not being a good parent and keeping a closer eye on their son.

CHAPTER 27

RAT PULLED INTO the gas station. The garage had two old gas pumps that had cranks on each side that you had to wind up to start the pumps. It looked like the last time the building was painted and cracked driveway was paved was back in the sixties. Bolt could see that there was only one person working at the station.

"What a shithole," Rat remarked.

"What are you talking about? This is perfect!" Bolt got out of the car and stretched his arms. "Get your ass in there, girl, and Rat, you take Savage in the back over there so he can shit and piss."

Shadow got out of the car and went into the office. Sitting behind the counter was a young man with curly hair. He smiled at her when she walked in. Shadow walked over and bent over the candy display so the attendant could get a good peak at her breasts. Shadow looked up just in time to catch him staring down her blouse. She gave him a naughty smile.

A few minutes later, Shadow came back out to the car and said that the guy agreed to her offer and that they would have to wait a few minutes until his friend came down to watch the station while he and Shadow went into the men's bathroom.

CHAPTER 28

IT WAS THE day before Thanksgiving. It had been a few months since Jordan had landed in Albuquerque, New Mexico. Jordan had grown tired of the road and found the city, which was located in the middle of the state to be peaceful and beautiful. The residents who lived there were a diverse population of friendly people who were very understanding.

Just off the Interstate, Jordan stumbled into a camp known as Hobo Flat. It was a community of tramps living there about eight miles northeast of town. The camp itself was located just below the Sandia Mountains foothills which straddled the Rio Grande.

Hobo Flat was a short distance from the train yard, which made it very convenient for travelers who were passing through. The population of Hobo Flat varied. Currently there was a group of fifty people, consisting mainly of males, with a scattering of women and a few dogs that roamed the camp. The ages ranged from the early fifties to the midtwenties. Jordan was pretty sure he was the youngest in the group. At least a quarter of the group that lived there were home bums who quit traveling and called Hobo Flat their home. The others were made up of vagrants and squat mattresses. (A squat mattress was a name given to women who were extremely easy to get into a sleeping bag for a night of fun.) These people came and went.

The camp itself was very organized. Each one of the home bums had their own individual campsite, which had a tent, mattresses, a garbage barrel that was used for making fires to keep warm at night, an ice chest to store food, and a kerosene lantern to be able to see when it was dark outside. Some sites even had worn-out furniture to sit on that was scavenged from the junkyard.

The leader of the camp was an older man in his midfifties named Captain Nathan Cooper. He had a rugged look of the old West with shoulder-length gray hair, a bushy graying mustache, round wired spectacles, a short-rimmed tarnished cowboy hat, with cowboy boots and a long coat. From a distance, he could pass for Teddy Roosevelt. Being an older man, he was still in very good shape. His daily hikes up in the hills with his old companion, a twelve-year-old German shepherd and Australian cattle Dog mix named Niko, kept him in good condition.

The captain first found Niko laying on the side of the road with a broken leg outside Memphis. The captain rescued the young puppy and nursed him back to health. Niko was not the friendliest dog. The older bums respected and stayed away from him. He was very territorial and protective of the captain. When he was younger, he would get loose and terrorize the camp. All the other bums and their dogs would run for cover. He had a very intimitating bark and could sense fear. As Niko got older, he stopped being a menace and mellowed out. Most of the time he preferred to just lie down beside his master.

The rules of the camp were simple: don't cheat, steal, or use hard drugs. There were two types of addicts that lived in the world of travelers, the ones that used hard drugs and the ones that preferred alcohol. Cooper was a firm believer that the hardcore drug addicts were troublemakers and could never be trusted. They would steal from their own mother. The alcoholics were a nuisance but were very manageable.

Everyone who lived at Hobo Flat had a duty to perform. The younger street punks did most of the garbage detail and finding scraps of wood for the campfires and cleaned up the dogshit. The younger kids also did the panhandling. The older bums birded for food and raided the garbage bins.

Captain Cooper got a piece of the panhandling. It was sort of like paying rent. He saved his percentage in a metal box that was secretly hidden where no one could find it. The rumor around the camp was that the captain was very wealthy and sitting on a fortune. The real truth was that the captain donated most of the money to the soup kitchens. Law enforcement appreciated that and stayed away from Hobo Flat. That allowed the camp to enforce their own regulations and kept the captain off the police radar because he had some personal history from his past that he was running from.

The captain lived in an old abandoned one-room shack that over looked the camp. His place had a few amenities, including a woodpellet stove, furniture, a bed with a full mattress and frame, and an outhouse in the back of the shack. The shabby building also had a front porch. Cooper spent most of his time sitting in his wood rocking chair with his dog, Niko, by his side. He enjoyed sitting there smoking his pipe and watching over the camp. The captain had a council made up of the older home bunms who had lived at Hobo Flat for a long time. They kept an eye on the camp for him. Unless it was a serious matter, he rarely got involved with any skirmishes that took place. He would get together with his leaders once a week on his porch and get caught up to speed on what was going on.

Cooper was not comfortable having the younger street kids around the camp. He was aware that Jordan was on the run, and that made him nervous about having the law snooping around the camp.

Jordan earned the captain's trust by volunteering to do any work that needed to be done. Cooper admired the Flintstone kid's work ethic. (Flinstone kid was the nickname that the old tramps gave the young travelers because they looked like Neanderthals.)

CHAPTER 29

AT THE CAMP, Jordan struck up a friendship with an elderly black man named Bags. He was in his midsixties and was the oldest home bum at the camp. Bags had a full head of curly gray hair and a scruffy beard. He always wore coveralls, an assortment of flannel shirts that had survived the test of time with patches on the elbows, and a pair of black shiny boots, which he polished every day.

When Bags was a boy back in Mississippi, he used to work at a shoeshine stand, which was located in front of Jackson's Barbershop. A good haircut and a shine made a man feel good about himself. Bags was very good at his trade and made a lot of good tips.

"Yessum, you can tell a lot about a man's character by the shoes he wears. And that's one of the first things a good woman notices besides having good looks is whether a man's shoes are shined or not," Bags would laugh and say. "Polished shoes are the sign of a true gentleman."

Nowdays, Bags had to use a cane to hobble around with because of his bum leg that he injured while hopping a train. He would never show it, but it was painful for him to walk. His leg never really mended properly. You could always hear Bags coming because he always whistled while he was walking. It was not really a melody. It was a continuous whistle that sounded like a bird chirping.

Home bums were a great source of information. They knew about town feedings, good panhandle spots, places to hop on trains, or were just fun to drink with. Captain Cooper trusted Bags and relied heavily on his advice. He was one of the last honest men that lived at the camp.

Bags took Jordan under his wing and allowed him to stay at his camp. His campsite was very cozy compared to the other tramps. The site had a couple of tents, kerosene lamps, and wicker chairs to sit on around the campfire, which was also used to cook food on.

The wise, old black man enjoyed sharing his experiences and liked the idea that he had someone besides the captain that he could trust and to talk to besides himself. Bags saw something special in Jordan. He liked the fact that Jordan was honest and told the truth. The only thing he didn't like about Jordan was that he never picked up after himself and left a trail of empty cans and cigarette butts all over the place. Bags was constantly nagging him to clean up after himself.

When Bags spoke, he talked very slowly and deliberately. Bags cautioned Jordan that times had changed since he was a young traveler and was trying to make his own way in the world. It was tough back then, especially during the freezing winters. But still, surviving was a lot easier, if there was such a thing because there weren't as many homeless people. That made less competition for a bed to sleep in at the homeless shelters. Also the lack of technology made the world a little slower, and it was easier to get away with things. He warned him that there was one thing that had not changed on the road.

"Yessum, it was still very dangerous out there, but you probably already know that," Bags said. "You need to make friends with fear because it will not go away and it will destroy you if left uncontrolled."

During their conversation, Jordan told Bags about his encounter with Frank Burke and the cattle prod.

"When it comes to us, society kind of looks the other way. It's like there are a different set of rules for law enforcement, especially in the little towns that take advantage of that." Bags paused and pondered for a few seconds. "We live in a world that doesn't know quite what to do with us. Life slips right through your fingers. Before you know it, the future's behind you. I hope that doesn't happen to you.

Anyway, I got a few things to give you that should keep you on your feet."

Bags handed Jordan a spare backpack that he had, which was equipped with some tools he would need to help make his life easier. The first things he gave Jordan was a P-38, an army-issue small can opener, and a flat thin piece of metal called a church key, which had a sharp curved end and a small hook for the rim. This tool could be used to open a bottle or tin can or make carb holes on a beer can to make drinking beer faster and smoother.

Next he gave him a squat key, which basically was a mini crow bar. This tool was very handy and could be used to break into an abandoned building. Jordan wished that he had a squat key back when he tried to break into that building in Winnemucca. He remembered how cold it was and the splinters he got trying to pry off the boards that were nailed across the windows and doors.

"The law don't think too kindly about squat keys," Bags cautioned Jordan. "They consider it to be a deadly weapon, and you could be arrested for a gross misdemeanor. Yessum, let me tell you something, it's no fun being incarcerated. You can't piss or shit by yourself. It's very lonely and claustrophobic as hell!"

The last item that he gave Jordan was a squat candle that was made by using chunks of wax, some paper, or most likely cardboard melted in a tin can. Squat candles were a lot bigger and hotter than a normal candle. Therefore, they produce more light and a good stove for cooking.

"So you are all set now," Bags laughed. "You are now a full-fledged road warrior. Yes, sir. I'm sure glad that I don't have to go through that anymore. Yessum, I am just content living here at Hobo Flat."

One of Bags's greatest pleasures in life was smoking a good cigar. His cigar box was his treasure, where he kept all his half-smoked cigar butts. He had an amazing collection of different brands that he found in trash cans. He even had a few Cuban cigars that he saved for special occasions. He was very protective of his cigar box. Over the years, several tramps had tried to rob him. Bags tried to teach Jordan the importance of keeping close tabs on his personal things.

Every night before he went to bed, Bags would light up a cigar and take a couple drags. After that was usually when he would share a story or two. Jordan was facinated with all his stories.

One of Bags's favorite subjects to talk about was riding trains. Bags was very proud of that skill. He would always start off by saying, "Yessum, it takes a lot guts and concentration to be able to jump onto a moving train." He would always smile and shake his head after saying that.

"Mind you, one false move, and you can lose a leg or get killed. One thing for sure, don't you be drinking while trying to hop a ride. I had to learn the hard way." Bags waved his finger and pointed down to his bum leg. "Yessum, I've seen more souls lost down a bottle of rum."

Although Jordan appreciated Bags's company, he missed being around someone his own age. Being the youngest, he couldn't relate to any of the other tramps that were at the camp. They considered him to be a nuisance.

A few weeks later, Jordan ran into a young traveler his own age named Jesse Clark. He was playing his guitar on a street corner for money. Jesse had been traveling on the road for almost two years. The two boys clicked immediately. They discovered that they had a lot in common. They enjoyed talking about the same things. They shared the same interest in music and playing video games. Jordan was impressed with Jesse's guitar playing.

CHAPTER 30

Jesse Clark

JESSE WAS CAUCASIAN with dark skin that made him look almost ethnic. He was a beanpole at six feet tall with shoulder-length Rastaman Vibration brown hair and matching eyes. He actually had some of Bob Marley's facial features with the same forehead, a skinny face, sunken cheeks, big lips, and a flat nose.

Jesse regretted never meeting his father, who was a drill sargent in the army and was based at Fort Ord. His mother, Julia, was a barfly who hung out at the Santa Cruz watering holes up the road from the base, where the military men frequented to pick up women. Her dream was to get married to a man in uniform and travel the world. She hooked up with Jesse's dad for a one-night stand, and the rest was history.

His mom tried her best to raise Jesse. Waitressing made it hard to pay the bills. Several different men came in and out of his life. His mother was never around much, and when she was, she was usually entertaining a soldier. Jesse witnessed a lot of things he didn't like. He lay in bed many a night listening to the headboard banging up against the wall. It was particularly troublesome when the landlord came over for some head to help pay the rent. He tried to cope with his situation at home. Jesse loved his mother dearly, but he hated the idea of her prostituting herself, and he knew that she was a dead end for him.

There was nothing shy about Jesse. He considered himself to be a ladies' man with his long hair and good looks. He was confident, outgoing, and outspoken. There was a rebellious side to him that made him very obnoxious and hard to be around when he was drunk. (Smoking pot was more his cup of tea.) When he was stoned, he mellowed and was fun to be around.

But mostly Jesse had a good heart, although he could be a bit of a used-car salesman at times. That came in handy when he needed something. He could sell cassettes to a deaf person, and it didn't bother him if he told a few white lies along the way.

Jesse learned how to take care of himself. He taught himself how to play the guitar. Strumming the guitar kept him company when he was alone at night. Playing songs on the street corner was a much better way to panhandle instead of holding up a cardboard sign. He thought of himself as an entertainer rather than a begger.

Like most kids with no supervision, Jesse quit going to school and got into trouble with the law. He got arrested for shoplifting. He had the knack for getting caught. (It was like he had a sign posted on his back or something.) He never went to jail peacefully, especially if he was intoxicated. He would become belligerent and end up being forced to the ground and handcuffed. In the back seat of the patrol car, he would rant and rave about how corupt our country was and that everything from Stop signs to not legalizing pot existed for the government to make money.

Social Services got involved, and everything went downhill from there. He eventually dropped out of school and hit the road.

CHAPTER 31

— ❧ —

It DIDN'T TAKE long for Jordan and Jesse to form a strong bond and become each other's road dog. (A road dog is someone that you can depend on and trust. Most street kids would fight to the death for their road dog.)

Jordan shared his dream of traveling to New York City. Jesse told him that he had only gotten as far as Chicago but would love to go with him to New York. Jordan appreciated the fact that Jesse had a little more experience on the road than he did, and he had no problem bragging about his adventures. He liked to crow about all the girls he had sacked in his sleeping bag along the way. He credited his guitar playing for his romantic success.

* * *

Bags didn't know what to think about Jesse. He didn't like the young boy's cocky attitude. When they were sitting around the campfire talking, Jesse would never listen to any of Bags's advice. He always had a better way of doing things. When the subject of hopping on trains came up, Jesse disagreed with Bags on how to jump on a boxcar. Jesse would always say it wasn't that big of a deal. Bags would just shake his head.

Many times Bags would take Jordan aside and tell him, "That friend of yours is pretty much a world champion pecker head."

But over time Bags got used to having Jesse around. The old man realized he was harmless and full of crap most of the time, except when he was drunk, when Jesse's rebellious side would leak out. Jesse disagreed with Captain Cooper's rule about sharing pan-handling profits. He pushed the envelope when he tried to get the other tramps' support. He had a huge drunken rage after being shot down. If it wasn't for Bags, Jesse would have been kicked out of the camp. He talked the rest of the council into giving Jesse a second chance.

What Bags most appreciated about Jesse was his loyalty to Jordan. He also enjoyed listening to Jesse play the blues. Jordan told Jesse that someday it would be cool to have him jam with his dad.

* * *

"That sure was a great meal, Bags!" Jordan said. That was one of the many benefits Bags had to offer was a good meal.

"I appreciate the kind words. Yessum, that's my Mississippi stew. My momma taught me how to make that. Just throw in some bacon and everything else you can find into a pot and let it simmer all day. Of course, it's not as good as Momma's."

"My mother was a shitty cook," Jesse said. "She couldn't even make mac and cheese."

"Well, we all have our special talents," Bags added. "Well, what do you say we clean up the dishes and put some more wood on the fire, and then I look forward to hearing you play some blues for these old tired bones."

"How about if I play now while you guys clean up?"

"No way, Jose," Jordan said. "It's your turn to take the plates down to the creek and scrub 'em."

Bags got a big kick out of Jordan calling Jesse out on his used-car-salesman attempt.

In between songs around the campfire, Jesse shared his experience on the road. He talked about the various factions that were located across the country. There were still the old traditional camps where the older bums lived. Jesse talked about the other camps that were springing up all around the country for the younger street punks who didn't respect the old ways and traditions. Those camps were more dangerous because there wasn't any clear leader or structure. It was more of a free-for-all. Whoever had the booze and the drugs was the king of the hill for the night.

"At some of those younger camps, there were more dogs than people." Jesse smiled.

Bags just shook his head. "Yessum! I wonder what this world is coming to? I have always said you can't let the inmates run the asylum. Heavens to Betsy! I am so glad that I am staying put right here. Mighty glad! Now mind you, Captain Cooper can be a pain sometimes, but at least you know where he stands on things."

An older tramp named Johnson stopped by the camp. He was quite a character, who used to be a professional baseball player. He almost made it to the big show until his arm gave out. He loved to talk about women. Johnson brought a bottle of rotgut whiskey with him and passed it around for everyone to have a share. Bags pulled out some cigar butts for the occasion.

"You two young kids have got a lot to learn about life." Johnson took a swig out of his bottle.

"And what's that, old geezer?" Jesse smarted off.

"Well, for starters, I bet that you didn't know that a sheep's vagina is the closest thing to a woman." Johnson laughed.

"Well, Jordan wouldn't know for sure," Jesse joked. "He has never seen a pussy."

"Fuck you," Jordan fired back.

"Is that right? Your still a virgin, boy?"

Jordan was embarrassed and took another swig of whiskey.

"I bet you could convince one our squat mattresses to cure you of that." Johnson laughed.

"Squat mattress?" Jordan asked.

"See, I told you that you whippersnappers didn't know shit. A squat mattress is what we call a loose woman. Martha Lynn over there by the creek is one of those types who would be delighted to show you the ropes."

"Oh my!" Bags smiled. "So you were a sheephearder and not a ballplayer, Johnson?"

"Why are you messing with me, Bags?" Johnson asked.

"All this nonesense that you are talking about is ruining our party. So, Jesse, why don't you play us another tune."

Jordan looked over and smiled at Bags. He appreciated him sticking up for him.

Jesse picked up his guitar and played a version of "Little Red Rooster" that everybody sang along with. A few other bums came over to the camp. One of them played along with Jesse on the harmonica.

Throughout the night, Johnson kept poking fun at Jordan and pointing out a few of the squat mattresses that came by to listen to the music.

After his evening walk with Niko, Captain Cooper dropped by to listen.

"It's kinda nice having some music to listen to. You are pretty good on that thing," the captain remarked.

"Thanks." Jesse smiled. That was the first nice thing that the captain ever said to him.

Bags nodded his approval. He figured the captain was getting used to having younger kids around. He never handed out many compliments, and that was something noteworthy when he did.

After a belly full of booze, Jordan started feeling guilty and sorry for himself. He thought about heading up the road to the convenience store and, using the pay phone to wish his Mom and Dad a Happy Thanksgiving. Back when they were all a family, the holidays were a very festive occasion with delicious food, a fire in the fireplace, and decorations all over the house. His dad always liked to put the tree up early. Jordan's job was to hang the lights outside. He felt sad not being there to help out. Things were different now with his parents living in separate places, so the holiday celebration was scaled down. Jordan wondered if his uncle had arrived at his dad's apartment yet.

Jordan hoped that his parents were okay with everything. He knew his dad would be disappointed and hurt that he ran away. He wasn't sure how his mom felt.

CHAPTER 32

JIMMY SUMMERS WAS up early getting ready for the day. He was a bit tired and hungover. This would be another Thanksgiving without a woman cooking the meal. Jimmy's brother, Donnie Summers, flew into town from Denver to spend the holiday with him.

The meal was already handled. Jimmy preordered a complete turkey dinner from one of the supermarkets. Jimmy and Donnie got a big kick out of the fact that all they had to do was run down and pick up the meal at halftime during the Cowboys game. They would be ready to eat just in time for the start of the second half of the game.

Jimmy's kids spent the night with their mother and would be dropped off at his apartment later in the day. Jimmy and Donnie stayed up late listening to music, playing Monopoly, and drinking wine. Usually Jordan stayed up with them and played board games. Donnie could tell how hurt and disappointed his brother was over Jordan running away.

CHAPTER 33

THE HOLIDAY DIDN'T start off so rosy for River Walker. She was sitting in a cold jail cell in Roseville, California. She was caught shoplifting some clothes. This was the first time that she ever got in trouble.

River was scared to death, wondering what was going to happen next. She was sharing her cell with two black girls named Sheila and Brenda, who had been busted for selling drugs.

"So what are you in for, girl?" Brenda asked.

"I tried to steal some clothes," River answered.

"First time?"

"Yeah."

"Well," Sheila added, "it probably won't be the last time either." Both girls cracked up.

A policewoman walked up to the cell. "Well, Ms. Walker, It looks like you are going to be getting out of here. Someone is here to pick you up." The officer opened up the cell. "Follow me."

River had a puzzled look as she walked down the hallway. She wondered who was there to bail her out of jail. She waved goodbye to the two girls, who wished her luck. She followed the policewoman through several clanging iron cast doors before arriving at the waiting area. The sitting area was a large room with several rows of chairs. There were several people in the room. River surveyed the room looking for someone that she might recognize. Her eyes almost bulged out of their sockets when she saw the person who was there to get her.

"Mr. Wilkens, she is now in your custody until the hearing."

CHAPTER 34

JORDAN AND JESSE spent Thanksgiving day with Bags. In the afternoon, they walked down to the Salvation Army and had a free meal, which included turkey and all the fixings.

After the meal, Bags went back to the camp, while Jordan and Jesse decided to hang around the soup kitchen and visit with some of the other young street kids. They promised Bags that they would be back before dark.

There were a couple girls hanging out that Jordan and Jesse flirted with. Actually it was Jesse that did most of the talking. Jordan just stood there and watched Jesse trying to put the moves on and get the girls to come back with them. It turned out the girls' parents worked at the kitchen and went home after the meal was served.

Jesse and Jordan took the long way back and followed the train tracks back to the camp. Jordan could tell that Jesse was getting restless by the way he was fidgeting.

"Hey, bro, what to do ya say let's you and I hit the road and head out to New York City," Jesse said.

"I don't know if I am ready to split yet. Bags has been awfully good to us."

Jesse pulled back his dreadlocks out of his eyes and jumped on one of the rails. He lost his balance and slipped off the track.

"Good thing you weren't walking a tightrope," Jordan joked.

"Oh yeah? Let's see you if you can do any better."

Jordan stepped on the rail and spread his arms out. He smirked as he floated down the track with perfect cordination.

"Well, smart-ass, at least I have seen a pussy," Jesse remarked.

Jordan jumped off the track and lit a cigarette.

"Come on, dude. There is a reason you and I hooked up. We are meant to carve out our own future. I want to play my guitar at Time Square and go see the Statue of Liberty, Yankee Stadium, and have a slice of that New York pizza. What do you say?"

Jordan gave Jesse a crazy look. "Man, you should go door to door and sell steak knives. All right, I'm in."

"Dude!" Jesse smiled. "This is going to be cool."

"All right then. We'll tell Bags when we get back. One thing, though."

"Huh?"

"I want to see the country riding on a train."

"That's fucking dangerous, bro," Jesse replied. "It is so much easier hitchhiking."

"Come on, man. The view will be awesome. We will see parts of the country that you can't see from a car window. Bags will show us how to do it."

After, they returned to camp and they told Bags the news.

He just sat there for a minute and gathered his thoughts.

"Yessum. The way I figure, it was just a matter of time before you boys headed out." Bags paused and took out his snot rag and blew his nose. "If it all boils down to gravy, there isn't enough here to cover over a plate of fresh-baked biscuits for you boys. I understand that. Life without purpose is not worth living."

Bags then pulled out a bottle of whiskey and gave each of the boys a cigar that he had been saving for special occasions.

"Here's to your new adventure." Bags took a snort of whiskey and passed the bottle. All three of them sat around the campfire and drank the whole bottle. Jesse pulled out his guitar and played the blues. Jordan just sat back and listened to the music.

Bags started telling stories about the good old days. He was in good spirits and was quite drunk. He was slurring his words together.

"You know, boys!" Bags burped and laughed. "Hahaha! Oh my! Pardon me." Bags hesitated for a second and then scratched his nose. "I wish y'all could have been with me back when I first visited New Yor-k. Yessum, it was in the summertime of 1960. I was traveling with a kid named Racer. He was about your age. He was originally from there, so he showed me around. He even got me in to see a Yankees game once. I still don't know how he pulled that off. I got to see Mickey Mantle hit a homerun. My god, that was something to see."

Jordan enjoyed watching Bags's eyes light up when he told stories about the good old days.

"So tell us about where you grew up and stuff," Jesse asked.

"Not much to tell. I grew up on a farm in Mississippi. My father and mother worked hard all their lives. Yessum, they were farmers and had a little spread outside of Jackson. They were good folks. I have a couple of brothers and a sister."

"So why did you leave?" Jordan asked.

"Times were rough in Mississippi if you were a Negro. Being called the n word all the time and having to drink out of separate water fountains and shit like that was humiliating."

Jordan could see the pain in Bags's eyes.

"Yessir, there was this Negro farmer who lived down the road, a piece named Samuel. He raised pigs and grew all kinds of vegetables that he sold at the farmers market. He used to wave at us with a big smile when he was out working in the field. One day we drove by his place, and it was empty. I asked my daddy why. He told me that the Klan burned Samuel's barn down and ran him off his property. They threatened to kill him if he stayed. After that I was pretty sure we would be next. I couldn't take it anymore. I just knew that there was a better place for me. So I took off."

"So do you stay in touch with your family?" Jordan asked.

"My momma and daddy are gone. I sure miss them and wish that I could tell 'em how sorry I am for leaving without saying good-bye." Bags looked up into the sky. "From time to time I check in with my sister. My younger brothers won't have anything to do with me. They think I am a worthless bum. That's all right, though. I don't blame them for thinking that way. How about you, boys? Especially since it's Thanksgiving and all."

Through the flickering flames, Bags could see the emotion in Jordan's eyes as he shook his head no. There was no reaction from Jesse. A holiday was just another day for him. He had no sense of what celebrating the holidays with family was all about.

It was around nine o'clock in the evening. Jordan and Jesse stumbled into their sleeping bags and went to sleep. Before Jordan drifted off, he promised himself that he would call his family.

CHAPTER 35

EARLIER IN THE day at Jimmy Summers's three-bedroom apartment, Jimmy's simple plan of picking up Thanksgiving dinner with all the fixings blew up in his face. When they arrived at the grocery store to pick up the food, they discovered that the meal was not prepared for them like Jimmy had thought. The turkey was just defrosted, not cooked. Fortunately everything else just needed to be heated up. Jimmy and Donnie both laughed hard and agreed that this would be a story they would be talking about for years to come. It actually worked out great for Jimmy's kids. They were able to eat with their mom earlier in the day and were hungry enough to eat later with their dad.

CHAPTER 36

RIVER WALKER CLIMBED into bed after what ended up to be a really good day. She really appreciated the fact that Mary and Melissa were at the airport to greet her. Unlike Jeff Wilkens, they were excited to see her. Jeff pretty much ignored her on the flight back. They gave her a big hug and told River how worried and happy they were to have her back home.

When they got to the house, Mary took River into the den to have a private conversation with her. She wanted to know why River ran away. There was a moment when River considered telling Mrs. Wilkens about her husband, but she decided not to.

"I think that I was just confused. I am so sorry," River explained.

Mrs. Wilkens reached over and gave River a warm hug. "I know this a difficult time for you, honey, but we want you to know that we are here for you."

River looked up and caught Mr. Wilkens giving her the evil eye as he walked by the room. He quickly looked away.

Later that afternoon they had a delicious Thanksgiving dinner with turkey, corn bread stuffing, which was a recipe that was passed on by Mary's grandmother, baked ham, mashed potatoes, bean casserole, and homemade pumpkin pie.

After dinner, Melissa and River cleared the table off and put the leftovers in the fridge. The girls washed the hand-painted china and serving dishes in the sink because they couldn't be washed in the dishwasher. That was actually a good thing because it gave River and Melissa a chance to catch up and spend some time together.

Melissa was curious to find out about River's adventure. At first, the conversation started off with some small chitchat. Melissa complimented River on how cute she looked without all the makeup. River was embarrassed but thanked her.

"So that took a lot of nerve to just get up and leave in the middle of the night."

"I know! I didn't feel good about it. But at the time I thought that was the best option for me." After that, River opened up and told her about her first night on the road.

"Oh my god! I could not have handled that. I would have turned around and came back. Wow!"

"Yeah, well, believe me! I thought about it. If it hadn't been for Dorothy, I probably would have put my tail between my legs and did just that."

"So why did you leave?"

River and Melissa looked into each other's eyes. It was at that moment that Melissa realized River was aware that something wrong was going on. It was also the beginning of a great friendship.

CHAPTER 37

IT STARTED TO snow outside. Jimmy Summers was miserable sitting in the living room, wishing he hadn't gone back for seconds. He had stuffed himself earlier in the day with deviled eggs and snacks waiting for the turkey to cook. Jimmy's kids and his brother, Donnie, went to bed early. Tomorrow was going to be a busy day at work. Jimmy was looking forward to Black Friday. He could use the extra money. It was tough living paycheck to paycheck compounded by the alimony and child support.

Jimmy flipped through the channels and found a John Wayne Western on Turner Classic Movies. He started thinking about his son. He hoped that Jordan was all right. He was disappointed that he didn't hear from him. Jimmy thought that maybe tomorrow he would check in with Amaya Parks and see if she had any new information.

CHAPTER 38

IT WAS A brisk morning the next day. There was a few inches of snow on the ground. Hobo Flat was a mess after a day of celebrating. The campfires and fire barrels were smoldering with ashes, and there were empty beer cans, whiskey bottles, and other trash spreadout all over the camp, which was partially covered up by the snow.

Jordan and Jesse were still asleep. They both had huge hangovers.

As usual, Bags was up early. He had a slight headache but was able to maintain and go about his normal day. He was whistling as he started a fire and he tided up his campsite. He pulled out a pan and cooked some bacon that he had salvaged from the mini store down the street.

The smell of fried bacon woke Jordan up. He got out of his sleeping bag and joined Bags by the fire.

"Morning. You are not looking too chipper today." Bags laughed.

"Oh man, my fucking head is killing me."

"There's nothing better to cure a hangover than a greasy breakfast. Yessum, get your friend up, and we will have a couple of slices of bacon."

Jordan yelled at Jesse, "Hey, bro, get your lazy ass up and have some breakfast with us!"

They both laughed as they heard Jesse moaning in his sleeping bag. "I hate fucking alcohol."

"Come on, dude, get your ass out here!" Jordan yelled. A couple of the bums close to Bags's campsite hollered back to shut up.

"Yessum. It sounds like there are a few headaches in camp this morning," Bags joked.

"You know something, Bags, I never thought that I would like being outside in the cold snow, but it's kind of nice and peaceful."

Bags handed Jordan a cup of coffee. "I know what you're saying. It's funny, after a while, you just get used to it. I tried to stay in a motel one night. I couldn't stand it. I prefer sleeping outside in a tent. So when are you two heading out?"

"I'm not sure yet. Jesse wants to leave right away."

"How are you planning on getting around?"

"Jesse likes hitchhiking."

Bags could tell that Jordan wasn't thrilled with that idea.

"Well, let me tell you something," Bags added. "Unless one of you is a woman, nobody in their right mind is gonna pull over and pick up two street kids with dregs and a mohawk."

Jordan lauged. "Yeah! That's what I think too. Jesse's pretty hardheaded. He always has to learn the hard way. I want to do what you did, Bags, and ride trains across America."

"My sense is that Jesse's a little bit afraid of hopping trains. It's that fear thing I was telling you about. Well, when you're ready, I would be happy to teach both of you. Just let me know."

CHAPTER 39

RIVER GOT UP and jumped in the shower. She was pretty chipper. She enjoyed the feeling of the refreshing, warm water rejuvenating her body. It felt good to be clean and smell good. She got out of the shower and dried off. She looked at herself in the mirror. She noticed that she had lost some weight and was not as chubby around her belly. Except for her small breasts, she liked the way her body looked. Her curves were shapelier. She gave credit to all the exercise and all the walking she had to do on the road.

Being a traveler had taught River a lot about herself. She knew what it felt like being a woman living back in the days of the old West. She had learned to survive without all the modern conveniences, like having a toilet or a bed to sleep in every night.

Time moved much slower when she on the road. Each day, she only had a few things to worry about, and those were her next meal, drinking water, and a place to sleep for the night. Of course, being aware of what was going on around her was a given. She had learned to sleep with one eye open.

Suddenly a chill came over her. She had a creepy feeling that someone had been watching her. Her experience being alone had taught her to be able to sense things. At the same time, it was frightening for her.

She calmed down after a few minutes and dried her hair. She looked at herself in the mirror. Because of Melissa's compliment, she decided to not put on any makeup. She agreed with her. She liked the way she looked. She even thought she was sort of pretty. The only feature she would change on her face, if she could, would be to have fuller lips like Melissa.

River was anxious to continue her conversation with Melissa. She hoped that they would be able to be alone.

CHAPTER 40

⁕

AFTER BREAKFAST, JORDAN and Jesse felt a little better, but they still had splitting headaches. They crawled back into their sleeping bags to get more sleep.

Captain Cooper would have nothing to do with that. He hated a dirty camp. He looked around the camp as he was taking his morning walk with Niko.

"Come on, boy, let's go visit Bags. I am sure that he is up and at it."

Bags waved as he saw the captain coming down the hill.

"Good Morning, Captain."

"Morning, Bags. It's looks like we had a pretty good celebration. You get your hooligans up and make sure they do their chores today. It's a glorious day ahead, and I want this camp cleaned up and put back to normal."

"Yessum, Captain! I will make sure they get right on it."

Cooper nodded his approval. "Come on, Niko." The captain headed back to his shack. The captain was lucky to have a trusted man like Bags around the camp.

They bitched and moaned, but eventually Jesse and Jordan got up and did their work. They spent the morning cleaning up all the garbage. Later on they would have to panhandle for money. The day after Thanksgiving was usually a good day for begging because people were more generous during the holiday.

Jesse did not like being bossed around by Captain Cooper. He thought he was a selfish old man who was taking advantage of his position. Jordan asked Bags if the leaders at the other camps were just like Cooper.

"Let me tell you about the previous leader who ruled the roost at this here camp. He was a huge fat man by the name of Rufus White. Yessum, he was a real wing nut. At the drop of a hat, he would lose his temper. Especially when he was drunk. Oh, God Almighty! The littlest things would piss him off. He was very vengeful, and he believed in punishing anyone who broke his rules. He would discipline them right in front of the whole camp. Rufus had a Middle Ages thing. There used to be a whipping post that was located right next to that tree over there. For punishment, Rufus would tie people up and give them ten lashes. He almost whipped a man to death once. Yessum, Rufus was not a good man. At least Captain Cooper is a fair man."

Jordan and Jesse were completely engaged in the conversation. "So how did Captain Cooper take over?" Jordan asked.

"Well, it all started like this. Yessum, I was just about ready to hit the road again. I didn't feel very safe around the camp. Things started to change when Nathan Cooper showed up. There was something about him. I couldn't quite put my finger on it at first. There was a quality that he had that made you feel like he had your back. He was a natural leader and got most of the tramps to believe in him. They were already disgruntled with Rufus."

Jesse strummed his guitar and sang, "You say you want a revolution. Well, you know, we all want to change the world."

"Great song." Jordan smiled. "Go on, Bags."

"Yessum, it all came to a head one day. You see, Rufus had this Middle Ages law. I believe it was called prima nocta. He must of got the idea from watching *Braveheart*."

"I saw that movie. It was one of my dad's favorites," Jordan said.

"How did you know about that movie, Bags?" Jesse asked.

"Oh my! So you think that I was just a hobo and didn't enjoy the fruits of life?" Bags scratched his head. "Well, let me tell you something. There was a time when I had a job and money in my pocket. I used to take a lot of ladies to the movies. Yessum, and I even tried to pull the popcorn trick."

Bags could tell by the look in their eyes that the two streets kids were clueless about the popcorn trick.

"You know, maybe Johnson was right about you two boys." Bags laughed.

"So what the fuck is that, uh, prima whatever it is about?" Jesse asked.

"Supposedly, back in those days, to bless a wedding, British lords exercised their right to take a groom's wife for himself on their wedding night. Rufus took a portion of that idea and claimed the right to have sex with any of the new women who came to the camp."

"Dude, he should be called Ruthless, not Rufus," Jordan joked.

"Anyway, Rufus wanted to whip a woman for refusing to honor his demand. He stripped her naked and tied her up to the whipping post. Captain Cooper defended the woman and demanded that she be untied. Rufus tried to use his whip on the captain. Nathan grabbed the whip right out of his hand and started giving Rufus some of his own medicine. Yessir, from that time on, Nathan became the leader of the camp."

"So what happened to Rufus?"

"Well, he, uh, put his tail between his legs and disappeared."

After hearing that story, Jordan and Jesse gained a little more respect for Captain Cooper.

"And by the way, I didn't see *Braveheart* in a movie theater. I saw it while I was in jail in Memphis. They used to show movies every Saturday night for the inmates. And I know, Jesse, what your next question is. I was in jail for trespassing."

CHAPTER 41

RIVER WALKER'S BLACK Friday was a glorious day. Mrs. Wilkens took Melissa and her shopping. River always enjoyed doing that with her mother when she was younger. The mall was filled with shoppers. Most of them all seemed to be stressed and not enjoying themselves. Mrs. Wilkens was just the opposite. This was one of her favorite days of the year. She loved going from store to store looking at all the bargains. They ate lunch at the Olive Garden and ordered the all-you-can-eat salad with soup and breadsticks. River and Melissa stuffed themselves with breadsticks. The waitress had to refill the breadstick basket three times. Mary was amazed on how many breadsticks the girls ate.

On the drive home, Mary told River that she had nothing to worry about. Her shoplifting charge was just a bump in the road and that Mr. Wilkens was working on getting the charges dropped so she wouldn't have to go back to California for the trial. River thanked her and told her that she had learned her lesson and would never do it again.

Melissa and River locked eyes on each other. River could tell that Melissa was anxious to talk to her alone.

CHAPTER 42

BOLT AND HIS adherents made it as far as San Francisco before the Honda blew the engine. On the way there, Bolt had picked up a new follower named Blake who was hitchhiking outside Sacramento. He wasn't very smart, but he was big and strong. And that was exactly what Bolt needed, which was to have a big ox defend him. Rat liked the idea of having Blake around to do all the little shit that he usually had to do. (Rat was middle management now.)

The Bay Area seemed like the ideal place for Bolt. He blended in perfectly with the diverse population of freaks. He liked the idea that he didn't stand out in the crowd as much. But it was also a disability because he wasn't as intimidating. The street people from the city were not as naive, and there were a lot of freaks just as scary as he was. He also discovered that living in a bigger city was not as easy as he had anticipated. There was more law enforcement on the street, and there was also a lot more competition for panhandling and prostitution. Gangs controlled most of the street corners in the tenderloin district, so Bolt's operation had to operate outside the prostitution area. Shadow had to be very careful to not get busted. There were vice squads all over the city. The police were more lenient with prostitution in the Tenderloin.

As he stood in a dark corner off Poke Street, Bolt was keeping a keen eye on his latest recruit, a sixteen-year-old male prostitute, Billy Jackson, whom Shadow had introduced him to. Bolt had high hopes that Billy would be a gold mine for him in a city that was infested with closet homosexuals. Billy was very handsome, with long blond hair, bright-blue eyes, and a perfect body.

Even though Bolt had protection from Rat and Blake, he had to be cautious, because it was very dangerous in San Francisco. Especially now with Billy in his camp and the trouble Shadow had stirred up. Bolt had treaded into another pimp's territory who wanted his property back, one of them being Shadow.

* * *

Shadow first met Prince when she was walking down Market Street. He pulled over in his white Cadillac and rolled down the window.

"Hey, pretty lady, can I give you a lift somewhere?" Prince asked.

Shadow was impressed with the handsome black man dressed in a tailor-made suit with a thick Afro and a well-trimmed beard.

That night, Prince recruited Shadow to come work for him. She was tired of Bolt taking her for granted and was ripe for the picking. She fell for Prince's line of crap. He was very seducing and made her feel special.

"I will tell you what, pretty lady. Tomorrow I am going to take you shopping. You need some new clothes if you are going to be my girl."

Shadow smiled. No one had ever offered to do that for her.

Just like in the beginning with Bolt, Prince had her believing that she was his girlfriend. He wined and dined her. He let her stay with him, and she had a steady flow of heroin, which was always hit and miss with Bolt.

Prince's operation was pretty extensive. He had a harem of young girls and boys who worked the streets for him. He kept them in a run-down apartment off Fell Street. He used the same tactics to lure all his victims into his web, and after that, he considered them to be his personal property.

Shadow wondered what the girls on the street thought when she walked by them arm and arm with Prince. She assumed that they were jealous of her.

After Prince suckered her in, their relationship changed. She became just another one of his street girls. She realized then what all the other girls were whispering about. Unless he wanted to discuss business with her, Shadow no longer spent any more time alone with Prince. Instead she was forced to live with the others. Her deal was very black and white. As long as she brought money in, he supplied her with heroin. Just like all the others, he would beat her and punish her if she didn't earn her keep.

It was in that filthy two-room apartment where Shadow met Billy. They were sleeping in the same room together. He was a lost soul who had just recently run away from home. He was hooked on heroin too. Shadow formed a friendship with Billy and promised him that she would help him get away from the clutches of Prince someday.

* * *

Even though Bolt was angry that Shadow left, he still wanted her back. He would never admit it, but he had feelings for her. Rat spotted her working the streets and followed her back to her apartment.

Later that night Bolt with his dog and two hooligans showed up at the apartment.

"All right! You dudes ready?" Bolt breathed in and hissed.

"Fuck yeah!" Rat answered. He lived for this kind of stuff. Anything dangerous was exciting to him.

"How about you?" Bolt asked Blake.

"I'm ready," the quiet giant answered back.

They pulled out their smileys. They had to climb some stairs because the elevator wasn't working.

"You sure she is on the second floor?" Bolt asked.

Rat nodded his head yes. It always annoyed him when Bolt doubted him. The hallway on the second floor was dimly lit and had a musky smell that stunk like dog piss. The walls were mugged with graffiti, and the carpet was stained with huge blotches. The hallway was empty except for a hooker who walked by them and asked if they were looking for a party. Bolt glared at her with his sharp teeth. She quickly disappeared.

Shadow's apartment was the last door on the left. They wasted no time. Blake kicked the door in, and they rushed inside. There was a crowd of people, including three black girls and two black men, sitting on the living room floor. Rap music was blasting out of a ghetto blaster. They were passing a bottle around and smoking a joint.

"Sick 'em, Savage," Bolt commanded.

Savage charged the group growling and showing his sharp teeth. He attacked one of the black men and locked his jaws on his arm. The man yelled in pain. The women screamed in terror.

"Savage, let go," Bolt hissed. The pit bull backed off and stood next to Bolt. "You bitches shut the fuck up and get over there against the wall," Bolt demanded. They were definitly intimidated by him. He put the full show on scratching the walls with his sharp fingernails and scowling with his menacing hiss.

Rat and Blake searched the two black men and found a switchblade and a pistol. The black men were drunk, and both of their eyes buldged out like they had just seen a ghost. "Where is Shadow?" Bolt screamed.

One of the black girls spoke up, "She is an Indian, right?"

"Where is she?" Bolt glared

The black girl pointed to the room next to the bathroom with the door closed. "She is in there."

Bolt barged into the room. It took a few seconds for him to adjust to the darkness. There were several mattresses spread out on the floor. There were five people in the room sleeping. Bolt found Shadow lying on a mattress next to another person in the corner of the room. He pulled her up and slapped her across the face to wake her up. She was heavily smacked up and didn't recognize Bolt.

"Shadow, it's me, Bolt." He grabbed her and shook her trying to wake her up. Shadow was stumbling and having a hard time standing up.

"Huh? Bolt!" The room was spinning, and Shadow was confused. She wasn't sure what was going on.

"Yeah! It's me. Come on! Let's get the fuck out of here." Bolt was getting impatient. "Boy, you are sure fucked up, baby." Bolt dragged her out into the living room.

"Rat, give me a hand with this messed-up bitch." Bolt slung Shadow's arms around both him and Rat. They headed down the stairs. Shadow started to get her control of her faculties. She stopped them before they got to the bottom of the stairs.

"Hey, baby, I left my pouch up stairs."

"Are you kidding me?"

"I need my pouch," she answered.

"Shit! What do you need that fucking pouch for? Is it magic or something?"

"It is part of my blood," she insisted. "Come on. We have to go back."

Bolt was pissed, but he gave in. "Okay. All right! Shit!"

They rushed back up stairs and stormed into the apartment again. The people were caught off guard again.

One of the black men was on his cell phone. "Fuck! They are back here again."

"Sick 'em, boy," Bolt hissed.

Savage could sense the fear and lunged at the man with the phone. The man panicked and dropped the phone. He put his arms up to defend himself. "Okay, okay. I'm cool."

Blake walked over and stomped his foot on the phone, smashing it to pieces.

Shadow went into the bedroom and came out with her pouch and her friend Billy.

"What is going on, Shadow?" Bolt frowned at the street punk.

"He is coming with us. I promised him."

"All right! Let's get the hell out of here." They ran out of the apartment. "You are a pain in the ass, you know that?"

CHAPTER 43

JORDAN AND JESSE were relaxing around the campfire. Their hangovers finally went away. They were able to make a hundred bucks panhandling. Except for today, Jordan and Jesse had an agreement. Jordan would do all the cleaning up around the camp in exchange for Jesse handling all the panhandling duties. They gave half of their earnings to Captain Cooper, and the other half they used to buy a couple of steaks and some beer, which Bags bought for them at the store. Both boys were excited about tomorrow. They were going to get their first lesson on how to ride a train.

"Yessum. You boys get a good night's rest now. Tomorrow we are going to get started in getting you in shape so you can master the art of riding trains." Bags took a swig out of a bottle of beer. "Yessum, riding trains is special. Not everybody can do it."

"What do you mean by that, Bags?" Jesse asked. Jordan was curious to hear his answer.

"Boys, it takes a lot of guts and thinking on your feet. One small mistake, and you could lose your arm or leg or get pulled underneath the train and get your ass killed." Bags finished off his bottle of beer and tossed it in his plastic bag with all the other empty bottles. Bags made extra money recycling glass and plastic.

Bags got to his feet and smiled. "Yessum, those were the best days of my life. There is nothing better than traveling across the country in a boxcar or on a grainer. The scenery is spectacular. Well, good night." Bags got up and went into his tent.

Jordan and Jesse lit up a couple of smokes.

"Pretty cool stuff, huh?"

"Yessum," Jesse imitated Bags. Both boys busted up laughing.

CHAPTER 44

RIVER WAS IN bed staring at the ceiling. She hoped that Mrs. Wilkens was right about her not having to worry anymore about her shoplifting charge.

Earlier that evening, Mr. Wilkens was a lot more conversational at the dinner table. He asked River questions about what it was like to run away and be on her own. He also wanted to know what happened to her car. He was fascinated with her stories. It almost seemed like listening to her talk about her travels sexually turned him on.

Later that night, River dosed off to sleep. She dreamed about being with her mother. They were in a large room standing in different lines with groups of people heading in opposite directions. The look on her mother's face was sad as she waved goodbye. River tried to get out of the line she was standing in but couldn't move. She kept moving farther and farther away from her mother. She was startled by a noise outside her door.

She quickly jumped out of bed. She knew that she had to think quickly. She grabbed her handbag by the strap and stood right next to the door. She was ready to bash Mr. Wilkens over the head if he came in the room.

Whoever it was who outside the door walked past her room and headed down the hall toward Melissa's room. She could hear Melissa's door open and close.

CHAPTER 45

Jimmy Summers dropped his brother off at the airport to catch the red-eye flight. It was always good having his brother around for the holidays. They were very close and always kept in touch with each other.

On his way home, Jimmy's cell phone rang. It was his ex-wife calling him.

"Hello."

"Hey, I haven't received your check in the mail."

"Oh, I am sorry. I will mail it tomorrow."

"Fuck you, Jimmy. I am counting on that money. I am getting sick of you not following through."

Jimmy was in no mood to argue. Gina could be so ruthless.

"Well?"

Jimmy knew that his silence drove her crazy.

"Yeah, you can afford to put out a big fancy spread for Thanksgiving, but you can't pay me on time."

Jimmy smiled. He had a great comeback ready to fire back to her. He thought about zinging her with it but kept it to himself. "Speaking of spread, who were you opening your legs for tonight?" He knew his comment would have really pissed her off. He decided just to hang up, which was an equally effective maneuver.

Gina did her job once again. She got his blood boiling. Jimmy looked at his speedometer and noticed that he was driving sixty-five in a forty-miles-per-hour zone. As he slowed down, he looked in his rearview mirror. A highway patrolman was turning around and heading toward him.

"That's great! That's just fucking great!" Jimmy was frustrated. That was all he needed, a ticket and another expense he couldn't afford.

Jimmy started cussing up a storm at Gina. In the end, she had won once again.

CHAPTER 46

A WEEK LATER, Bolt was getting frustrated with his two addicts. Their addiction was testing his patience.

Blake slammed Billy up against a building. Bolt howled and hissed. "Look here, you pissant. You had better straighten up and get your act together. I don't have time for this shit."

Billy was bleeding from the mouth. The john whom he had been with wanted more that just oral sex. He liked to beat his sex partners up. Billy fought him off and got away. The bad news was that he never got paid.

"And you sure that you didn't get paid?" Bolt asked again. "Are you tellling me the truth?" Bolt slapped Billy across the face. "Well, are you?"

Billy started crying. "No, I am telling you the truth."

"You are pathetic, you know that? Go on and get the fuck out of my sight. I must have been out of my mind to take you in."

Billy headed over to the one-story abandoned warehouse that they were living in. The accomdations were atrocious, with no heat, a cold cement floor, no furniture, and no running water.

Shadow had just woken up and was standing outside smoking a cigarette. She was complaining constantly, and her bipolar personality raged out of control when she wasn't high. She would scream and yell at the top of her lungs. Bolt would have to slap the piss out of her to calm her down.

She saw the bruises on Billy's face. "What the hell happened to you?"

Billy started crying again. "I got the crap beat out of me by this creep and I didn't get paid, and now Bolt wants to kill me."

"That's screwed up," Shadow replied. "Bolt should go find that prick and make him pay. I'm sorry things aren't any better here, Billy. At least being with Prince, we had warm water, heat, and a pot to piss in. This shithole sucks."

* * *

Bolt looked out the corner of his eye and saw a white Cadillac SUV pull up and park across the street. Four black men got out of the car and headed straight toward him. He assumed the black man dressed to the nines with a leather jacket, designer slacks, a silk button-down shirt, polished snakeskin loafers, a gold necklace, and sunglasses was the pimp who stole Shadow from him.

Bolt stood his ground with only Savage by his side. Blake was down the street keeping an eye on Shadow, and Rat was out pick-pocketing tourists. Savage started growling and showing his teeth.

Prince was cautious. He didn't want to mess with an angry pit bull. He took his sunglasses off, opened his jacket, and slid them in his side pocket. At the same time he conveniently gave Bolt a sneak preview of his pistol that was stuffed inside his pants.

"Well! Look what we have here." Prince glared directly into Bolt's eyes. "A purple-faced freak who thinks he can get away with stealing my property. Isn't that right, freak?"

Bolt just stood still and didn't say a word. He was outmanned and had to be careful with what he said.

"Cat got your tongue, boy?" Prince snarled. "What do you got hiding behind that grotesque, tatooed face? And I gotta say, that is one messed-up-looking tatoo," Prince continued to throw out the insults. "You are one ugly muthafucker. And what's with those fingernails?"

"Hmm," Bolt hissed.

"What did you say, freak?"

Bolt looked down at Savage, who was waiting for his master to give the attack command.

"I am not going to waste any more time on this. I think that you are a chicken shit," Prince continued to push the issue. "I want my property back, and I want them back now. Do you understand me, freak? And if I have to, I'll shoot your damn dog."

Bolt smiled back. "Did you hear that, Savage?"

Bolt pulled Savage's leash back. He could sense the fear in Prince's eyes. He crossed his arms and gave Prince a harsh look.

"I will tell you what. I have some business to attend to. Let's meet tomorrow after the sun goes down, but at a more private location, and then we will settle this once and for all," Bolt hissed.

Prince looked confused. He wasn't used to having someone stand up to him. "What's with the hiss, creep? You think that you are some kind of vampire or something? That don't work for me. I want my two whores back now! You hear me? Now!"

Bolt could see the muddled expression on Prince's face.

"No, it is not quite as simple as that." Bolt was enjoying taunting Prince. By now, most of Prince's previous foes would have folded their cards. Bolt knew that the last thing Prince wanted was to get into a confrontation in the middle of the steet.

"So tomorrow." Bolt pointed across the street with his sharp, long fingernail like the Angel of Death did to Scrooge. "Right down that alley over there. Let's go, Savage." Bolt turned and walked away.

"Fuck you! Freak!" Prince shouted.

Bolt turned back, smiled at Prince, and kept on walking. There were a couple of things that he had just learned. He was smart enough to outwit one of the toughest pimps in the city, and he also knew that staying in San Francisco was not in his future anymore. However, he could use his newfound skills and confidence out on the road in a smaller community with less competition.

CHAPTER 47

JORDAN TOSSED AND turned in his sleeping bag. He had a lot on his mind. He was excited about tomorrow, but he also felt guilty about not calling home. He missed his sister and little brother. He hoped that they were okay. While lying there in the dark, Jordan remembered the day that changed his life. He didn't want to go to school that day. A matter a fact, he didn't ever want to go back again. He felt like he was the dumbest kid in his class. It was humiliating for him to sit in class knowing that all the students thought that about him.

He continued thinking about that day. His father was driving him to school. Jordan could tell that his dad was not having a good morning either. He was not his old jovial self. He was very quiet and didn't have much to say. He had no idea how deep in trouble his father was. Later on in life, his father would share with him the stress he was going through being two car payments behind, his car registration was expired, and he was a couple of days late paying his rent, not to mention all the other wolves that were hounding him.

They pulled up in front of the school. Jordan's dad had tears in his eyes. He told Jordan that everything was going to be all right. He got out of the car and gave Jordan a hug. They both stood there crying in each other's arms. He told Jordan how proud he was of him. That was a memory that Jordan would never forget. It made him feel sad and guilty for leaving.

In the distance, Jordan could hear an old blues song drifting in the wind from some other tramp's crack box who was still up in the middle of the night. The sad tune fit the mood and helped him drift off to sleep.

CHAPTER 48

THERE WAS AN early knock on River's door Sunday morning. Mrs. Wilkens was all dressed up and ready for church.

"Come on, dear. It is time to get up and get ready for church. Everyone is downstairs having breakfast."

River was not looking forward to going to church, but she knew that there was no other choice. Church was very important to the Wilkens family.

Mrs. Wilkens believed that going to church would help River get her feet more solidly on the ground. Mary was impressed with River. She was amazed how smart she was and how she was able to adapt to the challenges that surrounded her. Unlike her husband, Mary was not bothered by River's appearance. The gothic look was her own personal style that Mrs. Wilkens accepted. Just like River's mother, Mary believed that River would grow out of it when she got older.

Today, River decided not to push the envelope. She dressed moderately in a blue dress that her mother had bought her for special occasions. She took her nose ring out and limited herself to a small amount of jewelry on each ear. She did not want to cause any friction or embarrass the family.

Jeff Wilkens was a deacon at the church and was well respected by everyone. He volunteered to help with all the community service that the church was involved in.

Mary smiled when River walked into the kitchen. "You look very nice today, dear." She was serving pancakes for breakfast. "Don't you agree, honey?"

Jeff Wilkens nodded his head in agreement. He took his last sip of orange juice and got up from the table. "Well, I have to leave early this morning. We are honoring Martin Jesup today. He just finished up his mission. See you later at the church." He gave his wife a hug and winked at Melissa.

"Goodbye, Daddy." Melissa smiled back. She took a quick glance over at River and saw that she had witnessed their exchange. It embarrassed her. She looked away and poured more syrup on her pancakes.

River wanted to reach out to her. She was very fond of Melissa. They were becoming real good friends. River's intuition sensed that it was just a matter of time before they would start to trust each other.

After breakfast, Mary Wilkens and the girls jumped in the family SUV and drove down to the church, which was located a couple miles away.

River was sitting in the back seat looking out the window. She was daydreaming and wishing that her life was different. She appreciated all the help from the Wilkens, but there was something missing in her life. The adventure of being a street kid was exciting for her. She enjoyed being on her own.

A block away from the church, River noticed a street kid standing in front of a convenience store. As she looked more closely, she recognized him. When they parked the van, River looked back where Jordan was standing.

"Would you mind if I walked down the street and talked to that boy? I know him. I would like to say hello to him."

"I don't think we have time, dear," Mrs. Wilkens answered. "Church is almost starting."

River was disappointed but excited at the same time. She was happy to see that Jordan was in Albuquerque. She knew that there would be another time to catch up with him. Even though they had only spent a small amount of time together, River felt a special bond with him.

CHAPTER 49

JESSE HAD DITCH watch today, which meant he had to stay back at the camp and keep an eye on everyone's gear. There was always a bonus for the person who had that job. Tonight he would get smokes and free drinks out of everyone's space bag (see definition of terms). Because of their special arrangement, the only time that Jordan panhandled was when Jesse was on ditch watch.

Jordan's feet were hurting him from standing on the pavement, so he sat down on the end of the curb. He had an hour to kill before the church service let out. He usually did pretty well panhandling at this spot, because the worshippers were very generous when they got out of church. Back in the day, this was Bags's favorite location when he panhandled. Jordan appreciated Bags passing on his offbeat location to him. He was also jacked up to find several half-smoked snipes (cigarette butts) lying on the ground next to the dumpster. Later on, he would share the butts with Bags and Jesse. He also considered doing more panhandling at Bags old location.

He was looking forward to getting started on learning how to ride trains. He smiled thinking that he would have stayed in high school if they offered hopping-trains classes. After training, they were planning on going to the soup kitchen for dinner.

CHAPTER 50

BOLT HAD BOUGHT himself some time with Prince. He knew that staying there was a losing proposition for him. He decided to skip town. He spotted two of Prince's spies staked out across the street. As a test, Bolt sent Rat and Blake out in different directions to see if they would be tailed. He was happy to see that the moles were only there to keep an eye on him.

Earlier that day, Rat had struck it rich on a cable car by pickpocketing an older gentleman who was carrying $1,500 cash in his billfold. They now had enough money to buy a vehicle.

Rat slipped out the back door of the abandoned building and made his way down to Van Ness Boulevard and bought a Volkswagon van from a used-car lot. Bolt gave Rat instructions to park the van a couple blocks down the street from the warehouse.

Bolt sent Blake out to find a couple intoxicated bums and bring them back to the building. Bolt planned to set up a diversion by staging a party. Bolt hoped that would sidetrack Prince's stalkers when his escape plan was put into action.

* * *

There is a golden rule in the drinking circle during a street kid party: never pass out with your shoes on. If you do, you are fair game to be elfed, and the other street kids can do whatever they liked to you if you were passed out.

The most common trick was to take a marker and write on the person's face. Some kids were more twisted and would sew the victims' clothing together or attach them to whatever they were passed out on, like a chair.

Bolt's followers were more extreme. Their elfing usually ended up being a boot party, which consisted of stomping on a helpless drunk and then taxing (forcefully taking) whatever they wanted.

* * *

"So are we going to have a boot party with those two snitches across the street?" Rat asked.

"I thought about it, but it's too risky," Bolt answered. "I have a better idea. Go make sure that Shadow is sober and alert. The last thing that we need is for her to be messed up."

At midnight, Bolt and his band of thieves implemented the first part of his strategy. Rat and Blake dragged one of the passed-out bums outside and dumped him in front of the building. Rat pulled out a magic marker and started drawing pictures on the tramp's face.

Across the street, Prince's motley crew was getting a big kick out of watching the drunk being elfed.

"Shit, man! That poor muthafucker! He is going to have more than a hangover to deal with tomorrow, especially if that marker is nonerasable."

"Oh man, can you imagine that? I am glad that I am not him." The other black man laughed.

Suddenly a medium-size rock rocketed from across street and nailed one of the Prince's men in the center of his forehead. He tumbled to the ground.

Before the other man could pull out his gun, another rock zinged him on the side of his head just below his temple. He crashed to the ground and smashed his head on the pavement.

"Yeah, baby!" Bolt hissed and raised his fist in the air. "Let's get the hell out of here. We have some rubber tramping [traveling by car] to do."

Shadow rushed across the street and joined Bolt. He gave her a big hug. She cherished that moment because she rarely got any love unless Bolt wanted some pussy.

"Good to see that I haven't lost my touch," Shadow boasted.

"And a good thing that you weren't fucked up," Bolt snarled. "But don't get too cocky. We wouldn't have had this shit to deal with in the first place if you kept your hand out of that asshole's pants."

Rat chimed in his two cents. "Wow! That was amazing. I hope that I never have to be on the other end of your slingshot. Shit! That was cool!"

"Where's Billy?" Shadow asked.

"He is upstairs and higher than a kite! He isn't coming with us. I can't afford his habit anymore. Come on. Let's get out of here."

"Bolt! Please! Come on, baby! We can't leave him here."

"Shit happens. We don't have time. Let's quit messing around." Bolt grabbed Shadow's arm and tried to pull her down the street.

Shadow jerked her arm away. "I'm not coming."

"So you want to stay here and face the Prince? Is that what you want? Are you crazy? That son of a bitch will beat the shit out of you and maybe even kill you!"

"I don't care! I am not leaving Billy here."

Bolt knew Shadow like a book and was prepared for her to throw a fit. He looked over and nodded at Blake. He came up behind her and whacked her on the back of the head and caught her before she hit the ground. He slung her over his shoulder, and they took off.

"I told you we would have to knock her ass out," Bolt said. "That stubborn Indian just won't listen!"

They raced down the street and got in the van and headed over the Bay Bridge toward Sacramento. As they were looking out over the water, Bolt told them their next destination was New Mexico.

CHAPTER 51

JIMMY SUMMERS GOT off the phone with Amaya Parks. He always enjoyed his conversations with her. She was very supportive in trying to help find his son.

He was attracted to her and wondered if she was single. He wanted to ask her out, but his lack of confidence derailed that. It was amazing how a divorce and being overweight could affect a person's self image. He avoided looking at himself in the mirror. He wished that he still looked like when he was the lead singer for Spider and the Crabs. The rock band had a huge following and played all the popular nightclubs. He was very good-looking with his long brown hair. He never had a problem getting women. They were standing in line waiting for their chance to be with him.

Jimmy picked up his acoustic guitar and sat down on the couch and strummed a few chords. His fingertips were hurting from not playing. He used to know how to play a lot of songs. But like anything else, you lose it if you haven't practiced in a while.

The doorbell rang. Gina was at the door dropping off Rose and Tommy. Gina was dressed like she was going out on the town. She had her heavy makeup caked on. Jimmy called it her rock and roll slut look.

"Hi. I hope you don't mind if I drop the kids off early?"

"That's cool," Jimmy said. "Have fun."

CHAPTER 52

JORDAN HAD A huge grin on his face when he returned to camp. He had scored eighty dollars and had a pocketful of snipes. So far it was a very good day.

Bags took them up the road apiece to where the railroad tracks were located. On their way there, Bags had to find a private place where he could squeeze one off.

"Yessum," Bag remarked. "I can't remember the last time I sat on a toilet. I know one thing for sure, though. Taking a good crap is still one of life's great pleasures."

Jordan and Jesse had a good belly laugh over that.

"Up ahead is an open area where we can begin your education on the refinements, rules, and regulations of riding trains. Yessum, sometimes I wish that I was young and westbound again. I remember those days back then when I was looked at as an oogle who didn't know shit about anything. I was just like you two Flintstones." Bags chuckled. Jordan smiled and Jesse scowled back at Bags.

"See them jewels up ahead, boys? Those are the tracks that will take you to ends of the earth. Yessum. Now, one thing you need to know from the very beginning, them there tracks have to be respected." Bags lit up one of the snipes that Jordan gave him. "Yessum, when it comes to riding trains, respect is very important."

Jordan could see the pride beaming from Bags's eyes.

"So what's the big deal about respect anyway?" Jesse asked. "The way I see it, all we have to do is learn how to jump on and off we go."

Jordan could see Bags's enthusiasm turn to disappointment.

"Well, young man, I promise you one thing. You won't last long out there. If the tracks don't get you, the bulls will."

Jesse knew that he blew it. "I'm sorry, man. I am just anxious to get out of here."

Bags finished his snipe and dropped it on the ground next to the tracks. He took a deep breath and continued.

"All right then, let's get started." Bags reached in his coat pocket and pulled out two bandannas and handed one to each of the two boys.

"It all begins with these here rags, boys. It is very important to have your bandanna with you at all times." Bags could see the sarcastic look on Jesse's face. "So you are probably saying to yourselves, 'This old man is a real wing nut [crazy].' Yessum, I can see it in your eyes, Jesse, but not so much in yours, Jordan."

"I just don't see the big deal with this rag you gave me."

Jordan just kept quiet and listened. He was fascinated with the whole tradition. He trusted Bags and knew that what he had to say was important.

"Well, you would think differently if you are on a train going through a long tunnel with all the exhaust from the engine choking you and stopping you from breathing. Yessum! You are lucky, Jesse, you have a Flintstone kid like Jordan looking out for you." Bags put his fist over his mouth and coughed. He then cleared his throat.

"I had a road dog named Georgia. She was a wonderful woman who road trains with me. When I first started out, I was kind of like you, Jesse. I had to learn things the hard way. I lost Georgia many years ago to a member of the Freight Train Riders of America. It broke my heart to lose her. I learned a good lesson. Your heart heals, but my leg never did. I will get into all that and what the train riders are all about later on."

Bags took his bandanna out from his back pocket and wiped his brow. "There is one more thing that I have to put on the table for you two to digest. It is a very important part." Bags paused, looked up at the sky, and pointed at the two boys. "Trust."

Jesse and Jordan looked at each other. Jesse gave Bags a look like what the hell. "What do you mean? We trust each other! Right, dude?"

"Yeah!" Jordan agreed.

"Well! You say that, but I beg to differ, and don't get me wrong now. I believe to some degree that you both have each other's back. But do you truly know each other?" Bags continued, "What I am saying here is when that moment comes, and it will, the both of you will need to know exactly how each other will react. Yessum, it is very important. Trust! So that's it for today."

Jordan looked at Bags and gave him a puzzled look.

"That's it?" Jesse blurted out sarcastically.

Bags shook his head. "Yessum! That's it for now. It is quite clear to me that you two boys aren't ready yet. There's more to it than meets the eye. Both of you have to make up your minds now, whether you are going to be committed to this. I don't want to waste my time if you boys aren't going to listen. Besides, I'm getting hungry for some of that soup kitchen spagetti." Bags took off, walking down the road.

Jordan and Jesse stepped back and allowed Bags to walk ahead of them so they could talk.

"Bro, are you buying into all this? What the fuck does this rag have to do with riding a train? This is stupid shit if you ask me."

Jordan had a disappointed look on his face. He was always very quiet when he was upset. He used to drive his father, Jimmy, crazy when he went into his cave and didn't say anything.

Jesse knew that he had crossed the line and upset both Bags and Jordan. He just wanted Bags to cut to the chase and teach him the ins and outs. He didn't like being preached to.

"Look, bro, I am sorry I got Bags all fired up. Man! I just want to hit the road and get to New York City."

Walking up ahead of the two boys, Bags could hear Jesse trying to plead his case. Bags had a lot of respect for Jordan. He liked his honesty and the respect he had for the traditions for being a traveler. Jesse was a different matter. Bags could relate to being a rebel and challenging the rules. It was Jesse's dishonesty and selfishness that concerned him. It was just the little things he did, like guzzling more than his share of a bottle of vodka when he thought no one was watching, that bothered Bags.

"Dude, you and I are just couple of dirty kids who could use all the help we can get. We don't know shit about anything. Bags has taught me a lot of stuff," Jordan said.

Bags smiled. It made him feel good to know that Jordan was buying into what he was saying.

"Jordan. We don't need anybody to tell us what to do. You and I are road dogs."

"Well, this road dog wants to learn things the right way. Bags knows what he is talking about. Shit! He has taken us under his wing. So let's not fuck this up. We should listen to what he has to say. That's what I think."

Jesse just shook his head. He still didn't think having a rag and trust was that big of a deal.

CHAPTER 53

RIVER SPENT MOST of the afternoon in her room covered up underneath her blankets reading one of Anne Rice's vampire books. She fantasized what it would be like to be a vampire. One problem she would have was her claustrophobia, so obviously, sleeping in a coffin did not work for her. One thing for sure, though, if she were a vampire, Jeff Wilkens wouldn't be a problem anymore. She would be stalking him instead of vice versa. That made her smile.

Earlier, Jeff wanted to know how she liked church. He thanked her for coming and appreciated that she didn't dress in her normal gothic wardrobe. River was cautious and very careful when she answered his questions. She wondered what his real motive was. When he stared at her with his eyes, he looked at her in a very lustful way. It was almost like he was undressing her. He always stared at her breasts, which made her feel uncomfortable. Every time he did that, River glanced over to see if Mrs. Wilkens noticed the way he was gawking at her. But Mary never paid attention to her husband's behavior. River wondered if Mary had any notion that her husband had a dark side to him.

There was a knock on the door. River's heart started pounding. She remained quiet hoping that whomever it was at the door would go away. There was another knock.

"Yes?" River finally answered.

"Hi, River. It's me, Melissa. Can I come in?"

River breathed a sigh of relief.

"Sure." She put the book on her nightstand and straightened up her hair.

Melissa came in and closed the door. River was glad to see her. She had a lot of her mother's tenderness, and she was fun to be around. She was one of the few people that treated River like an equal at school. River admired her. River had never had a close friend before. Her sense was that Melissa was in the same boat as her.

She sat down on the corner of the bed. River noticed that she was acting a little nervous because she was fidgeting around, rolling her fingers through her hair. Melissa looked over and noticed the book on River's nightstand.

"You like Anne Rice vampire books too?" Melissa asked.

"You do too?" River's face lit up with a wonderful smile.

"She is a great writer," Melissa said. "My father doesn't approve of me reading those type of books."

River could tell Melissa had something on her mind. "So what's up?"

"I need to talk to you about something. It is very personal."

"Okay."

Melissa moved closer to River and grabbed her hand. "Can you keep a secret?"

"Well, it depends on what it is."

"That's what I appreciate about you, River. I admire your honesty. I wish more people were like you."

Now it was River's turn to be uncomfortable. She pulled her hand away. She briefly looked away from Melissa.

River was not as compassionate or gentle as Melissa. She was more black and white and preferred to get to the point. "So what's the big secret?"

"I don't know really how to say this." Melissa paused and cleared her throat. "I have, uh, noticed how my father has been staring at you." Melissa eyes teared up.

River could see the pain riveting from the expression on Melissa's face.

River's eyes swelled up too. The two girls hugged each other and cried in each other's arms. Melissa didn't have to say another word. She knew that Melissa was being molested by her father.

CHAPTER 54

By the time Bags and the two kids arrived at the soup kitchen, the sun had disappeared below the Sandia foothills. The night was chilly with a swirling wind. There was a line of people standing outside waiting to get in. Bags figured that it would be a least an hour before they would get inside.

"This is fucked up, man. We are going to freeze our asses off," Jesse bitched. The other people in line grumbled with Jesse.

Jesse got out of line. "Hold my place just in case."

"Where you going?"

"I am going to try something." Jesse walked up toward the front of the line.

Bags shook his head. "Yessum, Jordan, there goes that Flintstone kid trying to take shortcuts again. Oh my! That boy only gives a damn about one thing—himself!"

Jordan was irritated as he watched Jesse reach in his pocket and pull out a handful of snipes and offered them to a couple of the gutter punks. Jesse smiled and waved back as he got in the front of the line.

"Son, are you sure that he is your road dog?"

Jordan heard a bunch of the older bums in line bitching about Jesse. He also overheard a group of young travelers in line behind him talking.

"I'd like to kick the shit out of that dirty kid."

"Yeah, that's not cool taking cuts," a girl in line commented.

Jordan stared at the girl. He remembered seeing her before. He also remembered the young punk with the rat-looking face standing next her. He wondered where the dude with a purple-tattooed face was.

* * *

The next day, Jesse apologized to Bags for his behavior and told him that he was ready to continue. Bags still had his doubts about Jesse but agreed to move forward. Jesse could be very charming when he needed something. But one thing Bags knew for sure, Jesse was a pompous ass, and he was worried about Jordan's welfare.

They returned to the same location by the train tracks.

"Looks like it might rain today," Bags said.

"Damn weather," Jesse whined.

"I enjoy listening to a thunderstorm. It's Mother Nature at her finest," Bags replied. "It's almost as good as hearing a lonely train whistle." Bags took in deep breath and paused for a few seconds. "Okay then, let's continue where I left off. Do you both still have those bandannas I gave you?"

Jordan pulled his out of his back pocket. Bags was pleased.

"Sorry, I, uh, left mine back at the camp," Jesse answered.

Bags could tell that Jesse was not telling the truth, but he decided to not make a big deal about it. He could tell that Jordan was disappointed too.

"Well, make sure you have it with you when you hit the road." Bags pulled out his rag. "All right, boys, I want you to take a whiff of my snot rag."

Jordan grabbed the rag and smelled the rotten odor. He handed it over to Jesse.

"Man, that smells like piss." Jesse handed the rag back to Bags.

"Yessum, there is some history with this here rag. Yessir, a lot of miles and lot of stories." Bags had a satisfying look on his face. "The condition and smell of your rag determines how many miles you've traveled and gives you creditability on the road. The longer you have traveled, the more respect you will get from the other riders."

Bags could tell that Jesse was still annoyed with all the ritual mumbo jumbo stuff. Jordan, on the other hand, was fascinated with all the tradition.

"There is more to it. Like I said before, you are going to need your rag if you are riding a train. It is important for you to remember this. Listen up now. When you are going through a tunnel, you need to wet your rag with water and cover your nose and mouth and always breathe slowly. Like I said before, never, I say never hop a train without your rag. You could choke to death without one."

Bags could tell from the look on Jesse's face that he was finally making some headway.

"So you can see there is a lot to learn about riding trains. Another thing you should know. This rag can keep you warm when you wear it on your face when it's cold."

"Pretty cool, Bags." Jordan smiled.

"So what about the Freight Train Riders of, uh, what were they called? Shit! I can't remember," Jesse stumbled.

"All in good time, Jesse, all in good time. If you don't mind, I am going over to those bushes and squeeze one off again." Bags hobbled off." When I get back, we'll talk about the different train cars."

Jordan waited for Bags to go behind the bushes so he couldn't hear. "So were you telling the truth about your rag?" Jordan asked.

"No, I lied. I don't know where it is. It must have fell out of my pocket. It's no big deal. I will get another one."

"Maybe not to you." Jordan looked over at the bushes where Bags was relieving himself. "Your bullshit is getting us nowhere. That old-timer over there squatting behind the bushes has been around a lot longer than you and I. And he sees right through your bullshit. You need to pay attention. This is important stuff. Maybe you don't think so, but you have to trust me. So quit fucking up."

"All right, bro, I hear what you say."

CHAPTER 55

EVER SINCE THAT emotional day, the relationship between Melissa and River grew to another level. It wasn't easy for Melissa to confess to River that she was having sex with her father. She was ashamed, and it was painful for her.

Although River's sexual experience with her teacher was much different from Melissa's, she knew what Melissa was going through. Together they were both able to express and share their true feelings. They both agreed that they were taken advantage of because of their youth.

Melissa was thankful to have River in her life. It was a complete change for her. On the outside, she was as perfect as a homemade apple pie on a July morning. The click of teenagers that she hung out with sometimes were members of the church and came from rich families. They were very snobby. They thought that they were better than anyone else. They looked down on people like River because of the way she dressed.

Melissa was the only person in her group who didn't think like that. She treated everyone with respect. It was a great quality that she inherited from her mother. She was always friendly, full of life, and had a beautiful smile. She acknowledged anyone that she came in contact with. Heck, she even had a friendship with Lyle, the school janitor. It made Lyle's day every time she greeted him with her wonderful smile. No one could ever tell that she was keeping deep inside her an agonizing nightmare.

Her dark side was very dysfunctional. Part of her was ashamed of her incestuous love for her father and the other half was her sexual attraction to it. Her father treated her like a princess. He told her how much he loved her and how special their relationship was. He told her how glad he was that he had sexual desires for her instead of other women outside the family. He convinced Melissa that her mother and him had a different relationship together that had nothing to do with sex. He told her that their love for each other was special.

Early on her sexual relationship with her father, which began when they lived in Salt Lake City, was amazing for her. She got to experience what it was like to be loved and adored by a man. But as time passed and she grew older, her dark secret tormented her. It was like an addiction that she couldn't stop. In her mind, she related to being stalked by a vampire who would come to her in the night and do forbidden things to her.

The painful guilt was growing deep inside her, knowing that she was cheating on her mother and how destructive it would be if she found out the truth.

All those hideous thoughts that raced through her mind had finally taken a toll on her. It was becoming more difficult to pretend that she was the perfect little girl living a wonderful life. It finally came to a head when Melissa saw how her father was acting toward River. She knew that he desired her and that made her jealous.

And that was why when she came into River's room and saw her reading the vampire story that she knew that it was the right thing to do to share her secret with River. It was a real relief for Melissa to finally have someone to talk to about it and express her feelings about how it really felt to be preyed upon in the middle of the night.

CHAPTER 56

JEFF WILKENS WAS startled by the turn of events. He was not pleased witnessing the bonding that was taking place between the two girls. It drove a wedge between him and his daughter.

He was caught off guard that first night when he tried to get in to Melissa's room and discovered that her door was locked. He looked around to make sure nobody was watching and knocked gently on the door again. He tried several times before giving up and heading back into the study to think about what had just happened.

Jeff wasn't positive, but he was afraid that River was now aware of what was going on. He first reaction was anger toward his daughter for betraying him. He was also frightened and knew that he had to be very careful. He had to tread softly. It would be an awful scandal if anyone else found out. His life would be ruined. The sad thing was that he only cared about what the consequences would be for him. He never even considered the harm that he had caused his daughter mentally or what it would do to his wife if she learned the truth.

The first thing he had to do was repair the damage between him and his daughter. Secondly, he had to figure out what do about River. He made up his mind that she was dangerous, and he knew for sure that he wanted her out of the house.

CHAPTER 57

FOR THE FIRST time in her life, Melissa was feeling better about herself. With River's support, she had made the first step to heal herself. In time, she hoped to be able to cope with her shame and even confess to her mother. But she also still loved her father. She didn't want to hurt him. She wrestled back and forth with her mind trying to find a solution to the problem.

The aching truth made it very cloudy and difficult for her. River's strong opinion on the matter guided her and gave her the strength and patience to work her way through the complicated mire.

CHAPTER 58

BOLT WAS NOT welcomed with a ticket parade when he arrived at Hobo Flat. From the first time he laid eyes on him, Captain Cooper knew that there was trouble. (Having that creepy tattooed face didn't help matters.) Besides his dubious hygiene, something didn't smell right. The captain was sure he was up to no good. His dog, Niko, also sensed the danger, especially with Bolt's pit bull invading his territory. Both dogs growled at each other. It was clear that the two dogs had alpha male issues.

Captain Cooper had worked hard to stay out of the Albuquerque Sheriff's Department spotlight. The last thing he needed was for this young punk to bring more attention to the camp.

* * *

Sheriff Deputy Rhett Morningstar's territory was Hobo Flat. Sheriff Miles Cotton introduced Rhett to Captain Cooper. That was the only time that Rhett set foot inside the camp. Sheriff Cotton made it very clear to Rhett that Hobo Flat was off limits. Rhett respected the sheriff's wish, but from time to time, he showed a presence by driving by.

Rhett was half-Cherokee Indian. He was a very handsome man of average height, with dark-brown skin and straight black hair. He grew up on the Pyramid Lake Indian Reservation outside Reno. He was always interested in how things worked. Norman Meeks, the tribal chief, recognized Rhett's talent and offered him a position with the reservation police after he graduated from school. He stayed there a few years and gained some valuable experience. Rhett's goal in life was to become a homicide detective. He knew that would never happen if he stayed on the reservation taking care of drunk Indians on a Friday night. So that was how he ended up in New Mexico. He got a job with the Albuquerque Sheriff's Department.

Captain Cooper could tell by the look in Rhett's eyes that he was curious, unsatisfied, and had half a brain. Those qualities were the mark of a good police officer. Nathan just hoped that Rhett wasn't too eager to learn more about him.

Rhett was facinated by the drifter life. He was amazed how they were able to survive without any of the modern conveniences. He wondered why a man like Captain Cooper lived the life of a tramp. He seemed to be very intelligent and capable. He searched the police database and found no information on him. Rhett assumed that was not his real name. He hoped someday to be able to sit down with the captain and pick his brain.

* * *

Bolt wasn't expecting to have this kind of resistance from the older tramp community. He thought they would be just a bunch of old complacent drunks that would just sit around and let him have things his own way. Even though he was older, Nathan Cooper was a very competent adversary. He had wisdom and experience on his side, and Bolt could tell that the captain wasn't buying into his voodoo shit.

Bolt was convinced that Cooper would be an easier challenge for him to overcome than dealing with the pimp from the Bay Area. For the time being, he decided to step back and be patient.

"Rat, you need to use your rodent ears and keep your weasel nose to the ground," Bolt hissed. "We need to find a weakness in that old man's armor."

"I think the first thing we need to do is have Savage take that old fart's dog out," Rat snarled.

"I will consider that, but let me do the thinking," Bolt spoke softly. Although it wasn't a bad idea, Bolt didn't want Rat to know that. The last thing he needed was for Rat to start making his own decisions.

Bolt's first move was to set up his own camp a few miles up the road. He made the Volkswagon van the main headquarters and a place for him to sleep. He parked the car between two huge boulders up against a hill, which served as a fort and protected the car from the wind.

Rat, Blake, and Shadow set up their sleeping quarters fifty yards away from the van. Rat found a large canvas at the city dump and converted it into a tent. They mounted it to the side of one of the jagged boulders and secured it by driving stakes into the ground. At night, all three of them snuggled up together to keep warm. The only time that would change was if Bolt wanted sex and would have Shadow spend the night with him. Otherwise, she slept with Blake and Rat.

An unexpected problem surfaced with Blake. Normally he just kept to himself unless Bolt needed him to do some heavy lifting or rough somebody up. Blake developed a thing for Shadow. When he was around her, he behaved like a sick puppy. There wasn't anything that he wouldn't do for her. He would get up early and bring her a fresh cup of coffee. He washed her clothes for her in the creek. Shadow was aware of his feelings and took complete advantage of it. She would flirt with him and compliment him on how handsome he was. Blake fell for it hook, line and sinker.

Bolt was aware of Blake's little crush. At first he didn't take it too seriously. He would joke back and forth with Rat about it. He did warn Shadow to not push things too far, but it was too late for that. Blake had fallen madly in love. He started to resent Bolt and became jealous. It became harder and harder for him to control his anger whenever he heard the van rocking up and down. He would storm out of the tent and walk up into the hills. A few times he took his frustration out on some of the other tramps who happened to be in the wrong place at the wrong time.

Bolt decided to not screw Shadow when Blake was around. He told her the importance of having Blake on his side until he had figured out a way to get rid of Captain Cooper. Shadow understood and backed off.

* * *

It didn't take long for Shadow and Rat to figure out the landscape. Most of the people who lived in Albuquerque were very friendly. There was a religious element that frowned on having drugs and prostitution being right out in the open. The two seedy parts of town were Central Avenue, where the strip clubs, bars, and run-down motels flourished and an area around the fairgrounds where the gangs hung out.

Rat's sneakiness and street savvy helped him get things done. For a bottle of whiskey, one of the home bums hooked Rat up with a drug dealer, and he was also able to find someone downtown who would exchange used needles for clean ones for free.

Bolt started his propaganda by sending Rat out to spread the word that there was now a new place for traveling kids to camp that didn't have the all strict rules like Hobo Flat. Bolt's new camp attracted weekend street kids. (Oogles who were fresh on the road and not street smart. Usually when times got tough, most oogles would run home to Mommy.) Even though it was a pain in the ass to put up with the obnoxious young punks, Bolt used it as an opportunity to recruit new soldiers and prostitutes for his business.

It didn't take long for Shadow to find her first customer. He picked her up while she heading back to camp.

Shadow had a big smile on her face when she saw Bolt. She pulled out a hundred-dollar bill and proudly handed it over to him. "Here you go, baby. I hitched a ride back with this guy and fucked him. He might be a regular john."

"Oh yeah?"

"Yeah, he wants to meet me again on Saturday afternoon."

"Nice," Bolt whispered.

"He's is well-off for sure. He was driving a nice car," Shadow explained. "He told me his name. Hmm, what the fuck was it? Huh, shit! Jeff. That's it! His name was Jeff."

"Nice work!" Bolt pulled a plastic baggie from his coat pocket containing a syringe, a spoon, and a folded square piece of aluminum foil. He handed it to Shadow. "Here you go. Take a little taste. Not too much, though. I don't want you to get strung out. We have a party tonight."

Bolt woke Rat up from his afternoon nap. "Hey, it's time to get your ass up and start setting shit up for the party tonight. I am expecting a large crowd. Lots of oogles, and hopefully, some of those older home bums will show up too."

Rat crawled out of his sleeping bag and nudged Blake. "Come on, big boy. Let's get this party rolling. We have to go to the dump and find some extra barrels for campfires.

"Hey, Bolt. Do you remember that dude that I told you about?" Rat asked.

"Huh?"

"Remember? That dude I told you about that could save us all the hassle of having to go through all that bullshit to buy booze."

"So?"

"Well, he will be dropping off the stuff soon." Rat realized Bolt was playing him. "Aw, you're screwing with me, man!" It bugged the crap out of Rat when Bolt was messing with him.

Bolt enjoyed teasing Rat. He smiled and looked over at Shadow. "Hey, baby. Come here a minute." He whispered softly into her ear, so Blake couldn't heare, "You have to take care of Rat's delivery man after he drops off the booze. Make sure he has a good time. And make sure your boyfriend isn't around."

Shadow rolled her eyes.

CHAPTER 59

JORDAN AND JESSE learned a lot about trains, especially Jordan, who was like a sponge, soaking in all the small details. Most of Bags's classroom took place on a hillside that overlooked the train yard that was a few miles up the road from Hobo Flat. Jordan was amazed on just how much he really didn't know. He never realized that there were so many different types of boxcars, including G trains, tankers, gondolas, flatbeds, lumber cars, 48s, 53s, piggybacks, units, slave units, coal cars, and hazmat cars. It was very helpful to actually see what all the cars actually looked like.

"You boys see that flatbed over there sitting by itself with the semi trailer on top of it?"

Jordan and Jesse nodded yes.

"That there thing is called a piggyback. Now, boys, the best place to stay hidden on one of those cars is for you to find a spot between the semi wheels. But let me warn you that you still will be open season for the bulls to spot."

"Bulls?" Jesse asked.

"Yessum, the railroad police. We call them bulls! They are not your friends. Their job is to keep people like you off the trains. They patrol the rails and train yards in their white SUVs. Bulls have more flexibility than most law officers. They are not supervised as much, if you know what I mean. They are given a lot of rope, and they get away with a lot of stuff. In their minds, the bulls consider us to be tramps without any rights."

"Screw them!" Jesse snarled.

"Now you are getting it. Once they beat the crap out of me for just walking on the tracks. Yessum, I lost a couple of teeth over that. So don't mess with them if you don't have to, especially you, Jesse."

Jesse exchanged a mischievous smile with Bags.

"I am just warning you. They are nobody to mess with. No sir! But knowing you, Jesse, I suspect that you are going to have learn the hard way."

Both Jesse and Jordan laughed.

"There are a few bulls out there that are different from the rest and understand us. I met one of them around Klamath Falls. His name was Charley Babbit. He found me hiding on a train and let me go with just a warning. He even gave me a couple bucks for a cup of coffee. Yessum, he was a good man."

One of the other home buns from the camp, Big Mike, yelled up at Bags from the bottom of the hill, "Hey, Bags! The captain wants to have a meeting with everyone up at the shack in an hour."

"All right then!" Bags shouted back.

"Don't be late, old fool," Big Mike grumbled and walked off.

"Well, boys, it looks like we will have to pick this up later. We don't want to keep Captain Nathan Cooper waiting."

"You guys go ahead. I don't feel like going. I'm tired," Jesse said.

"Come on, bro, we have to go," Jordan answered.

"That's a wise decision, my man!" Bags just shook his head at Jesse.

Jesse decided not to argue about it, and so they headed up the hill to the captain's shack.

"So, Bags, what about the FTRA you were telling us about?" Jordan asked.

"Well, I guess now is as good as any to tell you about the Freight Train Riders of America. Yessum, they are a distinguished group that consists of mostly older tramps nowadays. The gang is well-known for being brutal and trifling. I have known and met many FTRA members and found that none of them were either brutal or trifling. Unless you wanted to mess with them, and then they can be a handful.

"So how do you become a member?"

"Well, not by being a smart-ass like you!" Bags smiled at Jesse.

"Shit! What are you talking about, old man?" Jesse joked back.

"Well, first you have to know how to ride trains, and second, you have to be trusted with the secrets of the order."

"Sounds like the Klan," Jesse fired back.

"Well, there are some similarities. I mean, they are a brotherhood. But it is not racial, thank God. An FTRA member has to nominate your ass to be a member. The initiation is pretty simple. Remember that rag I gave you? The night of your initiation, the rag is placed on the tracks. All the FTRA members who are present take turns pissing on it. Then the one being initiated has to wear the piss-soaked rag on his head until it dries."

"That's pretty stupid."

"Well, you lost your rag, so it doesn't matter anyway. Hey, by the way, you boys already know an FTRA member."

"We do?"

"Yessum, in just a few minutes, we are going listen to what he has to say."

* * *

The whole camp, including the older hobos, the squatter women, and some street kids, were gathered at Captain Cooper's shack. Captain Cooper was sitting in his rocking chair on his porch with his dog, Niko, sitting by his side staring out at the crowd.

Bags and the two boys were the last to show up. Captain Cooper made eye contact with Bags and waited for him to find a place to sit down.

The captain stood up and cleared his throat. He looked very distinguished with his thin steel-rimmed glasses, dressed in his long hanging Pale Rider coat, cowboy hat, and boots. His face was rugged and weather-beaten. But he still looked pretty good for an older man.

"Thanks, y'all, for coming. I just wanted to get together and go over a few things. I know many of you are thinking about planning on attending the big party at that other camp down the road. I can't stop you from going. I know a lot of you younger kids don't necessarily like the rules here at Hobo Flat. And most of you think us older tramps are a bunch of wing nuts."

All the older bums, including Bags, chorused in agreement. He winked at Jesse.

"Just remember, we have been around a lot longer than you. I have heard all the talk about how much easier it is to live over at that other place. Well, the grass is not necessarily greener on the other side of the hill."

Bags once again glanced over at Jesse. He knew Jesse was considering that option.

"Y'all, I have seen it all and lived it all. I rode trains all over this blessed land, from flatbeds to junk trains. I have had to put up with choo choo riders, railroad bulls, drug addicts, you name it. Please be careful tonight, and don't travel by yourself. I do not trust that tattooed-faced gutter punk up the road. I got a bad feeling about him. There are also going to be some other kids from town there. Alchohol does a lot of strange things to people. Some folks get mean and want to prove their manhood. Us older tramps just pass out and go to sleep. So take care and have a good evening. And oh, there is a storm blowing in, so tie your stuff down so it don't blow away."

Captain Cooper and Niko stepped off the porch and walked toward Bags. "Come on, boy! Let's take a walk before the weather turns." He nodded his head. "Bags, come by my place later and have a drink with me."

"Yessum."

"Keep your eyes on your boys tonight. I have a bad feeling about things." Captain Cooper headed up the hill.

"So you two thinking about going over there?" Bags asked Jordan.

"Yeah, we were thinking about it. Jesse wants some pussy tonight. He has got his eye on a squat mattress who is going to be there."

Jesse had a big smirk on his face.

"You two stick together tonight, you hear me now?"

"Don't worry! Jordan and I can take care of ourselves."

Bags gave them both a disappointing look as he lit up a snipe.

"So will you keep an eye on our gear for us Bags?" Jordan asked.

"Yessum, just like the Captain said, I'll make sure your shit doesn't blow away. The captain is right, you know. There is a storm coming, and it is just not the weather."

CHAPTER 60

RIVER AND MELISSA'S friendship grew stronger. They were inseparable. They learned a great deal about each other. River appreciated how grounded Melissa was. She had a very positive attitude about the world. Her positive energy was an inspiration, although from time to time River could see the sorrow in Melissa's eyes from her troubled past.

Melissa appreciated River's strength and courage to be able to survive on her own. She wished that she had River's independence.

Also Melissa's friendship was a great benefit for River. She was given more freedom. She was allowed to go places as long as Melissa was with her.

The girls' friendship continued to not bode well with Jeff Wilkens. His maneuvers to persuade Melissa failed. It frustrated him that his intimate relationship with his daughter was on hold. He knew better than to try to push it any further than what he was already doing. Now that River was in the picture, he was afraid that his wife would find out.

River's influence on Melissa was changing her. Her friends at school and church noticed that she wasn't hanging around them as much. She preferred to be with River. Melissa started to wear more makeup. She was no longer the innocent little prep girl. She even put a small ring in her left eyebrow, which infuriated her father and embarrassed him around the other members of the church.

Jeff Wilkens complained to his wife about the changes that were taking place with their daughter. Mary disagreed with her husband. She told him that it was just a phase that she was going through.

Vice versa, Melissa was also a good influence for River. She taught her how to play chess. Things were turning around for River after the shoplifting charges were dropped. She was feeling good about herself.

* * *

The girls were in Melissa's bedroom listening to old-school punk rock.

"Wow, this band is really angry."

River smiled. "Hey now! What do you mean? This is a love song." Melissa watched her dancing around the room to the throbbing song. "I love Black Flag. I can relate to them."

Melissa laughed out loud. "You are crazy, River Walker!"

"Hey, I have an idea." River jumped back on the bed and grabbed Melissa's hands. "Do you want to do something different tonight?"

"What do you mean?"

"I mean, really out of the box!"

"Okay. What?"

"We have been invited to a party with some street kids." Melissa could see the enthusiasm in River's expression.

"You mean hanging out with homeless people?"

"Yeah, are you up for that?"

"Wow, I wasn't expecting that."

"I told you that it was out of the box. I have a good friend who invited us. Don't worry, I will protect you."

Melissa knew that she would be taking a big risk. She felt nervous about it, but she was also sort of excited. She knew her parents would not approve of her taking such a risk.

"So what do you think, punk rock girl?"

Melissa smiled and sighed as she nodded her head. "Okay! But we can't tell my parents."

"Of course not, silly. What do you think, that I have a lopsided skull?"

They both hugged and laughed with joy.

CHAPTER 61

JIMMY SUMMERS DROPPED the kids off at Gina's house. He had butterflies in his stomach as he drove down across town to meet Amaya for a drink. This was his first real date with a woman that he actually cared about since his divorce. He really liked her, even though it was a bit odd for him to be going out on a date with a police officer.

They were meeting at Big Red's, an old college hangout located across the street from the University of Nevada. Jimmy never went to college, but his band played a lot gigs at the saloon. Amaya graduated from UNR with a BA in law enforcement.

Jimmy was impressed with Amaya. She had a beautiful face with full lips and short blond hair. She was fun to talk to. She very smart and could converse about a lot different topics, including music and sports. She seemed to be levelheaded and easygoing. Jimmy liked that about her.

When Jimmy arrived at Big Red's, he spotted a few old friends at the bar.

"Well, look what the cat dragged in! Good old Jimmy Summers."

"Hey, Karl. Hey, Ryan." Jimmy gave each of his friends a hug.

"Jimmy! Is rum and Coke still your poison?"

"Hell no! I am a lightweight now. I stick to beer."

"I can tell by that beer gut you have been cultivating," Karl joked.

"At least I still have my hair!" Jimmy smirked.

"Ha! I see you haven't lost your sense of humor."

Karl got the pretty bartender's attention. "Hey, Shelly, get this lightweight a beer."

"So what are you up to, Jimmy?"

Jimmy filled his friends in about his divorce and about his date tonight. They teased him a little bit. It felt good for Jimmy to see his old friends. It was good to catch up with them. Karl was married with two kids and was a financial broker. Ryan was divorced but owned his own landscape business. Jimmy was sort of envious that his friends had careers and was sort of embarrassed to tell them that he was a salesman at Sears.

"Well, here's to the Wolf pack!" Karl hoisted his glass up in the air.

"So are you still playing music?" Ryan asked.

"Yeah, I pick up my guitar and strum a few chords once in a while."

"Man, Jimmy! I remember watching you playing up there on stage. You were quite the rock star." Ryan smiled.

"Yeah, let's drink to that!" Karl raised his glass.

"Shit, I was always jealous of you, Jimmy. You had all the women after you," Ryan added.

"Man, those were great memories. I would get those ladies back to my apartment and pour a couple of rum and Cokes down them." Jimmy smiled.

"Good old rum and Coke."

"Yep!"

Karl looked over and noticed a woman walking through the door. "Wow, look at that beauty that just walked in."

Jimmy couldn't believe his eyes. Amaya walked up to him with a big grin on her face. For the first time, he got to see her dressed like a woman.

"My, my, my, said the spider to the fly." Karl laughed.

She was everything Jimmy had hoped for. To go along with her beautiful features, she also had a curvaceous body.

"Boys, I would like you to meet my friend, police officer Amaya Parks."

Karl, who was always the smart-ass of the group, blurted out, "Please arrest me now."

CHAPTER 62

JUST AFTER SUNDOWN, Bags showed up at Captain Cooper's shack. He knocked on the door. Captain Cooper's dog rushed to the door barking furiously.

"It's all right, boy! Quiet down." Captain Cooper opened the door. "Well, hello, Bags, come on in and make yourself at home."

Niko walked up and smelled Bags and then went back over to his regular spot next to the stove.

Bags always enjoyed spending time with the captain. He felt special being invited to his shack. For being so weathered and run-down on the outside, Bags was impressed with how well-kept up the inside was. The one-room building was no more than five hundred square feet. Bags was not sure what the building was used for before the captain moved in. It had a cement floor, so he thought maybe it was a storage building. In the left-hand corner was the wood-burning pellet stove. There was a double bed and a makeshift dresser at the opposite end of the room. In the middle of the room was a tattered rug with a worn-out couch, a comfortable chair, and a stained coffee table. The room was lit by a couple of kerosene lamps that were sitting on small wooden tables in opposite corners of the stove.

"Mighty comfortable place you have here, Captain." Bags took a seat on the couch.

The captain pulled out two shot glasses and a bottle of Jack Daniel's. "Help yourself, old friend."

Bags reached in the side pocket of his coat and plucked out two wrapped cigars. "I have been saving these two for a special occasion." He clipped off the ends of the cigar and handed one to the captain.

"That is wonderful." The captain unwrapped his cigar and smelled the tobacco. "Ah! There is nothing like the smell of a good cigar."

Captain Cooper then went over to the stove, grabbed a small shovel, and stirred the burning pellets. He then came back, poured himself a shot, and sat down.

The captain raised his shot glass. "Here's to good friends. Bags, you and I have lived here at Hobo Flat for many years."

"Yessir, Captain, it will be ten years at the end of March." Bags took a swig of whiskey.

"My goodness, how time flies."

"Yessum, Captain! We have seen a lot."

"Well, then you know how concerned I am about this other camp. I spoke with Deputy Morningstar. He's not thrilled with having another camp either."

"Yessir, I can see why you are concerned about things." Bags took a drag of his cigar.

Captain Cooper lit his cigar and took a puff. He set the cigar down on the edge of the table and poured himself another shot. He paused a few minutes before he broached what was on his mind.

"Bags, I got a feeling this Bolt kid has intentions to take over Hobo Flat. This is the first time that I have ever been challenged. Of course, I am not perfect, and I am sure some of the decisions that I have made over the years weren't popular, but I have tried my best to be fair."

"Well, Captain, it's not easy being in charge. In my travels, I have seen far worse places. I am blessed to have a place to stay. There aren't many camps around the country. Just a bunch of cement paving and bridges to sleep under."

Captain Cooper filled both shot glasses.

"Bags, I need your help with something."

"Yessum."

"Over the past few months, the population of younger travelers has increased at Hobo Flat. It is hard for me to relate with them. They have a whole new way at looking at things. They come from a different breed. A lot different than growing up in Texas."

"Captain, being a Negro and all, I was born with two strikes against me." Bags took a drag from his cigar. "I think this younger generation thinks they have been shortchanged too! That is why there are so many of them nowadays. They are truly misunderstood. They had to grow up too fast. They are still just kids who don't fit into regular society. My momma used to say even a train has to stop somewhere. So here they are on our front steps."

"Bags, I know that you have a couple of the Flintstone kids' ears."

"Well, sort of, Captain. At least one of them." Bags laughed.

"And is that Jordan, right?"

"Yessum. He is a good, honest boy."

"I know that the young street kids are going back and forth from camp to camp."

"Yessum, they are being enticed by all the freedom and no rules to follow."

"So do you think that you could talk to him and see if he would keep an eye out for us at the other camp in case anything comes up that I should know about?" From the tone of his voice, Niko raised his head and looked at the captain.

"Niko sure is a smart dog."

"Yep, he can smell it in the wind. So what do you think, Bags?"

"I'll ask him, Captain. I don't mind doing that. I know one thing, he does not like being a snitch. I will keep my eyes and ears to the ground here too. By the way, I told both boys that you were FTRA."

Captain Cooper refilled the glasses. "Boy, that was a wild time in my life." He raised his glass. "Here's to the FTRA."

"All except for the one member, Yankee Wallace. He stole my woman."

They clanked shot glasses.

"I sure miss that woman. I wonder if she is still alive."

"Bags, you and I will be known forever by the tracks we leave behind."

"Yessum! I reckon that you are right about that, at least in our small pond! So, Captain, let me ask you something. How did you end up being a tramp? It seems like you could have had a great life in the real world."

Captain Cooper poured another shot. "Yeah, you're right. I could have. I mean, I was on my way. I had a good job, but I got derailed. My bailiwick is that I like younger women. One night, I ended up with this underage girl who lied to me about her age. She came from a wealthy family, and they wanted me sent up river. So I took off and kept running ever since."

"Yessum! Here's to Hobo Flat!"

CHAPTER 63

BY NINE O'CLOCK, the party was rocking. It was an icy-cold night with a chilly blowing wind whipping through the camp. The weather didn't bother the twenty people who were standing around the three huge woodburning barrels. It was electric with Judas Priest blasting out of the crack box. The hooting and hollering revelers included street kids that were made up mostly of boys and a handful of girls, including Shadow.

There was a variety of different types of alcohol being passed around, including space bags (a cheap wine that comes in a big box that could be discarded and the silver birthing bags were used to drink out of). Thunder chicken was the most popular drink for large groups of street people. (It was fortified Thunderbird wine mixed with half gallons of hard liquor and a packet of Kool-Aid.) In the drinking circle, it was called swilling, pass, and chase it. The half-gallon jug would be passed around from person to person. Each person would take a swig and consume as much as they could with one drink and then pass it on to the next person and chase it with either Coke, if it was whiskey; fruit punch, if it was vodka; or root beer, if it was rum. Ninety-five percent of travelers enjoyed the same thing on the road. (Life was quantity, not quality, for the least amount of money when you drink.)

Melissa, River, and her friend Marco Frazier arrived at the party at around ten. Marco and River were old high school friends. They hung out together at Smokers' Row. Marco was not sure what to do with his life. He was intrigued with the traveling world, but so far he had just stuck his toe in the water. He still liked having a roof over his head and bed to sleep in.

Marco parked his car on the side of the road. From there they walked a hundred yards to get to the camp. When they arrived, they were greeted by a lot of bumbling, stumbling drunks. Melissa wished that she had dressed warmer. The ice-cold air was cutting right through her thin jacket, sweatshirt, and tight black jeans. This was a very a strange scenario for Melissa. The surrounding was very creepy, with the pitch-black night combined with the shadows of the crackling flames shooting out of the fire barrels and flickering off the faces of the people. She was very uncomfortable. It was almost like she was in the movie *The Night of the Living Dead*. All the people standing around looked like zombies in the darkness gawking at her with their piercing eyes and rugged faces. She was spinning with all the attention she was getting. She could swear that she saw a scary-looking dude with his whole face tattooed staring at her with a lustful smile.

River was not bothered at all. This was old hat for her. She had been to a few street kid parties on the road. She put her arm around Melissa. "Hey, it's cool. Don't be freaked out. I won't let anything happen to you. Let's go stand over by the bonfire and get warm."

"This is really weird!" Melissa expressed her feelings.

"If this is too much for you to handle, I will have Marco drive us home."

Melissa could see that Marco had found a few of his friends and was giving them hugs and handshakes. He motioned for River and her to come join him.

"Uh, well, okay! I will give it a chance."

"By the way, you look marvelous tonight, darling," River joked. "I would believe your friends at school would say you are now fashion deficient."

Melissa laughed. "I don't normally use this word, but it is fucking cold out here."

"That cracks me up to hear the f-bomb come out of your mouth. Let's go get a swig of that Thunder chicken that Marco is sipping on. That will warm your ass up."

"I am not sure about drinking alcohol."

"Oh, come on, now! You need to go for it. It's up to you, though. But trust me, you need to loosen up a little bit. Remember, I've got your back."

As they walked over to Marco, Melissa stepped on a rock and twisted her ankle. "Oh my god!" She screamed in agony as the pain shot up her leg. She stumbled to the ground grabbing her ankle. As she fell, her purse hit the dirt, and her cell phone fell out on the ground.

"Shit, Melissa! Are you okay?" River knelt down beside her.

"I sprained my ankle!" Tears were running down Melissa's cheeks. "Man, that hurts!"

Jordan saw what was happening and came over to help. He could see Melissa was crying.

"Here, take it easy," Jordan said. "I got you." Jordan picked Melissa up and carried her over to a stool that was sitting next to a tree.

"Here, take a swig of this." Jordan handed Melissa a bottle of vodka. She took a drink and gagged at the taste of the liquor.

Jordan was amused by the retched expression on her face. "I am not laughing at you. It was the face that you made."

"Man, that is the worst thing that I have ever tasted."

"I know, it tastes like shit at first, but it will make you feel better. And it already has taken your mind off your pain." Jordan gently grabbed her ankle. "Whoa! Your ankle is really swelled up."

"Oh my god! It really hurts!"

Jordan found another stool and set it down in front of Melissa. "Just keep you foot elevated on this for a while."

Melissa cringed in pain as she raised up her foot. "Thank you for helping me."

"No problem. I'm Jordan."

"I am Melissa, and this is my friend, River."

"River and I have met before."

River's eyes sparkled with joy knowing that Jordan remembered her. "Hi!"

"Hello," Jordan answered back bashfully.

"It's so good to see you again."

"I am glad too!" Jordan smiled. "Here, you want a sip?" Jordan handed River the vodka.

"Thanks." River took a huge swig. "And thanks for helping my friend. You are pretty good at rescuing damsels in distress."

"I guess so!" Jordan laughed. He never thought of it that way before.

Jesse walked up and joined them. Jordan introduced him to River and Melissa. Jesse smiled at River and bowed his head.

"It is a pleasure to meet you."

Jordan shook his head. He couldn't believe how lame that was.

River got a kick out of it and laughed. "You're not serious?"

"Of course I am," Jesse answered. "You are beautiful!"

"Yeah, right!" River smirked.

Jordan crouched down toward Melissa. "How's your foot?"

Melissa took another sip of vodka. "It still stings. Have you ever twisted your ankle?"

"Yeah, on the road and once when I was in Little League. That motherfucker hurt for weeks."

"So you like sports?"

"Not really! My parents signed me up and made me play. Do you like sports?"

"Not really!" They both cracked up. "I was kind of forced into trying out for cheerleader too. So where did you first meet River?"

"I, uh, changed a flat tire for the family she was traveling with. Small world, huh?"

"It sure seems like it. So are you a runaway?"

"I am a traveler. How about you?" Jordan asked.

"I still live at home with my family. River lives with us. Boy, this stuff you gave me to drink is making me light-headed."

"It kind of numbs the pain." Jordan was amazed how easy it was to carry on a conversation with Melissa.

"Yep, I am feeling better." Melissa smiled. Melissa was enchanted with Jordan's kindness. She could tell that hidden beneath his scruffy and unwashed, filthy appearance was a down-to-earth, honest boy.

"Looks like your friend, uh, what's his name?"

"Jesse."

"Yeah, Jesse is having a good time." Melissa burped and laughed. "Oops, I'm sorry."

Jordan looked over and spotted Jesse and River standing in the drinking circle next to one of the fire barrels laughing and taking a swig of Thunder chicken. He saluted Jesse.

Jesse smiled and looked at River. "I will be right back. Don't you go anywhere."

"I won't." River looked over at Jordan. He was more her type than Jesse. She was disappointed that she wasn't with him, but she understood his attraction for Melissa.

Jesse walked over to Jordan. "Everything cool?"

"So far. Looks like things are going pretty good for you too!"

"Yep! It's shocking how much she wants me!"

"Dude! You are so full of shit."

* * *

A few feet away from them, Bolt was staring with lustful eyes through the flames at Melissa.

"Hey, Rat, do see that girl over there?" Bolt hissed.

"The pretty one sitting down? It looks like she might have hurt her foot."

"I want you to go over there and figure out a way to get her away from her group of friends and bring her over to the van."

"I know that dude Marco that is hanging with them. I will go over and see what's up."

"Good. You also need to find out how she got here."

"I am pretty sure Marco drove her over here in his car."

"If that's the case, you need to send Blake out to find it and make sure that it won't start."

"I am not sure about that. He can't handle his booze," Rat replied. "He just puked and is passed out over there.

Bolt had a disgusted look on his face. "Well, I guess you'll have to do it then." Bolt then looked at Shadow. "Hey, baby, I need you to do something for me. See that street kid who is with that chick over there?"

"Yep, I remember seeing him before."

"I want you to make sure that he is really drunk and make sure he has a good time."

"I would be happy to do that," Shadow answered. From the first time she briefly brushed by Jordan at the convenience store, he had made an impression on her.

"So do you recognize that other girl standing over there?" Rat asked.

"Which one?"

"The porky one."

"Oh yeah!" Bolt smiled. He flashed back to smashing in her car window and bashing her on the side of her head. "Huh! Well, I wonder if she remembers us watering her hole?"

"I think she was pretty much out of it when we humped her," Rat replied.

"She was wet and moaning when I was inside her," Bolt answered. He took a drink from his space bag. "Keep an eye on her. We don't need her to fuck things up."

"You sure you want to do this, dude? You have new followers. The party is going really well."

"Look! I know what I'm doing. Don't argue with me," Bolt spat back.

"I'm just saying!"

"Shit, dude! Sometimes you are a pain in the ass. Now get going, and don't disappoint me."

The predicted storm arrived. Heavy snowflakes began to stick on the ground.

CHAPTER 64

JIMMY AND AMAYA were having a wonderful time. They felt very comfortable with each other. Jimmy liked her style and personality. She was easily amused and laughed at all his jokes. There was one thing that he noticed that could be a red flag. She was very straightforward and had her own opinions on how children should be disciplined. Jimmy skated the issue. He knew this wasn't the time to be getting into a heavy parenting discussion. He definitely could feel the chemistry brewing between them.

Amaya had the same feelings about Jimmy. It was refreshing to be around someone who wasn't in law enforcement. She shared with Jimmy about her two previous marriages. Both ex-husbands were cops.

After having three drinks, things loosened up between the two of them. They started holding hands and hugging each other.

"You two want another round?" the cocktail waitress asked.

"What do you think? One more?"

Amaya smiled. "Sure. Why not! I don't have to work tomorrow."

Jimmy was not as lucky. Saturday was always very busy at Sears. He was hoping that he wouldn't have a hangover to deal with. But he thought it was worth it because of the great time that he was having with Amaya.

"Hey, do you remember that sheriff's deputy, Frank Burke, that I was keeping in touch with from Winnemucca about keeping an eye out for Jordan?"

177

"Of course. Why?"

"He got a new job with the railroad police in Albuquerque."

"Really!"

"So he can still be useful and keep an eye out on the rails for us."

"I would be surprized if Jordan hopped trains."

"I think that we should keep all our options open." Amaya hugged Jimmy.

"Wow, just the thought of Jordan riding trains scares the shit out of me."

It was midnight by the time Jimmy and Amaya finished their last drink.

Jimmy put his arm around Amaya.

"So where are you parked?"

"About a block away. But, sir, you and I aren't driving tonight."

"Are we taking a cab?"

"Yep, our own private cab." Amaya pointed over at a police car that was parked across the street. "My partner, Paul, is going to drive us home. Is that all right?"

"Cool!"

"What time do you have to be at work tomorrow?"

"Ten o'clock. Why?" Jimmy asked.

"Paul will come by and pick you up tomorrow at my house around eight. Does that give you enough time to get your car and get back to your house and get dressed for work?"

"Absolutely." Jimmy's face lit up.

CHAPTER 65

THE WIND HAD calmed down, but the snowstorm continued to fall. There were several inches on the ground.

Back at Hobo Flat, Captain Nathan Cooper and his dog, Niko, stood out on his front porch watching the snow mount. "Well, boy, go on and have some fun." Niko jumped off the porch and started rolling in the snow. It was one of his favorite things to do. The captain laughed out loud. He got a big kick out of watching Niko playing in the snow like a little puppy. It took the edge off the stress and the loneliness that the captain was feeling. He wished that he had a woman to share his life with. Having Niko as a companion was fine, but it didn't fill the void in Captain Cooper's life.

"Well, boy, are you ready to call it a night?" Niko gave a quick bark. "You are such a good boy! Come on, let's go."

Even though the storm had a quiet, peaceful feeling, the captain knew that there was a new change in the weather that he had to prepare for.

* * *

At the other camp, Marco welcomed Rat and Shadow with open arms. They brought him a pack of cigarettes and a full space bag for everyone to share. Everyone gave them a high-five except for River. She was hesitant and had a bad vibe about them.

"Here you go, dude." Shadow walked over and handed the bag to Jordan. She tried to flirt with him and make eye contact with him. He briefly exchanged looks with her. He returned his attention to Melissa. Jordan took a hefty gulp and passed the bag over to Melissa.

"I don't know if I should have any more. I am not feeling very good. My stomach is upset." Melissa belched again.

"Ah, come on, girl, one more will do you good. Besides, it's snowing. It will warm you up," Rat said.

"Yeah, come on, dude, one more. It made your ankle feel better, right?" Jesse asked.

"Dude? I am not a dude," Melissa answered.

Shadow looked at Melissa with a sarcastic look. "Well, excuse us! We have a princess among us, dudes!" Everyone laughed.

"Melissa, you don't have to do shit if you don't want to," River piped in as she stumbled into Jesse. She was very drunk and held on to Jesse to keep her footing.

Jordan smiled at Melissa. "It's cool. We're getting pretty fucked up here." It was his turn to belch. Jordan and Melissa both laughed out loud. For the first time in his life, Jordan had fallen head over heels over a girl.

Jesse, on the other hand, lost his virginity to a squat mattress when he was hitchhiking across Arizona. Tonight he had his sights on River. He was really attracted to her. River was drunk and having a good time but was not attracted to Jesse. She still longed for Jordan.

Shadow was frustrated. She was having a hard time getting Jordan's attention away from Melissa. Her tool chest of naughty looks wasn't working. It was like he was under a spell. There was still hope though. The alcohol was kicking in, and Jordan was getting drunker. The storm was getting worse, and the thickness of the wet snow was becoming a problem.

Jesse took another swig from the space bag. He smiled at River and stared her body up and down.

"Hey, cowboy, leave something on me. I might catch cold," River reacted sarcastically to Jesse's lustful look.

Jordan looked over at Melissa. "Are you all right being out here in the snow?"

"For a little bit, I guess so. River and I should be heading home soon."

"I have to take a piss. I will be right back."

"Okay," Melissa answered. "Hurry back!"

Jordan stumbled off into the snow. He was so happy to be with Melissa. He was beside himself. It was like a fairy tale coming true.

Rat approached Marco and pointed toward some rocks. "There's some cover over there, and we can wait out the storm. You guys head over there." Rat bent down toward Melissa. "I will grab little princess and follow you over there."

"Wait a minute, we have to wait for Jordan," Melissa answered.

"Ah, Jordan will be fine. He'll find us. Come on, River," Jesse said.

River was very drunk and not in control of her senses. "It will be all right, Melissa." She looked at Rat. "Be careful with her."

"No problem! I've got her." Rat picked her up in his arms. He winked at Shadow. "Hey, Shadow, why don't you stay back and wait for Jordan."

Shadow smiled. "Good idea! I will bring him right to you."

"Thank you," Melissa answered.

"Of course!" Shadow replied. "Anything for our princess."

CHAPTER 66

MARY WILKENS WAS getting tired of waiting up for the girls to come home. It was after midnight, and Mr. Wilkens had already gone to bed.

Mary had a gut feeling in her stomach that something was wrong. She knew the girls should be home by now. She looked out the window and saw the snow falling. She tried Melissa's cell phone again and got her voice mail.

* * *

After relieving his bladder, Jordan found it hard to find his way back through the heavy snow. When Jordan returned, he noticed everyone was gone except for the Indian girl. She walked over and locked her arm around Jordan's arm. Jordan was pretty hammered and was confused.

"Looks like it's just you and me, dude."

"Where did everyone go?" Jordan asked. He could see that most of the crowd at the party had thinned out.

"Well, your friend Jesse stumbled off with my friend Rat, and the other three oogles split for home." Shadow handed the space bag to Jordan. "Here, I saved a swig for you."

"That fucking Jesse!" Jordan was pissed that he took off without him. He swallowed the final drops from the wine bag and tossed it in the burning fire barrel. He was also agitated and disappointed that he didn't get to say goodbye to Melissa.

"Come on, dude. I have a nice, warm sleeping bag we can go crawl into and get away from the storm." Shadow tilted her head and opened her mouth for Jordan to kiss her. Jordan wasn't sure what to do. He just stood there looking at her.

Then Jordan put his arm around Shadow. "All right, sure. What the fuck, why not!"

* * *

Rat dredged his way through the snow carrying Melissa in his arms. He was having trouble keeping his balance with the wet sludge. He headed toward Bolt's van.

"I don't see my friends," Melissa said anxiously. "Where are they?"

"Just be patient, princess. I am sure that they are right up ahead here." Rat's arms were getting tired holding Melissa. He was relieved to see the van up ahead. He picked up his speed. When he got to the car, he let Melissa down and opened the sliding door. "Here, climb inside. I will go find your friends."

Melissa hobbled inside. Rat slid the door shut. It was dark inside the van. Melissa could sense that she wasn't alone. As she looked clearer, she could see the outline of another person.

"Well, hello, beautiful. I have been waiting for you."

CHAPTER 67

THE GRANDFATHER CLOCK struck one in the Wilkens' living room. Mary Wilkens concern turned to fear. Mary walked down the hallway and woke her snoring husband up.

Jeff Wilkens got out of bed, put his robe on, and joined Mary in the living room. He saw this as an opportunity to paint River as a bad influence.

"I warned you about all this before. We should have put a stop to her and River's friendship a long time ago."

"Sweetheart! I don't need a lecture right now. We need to find our daughter." Mary was still beating herself up over not getting more details on where the girls were going.

Jeff looked at the clock. "Well, it's almost one thirty." He yawned and scratched his head with his messed-up hair from sleeping in bed. "Do you have Melissa's friends' phone numbers?"

"Most of them, but she hasn't been socializing with them ever since River and her became close," Mary answered.

"Well, I think we should at least try to call them and find out what they know. Here, hand me the phone. I will try her cell again."

* * *

The snowfall lightened up considerably, and a gentle wind began to blow while Jordan and Shadow were cuddling together inside a small cave that only Shadow knew about. She kept it covered up with brush. The cave was located up the hill from Bolt's van.

Shadow was enjoying Jordan's company. She was attracted to his quiet nature and, of course, his good looks. She did most of the talking. She told him about living on the reservation back home in Tulsa. Jordan wasn't so forthcoming about himself. He just listened to her talk. Shadow knew that if they were going to have sex, she was going to have to be the one to make the first move.

"So what was the hardest thing for you to get used to beside the cold weather?" Shadow asked. At the same time, she was stroking his leg.

"Huh." Jordan paused for a second. "I would have to say learning to how to sleep on a cold slab of cement. That was a bitch."

Shadow laughed. "You got that right. That is fucked up."

As they nestled together with their clothes on, Jordan could hear a muffled sound in the distance of someone screaming.

"What's that? Did you hear that?"

"Sounds like someone's not getting along as well as you and I are." Shadow kissed Jordan's neck. She reached down, unzipped his fly, and stroked his hard penis. "Don't worry about it, baby, it's okay."

Being his first time with a woman, Jordan wasn't able to control himself and exploded in her hand.

CHAPTER 68

RIVER WAS STARTING to panic. Her and Jesse were staggering in the dark through the blinding snow searching for Melissa. Rat had done a good job of confusing them and sending them off in the wrong direction.

Jesse spotted the Volkswagon van up ahead. Bolt's pit bull was chained to a stake right next to the van. The dog was yelping and violently trying to set himself free.

River could hear Melissa screaming for help. She tried to open up the van, but it was locked. She looked in the back seat and saw that Melissa was pinned down with a man on top of her with his pants pulled down around his ankles.

Jesse smashed in the back window with his smiley. River reached in and unlocked the sliding door and dug her nails into Bolt's back.

"Get off her, you son of a bitch!" River screamed.

"You whore!" Bolt shrieked in pain. He twisted his body around and kicked River in the stomach, knocking her to the ground. He quickly pulled his pants up and jumped outside the van.

Jesse picked River up and confronted Bolt. "You are a fucking asshole."

Rat came from out of nowhere and blindsided Jesse with a punch to the left side of his face. Jesse fell to the ground.

"You cocksucker!" River screeched. She attempted to kick Rat in the groin. He caught her foot. She slipped and tumbled on to the slushing snow.

Savage's barking grew louder. He was tugging as hard as he could to set himself free. A group of kids who were still at the party heard the loud barking and approached the van. They kept their distance and watched.

The adrenaline kicked in for Melissa, and she overcame the pain from her sprained ankle. She pulled her jeans up and came flying out from the back seat of the van and jumped on Bolt's back. They both collapsed on the ground. Melissa restrained him with a hold that she had learned from karate lessons. Bolt broke free and got to his feet. He pounced on her and grabbed her by the hair and slapped her across the face. She struggled to get free but was not strong enough. Bolt grabbed her by the neck and started choking her. She was fighting trying to get loose.

From out of nowhere, Jordan struck Bolt in the middle of his back with his smiley. Bolt let go of Melissa's neck and staggered on top of her. Jordan grabbed Bolt by his shirt and pulled him off her. Rat tackled Jordan, and they both fell to the ground. Rat was able to get to his feet first and tried to hit Jordan in the head with his fist. Jordan ducked as Rat's fist sailed over his head and ricocheted off the side of the van.

Rat fell to his knees and grabbed his hand. "Son of a bitch. I think I broke my fucking hand."

Bolt lunged at Jordan and tried to kick him in the side. Jesse stepped in and caught his foot. Bolt slipped and banged his head on the ground.

River and Melissa held on to each other and watched all four of the punks wrestling around in the snow. It was tough sledding for everyone to keep their footing.

Bolt got to his feet and stumbled over to try to unchain his dog. Before he could get there, Jordan tackled him, and they crashed into the side of the van.

Savage leaped at Jordan barking ferociously. The chain wasn't long enough, and he ended up twisting and running around the pole until the chain tightened up and wrapped around the pole and choked him like a noose.

Blake woke up from his drunken stupor and joined in on the ruckus. He pulled Jesse to his feet and smashed him in the nose. The sight of blood spirting out of his nostrils enraged Jesse.

"You motherfucker!" He put his head down and piled into Blake and drove him into the ground. Jesse was swinging wildly like a madman pounding Blake.

Jordan got to his feet and pulled Jesse off Blake. They both stood toe to toe alongside River and Melissa, ready to confront Bolt and his road dogs.

"You want more? Come and get it, freak!" Jesse sneered at Bolt.

"Scumbag! You're the one that is all bloody!" Rat shouted.

"No, screw you!" River screamed.

Jordan intervened by swinging his smiley. He looked into Bolt's eyes. "We can carry on with this if you'd like?"

"All right. You fuckers get the hell out of here while you still can," Bolt hissed.

Jordan didn't back down. "We will see about that another time. That is, if you have the guts to face me without your two wing nuts."

"I look forward to that," Bolt scoffed back. He looked at Melissa and River. "I hope you two oozies had a good time, especially you!" He gave Melissa a despicable stare and licked his lips in a disgusting manner.

Bolt's insults were getting to Jordan. He was getting angrier by the second and was ready to explode. He wanted to hurt the tattooed lunatic for his degrading remark.

"Ah, so you are sweet on that little whore." Bolt laughed. "I bet you haven't even fucked her yet. Ah, I'm right, aren't I?" Bolt smirked. "I am glad I had her first. And by the way, she's been tasted before me," Bolt hissed.

Jordan charged toward Bolt. Jesse grabbed him and held him back. "Come on, bro, it is not worth it. Look how pathetic he looks with his mutant face."

"Yeah! Well, this mutant fucked your fat friend too!" Bolt smirked at River.

River's face swelled up with anger. "You worthless pig!"

"Fat-ass!" Bolt screamed almost coming out of character.

"You're disgusting!" River responded. "You'll get your karma soon, creep."

Jordan, Jesse, Melissa, and River looked at one another.

"Let's get the hell out of this toilet!" Jesse shouted. Jordan continued to stare at Bolt. He finally turned around, and they walked away.

"Wow! You put that asshole in his place!" Jesse said to River.

"Well, I am sure that won't be the last time we have to deal with that piece of shit." River shook her head in amazement. "Quite a night." She looked closely at Jesse's nose. "So you might have broken your nose, dude?"

Jordan reached in his back pocket and pulled out his bandanna and handed it to Jesse to help clean his face.

"You okay?" Jordan asked Melissa.

Tears came to her eyes. "Yes, I'm fine, a little scared. Thank you for everything." Melissa looked over at River and Jesse. "You guys too!"

"No problem. It was all in a day's work," Jesse spouted out proudly. He patted Jordan on the back. "So how about that, bro, our first brawl together."

"Hmm," Jordan answered. He was stunned that he actually got in a fight. There was something special inside him that made him come to his senses and rescue Melissa.

Jesse's nose stopped bleeding, but there was still dried blood on his face. He handed the bandanna back to Jordan. "Now there is some of our history on this here rag."

Jordan nodded his approval as he put the bloodstained bandanna back in his left jean pocket. Jordan knew for the first time he could count on Jesse if things got tough.

River felt guilty and sorry for Melissa. She hugged her and kissed her on the cheek. She admired Melissa's strength. Being sexually assaulted once again was not an easy thing to handle. River was curious what was going on in Melissa's mind.

Melissa appreciated River trying to comfort her. Melissa knew that her concern was genuine. Thoughts were racing through Melissa's mind on what she should do.

Jordan looked at both girls. "So I know this is a tough thing that you just went through. I am hoping that you won't press charges against that freak."

"Are you shitting me?" River answered. "He can't get away with this."

"I know, and trust me, he won't. We need to handle things here. We don't need the police meddling in our stuff. There are too many secrets here. Captain Cooper back at Hobo Flat will know what to do."

Melissa and River hugged each other.

They were glad to see that Marco's car was still parked where they had left it. They found Marco inside lying in the back seat drunk and trying to stay warm.

"The car won't start," Marco moaned.

Jordan knew that Marco would have left them if his car had started. He could see in River's eyes that she was thinking the exact same thing.

"Well, let's all cuddle together and keep each other warm until the morning comes."

"I wish I could call my mom. I dropped my purse when I sprained my ankle."

"Don't worry!" Jordan said. "When it gets light outside, we will go look for it."

"I bet my mom is really upset."

"We can always hitchhike," River joked. "Melissa, I want you to know that I am taking full responsibility for everything. It wasn't your fault. It was all my idea."

"Thanks, but we are all in this together." Melissa grabbed River's hand and gave her a hug. "And besides, I wouldn't have met these guys." She smiled at Jordan.

Jordan returned her smile. He was wondering if he found Melissa's phone, maybe she would let him borrow it to call his mom and dad.

They all climbed in Marco's car and snuggled together in the back seat.

River closed her eyes. She started thinking back about that awful day at the rest stop. She was happy that she didn't remember much except for her car window being smashed in. Everything else was a blur.

CHAPTER 69

BOLT WARMED HIS bruised hands over a barrel that was still burning. He glared at Shadow across the flickering flames and looked like a demon in the darkness from the glow from the flames fluttering across his tattooed face.

Shadow was frightened of Bolt when he was pissed off. She had felt his wrath many times before when she had let him down. In one of his lunitic rages, he slammed her head to the ground when he was too drunk to get an erection to have sex with her. This was a bigger problem. She had let Jordan slip through her fingers.

"I'm sorry I couldn't get Jordan to stay with me," Shadow said, cowering up to Bolt. She could see the anger on his face.

"Yeah, where were you? We could have used your slingshot," Bolt said. "So that's what that prick's name is huh, Jordan. So you're on a first-name basis with him now, huh? You got a thing for him, bitch? And that is why you didn't come and help." Bolt was getting angrier by the minute.

Shadow was prepared to get roughed up. She looked over at Blake for support. He had a worried look on his face.

"You let me down!" Bolt bellowed. He was aware that Blake might try to defend her. Bolt decided not to physically abuse her and take another approach. "Guess what, I'm cutting you off, so you can go find your own shit to stick in your veins. Get the fuck away from me."

Shadow walked back to the cave and crawled back in her sleeping bag. She was pretty much done with Bolt. She was sick and tired of being treated that way. Now she had to figure out what she was going to do about it.

Blake had followed her back to her cave. "Are you all right?" he asked.

"I'm cool, dude! Why don't you come in and get warm." It made her feel good that someone cared about her.

* * *

Bolt calmed down after Shadow left. He unchained Savage and climbed inside the van.

"Mind if I join you?" Rat asked.

"That's cool. So how is your hand?"

"It fucking hurts, man."

"Here, take a slug of this." Bolt handed Rat a bottle of rum.

Rat grabbed the bottle and took a huge gulp. "So what are we going do now? You should have listened to me, bro. Our party went to shit, and everybody that we recruited bailed on us."

"It's no big deal. I learned a few things tonight. I know that you and Savage are the only ones that I can trust."

"I'm your man. You can always count on me." Rat petted Savage on the head. "Poor boy. You got twisted up on that pole just like a tetherball."

"For the time being, we need to keep that bitch and her fat friend around. We'll get rid of them after we take over Hobo Flat."

"Are you kidding me?" Rat asked. "We just got our asses handed to us, and everybody knows about it."

"Yeah, that's a good thing. I am hoping that old captain won't feel as threatened and will let his guard down."

"I never thought of it that way," Rat said.

"Also we know that Shadow's buddy and that other kid are on the captain's side. Everyone else who was here tonight doesn't give a damn as long as there is some Thunder chicken to drink.

* * *

By 3:00 a.m., the usually calm and levelheaded Mary Wilkens had become hysterical. She had called all of Melissa's friends and got nowhere. "We have to do something, Jeff. Our daughter is in trouble. I just know it. Please, God, please protect our beautiful daughter."

Jeff Wilkens was trying to be strong. He grabbed his wife in his arms and tried to comfort her. He stroked the back of her head, which always relaxed her. He kept looking out the front window hoping to see a car drive up. "All right, we had better call the police."

CHAPTER 70

FRANK BURKE WAS on late patrol. He loved his new job working for the railroad. It kicked the hell out of being a deputy sheriff in Winnemucca. It also paid a whole lot more. He was sad, though, that he wasn't able to talk his girlfriend, Josie, into moving with him. She was born and raised in Winnemucca. She told him that was her home and she didn't want to pick up and leave.

Miles Phillips was Frank's partner. The fifty-one-year-old was on the downward slide of his career. He didn't want to work too hard. He was at least fifty pounds overweight with a big belly and no chin. His shirts were never laundered and were always wrinkled. He had a scruffy red beard and was in need of some dental work. He enjoyed chewing snuff and spitting it in an empty Coke can that he kept on his desk. That grossed Frank out every time Miles discharged in the cup. Miles was bitter that he had never been promoted. After twenty years on the job, he still worked the late shift. He had the reputation of having two speeds, which were slow and stop. It was known in the bum community that it was much easier to maneuver on and off trains during the late shift when Miles Phillips was on duty.

One of the great spots for tramps to hop on or off trains was at two-mile. At this location on the rails is where two sets of tracks lie parallel with each other. This allows the lesser-priority trains to pull aside to let the higher priority trains pass. The closest two-mile track from the train yard was located three and a half miles away. Miles rarely drove out that far.

Miles was used to having young, inexperienced whippersnappers on his shift. They always started off very gung ho about the job. Only the really serious career men kept up the enthusiasm and were promoted to daytime shifts. The rest of them fell right into line with Miles's way of thinking. They just rode around in the company SUV with Miles gossiping, spending time at the train yard, watching television or drinking coffee at the diner up the road. They didn't last long. The late shift had constant turnover.

Frank Burke had no intention of staying on the late shift. He was a go-getter and wanted to do a good job. He saw this as his big chance to be successful. It was exciting for him to patrol the area looking for bums and street kids trying to hop on trains. He felt really important. He was working for the railroad now! He had a big responsibility. He was protecting the rails from all the vermin.

It didn't take Frank long to figure out Miles's shortcomings. He was annoyed with his laziness and bullshit. All Miles could talk about was how much he was screwed over by the company and his long-winded, boring stories about how wonderful he was. Occasionally on their rounds, he would stop and let Frank get out of the SUV and shine his flashlight on the junk trains, which were low-priority trains loaded with boxcars, gondolas, and tankers. Junk trains never go far, but they are easy to stay hidden on from the bulls.

Most nights, Miles would stay at the train yard or he would have Frank drop him off at the diner up the road to stuff his fat face. Frank would then drive around by himself checking out locations including two-mile. He also paid particular attention to the crew change, which was a good opportunity for bums to hop on and off trains.

Word was spreading fast around the traveling community to watch out for the new bull who was taking his job serious on the late shift. Frank's diligence was making it more challenging for riders to hop on and off the trains. However, the veteran tramps still had the advantage with the pitch-dark nights and Frank's lack of experience.

Captain Cooper had been through this before with brand-new bulls. He knew that it would just be a matter of time before the new guy would be promoted to a new shift. The captain did have some real concerns about this new railroad bull. He had a mean streak in him that made him very dangerous.

Most bulls were stern when they confronted travelers on trains. They would give them a strong warning that if they were caught again, they would be arrested and locked up for trespassing.

Just like back when he was deputy, Frank took liberties with his new job. He was very intimidating with his stout body. It had been that way for him his whole life. Nobody messed with Frank Burke on or off the football field.

* * *

Because of the storm, tonight's late shift was very quiet. Frank spent most of the evening at the train yard. He had a couple of more hours to kill until the next shift came in. He sat behind his desk reviewing his email. He responded to a message from Amaya Parks. He told her that he would keep an eye out for Jordan Summers. He chuckled to himself, "I'm sure Jordan would be pleased to see me again."

Frank got up from his desk and walked outside the office. There was still a light snow falling. The chilling wind was refreshing as it blew across his face. It gave him a new zest of energy. He watched a crew of a junk train preparing to pull out with a G train and gondola attached to the engine.

CHAPTER 71

MELISSA WOKE UP as Jordan got back in the car. She yawned and smiled at him. Jesse, River, and Marco were all sound asleep in the back seat.

"Where have you been?"

Jordan handed Melissa her purse. He found the purse and cell phone buried in the snow next to one of the barrels.

"Thank you."

"No problem." Jordan smiled.

Melissa opened her purse and took out her cell phone. She had twenty messages from her mother. She listened to the first one and could tell by the tone of her mom's voice that she was upset. Melissa dialed the home phone number.

"Mom!"

"Sweetheart, where are you? Are you okay?" Mary Wilkens asked.

"I am fine, Mom. The car I was in broke down, and I lost my purse in the snow."

Mary was relieved and told Melissa that the police would be out to get her. Melissa gave her mom a description of Marco's car. Mary wrote down all the details on a notepad that she kept by the phone.

"Here, talk to your father."

"No, it's okay mom. I will see him when I get home. I love you, and I'm sorry that I worried you."

"It's okay, sweetheart. Is River okay?"

"Yeah, she's fine. Please don't be mad at her. It's all my fault."

"I am glad that you two are safe. We will talk more about this when you get home. Are you cold?"

"Yeah, I can see my breath. We are keeping warm by snuggling together. Bye, Mom, I love you."

"Keep the phone on."

"I will."

Mary hung up the phone. She looked at her husband and handed him the directions where their daughter was. As Jeff Wilkens dialed the police, Mary wondered why Melissa did not want to talk to her father.

By the look on her face, Jordan could tell how relieved Melissa was to talk to her mother. It made him think about his family. He really missed them and felt really guilty inside.

Melissa had a sense that Jordan wanted to use her phone. "Do you want to make a call?"

"Cool! I would like that." Jordan grabbed the phone and dialed the number. He was nervous and anxious as the phone was ringing. The message machine picked up, and he could hear his dad's voice on the recording.

"Hi, Dad, it's me Jordan." He choked up and paused to get his emotions under control. "I miss, uh, you." Tears welled up around his eyes. "I just wanted to let you know that I am okay. Tell Rose, Tommy, and my mom hello. I love you, Dad. Bye."

He handed the phone back to Melissa and wiped the tears from his eyes. Melissa gave Jordan a hug and gave him a kiss on the cheek. The hug felt really good.

Jordan then reached in the back seat and nudged Jesse. "Hey, wake up, bro. The cops will be here soon. We have to get out of here." Jordan hugged Melissa goodbye, and they headed back to Hobo Flat.

* * *

When his phone rang, Officer Morningstar was sound asleep in bed next to his wife, Kate.

"Hello."

"Sorry to bother you so early in the morning," the dispatch operator answered. "We just got a call that there are some stranded teenagers out by Hobo Flat."

"All right. I will head out and get them."

"Drive carefully. We had a pretty good snowstorm. And I'm sure the snow plows haven't cleared the roads yet."

"Thanks," Rhett answered. He reached over and kissed Kate on the cheek. "I have to go out and pick up some kids that are stranded."

"Can't somebody else do it? I was looking forward into sleeping in," Kate replied.

"I'll be back as soon as I can and make you breakfast. I love you."

Rhett got dressed and headed out.

CHAPTER 72

Later on That Day

JIMMY SUMMERS WAS dead tired when he finally walked through his front door at around six o'clock. The clock moved like a snail, and his hangover was extra painful because of the mixed drinks of tequila and beer. He did have a fun night and did his customary promise to never drink like that again.

He got out of his work clothes and put on his leisure pants and a long-sleeve T-shirt. He looked over and noticed that his message machine was blinking. He figured that it was probably his wife or a bill collector after him. He sat down in his favorite chair and rested for a while.

Jimmy yawned and stretched out his legs. Finally the tormenting headache was starting to subside. The kids would be dropped off soon. He hoped that they wouldn't be so demanding because he wanted to get to bed early.

He got up and pulled out a frozen pizza from the freezer and turned the oven on. He decided to check his phone messages. The first one was from a credit card company. Jimmy deleted that call immediately. "Vicious bastards!" he shouted. He was trying his best to catch up on his payments. The second message was from the

American Heart Association, and the third message took him completely off guard.

Tears came to Jimmy Summers's eyes as he heard Jordan's voice trembling out of the speakerphone. He played the message over and over again. He was relieved that his son was okay.

CHAPTER 73

FOR THE NEXT couple of days, there was a lot of friction at the Wilkens residence. Both girls kept quiet about what really happened. Their story was that they had gotten roughed up by a couple other girls at the party.

Detective Morningstar suspected that there was more foul play but didn't push the issue. He wrote in the report that there was a minor scuffle between a bunch of teenagers at a party.

Jeff Wilkens saw this as an opportunity to get River out of the house. He took a calculated risk and insisted that she be turned over to Social Services and placed in a foster home. He was hoping that River would get the message and disappear before they moved forward and contacted the agency. He had hopes with her out of the picture that things would get back to normal.

Mary Wilkens was on the fence on whether that was a good idea. Of course, she was concerned about her daughter's bad decisions. She wasn't so sure that River was fully responsible for her daughter's actions. Besides, she liked River and had developed a relationship with her.

It reminded Mary that she wasn't the perfect angel. When she was a sophmore, she had a crush on a Hispanic boy named Rollie. Her parents had forbidden her to date Rollie. She smiled to herself as she remembered calling her father a racist and storming out of the living room. She never listened to her parents. She sneaked around and carried on a secret relationship with Rollie, which lasted for almost a year.

Mary made the decision to disagree with her husband. She knew deep down inside that her daughter and River were just young girls making their way in the world. This would be the first time in their marriage that Mary would take a stand and not go along with her husband's wishes.

* * *

Even though it ended up being a nightmare evening, River knew being a traveler was still in her blood, and now she had a friendship with two young travelers that she could relate to. She was aware that Jesse was a loose cannon and had other intentions besides just being her friend. She had a lot of respect for Jordan and looked forward to nourishing their friendship. She liked their free spirit.

* * *

Melissa was able keep up her friendship with Jordan. Because of her, Jordan volunteered to panhandle every Sunday by the church. After the service, Melissa would walk over to the convenience store and visit with him. Her father was embarrassed to see his daughter have a friendship with a homeless person.

Mary Wilkens thought just the opposite and was proud of her daughter. Melissa had told her all about Jordan and how kind he was to her.

CHAPTER 74

BOLT'S CONFIDENCE WAS growing stronger every day. He continued to put on the notorious bonfire parties that were growing in popularity and attracting large crowds, including upper crusties (CCR, or choo choo riders, who were stuck-up street kids who thought they were better than the other street kids).

Jesse and Jordan still went to the parties. They enjoyed getting shit-faced and socializing with most of the other Flintstone kids. They kept their distance from Bolt's drinking circle.

Everytime Bolt looked at Jordan, he had an evil smirk on his face, like he had some sort of revenge in the works.

Jordan and Shadow became friends and enjoyed partying together. Jordan liked Shadow, but he wasn't in love with her. His heart belonged to Melissa. He was realistic, though, and accepted the truth that he would never be with her. She was out of his league.

Shadow was getting attached to Jordan. He was the first boy in her life that made her laugh and treated her with kindness. They had to be very careful being seen together at the parties. Bolt was very jealous and would punish her if he found out. During the week, they would meet secretly and have sex up the hill from the camp. It was also when Jordan first started using heroin. It was an increditable high and escape for him. He would just lie on a blanket and float away.

CHAPTER 75

"HI, FRANK, IT'S Amaya Parks."

"Hey there. How's things in Reno?"

"It's alright. We busted a bunch of big shots for trying pick up some hookers on Fourth Street."

"No shit!"

"Yeah. It was quite the sting. One of them was the president of the Little League. He was married and has kids."

"If you ask me, it's an unhappy married man who's not getting any at home."

"I don't understand why they just don't go out to the brothel."

"Have you ever been out to a whorehouse?" Frank joked.

"Yeah, right."

"Well, let me tell you, going out there is weird and uncomfortable. As soon as you walk in the door, the girls line up and put the pressure on you to pick somebody. Then you go into a room, and they put you on the clock, and it's expensive as shit. On the street, you can get head for twenty bucks."

"Sounds like you are a man with experience."

"There are only so many girls to go around when you live in a small town like Winnemucca."

"Men are pigs."

Frank changed the subject and bragged about busting two street kids who were trying to hide on a flatbed that was loaded with a semi trailer on one of the priority trains.

Hotshot trains are always in a hurry and traveling long-distance. The trains usually pull 48s and 52s. There are not many places to hide on those trains. You could hide on a 48, if the bucket has a floor.

"Those dumb shits' biggest mistake was hiding in plain sight. It made it so easy for me to spot them." Frank left out the details about zapping them with his cattle prod and pointing a gun at their heads. He was quite proud of himself.

"It sounds like you have found your place in this world," Amaya said.

"Ah, you never know. I wouldn't mind being a homicide detective someday. Maybe I'll come and work with you."

He recommended that Amaya should contact the sheriff's department and see if Jordan was living out at the hobo camp. She told him that she had already talked to a Deputy Morningstar about going out there. She thanked Frank for his help and told him that she owed him a favor.

Frank was curious what Amaya looked like. Her voice sounded very sexy on the phone. He thought most policewomen were not very attractive. There were a few, though, like Millie, who worked dispatch in Winnemucca. So that gave Frank hope that Amaya was just a sexy as her voice sounded.

CHAPTER 76

CAPTAIN COOPER WAS very concerned about Bolt. The number of boot parties were on the rise. Several of the older tramps were afraid to go out by themselves.

That afternoon, Deputy Morningstar drove out to Hobo Flat to meet with the captain. He walked through the camp toward Cooper's shack. All the older tramps, except for Bags, scattered like by a bunch of flies as soon as they saw Rhett pull up. He got a big kick out of that. He was sure that they were all guilty of something and he could fill up his jail with the whole camp.

"Good afternoon," Rhett said as he walked past Bags's campsite.

"The same to you, sir," Bags answered back. "Are you here to see Captain Cooper?"

"Is he around?"

"Yessum, I see him sitting on his porch up there."

"You have a good day."

"You too, sir. It's a pretty day today. Spring will be here soon enough."

Rhett wished that he had more time to talk to the old black man. He bet that he had some great stories to tell.

Captain Cooper waved at Rhett.

"Hello, what brings you up here?" The captain trusted Rhett and appreciated the fact that he was respecting the camp's authority.

"Well, the sheriff wanted me to come up and meet with you."

"Would you like a cup of coffee?"

"I appreciate the offer. I pretty much drank a whole pot back at the station."

"Suit yourself."

"Nice dog you have there."

"Yep, Niko has been by my side for many years."

Niko looked up and could tell that they were talking about him.

"What are your thoughts on this other camp?" Rhett asked.

"It makes me real nervous. We have a good thing going here, and I hate the idea of those kids screwing things up. By the way, I am grateful that you are not butting in."

"Well, it's gathering a lot of attention in town. The sheriff is concerned about all the fights and underage drinking. He's getting a lot of complaints from upset parents."

"Yeah, I was hoping that this street kid, Bolt, would just move on. But so far that's not the case."

The captain told Rhett that he was setting up a meeting with Bolt to tell him to hit the road.

"Would it help if I stopped by over there?"

"Thanks, but I can handle it. He is just a young punk who needs to understand how things are around here."

"By the way, I understand that there might be a runaway kid named Jordan Summers living here at the camp. This was dropped off at the station with a note on it." Rhett handed Nathan a copy of the flyer with Jordan's picture on it.

"Yeah, he was here for a bit, but he hopped a train and took off. That was about a week ago. He was a good kid."

"His family misses him, and there is this policewoman in Reno who has taken an interest in finding him. So you let me know if you see him."

Rhett wished Nathan good luck and said he would check back with him next week.

* * *

Later that day, Cooper met with his council. Bags volunteered to contact Bolt and arrange for a meeting at the abandoned service station up the road.

* * *

The captain got up bright and early the next day. He and Niko warmed up next to his stove waiting for the sun to rise. A crow was cawing in the distance as Captain Cooper and Niko walked down the hill to Bags's campsite. He was happy to see that Bags was up early brewing a pot of coffee on his little stove.

"Morning, Captain!"

"Good morning, old friend."

"You are sure up bright and early today."

"It is the best part of the day, don't you agree?"

"Yessum! It surely is. Would you like a cup of coffee?"

"Yes, please! That sounds mighty good to me."

Bags poured the captain a cup of coffee and handed it to him. "Be careful, Captain. It is a little hot."

Captain Cooper took a small sip. "That's mighty good, Bags." The captain took another sip. "I am not sure how things are going to, uh, wind up."

"Yessum, Captain, I understand. What's your plan? Are you going there by yourself?"

"Well, that's part of the reason that I am here." Captain Cooper pulled out a snipe and handed one to Bags. He struck a match and lit up the smokes.

"Of course I will have Niko with me. I am thinking that this is going to be a good opportunity for Bolt to lay out his cards."

Bags knew what the captain meant. "Besides Niko, it would be good if you had somebody else watching your back. If I were younger, I would do it, but I would just be a distraction and someone else for you to worry about."

Captain Cooper chuckled. "I appreciate that, Bags." Cooper patted Bags on the back. "Is Jordan and Jesse around?"

Bags looked inside Jordan and Jesse's tent.

"Jordan! Are you awake?" Bags could hear Jordan snoring inside his sleeping bag. "Hey, psst, I know you and Jesse partied it up last night. Come on, boys, wake up. Captain Cooper wants to talk to you."

"What now, man?" Jesse grumbled.

Jordan and Jesse stumbled out of the tent. They both reaked of alcohol.

"Here, boys, have a cup of my famous coffee."

"Thanks." Jordan took a gulp. "Man, I feel like death."

Jesse just sat there staring at the ground.

"Yessum, once again, you've got to sweat that devil juice out of your pores," Bags said.

"Boys, you're pretty young to be drinking so much. I would be careful if I were you. Once that devil gets a hold of you, it's mighty hard to get rid of." Captain Cooper shook his head and gave Bags a doubting look. "I don't know, Bags! So these Flinstone kids think they can ride trains?"

The captain's comment got Jordan's attention. He could tell that he was being tested. He also knew that the captain wouldn't be standing in front of him if he didn't have something important on his mind.

Jordan stood up straight. "So what's up?"

"Well, a couple of things. I know that you two have been going to those parties down the road. They are causing a problem for us here. The sheriff wants it to stop. I have a meeting later on with your friend Bolt."

"Yeah, he's our best buddy." Jordan smiled.

"Anyway, I heard about your scuffle with him. Word is that you put him in his place."

"We kicked his ass!" Jesse answered proudly.

"I know that you two are moving on and probably don't give a damn about Hobo Flat, but someday you might just come back, and besides Bags here needs a safe place to live. I am hoping that you two will watch my back and come with me to the meeting?"

"Wow!" Jesse answered. "Is this going to be a showdown like in the cowboy movies?"

"I sure hope not," the Captain answered. "And hey, Jordan, someone tipped off the sheriff's office about you being here."

CHAPTER 77

BOLT POLISHED OFF a bottle of tequila that he had stashed in the glove compartment of the van. He walked over to where Shadow, Rat, and Blake were standing around a fire barrel warming their hands.

"So the way I see things, we have a real opportunity to take over that camp."

Rat's and Blake's eyes perked up. Shadow was coming down from a high and had the shakes. She was trying her best to act interested.

"Here's how it's gonna go. How many of those new crustees can we trust to help us out?"

"Help us do what?" Rat asked.

Bolt looked up at the sky and rolled his eyes at Rat. "Help us take out that old fart, you fuckhead!"

"I wouldn't count on any of those pussies," Rat answered. "Those choo choo dudes are just pretenders. They still live at home with their mommy."

"We just need them to pretend that they are on board. They don't have to do a thing except stand around so I can show the captain that he is outnumbered." Bolt frowned at Shadow. "Are you steady enough to have a good aim?" Shadow nodded her head yes. Bolt threatened her, "If you screw this up, bitch, you'll pay for it." He looked over and could see that Blake did not like the way he was treating Shadow.

"If you don't like it, big boy, you can get the hell out of here."

Blake backed off and looked the other way.

212

"All right then. I think we're ready to go. Right, Savage?"

Savage growled as he looked up at Bolt.

"I look forward to moving into that old coot's shack. And, Rat, you can live in the van. How's that sound?"

"Right on." Rat smiled.

"I saw a police car heading towards Hobo Flat." Bolt smiled.

"Let's hope our little tip was the reason they headed out there."

CHAPTER 78

RIVER WALKER AND Melissa Wilkens held on to each other. Melissa kissed River on the cheek.

"I am really going to miss you." Tears were rolling down Melissa's cheeks. River was having trouble holding back her emotions.

"Thank you for being my friend. And thank you for understanding me and sharing with me that beautiful heart that's inside you."

They both balled like little babies and ended up laughing in each other's arms.

"Are you going to say goodbye to my mom?"

"Will you say goodbye for me? I couldn't face her."

"I will."

"Tell her I love her and thank her for everything."

They both hugged each other again.

"What are you going to do about your dad?" River asked.

"I am sure he will try to make his move, but that's in the past. It sickens me to even think that I did that with him."

"You are an amazing person, Melissa Wilkens. Not many people can handle what you have been through."

"You're pretty remarkable too!"

"I suppose you are going to return to being a preppie?"

"Excuse my language, fuck no." They both laughed out loud.

"So I will be gone in the morning. You take care of yourself."

"I will. You too. Hopefully we will see each other from time to time."

It was a day that both girls would never forget.

CHAPTER 79

JESSE AND JORDAN were sitting on a hill overlooking the train yard. They were observing the railroad police building, which was a multiplex aluminum structure. Four white SUVs were parked in front.

"I don't know about you, bro, but I want to get the hell out of here and get going to New York."

"What's your hurry? I'm the one that should be worried," Jordan responded. "Melissa told me last Sunday that River is coming to live with us. I thought you might want to stick around a little longer."

"So she says. I will believe it when I see her."

Jordan noticed a couple of the bulls getting in an SUV and driving out of the yard.

"What about you, bro? You have two girls that you have a shine for."

Both boys watched the SUV drive by them.

"I wonder if that new gung ho bull is in that truck?" Jesse asked. "I've heard that he likes to torture people with a cattle prod."

Jordan knew what that felt like.

"Well, he can have at it. I will kick his ass."

"We have to be careful and watch out for him. I think that we are going to have to jump a train on the fly. You up for that?" Jordan asked.

"Oh yeah. It will be a piece of cake."

"See that junk train down in the yard?" Jordan pointed at the corner of the yard.

"That old, rusty-looking bastard. What about it?"

"Remember, Bags told us those junk trains will be easy for us to jump on and stay hidden from the bulls."

"Bags, Bags, Bags! You love that guy! You think everything he says is the Gospel."

"Absolutely! You see that freddy blinking on the end of the train?"

"You mean that red light?"

"Do you know what that means?"

"Yeah. There are hookers on board."

Jordan shook his head. "You are a piece of work."

Jesse slugged him on the shoulder.

"You don't remember, do ya? Didn't you learn anything from Bags?" Jordan was disgusted. "That means that the trains will be leaving soon."

"Yessum!" Jesse imitated Bags. "I knew that. I was just fucking with you."

"So, dude, what do you think about watching Captain Cooper's back?"

"I don't know. What has he done for us lately besides give us shit details to do?"

"He let us stay here at the camp. My gut tells me it is the right thing to do. And if anything, we should do it for Bags."

"Bags, Bags, Bags. You love that old man. So you willing to get your butt kicked over who wants to be the big muckety-muck? Maybe we should go talk to Bolt and see what he would offer us."

"Are you nuts? That purple-faced psycho is an idiot."

Jesse took another hit off his snipe and looked down toward the train yard and watched the junk train pulling out.

"There she goes. Dude, we could be riding on that right now. Look at the grafitti on that gondola."

Jordan studied the gondola as it rode by. "I can hardly wait to tag my first boxcar. Bags said some riders write down good information about train yards on those tags. I wonder what that one means?" The tag sign read RWN 2000 Northbound with railroad tracks drawn underneath.

Jordan got up. "Well, I have to go. I have to meet up with Shadow."

CHAPTER 80

MELISSA WAS IN her bedroom reading one of Stephen King's books that River had given her to read. King was not the easiest author to understand. She was confused and had to read some of the paragraphs over a couple of times. She was distracted by a knock on her door.

Her dad walked in and shut the door.

"I am not interrupting anything, am I?"

"A matter of fact you are," Melissa replied.

"Look, young lady, disrespecting your father is not going to be tolerated anymore. River was a bad influence on you. But now that is all over." He walked over and started rubbing her back.

Her father's touch sent chills down Melissa's back and made her feel creepy. She shrugged her shoulders and removed his hand from touching her.

"Please don't do that to me anymore."

Her father backed off and sat on the edge of the bed. He took a deep breath.

"It's been a long time since you and I have, uh, you know."

"Please get out of here and leave me alone." Melissa was angry and started to cry.

"Shh. Quiet down. It's all right. I just wanted to show you something." Jeff reached in his coat pocket and pulled out a piece of paper. "I saw this flyer posted on a bulletin board at the post office."

He handed the piece of paper to Melissa. Jeff could tell by the look on her face that he had struck a nerve. He took off his glasses and grabbed a Kleenex that was on Melissa's nightstand and started cleaning his glasses.

"That's a photo of that boy that you hang out with after church. He is on the run and the police are looking for him. Of course, I haven't said anything yet." Wilkens put his glasses back on. "I have a proposition for you to consider. I'm going to come back later after your mom goes to sleep. I will keep my mouth shut as long as you cooperate with me."

"How dare you. Fuck you," Melissa reacted.

Melissa's father turned red in the face. "My little girl has a potty mouth now. River has taught you well." Wilkens got up from the bed. "It's all up to you. Like I said, I won't go to the police. I am not asking for much. I will see you later." He touched her shoulder and walked out of the room.

CHAPTER 81

Bolt had a wicked smile on his face. "Here's to the new sheriff in town."

"I will drink to that." Rat snagged a bottle of opened beer and toasted Bolt. "I am looking forward to pulling that old bum apart like warm bread."

"Well, I have to go. I am meeting up with that john again," Shadow said.

"Don't be late and screw things up," Bolt hissed.

Shadow smiled at Bolt and walked off.

"Do you hear me?"

Shadow ignored him and just kept walking.

CHAPTER 82

CAPTAIN COOPER WAS sitting on his porch on his old, wooden rocking chair. He was very stressed. His life was fairly simple until Bolt arrived. This was going to be the first time that he had ever been challenged to be the leader of the camp. He knew that his age was a disadvantage for him if any physical violence broke out. That was why it was important for him to have the support of Jordan and Jesse.

The captain trusted Jordan to a certain degree. He was always respectful, and Bags's endorsement gave Jordan a lot of creditability. Because of Jordan's age, Cooper was still skeptical and rightfully so.

Cooper was also still on the fence about Jesse. He knew Jesse was a smart kid and very likeable. He did recognize his potential dishonesty and selfish side, which made him questionable. He smiled as he remembered what Bags had said about him. "Yessum, Captain! Jesse is like a caged dog in the backyard. You don't know what he's gonna do when he gets loose."

The ruckus earlier between Bolt and the two Flinstone kids did give the captain a sense of which side they were on. The loyalty part was still up in the air. The captain looked down at Niko and stroked his head. He struck a match and lit his pipe. "Well, boy, I hope those two boys won't be tying knots in our tail."

* * *

Shadow had reached a crossroad in her life. Her distain for Bolt had blistered. She had enough of his controlling and abusive ways. She had to make a decision on where she was heading from here. She brought her leather pouch with the sling along with some sharp rocks. Her job today was to take out Captain Cooper's dog. Bolt was convinced that would demoralize the captain and his confidence would soon collapse after that. At the moment, Shadow was leaning toward not following through.

She hurried down the road to the train yard. She looked up the hill and saw Jordan waving at her.

CHAPTER 83

FRANK BURKE WAS in a great mood. This was his first day on day shift, and he was excited to not have to be on the graveyard shift anymore. Frank's new partner, Shoog Martin, and him were like two peas from the same pod. Shoog had a mean streak too and was very dedicated to his career.

When Frank arrived at work, Shoog was already there and looking out the office window through a pair of binoculars.

"Looks like there's a couple of street punks up on the hill trying to scope out things. Here, have a look." Shoog handed the binoculars to Burke.

"So should we head up there and scare the shit of them?" Frank asked.

"Maybe later on. Let me see that cattle prod that I have been hearing so much about."

CHAPTER 84

AFTER SPENDING A couple of hours with Jordan scoping out the train yard, Jesse returned to camp. He smelled fried bacon sizzling from Bags frying pan.

"Hey, Bags! That sure smells good."

"You are welcome to join me." Bags stabbed the slices of bacon and turned them over in the pan. "Where's Jordan?"

"He is hanging out with his friend Shadow."

"Yessum. Uh, maybe that's a good thing for him to stay away with the sheriff snooping around."

"Yeah, I am not sure that she's a good influence. She likes heroin. I don't trust her."

"Oh Lord. I would hate to see Jordan get hooked on that stuff."

"Yeah, she's got him hooked on her pussy right now. It's his first piece of ass."

"Can't be all bad then. I remember my first piece of tail. Her name was Betsy Lou. Yessum. She was a white woman that I met riding a train up to New Orleans. She had a hot temper like boiling water, but in the sack she was something else."

"I wonder who the snitch was that told the cops about Jordan? I bet it was that prick Bolt. Sounds like something he would do."

"Maybe so, but what's done is done."

"Guess, I'll get his sleeping bag and bring it out to him."

"That's mighty nice of you. Here, have something to eat first." Bags handed Jesse a couple of strips of bacon on a plate. "You make sure that he is still planning on showing up for the captain. He is counting on the both of you."

Jesse looked up and saw River walking toward him. They both smiled at each other and gave each other a hug.

River backed off immediately as the fowl stench of Jesse's bad breath and unbathed body shot right up her nostrils. She almost gagged. "Whoa, dude! You are ripe. Gross!"

Jesse ignored her comment. "Wow, you actually showed up."

"I told Melissa to tell you guys that I was coming."

"So anyway, I have to go find Jordan. The cops are looking for him, and I will fill you in on some of the heavy stuff going down. Come on, let's go."

"Hold on! I just got here. Can I rest a minute?"

"Come on. We don't have much time."

Bags stood up and took his hat off. "Well, since your gentleman friend won't introduce me, my name is Bags. You must be River. I've heard about you. It's a pleasure to meet you, young lady."

"I've heard about you too. You are just exactly what I imagined you would be."

"Well, thank you, miss. It's apparent to me that you don't like to be ordered around, yessum!" Bags smiled. "But unfortunately we have a situation that needs to be taken care of, so you can stay here with me if you'd like. Jesse has to go find Jordan, and then in a few hours there is an important meeting between the leader of our camp, Captain Nathan Cooper, and that new street kid. I think you know who I am talking about."

"Bolt?" River shook her head. "That creep just won't go away. All right, I am in. I still have a bone to settle with that dickhead."

Bags was impressed with River's moxie. However, he knew that she was too much woman for Jesse. "Here, take this with you and give it to Jordan." Bags handed Jesse his flashlight. "He might need it later. I suspect that he should hide out for a few days and let the dust settle. Now don't you lose the damn thing, you hear me?"

CHAPTER 85

MARY WILKENS WAS very sad that River had ran away. She couldn't understand why. Everything seemed to be going fine. She felt like River was starting to be part of the family. The only friction that Mary was aware of was between her daughter and her husband. She was curious why her daughter was not as close to her husband as she was before River entered into the picture.

Jeff and Mary were sitting in the living room. Mary was on the couch reading a book, and Jeff was sitting in a chair watching Sports Center.

"I miss the good old days when Melissa would be sitting here with us," Mary reminisced.

Jeff nodded. "I think about that too. Our little girl is not the same person anymore."

"Well, she has grown up. She has a mind of her own. Who do think she got that from?" Mary smiled at her husband sarcastically.

"Who? Not me."

"Yes, dear. I am quite sure it's you."

Jeff smiled. He had never thought about that before. He had pretty much blamed River for Melissa's behavior change. Although River had exposed his daughter to a different way of life, he now had to come to terms with the reality that Melissa was making decisions on her own. Tonight, he would be testing her will to give in to him, when Mary was sleeping.

Earlier when they were having dinner, Jeff thought he was making some headway with Melissa. For the first time in a while, she was staring at him and joking with him. He took that as a good sign that she was coming around. He was starting to get anxious thinking about being naked beside her as he was sitting there in the living room with his wife. Mary's banter was starting to agitate him.

* * *

Melissa sat in her bedroom listening to her stereo. She was playing a Clash CD that reminded her of River. She was weighing her options. She knew that later on her father would be sneaking into her room and expecting to have sex with her.

One option would be for her to run away and join River. Melissa turned up her stereo as the song "Should I Stay or Should I Go" came on. What timing, she thought, for that song to be playing when she was considering leaving.

She could play the confess-everything-to-Mom card, but the pain that would cause her mom was not worth it.

The other choice was the one that she couldn't even believe that she was still even contemplating. Even though she was disgusted with her father, having sex with him was the most logical choice, and that way, her dad would keep his mouth shut about Jordan.

The scary part was that she had the urge to have sex. It aroused her thinking about having forbidden sex. Being raped by Bolt excited her, and at night she would masturbate thinking about it. It disturbed her that she would secretly fantasize about things like that. She wondered if she was mentally ill. Was this a sickness that was passed down to her by her father? Was she a nymphomaniac?

River's favorite Clash song, "London Calling," blasted out of the stereo. It took Melissa's mind off thinking about sex.

227

CHAPTER 86

FRANK AND SHOOG drove their SUV a mile up the road from the train yard. They pulled over and parked.

"Okay, Frank, let's be real quiet now and sneak up on those two punks." They both got out of the truck and headed back to the area where they had spotted the two kids watching the train yard.

"Shoog, you are a man of my own heart."

"All right, we are going to teach those assholes a lesson, so no more talking until we get there."

CHAPTER 87

THE WEATHER HAD turned colder. The wind had picked up, and the cloudy skies were hiding the sunlight. Bolt walked over to the campfire where Rat and Blake were huddled around.

"Where the fuck is Shadow?"

"Do you want me to go find her?" Rat asked.

"No, you need to stay here and wait for those choo choo riders to show up."

"If they show up," Rat answered back, taunting Bolt.

"Shut up, Rat. I don't need your shit right now."

"I'm sorry, man," Rat apologized.

Bolt stormed off back to his van. He opened up the sliding door and climbed into the back. The stress was getting to him. He had a gut feeling that Shadow wasn't loyal to him anymore. If that was the case, he was glad that he had Savage, who was always ready for a good scrap.

By the end of the day, he would be either the king of the hill and sleeping in Captain Cooper's shack or in deep shit. Because of his limited vocabulary, Bolt knew he had to choose his words wisely. The captain was a lot wiser than Prince. His objective was to convince the old man that the world had passed him by and that it was time for new leadership. In exchange for Captain Cooper stepping down, he would leave the captain alone, which of course was a bunch of bullshit.

All he needed was for Cooper to let his guard down for just a brief moment.

CHAPTER 88

JESSE WAS HAPPY to see River.

"I am blown away that you actually showed up."

"Why? What's the big deal? I've been on the road before."

Jesse tried to hug her.

"Hands off until you take a bath."

"A few more days here, and you'll love the smell of my sweat."

"Yuck.

"So did you bring any music with you?"

"Yeah, I have a few cassettes in my backpack. I thought I might need to sell them to get some money."

"I found a squawk box in the one of the trash bins in town and brought it back to the camp. I think all we need is batteries."

River smiled. "Cool!

"Hey, look up ahead. Do you see that SUV parked over on the side of the road?"

"What about it?"

"Shh. It looks like a railroad bull SUV." Jesse grabbed River, and they both crouched down on the ground. Jesse looked around to see if he could spot the bulls. He wasn't sure how many of them there were. He knew that they usually traveled in pairs.

"We better get the fuck out of here."

"What about Jordan?"

"Come on. Let's go. We will come back later."

Before they could get to their feet, Frank Burke was right on top of them.

"Hold it right there!" Shoog shouted. "Don't you two assholes move an inch."

Jesse could see that they both had their guns drawn from their holsters. "Well, lookie here, Frank. We have a couple of train riders."

Frank put his pistol back in his holster and took out his cattle prod. He nudged Jesse with the club. "Is that what you two street punks are up to? You are going to jump a train?"

"No, sir, we are just out for a walk," Jesse answered.

"You think that we are a couple of idiots?" Frank poked Jesse with his stick. "That 'yes, sir' stuff doesn't work here. What do you think, Shoog?"

"I think we should run the both of them in and arrest them for trespassing." Shoog stared up and down River's body. "What about those other punks that we spotted?" Frank asked.

"We'll deal with them later." Shoog replied.

River could see the lust in Shoog's eyes.

"Well, we have a pretty little pork chop here, Frank."

"Looks like you're a new, street kid. You're still pretty clean looking. I bet that you had a shower today. Am I right?" Frank rubbed his prod on one of River's breasts. "I like little chunky girls. How about you, Shoog?"

River pushed the club away from her breast. "You pigs keep away from me! You have no right to be touching me!"

"Oh, Ms. Pork Chop! You have no idea what we can do."

Jesse stepped in front of River. "Come on, dudes. Give us a break. We aren't doing anything wrong."

"Well, lookie here, Frank. This young punk thinks he is a tough guy."

Frank whacked Jesse on the side of his head, and then he zapped him with the cattle prod on the arm. Jesse grimaced in pain as the electric shock riveted through his shoulder. River dropped down to the ground beside Jesse as he tried to get back up on his feet.

"I would tell your boyfriend to stay down if I was you, pork chop."

"Cuff him, Frank." Burke twisted Jesse around and cuffed him. Jesse remained on the ground.

River looked up at Shoog. "So what now?"

"Ah, so don't be in such a hurry little, pork chop. We have a couple of ideas. We could run both of you in and lock you up or, little pork chop, you could provide us a little service and pleasure us. If you're willing to do that, we will be more lenient, and we might even let you go. What do you say, Frank? Do you want to get a little?"

"So that's what this is all about?" River spouted out. "Sex and power for you two pricks. What's the matter, can't you find anyone to give you head without threatening them?"

Shoog slapped River across the face. "Don't you disrespect me, you little bitch! So if I were you, I would cooperate and don't piss us off anymore."

"Well, pork chop? Are you ready to do your duty?"

River was pretty sure that she had no other choice but to go along with the one bull's request.

"Well, you ready, little missy? I have a nice comfortable spot in the back seat of the SUV. We will have plenty of room when I put the seats down."

"Don't do it, River," Jesse screamed.

"Shut the hell up, boy, or I will hit you again." Frank raised his club.

River got to her feet. "No, don't hurt him anymore. Okay! Let's go."

"Good choice, pork chop. Frank, you keep an eye on that fuck-head. We will be right back, and then you can have your turn. Come on, honey. Let's go have some fun." As the two of them strolled off toward the SUV, Shoog put his hand on River's ass and squeezed her left cheek.

From out of nowhere, a rock came flying through the air, and another rock shimmered off Shoog's back. He tumbled to the ground. Frank drew his pistol and fired off a couple shots. Another rock soared through the air and knocked the gun out of Frank's hand. He grimaced in pain. Shoog tried to reach in his holster to pull out his gun. Another rock bounced off his shoulder.

"Don't move, asshole!" Shadow screamed. "We have more coming your way."

Jordan shouted, "You two get out there now!"

Shoog and Frank didn't move. They were bleeding from the blows delivered by the rocks.

River got Jesse to his feet, and they took off running. Jesse was stumbling around because it wasn't easy running with his hands cuffed behind his back. He fell a few times trying to keep up with River.

Jordan and Shadow took off and headed in the opposite direction up into the hills.

"Man, that was amazing! How did you get so good at throwing rocks?" Jordan asked Shadow.

"Back on the reservation, my brother, Charlie, and I used to practice slinging rocks all the time. We used to bird for food."

"Like what would you kill?"

"My brother and I got really good at hunting rabbits. We have part Cheyenne and Navajo in our blood. They were famous trackers who used rocks to kill their food. They used slings made out of buffalo hide to catapult the rocks for long distance tosses. Charlie Little Hawk and I carried on the tradition."

"Wow! So how did you end up with Bolt?"

"It's a screwy story. Growing up on the reservation as a kid was great. I was free to run wild with my little brother. We were always exploring the countryside for the next adventure." Jordan could see the gleam in her eye. "Charlie and I had a fascination for quicksand."

"No way!"

"Yeah way! We were always out searching for it."

"Me too!" Jordan laughed. "I love the quicksand scenes watching all the *Tarzan* movies with my dad."

"Pretty funny!" Shadow smiled. "When my mom died, I was kind of left on my own. I started making bad decisions. Unless I wanted to be a hotel maid, it wasn't easy finding a job. Not many people wanted to hire a Native American. So I hooked up with the wrong crowd and started making money selling drugs. My father found out, wrote me off."

"That sucks."

"Yeah. So anyway, things were never the same after that. He started calling me a whore, especially when he was drunk. And then I got busted for selling drugs and got sent to prison."

"Hmm." Jordan put his arm around Shadow. She cuddled up to him. She loved it when he held her. He was a good listener and didn't judge her. It made it easy for her to open up.

"So what was it like being in prison?"

"Very scary! And if you weren't a rich person, it was a bitch because everything cost money. Shampoo, soap, nothing was free. And of course, I had no money, so it was really tough at first. I didn't know the ropes. So I had to go cold turkey with my drug problem. It was brutal until this black chick, Puddin, took me under her wing. It was the weirdest thing. During mealtimes I kept getting ice cream and cookies on my tray. Another inmate finally filled me in that Puddin, who ran the kitchen, had put claims on me. After that, prison was like a vacation. Puddin took care of me. I learned how to be a con artist in there. I learned how to manipulate Puddin, and occasionally I would let her touch me.

Jordan was facinated with her prison stories.

"Out in the yard was where all the bad stuff happened. Sex and drugs were everywhere. A few of the girls were jealous of me. They tried to give me the business, but Puddin was there to straighten them out. I learned how to play the game and avoid the trouble spots, especially out in the yard. Everything was a con. The only person I trusted was Puddin. So anyway, I first met Rat on the street, and he took me back to his campsite and introduced me to Bolt. I have been with him ever since."

"So you have hopped trains before?"

"Fuck yeah!" Shadow pulled out her bandanna hanging from her back pocket.

"I wondered about that. I saw that hanging from your back pocket."

"Right! That's all you were looking at was my rag, huh?" Shadow playfully punched Jordan in the arm.

Her comment embarrassed Jordan. He didn't know quite how to react. He wasn't used to all the flirting and lovey-dovey stuff.

They walked a mile over the hill from where they had stoned the railroad bulls. They found a large formation of rocks that almost formed a cave that would serve as shelter from the cold wind that was blowing.

"This is a good spot for us to hide if we have to." Jordan and Shadow took a seat on the ground.

"You're not going back to Hobo Flat tonight?"

"I am not sure. Who knows who's waiting for me there. What about you? Won't Bolt be wondering where you are?"

Shadow nudged her head into Jordan's shoulder. "Yeah! He needs me to do something for him. I should probably get going. So why did you run away from home?" Shadow asked.

"I am not sure." Shadow could tell that Jordan wasn't comfortable talking about himself.

"Come on! Do I have to suck it out of you?" Shadow rubbed Jordan's leg. She could feel his member start to swell.

"You know I really can't tell you why. I mean, it wasn't that I had a horrible life or anything. I guess I was just confused and I didn't want to be a burden on my parents. They tried really hard, even though they are strapped for money. I miss my family."

"Sounds like you can always go home if things get too crazy." Shadow answered. "So it looks like your friend Jesse has found a girlfriend."

"Yeah, that was our friend River." Jordan paused for a second. Then he shook his head. "Well, I will be damned." Jordan chuckled. "She showed up just like Melissa said she would."

"She looks just like a vampire."

"She hates Bolt."

"Can you blame her? Bolt raped her, stold her car, and left her out in the middle of nowhere. I didn't have anything to do with that. It was all Bolt and Rat. So do you like that little princess?" Shadow asked. "Huh, whatever her name is."

"Melissa? Yep! She is pretty cool."

Shadow's dark-brown eyes turned ice-cold. Her jealous blood started to boil. Jordan could see that Melissa had struck a nerve with her. He was getting his first taste of how complicated relationships can be.

Jordan tried to sidetrack Shadow and change the subject. "So I am not sure what to do. I am not sure if it is a good idea to go back to camp. Jesse dropped off my sleeping bag, and I bet Bags had something to do with that. So he must think that it is a good idea to stay away for a while. Can we meet back here later?" Jordan asked.

"I don't know. We will see how it goes."

Jordan wasn't sure what to do next. "I would like that if you did." Shadow and Jordan got to their feet. They hugged each other.

"Look, Melissa and I are just friends. She is just very nice to me. That's all there is to it." Jordan was struggling trying to cover up his real feelings for Melissa. If today he had to choose, he would pick Melissa over Shadow.

Shadow didn't buy his line of crap for a minute. "Take care, Jordan." She started to walk away.

"You too! See you soon. I will be here waiting for you."

"Maybe. Wouldn't you rather be with that oogle chick instead?"

"No, not at all."

Shadow's attitude lightened up. "Are you going to the big meeting?"

"I don't know. Captain Cooper wants me to." Jordan paused, trying to be noncommittal. "You be careful heading back. Those two bulls are probably still looking for us."

Shadow headed off. She wrestled with the idea of just staying there with Jordan. She thought it best to head back.

Jordan went back and found his sleeping bag that was still lying on the ground. He staked out the place to make sure the bulls weren't still around. He also picked up the flashlight and walked back up the hill. He snuggled up in his sleeping bag in between the rocks that sheltered him from the wind.

CHAPTER 89

BOLT ARRIVED AT the meeting place early. A half-dozen choo choo riders also showed up. Bolt smirked at Rat and gave him the "I told you so" look.

Shadow got there a few minutes later. She appologized for being gone so long. Her excuse was that she had waited and waited for her date to show up.

Bolt was irritated with Shadow. He didn't believe her bullshit story for a minute.

"Just get over there behind those bushes and get ready to do your job."

At four o'clock, Bolt could see two men in the distance walking toward the building.

"Where's his dog?" Bolt wondered.

As the two tramps got closer, Bolt could see that neither one of them was Captain Cooper.

"Are you Bolt?" one of the tramps asked.

"Yeah, so?

"We have a message from Captain Cooper."

"Yeah? What's that?"

"Something came up, so the captain has to reschedule for tomorrow."

Bolt's facial muscles tightened. He hissed and snapped back. "Well, you can give him a message for me. I think that he is a chicken shit and that he had better not stand me up again. Now you two old pukes get the hell out of here before I take it out on you."

The old home bums, Herme and Johnson, quickly turned around and scurried off at a pace that they hadn't done in years.

"That old dude is playing games with me. Can you believe that?"

Rat tried to settle Bolt down. "Ah! What's another day anyway?"

Bolt looked over at the spot where Shadow was supposedly hiding. "Hey, bitch! Get your ass over here!"

There was no answer back.

Rat walked over to the place behind the building where Shadow was supposed to be hiding.

"Hey, you better come here!" Rat yelled at Bolt.

"I have had enough of this shit! What now, is she passed out or something?" His anger grew as he got to the hiding place. Shadow was gone, and left a message on the ground spelled out with rocks. It said, "Fuck you!"

Bolt howled and stomped around in frustration.

"I am going to get that whore. You wait and see. I am not finished with her."

CHAPER 90

Jeff Wilkens was sitting in the front room watching the eleven-o'clock news and waiting for his wife to fall asleep. He decided to go outside and stretch his legs. After a few minutes, Wilkens returned back into the house, hung his jacket up in the hall closet, and peeked in on his wife. He opened the door quietly and could hear her softly snoring. He shut the door and walked down the hallway to Melissa's room.

Melissa could hear him coming down the creaky hallway toward her room. Her heart was beating fast.

He twisted the doornob and was pissed to find out that the door was locked. He stood there as the anger surged through his brain. He wanted to pound on the door.

Melissa breathed a sigh of relief as she heard her father stomp off. She pulled the covers up and masturbated before finally drifting off into a deep sleep. Her final thoughts were about River. Melissa knew that she would have been proud of her tonight. River wouldn't be so proud of her if she knew that she had impure thoughts.

CHAPTER 91

———— ❦ ————

CAPTAIN COOPER HAD a satisfied look on his face after he got the report back from Herme and Johnson about how Bolt reacted to the delay. He knew that he had a mad dog on his hands. He had one more night to think things through.

* * *

The next morning, Captain Cooper headed out for his morning walk. He was once again greeted with another beautiful sunny morning.

Last night he considered the different choices that he had. One would be to have a vote and have the camp decide who should be in charge. Another plan would be for the captain to just simply step down and relinquish his authority.

The captain was comfortable with his role as the leader of Hobo Flat. Having to hit the road and starting over was not appealing to him. He was quite proud of his accomplishment of being one of the few people to be the leader of a subculture society. There were maybe a handful of others across the country that held such a position.

He felt he was a fair man who ruled with compassion and with a steel fist if that was needed. It was not an easy task keeping the inmates that lived in Hobo Flat in line. Many of them had no respect for anyone else and had learned to fend for themselves. Any disputes would be settled swiftly. Captain Cooper always had the last say. The law of the camp was very simple. No stealing, no raping, no drugs, and no fighting unless it was supervised, which meant if two bums had differences and weren't getting along, they could put on the gloves like in the movie Cool Hand Luke and slug it out on Saturday afternoon. Captain Cooper would be there to referee. There hadn't been a Saturday dispute in quite a while.

* * *

The captain was very proud that he was member of the Freight Train Riders of America, (a.k.a. fuck the Reagan administration). He was twenty-five years old when he first engaged the FTRA. He had heard of them. They were mostly older tramps that were well-known for being brutal and very loyal to the brotherhood.

He was traveling through Illinois on a hot summers day back in August of 1967. Back in those times, the cost of living was much different. Gasoline was thirty-three cents a gallon, fresh-baked bread was only twenty-two cents a loaf, and you could buy a new car for around three thousand bucks.

Cooper had been riding a G train and had found a hop out spot (a hidden place in a jungle area) where he could safely jump off right outside Chicago. He was immediately surrounded by four men. They wanted to know what the hell he was doing there. Cooper remembered being scared too death. He told them his name, where he was heading, and just stood his ground. One of the older bums got a kick out his name being Nathan Cooper. He said it sounded like an old gunfighter's name. He asked him if he was as tough as a legendary gunman of the old West. Cooper told them that when he was a kid, he used to always pretend that he was going to the OK Corral for a gunfight. That broke the ice with the older tramps, and he spent the night sharing a meal of baked beans and ham with them. That was a welcome meal for a starving traveler.

* * *

Earlier in the morning, Bags took a stroll by the train yard to see if he could find Jordan. He had no such luck.

Nathan smiled as he thought about the upcoming showdown with Bolt. It reminded him once again of the gunfight at the OK Corral. Only the captain's foes weren't the McLaurys, Clantons, and Claibornes. It was a Salty Dog who could be a villain in a *Star Wars* movie. This was a different time but similar circumstances.

Earp had his two brothers and Doc Holiday by his side. The captain was not as fortunate to have that solid kind of support. His Doc Holiday was his old dog, Niko, some street kids, if they showed up, and an old black home bum with a bad leg.

Captain Cooper knew his placid temperament would come in handy for him today. His ability to be calm in tense situations would give him the upper hand against an immature kid. It usually intimidated his opponents. This time, though, he wasn't so sure. His latest antagonist was unscrupulous and unpredictable. The captain himself was a little unnerved by Bolt.

CHAPTER 92

RIVER WALKED UP the road from the camp and bought a cup of coffee at a convience store so she wouldn't feel guilty using the restroom to clean herself up. It felt good to wash her body with warm water. As she walked out of the store, the clerk with the name Roy on his name tag, smiled at her.

She was thrown right back into the fire on her first day back on the road. Thank God she didn't have to submit to the wishes of the obnoxious bulls. She knew from her previous experience that danger was always a bit of life's cavalcade on the road. Today wasn't going to be much easier.

* * *

Jesse wondered how Jordan was doing and whether he would be at the showdown. As he sat by himself leaning up against a tree, his thoughts shifted back to River. She wasn't the most beautiful girl he had ever met. He liked her gothic look and outspoken personality.

In another month, Jesse would be turning eighteen, which would make him an adult and would change the way the law looked at him if he ever got arrested.

Jesse grinned as he saw River walking toward him with a paper bag and two cups of coffee.

"Dude, I brought you a nice, creamy filled donut."

"Awesome."

"No problem. What are you thinking about?"

"Uh, well, a lot of different stuff."

"I hope one of them is to hike up to the river and bathing yourself."

Jesse cracked a half-crooked smile. "Yeah, it was crossing my mind."

"Liar! You like to stink, mister. Don't bullshit me."

"You are something else, River!"

"So are you, Jesse, uh, I don't even know your last name."

"Clark. Jesse Robert Clark. Robert was my mother's brother's name."

"What about Jesse?"

"No other Jesses. I am one of a kind."

"So why did you become a street kid?"

Jesse filled her in on his life living next to a military base.

"So who's that walking towards us?"

"That's Captain Cooper. Watch out for his dog. He is very protective of the captain. First time I met him he scared the crap out of me."

As he approached them, Jesse and River started to get up.

"Morning. No need to get up. Y'all both look very comfortable sitting in the shade."

Nathan smiled at River and tipped his hat. She was the prettiest thing his old tired eyes had seen in a long time. "So this is the lovely lady that Bags told me about."

"This is my friend, River Walker. She just joined us last night."

"Ah! Pleasure to meet you. This is my friend, Niko."

Jesse was surprised and curious why the captain introduced his dog to River.

"So have you filled this lovely lady in on the rules here that need to be followed if she decides to stay with us at Hobo Flat?"

"Not yet." Jesse hated following the rules. Just hearing the captain bringing it up pissed him off.

"Then allow me to. We live a very simple life here. No cheating, stealing, or using drugs at Hobo Flat. If you can do that, you are welcome to stay. If not, the camp down the road allows all of that behavior."

"No thanks. I've been there. That's not for me." River got to her feet. "Is it all right if I pet your dog?"

"Huh, now that's something nobody has ever asked me before. Everybody is sort of afraid of Niko."

"I love dogs. When I lived with my mom, we had a retriever. She died of old age."

"Well, Niko is not one of those who you can just walk up to, are you, boy?"

Niko looked up at the captain like he understood what he said.

"Sit, boy." Niko immediately obeyed the command. "This pretty little girl likes you and wants to pet you. What do you think, old man?" Just like before, Niko looked at River and then back up at the captain.

Captain Cooper grinned. "Well, it's your hand, girl."

River didn't waste any time and walked right up to Niko. "Hello there."

At first Niko stood up on all four paws. This was unusual for him because he wasn't used to being approached. He could sense her confidence. There was a certain calmness about her. He dropped his guard and allowed her to touch him.

She stroked his neck and petted him on the head. "You are such a good boy." Niko responded by licking her hand.

"Well, I'll be. Huh. Looks like you have found a new friend, boy."

The captain was enchanted by River. She seemed very wise for her age. It had been a while since he had feelings for a woman. This was something new and exciting. He could tell by the way River looked at him that she was interested in him too.

Captain Cooper knew that this was the wrong time to pursue anything further with her. He needed Jesse to support him.

River could feel the chemistry between the captain and her. Even though he could be her grandfather, she was attracted to him and hoped to be able to spend some time with him.

"So the reason I am here is to make sure I can count on Jordan and you later."

"Don't worry! I will be there. I am not sure about Jordan."

"Well, hopefully he will show up."

River jumped in. "I'm coming too."

"I am not sure what is going to happen today, young lady. It could be dangerous!"

"Like I said before, I have been to that camp, and I have a score to settle with that scumbag."

"Well now, you seem pretty serious. I appreciate your passion. All right then! Okay! You be careful and stay close to Jesse." Cooper made a clicking sound to Niko. "Come on, boy." He turned and headed back to his shack. He looked back and waved.

The captain looked at Niko. "You never know, boy, what's waiting for us around the next turn. That River is a pretty one."

Captain Cooper would have never thought Jesse would be the one that he could count on.

CHAPTER 93

SHADOW GREETED THE new day with her usual hangover. But by the look on Jordan's face, it was worth it. She was happy that she made up her mind to part ways with Bolt. Shadow and Jordan partied hard together drinking vodka, and later that night she introduced Jordan to heroin.

For Jordan, it was the greatest high that he had ever felt. It was like an out-of-body experience. His veins were electric, and he was numb to the chilling wind and the rest of the world that was circling around him. And he was able to maintain his faculties.

Shadow knew that the dope thing would be a problem for her at Hobo Flat. The good news was that it was short-term and that Jordan and her would be traveling soon.

Shadow tried several times to get clean, but she wasn't strong enough. She couldn't withstand the painful withdrawals that attacked her nervous system and caused intense charley horses. She remembered waking up one morning after a night of drying out and seeing that she had kicked the wall in of a shed that she had been sleeping behind.

Obviously now with Jordan in her life, she would have to make some changes in her lifestyle. She wasn't certain, but she was pretty sure Jordan wouldn't approve of her hooking. But if push came to shove, she always had that in her back pocket if she ever needed to make some quick cash. Everything else seemed perfect. Their chemistry together was good. She was attracted to him sexually and liked the way he treated her. Being older gave Shadow an distinct advantage that she never had before. She was wearing the pants in the relationship.

* * *

"Yessum, Captain, our peaceful world has become complex. It's like a bunch of killer bees invaded our hive."

"Well, there's not much we can do about it." Cooper took off his hat and scratched the back of his head. "So, Bags, what do you think about Jesse's friend?"

"Yessum, she seems special to me. I wonder why she is here with us."

"Well, like all of us, we have a path that lead us here. She wants to go with us today. I have never had a woman volunteer before."

"We are kind of shorthanded. Another body would be helpful," Bags responded. "According to Jesse, she held her own against Bolt last time. She scratched him up pretty darn good."

"Yeah, that's what you told me," the captain answered. He took off his spectacles and cleaned them with his bandanna. "So tell me something, Bags, if you could choose anything in the world that would make you happy, what would that be?"

"Shucks! That's an easy one, Captain. I would like to have some room service."

Both Captain Cooper and Bags both busted out loud laughing.

"Thank you, Bags! I needed a good laugh. It looks like we had better head out."

Captain Cooper knew it would take a half hour get to the abandoned service station and maybe a little longer depending on how fast Bags could keep up with his hobbled leg. The Captain was happy Bags decided to go with him.

"Well, boy, you ready?"

Niko got to his feet and stretched his legs.

"No matter what happens, boy, I want you know that I love you and I appreciate your companionship." The captain petted Niko on the top of his head. By the look in his eye, the captain could tell that Niko understood what was going on. "Let's hit the road."

Captain Cooper had a nostalgic look as he stared back up the hill at his shack. It was holy ground to him. Sure, he had lived in apartments and other places, but this place was special to him. It was in shambles when he first moved in. But with hard sweat and tender loving care, along with the old stove and furniture he found at the junkyard, Nathan was able to make it a comfortable place to live in. He hoped that everything would work out and that he would be returning home.

Up the way, the captain could see Jesse and River waiting for him.

* * *

Bolt was already waiting at the abandoned adobe building that was nestled on the side on a dirt road off the main highway. Back in the day before the highway bypassed the road, it was a popular place to gas up and buy refreshments. Now the place had been taken over by overgrown vines and weeds. Inside the building was an old table with a couple of benches. There was garbage stacked up in the corner from travelers who had previously spent the night there.

Bolt was anxious to get the meeting over with. He was still angry at Shadow. He had counted heavily on her rock throwing, and now he had to change his plan of attack.

This time only two choo choo riders showed up. "See, I told you we couldn't trust those pricks," Rat said.

"Yeah, you love that they didn't follow through. I will deal with them later."

"What do you think is going to happen?" Rat asked.

"Hell, if I knew the answer to that, I wouldn't be so messed up," Bolt snapped back. "We are dealing with a cagey old bastard. I am pretty sure he is not going to want to step down without being nudged, you know what I mean?"

"Yeah, well, I am ready to do some nudging."

"I hope so. Shadow screwed up everything. What about Blake? Can I trust him?"

"Don't worry, B! It's all handled. We will be toasting some Jack Daniel's later tonight."

* * *

Bags was keeping up pretty good with Captain Cooper. His cane was very helpful as he limped along.

"You know, Bags, I appreciate you having my back. Your tired old bones didn't have to do this."

"Well, Captain, I figure I owe you something for making an old bum's life comfortable. Yessum, I appreciate being able to sleep at night all these years with both eyes closed."

"Ha-ha!" The captain shook his head with a grin on his face. "I love the way you put things in perspective." Cooper patted Bags on the back. "The building is just around the corner."

* * *

"Do you want to keep going?" Jesse asked River.

"Fucking right! No worries. I bet that chicken shit will back down. I think he is just feeling things out."

"Yeah, I am not sure this is our war to fight. I mean, what the hell, Jordan and I are planning on leaving soon. We could duck off right now and get out of here. I don't think Jordan is going to show up either."

"Come on, little boy. A promise is a promise." River was disappointed in how selfish Jesse was. She wasn't sure how much longer she would be hanging out with him. As they walked around the bend, she could see the deserted building off to the left.

"Here. Take this." Jesse handed River a smiley that he made out of rope with a sharp piece of broken pipe tied on the end.

CHAPTER 94

FRANK BURKE WAS still upset and very sore from the day before. Unlike his partner, Shoog, who took the day off, Frank showed up on time. He was embarrassed and preferred not to discuss what happened with the other bulls.

Old Tom Rowe, a veteran with the railroad police, was a smart-ass and loved to rub things in. He started right in on Frank. "Looks to me by those bruises on your face, some old bum got the best of you. What about your partner? I bet old Shoog is faking it and staying home because he is too humiliated to come in and face us. Have I got that right, Mr. Burke?"

"Fuck off, you lazy old fart." Frank gave him the finger.

The other two men in the office busted up laughing.

Frank put his jacket on and headed out to go on patrol. He got in the SUV and drove off. He drove by the spot of the incident last night. He pulled over and looked over the area. He never got a good look at the kids whom he saw earlier sitting up on the hill looking at the train yard. He wondered if they would be back anytime soon. He was pretty sure that the two street kids that Shoog and him roughed up knew the rock throwers.

Burke drove off and continued his patrol. It felt good being by himself for a change. Shoog could be annoying bragging all the time on how smart and tough he could be.

CHAPTER 95

Niko started growling as soon as he saw Bolt's pit bull. Savage growled back.

"Easy, Savage. You'll get your chance," Bolt commanded. He pointed out to Rat, "He brought that old black bum with him, and it looks like that Jesse dude, and oh look, it's the fat chick coming back for more."

"A piece of cake," Rat answered.

"I wonder where that other punk Jordan is? Shit! It would have been so much easier if we had Shadow," Bolt reacted nervously. "Just keep your eye on that dog, do you hear me?"

Bolt had a fear of dogs. When he was younger, he had a traumatizing experience when he went over to a friend's house that lived up the street from him. The family owned a Doberman pinscher that they usually kept pinned up in the backyard. The dog was very intimidating. That day, the screen door was left open, and the dog had gotten in the house when Bolt was alone sitting in the living room waiting for his friend to come out from his bedroom. The fierce animal came right up to Bolt and stood a few inches away from his face growling and showing him his sharp teeth. Bolt sat still and tried to ignore the dog. He tried to stand his ground and try not to show any fear. One bad move, and Bolt knew the dog would tear his face off. Bolt's friend eventually came out of his room and saw what was going on. His friend called the dog off and put him outside in the backyard. Bolt never forgot that day. Over the years, he still had nightmares about it and was the reason for the abuse on Savage. It was his way of getting revenge for his fear.

Niko could smell Bolt's fear. Even though he was an older dog, he still was a very worthy opponent. He kept his eyes focused on every move that Savage made.

Captain Cooper wasted no time and confronted Bolt. The captain could sense that Bolt was nervous and that gave him the advantage.

"So here we are."

Both dogs barked and leaped out toward each other.

Bolt's face was slightly twitching as he tried to stare Cooper down. The captain could see that he was afraid of Niko.

"So are you experiencing some old ghosts, punk?"

"I am not a punk, old man!" Cooper could tell he was getting under Bolt's skin. "I think it's time, old man, for you to step down and go into retirement."

"What makes you think that I am ready to do that, punk?"

Bolt hissed. He did not like being called a punk. "Like I said before, or maybe you are hard of hearing, I am not a punk, old man."

"I am afraid so. You are just a dishonest mole who hasn't earned an ounce of respect."

Cooper could tell that he was frustrating Bolt with his demeanor and choice of words.

Bolt attempted to sidestep the issue. He looked over at Jesse, River, and Bags, who were taking it all in. River was very impressed with Captain Cooper's strength and control.

"That is a sorry-looking army, old man! A chicken shit, a fat girl, and a old, washed-up spook." Bolt grinned.

Bags shook his head with a slight half-crooked smile. (He hadn't been called a spook in awhile.)

Bolt's comment about River pissed Jesse off. His face turned red, and he had a vindictive glare in his eyes.

River rolled her eyes and sneared at Bolt. "Yeah, freak! You're nothing but a worthless snail leaving your slime whereever you crawl. And that fake voice of yours is obnoxious."

"It is clear we don't like each other." Cooper agreed and nodded back at his three comrades. He turned his head and looked intently into Bolt's eyes. "I have no interest in giving up my position to, uh, how did she put it? Oh yeah, a worthless snail."

Rat stepped closer to the captain. Niko growled, showing his sharp teeth. Rat backed off and took a few steps back.

"Stay, boy. It's okay," Cooper said.

"You are pretty tough, old fart. I would like to see how tough you are without that fucking dog by your side!" Bolt smirked.

Cooper laughed. "Well, one thing, punk. If I were younger, I would love to teach you a lesson. So I prefer to have Niko do my dirty work. As you can tell, he is anxious to get it on. Aren't you, punk?"

Niko snarled at Bolt.

"Fuck you!"

"Don't embarrass yourself, punk. Foul language is so childish and shows me how weak you are."

Bolt had enough. He turned and motioned to Rat. "Let's get the fuck out of here."

"That is a wise decision," Cooper replied. "However, there is one final thing for you to take creed in. Oh, uh, pardon me. Do you know what the word *creed* means?" The captain was on a roll and continued to pile on the insults.

"Isn't that's a name of a rock band?" Bolt's replied with a feeble attempt at playing the game of malignment.

"Lame, just like your dick is," River scorned.

"Your pussy didn't think so," Bolt replied.

"Like I said, lame," River countered back.

"Well, we can belittle each other all day long. Frankly I'm getting bored. The bottom line is, the local law enforcement has sanctioned Hobo Flat. What the word *sanctions* means, in case you don't know, is that they leave us alone because we don't cause them any grief. Now your little camp is a different story. They don't like you being around. So if I were you, my Huckleberry, I would move on!" Captain Cooper looked down at Niko and gave his familiar clicking sound from his right cheek. "Come on, boy, let's go."

As they headed back, Captain Cooper had a satisfied look on his face. He enjoyed putting Bolt in his place.

Bags was relieved. There were some tense moments. The last time he had been in a ruckus was back in San Antonio when he was protecting himself from a hobo who was trying to steal his cigar box.

"Yessum, I believe we may have dodged a bullet, Captain."

"I hope so." The captain was cautious.

"Fuck yeah!" Jesse raised his fist in the air. "Oops! I am sorry for cussing."

"Well, son, I will give you a get-out-of-jail card this time," Captain Cooper replied. Everyone busted up.

River was beaming with pride. She smiled at the captain. She was amazed on how strong and tough he was without having to throw a punch. He returned the favor with a wink.

* * *

That all changed in a New York minute. Rat rushed out of the sagebrush, screaming like a wild banshee, swinging his smiley over his head. He charged straight toward Captain Cooper. Niko stepped in the front of the captain to protect him from the oncoming assault.

From the opposite side of the road, Savage blindsided Niko before he could react. He sunk his teeth into Niko's neck and tore his throat open, severing a blood vessel. Niko yelped and collapsed helplessly to the ground. Blood was spirting out like a broken water pipe. Jesse walloped Savage with his smiley. The pit bull was dazed by the blow and let go.

Captain Cooper ducked Rat's smiley as it sailed over his head. His agility was impressive for an older man as he raised his leg and kicked Rat in the groin. The blow knocked the air out of him, and he bent over in pain. Blake charged out from the backside, running straight toward Bags.

Bolt just stood in the background shouting orders, "Come on, dudes, let's get that old fucker! Sick 'em, Savage!"

The vicious pit bull surged toward the captain. River stepped in front of the captain and belted Savage in the ribs. The dog fell to the ground and quickly got back up. He leaped and grabbed a hold of River's pant leg and was intensely attempting to chew through her jeans to get to her flesh. Jesse pounded Savage on the head, but the determined dog was relentless and wouldn't let go.

"Let go, you son of a bitch!" River screamed.

"Chew her fucking leg off!" Bolt screeched.

Blake knocked Bags's cane out of his hand. The old man lost his footing and fell down. Blake jumped on top of him and tried to punch him in the face. Bags dodged the blow, grabbed a handfull of dirt, and threw it in Blake's eyes. The dirt disoriented Blake and gave Bags the chance to grab his cane and wack him over the head. The street kid stumbled back trying to get his bearing.

Instantly, several rocks sailed in the air. One was a direct hit and smashed Savage in his right eye. The dog yelped in pain and was knocked unconscious as blood squirted out of his head. Bolt and his henchmen kneeled down in a circle with their hands over their heads to protect them from the bombardment (just like the Vikings would have done if they were being assaulted by arrows).

"Shadow, you fucking bitch!" Bolt shouted as he voice slipped out of character.

"So that's what your real voice sounds like." Jesse laughed.

"You sound like a fucking whimp." River smiled.

Up the road, a white SUV raced toward them with the horn blaring and dust swirling in the air. Frank Burke slammed on the brakes and fishtailed to a halt. He jumped out firing two shots in the air.

"Knock this shit off!" Frank fired another shot in the air. "You assholes are trespassing on railroad property. Now get the hell out of here!" He pointed his gun at Bolt, who took off running, with Rat scurring off like a sneaky rodent right behind him. Blake picked up Savage and carried him off.

Captain Cooper was kneeling on the ground holding Niko in his arms. Blood was everywhere. The captain's eyes swelled up with tears. River came over and put her hand on the captain's shoulder and crouched down beside him.

"I am so sorry for your loss," River said.

"He was my best friend." Cooper held Niko tighter in his arms. "I am going to miss you, boy," Cooper sobbed.

Frank Burke walked up to Captain Cooper. "I have a shovel in the back of my SUV. If you want to bury him here, I am okay with that."

"Thank you," Cooper answered.

Jesse spoke up. "I will dig the grave."

"All right, come with me, and we will get the shovel."

Jesse and Frank walked over to the SUV.

"So we meet again, kid. By the way, what's your and that pudgy girl's name?" Burke asked.

"I'm Jack and she's Betsy," Jesse answered.

Frank knew he was lying but didn't say anything. "So when I drove up, I could see the rocks flying. I assume you know who was doing that, right?"

"Not really."

"Don't lie to me, jerk-off. You know who they are." Frank opened up the back of the vehicle. He took out a shovel and tossed it to Jesse. "So when you see them again, tell them that I am looking for them."

Jesse didn't say another word. He walked back over to where Niko was lying. Captain Cooper decided to bury his friend right next to the abandoned shack.

The ground was very hard from the cold winter. It took a while to loosen up the dirt and dig the grave. River and Bags gathered rocks to put on top of the grave. Captain Cooper stood off to the right by himself.

"So now that the genie is out of the bottle, what do you think the captain will do next?" River asked Bags as he bent over to pick up a rock.

"Not sure. I am not sure at all," Bags answered. "He is a very sad man right now. We need to respect that."

They stood for several minutes around the grave after Niko was buried. The captain took his cowboy hat off.

Burke stayed in his truck and waited for everyone to leave. As they were leaving, Frank drove up and rolled down his window. "I will report this to the local police."

"I appreciate it, but there is no need to do that, Officer. We handle things here our way," Cooper answered. "Thanks for letting us use your shovel."

Frank pointed at Jesse. "Whatever your name is, remember what I told you. You tell your buddies that this is not over yet. I am looking for them, and I sure hope that they try to hop a train."

The railroad bull rolled up his window and peeled off down the road, leaving a cloud of dust. Frank decided to go back to the office and write his report up and call the sheriff. They needed to know that there was a war brewing in Hobo Flat.

* * *

On the way back, the captain thanked everyone. Jesse filled Captain Cooper in on Shadow and Jordan. Bags's limp was more profound than usual. He had twisted his knee, and his body was aching from the commotion that took place with Blake.

River put her arm around Bags. "Are you okay?"

"Yessum. I am a bit shaken up. But other than that, a shot of whiskey will fix that." Bags smiled.

"You're one tough son of a bitch," Jesse bragged. "You kicked that young kid's ass."

"Well, I am proud of the both of you, and Jordan too. That was a brave thing they all did."

Captain Cooper was walking ahead by himself. It was a lonely walk back to his cabin.

CHAPTER 96

AN HOUR LATER, Jordan finally talked Shadow into going with him to Hobo Flat. He assured her that everything would be okay, especially after what happened. They were welcomed with open arms at Bags's campsite. Shadow was still a bit uncomfortable with River being there. Bags's recognized the tenseness between the two girls.

"Yessum, Jordan, you two have a seat over there, and I will get you something to drink. That was nice work with those rocks."

"The ones that hit the target came from Shadow," Jordan explained.

"Ah, you did good too! You just didn't have a slingshot," Shadow answered.

"You are quite good at that, young lady. Yessum! You were a lifesaver. That purple-faced young man wiggled away like a snake."

"How's the captain taking losing his dog?" Jordan asked. "I wanted to come down and join you all, but that bull was still there hanging out."

"Well, he will be sad for a while. That dog was with him for many years. So you two should go up and see him later."

River looked at Shadow and spoke up, "By the way, thank you for what you did."

"Sure."

Shadow was proud of herself.

Later that night, Jordan and Shadow walked down to see Captain Cooper. They knocked on the door of the shack. The captain opened the door.

"Ah, the rock throwers. Come on in and sit next to the stove."

Jordan and Shadow took a seat on a bench that was close to the stove. Captain Cooper opened the lid and poured some more pellets in.

"Want a belt?" The captain handed Shadow a bottle of vodka.

Shadow took a huge gulp and passed the bottle over to Jordan.

Captain Cooper took a seat in his wood rocking chair. He looked down to his side where Niko usually was.

"Sorry about your dog."

"Thanks. It is going to be tough for a while. He was the only family that I got." The captain stared over in the corner where he kept Niko's food and where his water bowl was.

"So I want to thank you for your help today."

Jordan nodded. Shadow was nervous and twitching.

"Where did you learn how to throw rocks like that?"

Jordan explained how Shadow had learned the skill when she was a child at the reservation.

Captain looked at Shadow. "You are a user, aren't you?"

Shadow nodded that she was.

"Heroin?"

She nodded again.

"What about you? Are you drugged up?"

Jordan nodded yes.

"Well, you won't be able to live here at Hobo Flat until you both get clean. I will let you spend a couple of days here. After that, you have to leave."

Captain Cooper could see the disappointment in Jordan's face. Jordan knew that there was no use arguing.

The captain stood up. "Well, thanks again for watching my back, and good luck, young lady. My advice for both of you is to get clean. I mean, it is hard enough surviving without that headache."

Jordan and Shadow headed back to Bags's campsite.

"That really sucks! We help him out, and we can't stay here. Shit!"

"Don't worry. It's time for us to hit the road. I am anxious to hop my first train." Jordan put his arm around Shadow.

"Sounds good to me."

"I will talk to Jesse and see if he is ready to leave too. I will do some panhandling by the church this Sunday and get us some traveling money."

"Speaking of that, I can't stand it. I need a fix. Do you mind if I go out for a while?"

"All right. Do you want me to go with you?"

"No! I will do better by myself." Shadow hugged Jordan and kissed him. "See you soon."

Shadow headed off down the road. She reached in the inside pocket of her jacket to see if she still had the piece of paper with Jeff Wilkens's cell phone number.

CHAPTER 97

IT WAS A beautiful Sunday morning with clear blue skies. Jordan woke up and quietly climbed out of the sleeping bag with Shadow and tried not to wake her up.

In just a few days, he would be riding his first train. He felt very confident, thanks to Bags. He walked over and joined Bags, who had a fresh pot of coffee on the fire.

"Morning."

"Well, you look mighty refreshed today, son. Yessum, no hangover!"

"Yeah, I went to bed early."

"See, I told you how much better off you'd be not drinking so much."

Bags pulled out a tin cup and poured Jordan a cup of coffee. "Watch out, it is still mighty hot. You don't want to burn your tongue."

Jordan had learned his lesson about gulping Bags's hot coffee.

"So you are finally going to take off, huh?"

"Planning on it. I am not sure about Jesse."

"Yeah, he is a little bit pussy whipped at the moment," Bags joked.

"I don't think River wants to go."

"Yessum, I think she has other reasons that are keeping her here."

Jordan would be sad if Jesse bailed on him after all the times they dreamed and sat around talking for hours about how exciting it was going to be to see the country and finally end up in New York City. He was aware of the circumstance that was holding Jesse back. Jordan remembered his dad telling him one day when they were going to the movies how a woman can get in the way of friendships and influence the way men think.

River also woke up early. She spent most of the night tossing and turning trying to avoid Jesse's foul body odor and his lame attempts to fondle her.

All River could think about was Captain Cooper. She was fascinated by him.

River walked up and warmed herself by the fire. "Good morning, dudes."

"Morning," Jordan answered.

"Well, good morning, young lady. You are up early today. Would you care for a cup of my famous coffee?"

"Thanks, Bags, I might take you up on that when I get back from taking my walk. See you in a bit." River strutted off toward the convenience store up the road. She was thankful that she still had a few dollars left so she could again buy something and not feel guilty about using the restroom to clean herself up. After that, she planned on visiting Captain Cooper. She hoped that he wouldn't mind her stopping by.

Bags stared at River as she walked away. "Oh my! That girl is a different one!" He laughed. "Yessum, she runs on her own clock. My gut tells me that Jesse is only going to be a cup of coffee for that girl. She is too much woman for him."

In a selfish way, Jordan knew that would be a good thing as he just sat there next to the fire and drank his coffee. He had his own set of female problems. Shadow was still very jealous of Melissa and didn't want him to panhandle by the church anymore. He still wanted to say goodbye to Melissa.

CHAPTER 98

MELISSA PUT ON her pretty new blue dress that her mother had just bought for her at Macy's to wear to church. She looked in the mirror. She had a sly smile on her face like she had just eaten a canary. She knew that her mom would be happy to see her dressed less New Wave for church today. Although she still had a small nose ring on her left nostril that she still wore in honor of River.

She had a piece of toast for breakfast with a glass of orange juice and then headed off to church with her family. It was such a beautiful day ahead for her.

Mr. Wilkens stared in the mirror at Melissa sitting in the back seat with a big smile on her face. In a few minutes, she wouldn't be in such a cheerful mood, after they drove by the 7-Eleven where her boyfriend was panhandling. Mr. Wilkens was excited to wipe that foolish grin off her face and teach her a lesson for not submitting to him.

The store was only a block away. Mr. Wilkens sped up the car. He was anxious to see if her friend was there already. He knew the police would be there any minute. He saw someone standing on the corner. He smiled at Melissa as they got closer.

"It looks like someone is filling in for my friend today," Melissa spoke up. "Too bad, I was looking forward to seeing him." She smiled at her father.

Mr. Wilkens turned red in the face. He was angry and embarrassed as he recognized the person begging on the corner. It was his hooker, Shadow. He turned his head to the left as he drove by hoping that she wouldn't see him or spot his car.

"What's wrong, dear? You look upset," Mary Wilkens asked.

"Oh, I forgot a book that I promised the bishop that I would bring with me to church today."

"Too bad, Daddy!" Melissa smirked. She looked out the window and made eye contact with Shadow, who recognized her and looked away. Melissa noticed how odd her father was behaving. It was like he didn't want Shadow to recognize him. She wondered what that was all about.

Mr. Wilkens looked back and gave Melissa the evil eye.

Shadow was a bit confused. She wondered why Melissa was riding in the back seat of her john's car.

CHAPTER 99

CAPTAIN COOPER WAS sitting in his rocking chair outside his shack, smoking a pipe. He glanced over to his left, where Niko would normally be. The captain looked up and saw River coming toward him. He waved at her to come join him. He got up from his chair and grabbed a folding chair that was leaning against the wall next to the door and sat it next to him.

The captain tipped his hat. "Well, good morning, young lady! Come sit a spell. Would you like to share a Bloody Mary?"

"Oh! No thanks. I am not much of a drinker. I hate the taste of it."

"It warms the belly and shakes the rust off, at least for me anyway! Besides, I forgot, you are still a young girl. You are, uh, um, about seventeen or eighteen?"

"I just turned seventeen."

"Well! You are getting up there. That would make you a senior in high school then?"

"Yep."

"Sure you haven't changed your mind now? I am going in and fix me one. I could make you a virgin if you like."

"Too late for that," River joked. The captain laughed. "Okay! I will try one. I just didn't want you to go to any trouble because of me."

"Be right back." Captain Cooper walked into his shack.

River was curious what his shack looked like inside. Did Captain Cooper have a bed to sleep in, a kitchen table, and maybe a bathtub? That was one thing she missed was not being able to take a hot bath every night.

Captain Cooper came back with two cocktail glasses and handed one to River.

"Wow! Fancy."

"I save these for special occasions like this one. It's not every day that I am joined by such a pretty girl."

River was shy. Compliments were a whole new thing for her.

"Sorry that I don't have any celery sticks for our drinks," Captain apologized. "That damn store down the road doesn't have any vegetables.

"It's all right. This is very cool." River paused and looked out over the camp. "So, Captain, can I ask you a question?"

"You probably want to know how old I am, correct?"

"Well, I was going to get to that. I am curious. How did you end up being uh, uh…"

"A bum?"

River was a bit embarrassed. "Yeah. I mean, you seem like you got your shit together."

"I ponder about that a lot. Here I am still doing this after all these years. I mean, when I was your age, color television sets were just coming out. But if you look around, everyone who lives here has a secret that they are hiding from. That's why I ended up here. Maybe someday I'll tell the truth."

"So you were around when Lincoln was president?"

"Ah, comedy!" Captain Cooper chuckled. "I like a good sense of humor. Would you like a smoke?"

"No! I quit smoking. I also didn't like having breath that smells like dog shit," River answered. "But the main reason is that my mom died of cancer."

"Ah, I gotcha. But consider this thought, and take it as you will. There are not many pleasures in this here world. I live a simple life. I just lost one of the greatest joys in my life. So I hope that you won't hold it against me if I indulge in a smoke?"

"Not at all, Captain Cooper. I understand. You do what you want. It's your life."

"You know, little lady, you are very wise for your age. I really enjoy your company." Cooper reached over and touched River's hand.

"Me too!" River replied bashfully.

"So are you planning on hitting the road?"

"It sounds exciting. I have never ridden a train before."

"I have some great memories. There are some beautiful places that you normally wouldn't see from the highway, like the snow-caps on the Sierra Mountains. I wouldn't trade that adventure for the world."

* * *

Later that night, Bags, Jordan, Shadow, Jesse, and River were feeding at the soup kitchen. Without Bags, it would have been a real challenge for the street kids to get in to eat all together. The Gospel Mission did not like serving too many young people at the same time because of the commotion it caused. It was difficult enough serving the homeless people dinner without the distractions of the young people raising hell.

Everyone was in good spirits. It was kind of like a farewell dinner. The meal that night was beef stew that consisted of mainly carrots with a few pieces of meat, but it was better than nothing, as Bags would say.

There was a lot of talk that came mostly from Jesse about the adventure that lay ahead. Jordan, for some reason, was very quiet. Bags was cautious and told everyone sitting around the table to pipe down and not talk so loud.

Shadow was happy to share the good news that she had earned almost a hundred bucks filling in for Jordan, which she lied about. She kept forty bucks to support her habit. She laughed when she talked about how pissed off the police were when they showed up looking for Jordan.

River proposed a toast to good friends.

Bags again cautioned everyone to keep a low profile. "You never know who is listening. Not everyone in this here soup kitchen is who you think they are."

"Oh, come on, old man!" Jesse wised off. "You worry too much."

"Yessum, I reckon I do." Bags cleared his throat. "I am just saying. I know one thing for sure, the railroad bulls are getting smarter. I believe one of these people, maybe even two in this room, could be undercover bulls. So I am just telling you to keep it down."

Jesse proposed a toast to Bags. "Here's to the old dude! Thank you! You're the man. And thanks for the copy of North Bank Fred's freight-hopping page."

"Shh!" Bags put his finger to his lips. Bags talked very softly, "See, that's what I am talking about. That there journal contains confidential information and connections to other hobo resources of where to hop trains and a lot of the stuff I shared with you. Like which cars are the easiest to ride and how not to get caught. The bulls wouldn't like that if they caught you with it."

"Sorry!"

Bags finished eating, burped, and got up from the table. "Well, I am going to head back to camp. Are you rascals coming?"

"Not yet. We are going to head downtown for a while," Jesse answered.

"All right then. You all be careful now! It would be a shame if you got arrested doing something stupid. New Mexico Police don't like young kids out late at night on the streets."

Jesse once again threw his two cents in, "Don't worry, old-timer. We have it covered."

"See you later, Bags. Thanks for your concern. You be careful too," River added.

"No problem, young lady. You keep an eye on those two hooligans." Bags was concerned about Jordan.

"All right, one more toast to our adventure." Jesse raised his cup to toast River.

River was hesitant to raise her cup. She had other thoughts on her mind.

Jesse looked over at River. "Hello! Earth to River. Come in."

She finally lifted her cup.

Shadow whispered in Jordan's ear, "Did you see that? I don't think that bitch is coming with us."

River stared at Shadow. She knew she was talking shit about her. As far as River was concerned, Shadow was not someone to be trusted. It was true that she helped out during the ruckus with Bolt and the bulls. It wasn't clear to River what Shadow's real intentions were.

One of the supervisors, a heavyset woman, walked up their table. "All right, kids, it's time to clear out. We have other folks who need to eat."

"We are not ready yet. We are celebrating here!" Jesse wised off.

"Come on, Jesse," River interrupted. "We need to go."

"Fuck, man! Shit! What's the big hurry?" Shadow spouted out.

River tried to get Jordan's attention. He was not great at handling confrontations. As always, when it came down to conflicts, he would try to avoid it. Tonight he was even more disengaged. He was in his own world. He just sat there staring at nothing in particular. River also noticed that he hadn't eaten much.

"See that woman who asked us to leave?" River said. "She is over there talking to a couple other people about us. Come on, let's split. We don't need a hassle here. We might need to eat here again."

Jesse, who didn't like being told what to do, was still being belligerent. "All right, fuck it. Let's get the hell out of here."

Shadow got up and helped Jordan get to his feet. Jesse made plenty of noise as he got up. His chair tipped over and made a loud clank on the pavement. Being obstinate, he walked away and left the chair lying on the floor.

River picked up the chair and apologized to the lady supervisor, who stood there with her arms folded shaking her head in disgust. It now made perfect sense to River why the soup kitchen was not thrilled to have a group of street kids in the room at the same time. She appreciated Bags even more and why the old gentleman had respect outside the camp.

When they got outside, River walked over to Jordan. "So what's up with you, dude? Are you doped up or something?"

Shadow put her arm inside Jordan and pulled him away. "Stay away from him, oogle. It is none of your business what he does."

River shouted, "Fuck you!"

Jesse stepped in between the two girls. "Hey, dudes! Wow! Remember, this is supposed to be a celebration."

"Yeah, well your friend is fucked up on junk. He is not going to do you much good on the road. And his girlfriend there is just using him because she has no other option. She stabbed her pal with the purple face in the back. There is no way he will ever forgive her and take her back. So do you get it now?"

"You are such a bitch," Shadow fired back.

"And you are a drug-addict whore."

"Fuck, man! Knock it off. I can't stand it!" Jordan yelled. "Shit! Yeah! I am fucked up on heroin. Is that what you wanted to hear?"

Jesse was stunned. "Dude! Are you shitting me? Jesus Fucking Christ."

"Shit, let's just head back to camp. Come on, let's go."

Jesse and River walked up ahead. Shadow and Jordan followed behind at a slower pace.

River spoke up, "I knew something was up with him. He left a whole plate of food on the table."

"Yeah, he normally would go back for thirds if he could," Jesse answered.

"So I have made up my mind. I am not going, Jesse. I am not ready to leave yet. I couldn't take it being on the road with that chick and the dope."

For a change, Jesse was quiet and just kept walking "Well, I might not go either."

"Hey, don't let me stop you. It is your dream to travel with Jordan."

"I know, but I feel the same way about that wing nut Shadow and now Jordan acting weird and is all messed up on dope."

Up ahead, Jesse could spot something lying in the road.

"Do you see that? What is that, a dead animal?"

As they got closer, River screamed out, "Oh my god! It's Bags!"

271

CHAPTER 100

RUMORS AND SADNESS riveted throughout Hobo Flat. The older bums were mourning the loss of one of their own. Bags was loved and respected by everyone.

This was the first death that either Jordan or Jesse had ever experienced. Jordan was the most emotional of the group. When he saw Bags's dead body, he lost control and fell to his knees crying out loud. The drug use was partly responsible for the outpour of regret and sorrow that Jordan was feeling. Bags was like family to him. He was almost like a father. Jordan cried out how sorry he was that he had never told Bags on much he appreciated and loved him. He also apologized for letting Bags down by using drugs. Bags had warned him that it was a big mistake and impossible to trust a user.

He remembered Bags sharing with him a story about an addict that he once traveled with who eventually stole from him and almost killed him over choosing to have a fix.

The facts were obvious. Bags was murdered by a brutal boot stomp. The local police would not be contacted. There would be no headline on the front page or obituary in the morning paper. A great human being was gone from this earth, and no one would know about it. What was done was done. Eventually the truth would come out and the people responsible would be dealt with. That was the law of the hobo jungle.

Captain Cooper picked out a beautiful spot up in the hills next to the Rio Grande that overlooked the camp to bury Bags. The whole camp except for Shadow attended the ceremony.

The captain had a stern look on his face as he stood over the grave dressed in his best old dark sports jacket that he only wore for this type of occasion.

"Today we are honoring and mourning the loss of a great man, my dear friend, Henry Jackson. You knew him by his rail name, Bags. He lived and enjoyed a simple life. He would give the shirt off his back if someone needed it. When he was young, he grew up in the South. He didn't fit into regular society, witnessing the racial bigatry had become a burden for him, so he packed his suitcase and traveled the country searching for a peaceful place where he could settle down. According to all the stories he shared with me over the years, he told me that if he had a choice, he would do the same thing all over again."

The captain pulled out the box of cigar butts that Bags kept in his tent. He took out one and lit it up. "Here's to you, old friend. I will miss our long talks. Thanks for all your advice over the years." He took a puff out of the stogie. "I will smoke one of these every night before I go to sleep and remember you."

River was so proud watching the captain standing there conducting the ceremony and gushing out his personal feelings. She knew the captain was going through some hard times with the loss now of two of his closest friends. She wanted to go over and put her arms around him and comfort him.

Jordan and Jesse stared down into the grave at Bags's dead body that was wrappped in his brown sleeping bag. It was almost surreal.

As a tribute to Bags, the Captain tossed his bandanna into the grave on top of Bags's body. The memorial ended with Stubbs, one of the older bums, playing his harmonica and Jesse strumming his guitar.

The music made Jordan think about his dad, who used to play his guitar and harmonica when the family would go camping.

After the song, Jordan grabbed a shovel and filled in the grave with dirt. When he was finished, Jordan and Jesse headed back to the camp. River told Jesse that she would be along in awhile.

"Well, I don't fucking get it," Jesse bitched. "Why didn't the captain do something? I thought the camp had its own way of doing justice. We should have finished that freak show off while we had our chance. Now he is fucking gone to who knows where, and Cooper just sat up there in his rocking chair moping like a little baby."

Jordan didn't respond. That really aggravated Jesse. "Ah, shit! Forget about it." He walked off.

As usual, Jordan was quiet when times were stressful. He inclined toward hanging out inside his cave trying to sort things out. He had blocked out Jesse's gibberish. Bags's death was devastating, and his emotions were all over the place.

He pulled out Bags's bandanna that the captain had given him to keep as a memento of his old friend. There was a lot of history on that old rag that he would proudly share with anyone who wanted to listen.

In just a short time, Shadow's domination along with the alchohol and drugs had turned Jordan into a feeble, apathetic person. He had lost his will and was her puppet now. All she had to do was spread her legs to get what she wanted. Her bipolar rages were occuring more. She would take her anger out on Jordan, demeaning him, which made him feel like he was a worthless piece of shit.

River walked up to Captain Cooper and locked her arm inside his arm and escorted him back to the camp.

"I am so sorry, Captain."

"Thanks for your concern."

"I didn't know him very well, but he was very nice to me and was a good mentor to my friends."

"Well, hopefully Bags is in a better place now. I loved that old coot. He was special."

"So what happens now, Captain?"

"Well, first of all, you can call me Nathan. I miss being called that."

"Okay. I feel privileged," River answered.

"I told Bags to call me Nathan, but he preferred calling me Captain. As for the other thing, we just sit and wait. It won't be long before someone opens his or her big mouth. It's hard to keep a secret around here. I know we all suspect Bolt, but you never know in this jungle that we live in with the homeless and mentally ill. That's why I am still curious why you are here."

River smiled. "Maybe it's my destiny."

"That could be. Huh, what do you know." The captain put his arm around River's shoulder.

"So, Nathan, does your place have a bathtub?"

"Ha-ha! Oh my!" The captain coughed while he was laughing. "I have never been asked that before. Why?"

"Just wondering. You don't smell too bad."

"Well, I've been told, a matter a fact it was Bags that said that besides appearance, people are attracted to each other's smell. You know over time you kind of get used to the foul smell of stench and don't even notice it."

"I don't know about that. I do know that I miss taking a warm bath at night."

"So will you be traveling soon, leaving with Jordan and Jesse?"

"Not if you get me a bathtub!"

Captain Cooper hugged River. "Ah, you are a sweet little thing." He kissed her on the lips.

River hugged the captain and kissed him back.

"It's kind of awkward for me. I haven't been with a woman for a long time, and besides, you could be my granddaughter."

"I know that you don't like to hear this word, but who the fuck cares? I don't."

"Well, I guess if Elvis and Jerry Lee Lewis can rob the cradle, it is just fine for me too!

They both laughed huge belly laughs.

* * *

Deputy Morningstar sat with a frustrated look on his face at his desk. He was ready to press the send button on his computer. He was once again disappointed by the sheriff's decision not to allow him to investigate the Hobo Flat murder case. He argued that the crime took place on public land, but the Sheriff shrugged it off and told Rhett to back off.

Rhett was getting tired of getting shut down. He didn't sign up for the job to just go on patrol and issue speeding tickets. If he wanted a career to just stand around, he would have gotten a job as a cashier. He scratched his hair and watched the dandruff flakes sprinkle on his shoulder. He pressed the send button and sent out his email with his résumé attached. He was applying for a job with the Albuquerque Police Department. There was a job opening in the homicide division.

CHAPTER 101

OVER THE NEXT few days, Melissa convinced her mom to drive her out to Hobo Flat to visit River. Mary Wilkens was very understanding. She was very happy to see River again. She missed her too and was confused why she would choose to live in such a god-forsaken place instead of enjoying the fruits of having a warm bed to sleep in. River hugged Mrs. Wilkens and apologized for not saying goodbye to her.

River took Mary and Melissa up to the captain's—excuse me, Nathan's—cabin and introduced them to him. Like a true gentleman, Nathan took his hat off, bowed, and shook both of their hands.

After their visit, Melissa was relieved when her mother told her that for the time being, their meeting with River would be their little secret. It also brought up the question just how much Mary Wilkens trusted her husband.

CHAPTER 102

AT SAM'S COFFEE Shop, Frank Burke took a seat in a booth and ordered a cup of coffee. A young street kid joined him a few minutes later.

"Hey, Marco, how's it going?"

"All right, I guess."

"Want something to eat?"

"No thanks. I have to get going."

"All right then. What do you have for me?"

"I don't know if you've heard, but a very popular black home bum named Bags was attacked and stomped to death."

"Really? So what happens in that culture? Do the local police get involved?"

"No, they handle all that shit themselves."

"So what else?"

"Well, I hear the two kids that stoned you are getting ready to do some train hopping."

"So you know them?"

"Yeah, one kid is named Jordan, and the other is a drug addict Indian woman who calls herself Shadow."

"Do you know where they are heading?"

"I think that they are heading east."

Frank reached in his pocket and pulled out a hundred-dollar bill.

"Here you go. Stay in touch. Let me know if you find anything else out."

Marco got up quickly and left the coffee shop. Frank could tell that he was not comfortable being a snitch, but Marco needed the money. He still lived at home and was a weekend street punk. At least that was how Frank put it when he pulled him over a month ago and found dope in his car. Burke threatened if he didn't cooperate with him, he would turn him over to the local sheriff's office. He told him that he had no loyalty to any of those kids, which was true. Marco wandered in and out of both camps. He partied with Bolt's clan and hung out with Jordan and Jesse.

Frank was proud of himself for planting a spy inside the hobo jungle. He was glad that he had followed through on the advice he had been given by Amaya Parks, even though he knew that she was only concerned about finding a runaway boy named Jordan Summers. He could have blown her off, but he had the smarts to see the value in doing something like that. It could give him the heads-up on what was going on in the bum community and maybe help get him a promotion.

* * *

Jesse was trying to read the traveling guide in the dark with a dim flashlight that needed new batteries. "Man, this sucks and is hard to read," Jesse whined.

To conserve space, the guide was typed in very small letters and abbreviations were used to describe the types of trains and highways. The purpose of the book was to point out the different routes and give tips on where the safest locations were to hop on trains. That was why railroad law enforcement would not be happy if they caught travelers with the publication that was shared across the country.

Jordan was high and sitting over in the corner. He had just finished shooting up with Shadow.

"Dude, look at this bullshit. This guide is telling us to catch a bus first before we can even hop on a train."

"Can I look at it?" River asked. Jesse handed her the pamphlet and the flashlight. He got up and pulled out a snipe to smoke.

River was amazed and impressed on how detailed the guide was. There were sections for each city and included routes and actual mileage. The section she looked at was Albuquerque. She started reading it out loud.

"It says here, in parenthesis, BNSF# Yd is BTN Broadway SE and Second Street and S of Central Avenue. Not all trains have CC here, but they may work here. If they do, CC is in Yd W of Amtrack STA. From DT, walk S on Second about 2m just past the big city baseball diamonds with the Santa Fe caboose in front."

Jesse lost patience. "Who can understand any of that bullshit?"

"I am not sure, but I guess it is the safest and best way to travel, according to the guy who wrote this. It is pretty simple, either follow his advice or throw this thing in the fire." One thing, though, River was glad she wasn't going with them.

"Hey, I have ridden the rails before," Shadow spoke up. "We don't need a fucking instruction Manuel."

"Yeah, well, do what you want, but this book is a detailed account from a dude who had been there before. It has everything in it that you need to know. He is saying that the further you get away from the bulls here at the train yard, the safer it will be." River added sarcastically, "But don't listen to me. I am just an oogle. Right, Shadow?"

"You don't know shit about anything except how to suck up to the captain."

"Yeah? Well, I know one thing. I am smart enough not to be a drug addict."

Shadow got to her feet. She staggered toward River. "I have had enough of you!"

River stood up, solidly planted her feet in the ground, and was ready to defend herself. Shadow took a wild swing and tripped herself.

"I am getting the hell out of here." River walked over and hugged Jesse. "Good luck, dude. Take care of Jordan. He is a mess."

"You take care, and here..." Jesse handed the train riding guide to River. "Put this to good use."

"All righty then. You sure?"

"Yeah! I like to do things on my own terms."

"I can see that. It seems like you have to learn things the hard way."

"That's me. See you later."

River disappeared into the night.

Shadow was sitting on the ground mumbling to herself. Jesse was trying to understand what she was saying. It sounded like she said "Good riddance," but he wasn't sure.

"Let me tell you something," Jesse said. "We are not going to do shit until Jordan comes down from his high. There is no way he can hop a train in his condition. Why did you get him on the shit anyway?"

"Man, it just happened that way. Just like it happened to me when I started. Anyway, we can't go back now. He will be better and be able to cope with the high." Shadow started to walk away. "I am going to start packing our stuff."

Jesse sat down next to his friend. "Fuck, man, this is not good. That Indian's got you messed up. You have to get straight, man. You are really screwed up, dude. We are never going to make it to New York."

Jordan just stared into space. "I know. I will. I will be okay tomorrow. This shit is helping me get over Bags." Jordan started crying. "I really miss him. I wish that we would have left the soup kitchen with him when he asked us to."

"It's not your fault, dude. Shit happens."

"I let him down, man. I messed up. I should have been with him."

Jesse was annoyed with Jordan's emotional breakdown. "Come on, dude! Quit being so soft like butter. You gotta get your shit together. Grow a pair. Come on! This act is getting old. We have to move on. There is nothing you can do about it now."

He got up and walked away, leaving Jordan to sob in his own misery. It was pathetic watching Jordan being so weak and crying out for help. That was something that Jesse swore he would never ever do. His friend was self-destructing right in front of him. He knew one thing he had to do was to get his friend away from the clutches of Shadow. She was a cancer to him and was filling him up with bad ideas.

CHAPTER 103

Jimmy put his guitar down and answered his phone.

"Hello."

"Hi, Jimmy," Amaya answered.

"Hey, baby. I was just working on a song I wrote for you."

"You are so sweet! Anyway, I just got off the phone with Frank Burke, you know, the cop who works for the railroad now."

"Right."

"He says he is getting close to catching Jordan."

Jimmy was a little shocked to hear the word *catching*. His son was not a fugitive. The thought of someone setting a trap for him was bizarre. In Jimmy's mind, Jordan was just a misguided kid.

"He is not in any trouble, is he?"

"He kind of is, but no charges have been filed yet."

"What do you mean?"

"I am just pulling in to get some gas. I will explain when I get home. Shall I pick something up for dinner?"

"Cool. How about Chinese?"

"Sounds good. I will tell the kids. See you soon. I love you."

"I love you too."

Jimmy hung up the phone. He picked up his guitar and started playing. As he was strumming, he started thinking about how fast things were moving between Amaya and himself. Once they started dating, they were inseparable. It was a Hollywood romance. Jimmy was a true romantic. He loved making Amaya smile. He sent her flowers, made handmade cards for her, and now he had written a song for her. They wasted no time moving in together. And that was when the trouble began.

Amaya had never been a mother. Her only experience with kids was working with the troubled runaways. She believed in running a strict household similar to the one she grew up in. Her father was a police captain and enforced rigid rules that she had to abide by. Her room had to be clean, she had chores that had to be done, and dinner was served at the same time every day. She could only watch television for one hour a day. There would be consequences if any of the rules were broken which was usually being grounded.

Jimmy, on the other hand, believed in a looser structure. There were no consequences. He wanted his kids to feel comfortable and enjoy being at home, not, as he put it, to feel like they were in prison. That was how he was raised as a child. His parents were very easy-going and let him and his baby brother pretty much do what they wanted to do. He figured he turned out okay.

Their different views made it very difficult for them to agree when it came to enforcing rules and discipline.

The biggest struggle was between Rose and Amaya. Rose was not willing to accept a new woman in her father's life. She still had hopes that her mom and dad would get back together.

Tommy was still too young to comprehend the politics of what was going on around him. However, because he was younger, it was easier for Amaya to develop a relationship with him. Rose did not like watching Tommy and Amaya's relationship blossom. She would play games with him and be very mean to him anytime he was enjoying being around Amaya. Tommy was impressed with Amaya being a police officer. She would let him pin her badge on his shirt and wear it around the apartment. She finally stopped letting him do that when she woke up one morning when she was late for work and couldn't find her badge. Tommy had taken it and put it in his pocket. Amaya lost her temper and screamed at Tommy. Rose used that incident to turn Tommy against her.

But even though the children made their relationship dysfunctional, Jimmy and Amaya adored each other. Without the kids around, they got along perfectly. They had great sex. They enjoyed taking walks together. Everything was great. Jimmy especially enjoyed the fact that he could sit around and watch sports without being bitched at. Amaya could thank her father for that, being that she was the only child and her dad would take her to watch the Nevada Wolfpack play, so she didn't mind watching sports.

Jimmy was a very patient man. He hoped in time that Amaya would see the light and realize that being too constrictive was not the path to a happy home.

CHAPTER 104

THE MORNING WAS cool with cloudy skies and a brisk wind whistling through the tree branches. Shadow, Jordan, and Jesse climbed up the mountainside and chose a position that overlooked the train yard. Their plan was to scope out the different trains that would be leaving soon. Bags had taught them that the easiest one for them to hop on to would be a piggyback, which was a flatbed with semi trailers. He cautioned the two boys that they could be easily spotted, so they would have to stay hidden between the semi wheels.

Jesse was getting anxious. The big moment that he and Jordan had been waiting for had arrived. Jesse was skeptical that Jordan would be able to pull it off considering the state that he was in.

"Hey, don't worry, dude. Jordan will make it," Shadow said.

"Man, he is useless. He can't even pack his own backpack. What makes you think he is going to get his shit together?"

"Well, smart man, we are just not going jump on any old train. This is going to take a while before we hop on. Jordan will be a little shaky, but he will be ready. Trust me!"

"Sure. That's what I am going to do is trust a junkie."

"What the fuck, dude? You and I have to be road dogs. This is important shit."

Jordan finally spoke up, "Come on, dude. She's cool and she's right. I will be all right. Quit worrying!"

"Yeah, right! Look at you! You are shaking. You need some more shit. Fuck, man." Jesse grabbed his backpack and stormed off.

This whole thing was driving Jesse nuts. There was a power struggle going on with Shadow. She had driven a wedge between Jordan and him. She had the edge because she was older and had experience riding trains. Jesse wished Jordan would get sober and start contributing. He was getting sick and tired of arguing with Shadow. Jesse climbed up the hill and found a hidden spot behind some bushes where he could squeeze one off. After he was finished, he climbed up a little farther and found a secluded spot between two rocks. Jesse pulled out his sleeping bag and spread it on the ground. He would sleep there tonight. Tomorrow morning he would go through his backpack again to make sure that he had everything that he needed.

* * *

Frank Burke opened the fridge and pulled out his roast beef sandwich that he bought on his way to work. His partner, Shoog, was not feeling well and went home early. Frank was disappointed that Shoog was flaking out and was not as passionate about getting even with the street kids that humiliated them.

Burke had spotted them up in the hills. He figured that they would making their move tomorrow afternoon to hop on the hot-shot, which was high-priority train that was scheduled to leave at noon.

Tomorrow, Frank was also planning on coming in early to work. He wanted to keep a close eye on the junk train that was pulling out early in the morning. His gut told him that the street kids wouldn't be hopping that train because junk trains don't travel far, but he wanted to make sure.

* * *

Shadow spread out the sleeping bags and zipped them both together. She shared a small dose of heroin with Jordan, who was dope sick. It helped calm down the shakes. They both climbed in the sleeping bags and cuddled up with each other.

"Get some rest, baby. We have a big day tomorrow."

"I know. I will be all right."

"I know, baby. After a while, you'll adjust to being high."

"I hope so. Jesse is pretty pissed off."

"Well, fuck him! We don't need him."

"Yeah, I guess you're right."

So far everything was working out fine for Shadow. Jordan was easy to manipulate. Jesse was the only loose cog. He was a thorn in her ass. But she had a plan in place for that. She also knew the train that they were going to ride. It was a high-priority train that was leaving tomorrow late in the afternoon. She got the information from one of the rail yard workers named Timmy, who was one of her regular johns, who worked in the hump yard where all the cars were individually disconnected. She could always count on Timmy to come through when she needed extra money or information. Timmy loved Shadow and would do anything for her.

The train was heading north to Denver. There were several cars attached, including a slave unit (a train engine at the very end of the train used for fully loaded trains climbing a mountain). Shadow was aware that the conductors always left that unit unlocked, so it was available to be used by riders. It was a great place to keep warm next to the engine. She knew that they would have to keep their eyes open for workers. Other than that, everything would be fine as long as they didn't touch anything and some other bums had beaten them to the punch and boarded the engine first.

Shadow waited till Jordan drifted off to sleep and sneaked off toward town. She was meeting Jeff Wilkens for one last time. The extra money would come in handy.

Jeff picked her up on the side of the highway and drove his SUV up a dirt road that overlooked the city. Shadow gave him head, which was his favorite thing for her to do. Giving head was a turn-on for her, especially the climax.

"So I have a question for you."

"Yeah?"

"Was that your daughter in the back seat the other day?"

"I was hoping that you didn't recognize me."

"Yeah, right. I have been spreading my legs in your back seat for awhile," Shadow teased back.

"Why do you want to know?"

"Because I know her. She had sex with one of my fellow travelers."

"I should have known." Jeff became angry. "Was it that Jordan kid?"

"No, a dude named Bolt."

"So you know River then?"

"I hate that bitch."

"Me too. She used to live with us. We took her in after her mother died. She turned my daughter against me. Everything I did for her."

"Well, if you want to get her back, she's living at the camp."

* * *

The next morning was a glorious spring day. The birds were singing with clear blue skies. There was a slight breeze, not cold enough to chill the bones.

River woke up early. Nathan was still sleeping. She was in a great mood. She loved waking up next to him and listening to him snore. She got dressed and headed out to the convenience store to clean up. She stretched her arms and legs. She loved getting up early in the morning. She walked at a very fast pace. She wanted to give herself a body wash and be back before Nathan woke up. He had given her some money to buy some food. River wasn't the greatest cook, but she did know how to fry eggs and bacon. She used to love to fix her mom breakfast. As she was walking, she was thinking how much she missed her mom. She hoped that if she was watching from above that she wasn't too disappointed in her.

Nathan had promised her that she would have her own bathtub by the end of the week. She felt like a princess. She was the only one in the camp to have a real bed to sleep in and have a roof over her head. Nathan pointed out that the roof did have some leaks in it and

289

that they would be emptying a lot of buckets full of water when it rained.

As River walked up the road, she spotted Jesse strolling up ahead.

"Hey there."

Jesse kept walking.

"Dude!" River shouted. He continued walking ahead.

"Hey, Jesse!" He finally stopped and turned around. He waved to River and waited for her to catch up.

"You okay?" River asked.

"Fuck no," Jesse answered. "At first I was all excited about leaving, but now I am not so sure."

"Why?"

"Jordan is screwed up over a woman and drugs. He is not the same dude."

"Well, if I was you, and I am not you, I would reconsider taking off at least until Jordan straightens out."

"Easier said than done, dude. Do you want a smoke?"

"No! You know that I quit."

"I know." Jesse smiled. "Where you headed?"

"You know me. I don't like to stink. By the way, you are pretty ripe! Do you want to come with me and clean yourself up?"

Jesse smiled. "Maybe next time. See you." Jesse hugged River and headed up the hill.

"You take care, Jesse, and be careful."

"If everything works out, we will be taking off this afternoon. I hope that we run into each other again."

"I hope so too!"

* * *

Frank Burke was getting anxious. His partner, Shoog, showed up to work but was still not interested in getting even with the street kids as Frank was.

"Man, you are serious about this?"

"Yeah, I am. Don't you get it, Shoog? I don't know about you, but I have a reputation to uphold. Those punks embarrassed us. I heard a couple of the yard workers joking about it. That shit doesn't sit right with me."

"Come on, man. Shit happens!"

"Yeah, but not with me? Come on! You're killing me here!"

Frank stormed out the door of the office. Shoog just sat there and shook his head.

* * *

Jesse showed up to the spot where Jordan and Shadow had camped.

"Hey, brother!"

"Hey!"

"Where's your squaw?"

"Fuck you!"

"Well, at least you are alert today."

"Yeah, I think I am kind of getting used to being high on this shit. It feels pretty good. You should try it."

"No fucking way. You should look at yourself. You might think it's okay, but you will need a fix soon, and I am scared that you are going to kill yourself trying to hop on a train. That's what I think, dude. And that squaw is only using you. And now you're dependent on her."

"I'm sorry, dude. She's my friend."

"Whatever! So let's check our shit out and make sure we have everything."

"Okay. By the way, She went to the store to get some snacks for us."

"All right, bro. I get it. Just remember what I told you. Did you bring your butt flap?" (A butt flap was a cloth of leather that hangs from the belt and prevents holes from forming in the back of your pants from sitting on concrete and sitting on the ground.)

Jordan smiled and pulled his out of his pack and waved it like a flag. "Couldn't forget that. That's all I need is a hole in the back of my pants with my ass hanging out. Good old Bags pounded that into my head."

Both Jordan and Jesse had a side bag to put all the important items so they wouldn't have to keep digging into their backpacks all the time. They each had a P38, church key, squat key, squat candle, matches, patches, and dental floss, which would be used to sow holes because it was stronger than using real thread.

"All right, well, I think we are good to go," Jesse said. He noticed Jordan was shaking and squirming. "You all right, dude?"

"Yeah, I am kind of dog sick, and I am trying to stay clean before we hop the train."

"And you want me to try that shit!" Jesse shook his head and took a seat next to Jordan.

* * *

Frank Burke came back into the office. He opened the left drawer of his desk and pulled out his cattle prod and stuck it in his gun belt.

"All right, Shoog. Let's get moving. We have some trespassers to kick the crap out of."

"Man, this is like Christmas morning for you, isn't it Frank?"

* * *

Shadow returned to the camp an hour later with a plastic bag full of food for the trip, including dried beef jerky, peanuts, chips, and candy bars. She was able to talk to her friend Timmy once more at the train yard. He assured her that there would be an open boxcar to hop on. Shadow knew if they missed that opportunity, the last option was the slave unit at the back of the train. She gave Timmy a hand job for that information.

The threesome loaded up their gear and headed for the jungle area up the road where they could hide and wait for the train to come. Shadow kept a keen eye on Jesse. He was carrying extra baggage with his guitar, which would make it cumbersome hopping on the train. There was a chance that Jesse would mess up and not be stable enough to get on the train. It would be her chance to kick him off the train. For the time being, she needed him being this was the first time for Jordan trying to hop trains. He would come in handy.

By the afternoon, the beautiful day had turned cloudy, and there was a possibility of a storm blowing in, which would make it more difficult and slippery trying to grab hold of the handles on the train.

Jordan was starting to get very anxious. He felt the same butterflies that he always felt when he was in a stressful situation. This time there would no quitting like it was in Little League, when he would give up on purpose so he wouldn't have to play. This was the real deal. It was dangerous and treacherous. One mistake could cost him his life.

In the distance was the sound of a train moving.

"Hey! Do you hear that?" Jesse asked.

"Come on! Let's get ready!" Shadow shouted. "The train will be slowing down for a few minutes, but it won't be stopping. It is heading toward us, so we won't have to catch up to it. Remember, Jesse, I will hop on the train first and be there to help out Jordan. Remember, we have to all be close together and move quickly."

As the train got closer, Jordan and Jesse started to panic. Shadow could tell that they were both uneasy. About a mile away, the train horn blew.

"All right, let's get close to the tracks. Get your gear. Remember to throw all the gear on first." They hurried out of the bushes and stood right next to each other.

They could see the train slow down up a head. They moved toward it. The loud sound of the horn and the breaks screeching spooked them. The time had come. There would be no turning back now. Everything they had learned from Bags was on the line. The engine roared past them followed by a lumber car, G train, and several boxcars. It was a very long train with lots of cars attached to the engine. It would take a few minutes to get to the end of the train.

Up the road, Shadow spotted a white SUV roaring in a cloud of dust toward them. "Shit! Here comes the bulls."

Frank Burke was behind the wheel driving at sixty miles an hour. Alongside him was his partner, Shoog, and two other bulls in the back seat.

"See, I fucking told you that snitch knew what he was talking about. Revenge is going to be so sweet."

Jesse screamed, "Shall we get the hell out of here?"

"No! Keep running. See it? The open boxcar is up ahead." Shadow yelled. "Come on, keep up!"

Jordan lost his footing and twisted his ankle. He tumbled to the ground. He screamed in agony. Jesse slung his guitar inside the boxcar and went back to help Jordan get to his feet. Jordan's backpack fell to the ground busting open and spilling out all of his gear.

"Go ahead, man! It's all right! Leave me."

"Come on, dude, don't give up."

"Hurry the fuck up!" Shadow screamed. She jumped and grabbed the handle on the boxcar and swung herself on board.

The SUV stopped, and all four men got out and stormed toward Jesse and Jordan. Frank Burke was leading the pack. He pulled out his cattle prod. Shoog pulled out his pistol and fired two shots into the air.

Burke screamed, "Hey, you fuckers, stop what you're doing! You are all under arrest!"

The boxcar was just a few feet away. Jesse screamed instructions for Jordan, "All right! See the handle. Grab on to it and swing yourself towards Shadow."

"I can't do it. Damn it!" Jordan grabbed his ankle in pain and stumbled to the ground. Jesse toppled on top of Jordan and stopped him from going underneath the train.

Burke was a few feet away. "Stop right there."

Shadow reached in her backpack and pulled out her sling. She fired a rock outside the boxcar and nailed Burke on his shoulder, knocking his cattle prod out of his hand.

Jesse got to his feet and had a decision to make. He had one chance to hop on the train. The slave unit was coming up right behind him. Should he leave his road dog behind?

Shoog and the other two bulls were on top of Jordan. Burke grabbed his cattle prod and jammed it into Jordan's side. Jordan screamed in pain from the sting of the electric shock.

Tears came to Jesse's eyes as he bellowed, "Fuck you! You assholes!" He turned and swung himself onto the slave unit. He got to his feet and looked back down the tracks. He could see the bulls dragging Jordan away.

The pain of guilt riveted through Jesse for deserting his friend, a road dog that he had promised that he would fight to the death for him. He crept into a corner of the old slave unit and wept.

CHAPTER 105

JIMMY SUMMERS GOT the news that Jordan had been taken into custody. The sheriff's department had turned him over to juvenile services, where he was being contained in their facility. Jordan had been formally charged with trespassing by the railroad police. Frank Burke wanted to file assault charges but was frustrated because Jordan was not an adult yet.

Jimmy got the day off from work and arranged for an early flight to Albuquerque. Amaya dropped him off at the airport. She advised Jimmy to take things one step at a time. She warned him that Jordan was going to be a different person than the son that he knew before. Jimmy was worried as he was sitting in the airport waiting to board his flight. He was angry, of course, to be put in this situation, but he was also relieved that he would be bringing his son back home. The special cases officer at juvenile services filled Jimmy in on the drug test results. Jimmy was shocked to find out that his son was using heroin. He never imagined that he would ever encounter having a drug addict in his family. In his younger years, Jimmy dabbled a little with cocaine and pot when he was in the band, but he never tried heroin.

The plane landed at ten twenty in the morning. He got a cab and headed over to the juvenile detention facility. Jimmy was impressed how clean the city was. The streets were wide, and there was no trash on the sidewalks or gutters. The streets were decorated with plants and trees. The cabdriver named Wally wearing a Packers football cap was very entertaining. He took the edge off. He bragged about going every year to Lambeau field with his buddies and going to the Packer-Vikings game. The day before the game, they would play a game of touch football at a local park in Green Bay and then end up the evening getting drunk at a topless bar.

"You know, the women back there are pretty large, but after a few beers, their big asses looked pretty good pole dancing at the club." Wally laughed.

The cab pulled in front of the detention center. Jimmy tipped the cabdriver and thanked him for the entertaining ride. He also said that he didn't know how long it would take him to get his son out of custody and that he needed a ride back to the airport. Wally gave him his card with his cell phone number on it for him to call him when he needed a ride.

Jimmy walked into the building. The first thing that he had to do was go through security. He emptied all the contents out of his pockets into a tray. After that, he had to put his wallet and cell phone in a locker. He checked in at the front desk and was told that Jordan would be released shortly.

He was very nervous as he took a seat in the front row of the waiting area. There was a cast iron door located to his right. He assumed that was the place where Jordan was being held.

There were three other people sitting in the lobby waiting for their kids to come out. Jimmy wasn't sure what was going to happen when he saw Jordan. He hoped that Jordan would be happy to see him.

To occupy his mind, Jimmy picked up an old *People* magazine that was sitting on a table with a picture of Tom Cruise on the cover. Jimmy was never a fan, and he wasn't sure why.

There was an echo of keys clanking. The iron cast door opened up. Jimmy put the magazine down. A security guard walked out with a young white girl following behind him. The girl's parents, who were sitting behind Jimmy, stood up and walked toward the girl. Jimmy watched them hug and leave the building.

There was one more person left in the room. She was an older Hispanic woman. She was sitting in the same row and a few chairs down from him. He assumed that she was the grandmother of one of the kids being held.

Jimmy stared down at the floor and shook his head in dismay. The old woman looked over at him.

"First time for you, senior?"

"You can tell, huh?"

The old woman smiled. "Oh, yes! That big door over there is pretty intimidating. My grandson has spent a lot of time here. His parents have given up on him."

"That's too bad!"

"I still love him and haven't given up yet."

"My son ran away and got caught trying to hop on a train."

"Well, at least he is not caught up in a gang like my grandson is. Well, good luck!"

"Thanks! You too."

Ten minutes later, the door opened, and the old woman's grandson came out. He fit the role of a gang member, with tattoos on his arms and neck. He had an angry look on his face with piercing eyes.

The kid caught Jimmy staring at him. "What the hell are you looking at?"

Jimmy looked away.

The old woman responded by shaking her finger at her grandson and reprimanding him in Spanish. The boy backed off and cowered to her wishes.

"I am very sorry." The old woman and the boy walked out.

"Wow!" Jimmy whispered under his breath. That was pretty scary stuff, and he felt lucky that he was inside the facility when the incident took place. That was a dangerous kid, and he remembered what Amaya had told him. He was even more nervous than before. He wondered what kind of person his son had turned into.

Another man and woman walked into the center and checked into the front desk. Once again, Jimmy thought, "Wow! What a busy place!"

Jimmy's heart started pounding as he heard the clanging sound coming from behind the door. The door opened, and a woman holding on to a clipboard came out. She walked over to the front desk and joked with the receptionist.

Jimmy was starting to get annoyed. He had been there for over an hour. He thought about asking the receptionist what the holdup was. He got up and went to the restroom. He pissed as fast as he could. He didn't want to miss being out there when Jordan finally came out. He didn't shake himself off properly. As he zipped up his fly, pee ran down his leg.

"Shit!" Jimmy's underwear was soaked. He hoped that it didn't smell. When he got out of the bathroom, nothing had changed. He took a seat again. He knew any minute his son would be coming out.

Finally! The door opened and out walked a security guard with Jordan. Tears came to Jimmy's eyes as he walked up to Jordan.

"Mr. Summers?" the guard asked.

"Yes, I am."

The guard handed Jimmy some paperwork. "Just initial here and sign at the bottom of the page." Jimmy signed the paperwork with his left-hand chicken-scratch signature.

The guard, who couldn't have been more than twenty-three years old, exchanged looks with Jordan. "Stay out of trouble, and don't hop anymore trains." He then shook Jordan's hand.

Jimmy walked up to Jordan and gave him a big hug. "Let's go home, son."

Jordan hugged his dad back. "I would like that. I would like that very much." They turned and walked out of the detention center.

CHAPTER 106

A FEW WEEKS later, River Walker woke up promptly greeting the sunrise. Being an early bird had become a familiar habit for her. No more sleeping in for her. It was like pulling teeth for her mother to get her out of bed in time to go to school. She smiled and wondered if her mom was proud of her.

River had a lot to look forward to. This would be the last morning that she would have to use the restroom at the convenience store to clean up. Nathan had located a bathtub at the garbage dump and was having a few of the tramps clean it up and deliver it his shack later that day. The porcelain on the tub had chipped off from the bottom. Otherwise, the tub was in good shape.

She was feeling like the queen of Hobo Flat.

She put on a light sweater and headed off to the store. She had a huge smile on her face and was prancing like a ballerina down the road. Up ahead to her left was a thick jungle area. She noticed some movement in the bushes. Before she could react, a man wearing a mask leaped out and dragged her off into the bushes. She screamed and tried to fight him off, but he was too strong for her and had a hold of her throat. He threatened to kill her if she screamed any more.

* * *

Nathan was starting to get worried. It had been a while since River had been gone. He sensed something was wrong. He put on his cowboy hat and decided to go look for her. As he was walking out the door, he glanced over at the corner next to the stove where Niko used to lie down. Old habits never die. Just for protection, he grabbed Bags's old cane, which he had kept to remember the old man by, and headed out.

He wasn't sure what to expect, but his initial thoughts told him that River was in danger. The captain had spontaneous energy and he was trucking right along at a very fast pace.

The captain's first stop was to the convenience store. The attendant at the store named Roy, who was a bit pudgy with curly brown hair and a scarred face from acne, told the captain that he knew River and had not seen her today. Roy told Cooper that he was kind of surprised to not see her and wondered if she was sick or something. He also told the captain how impressed he was that she always purchased something in order to use the restroom. The captain smiled at him and thanked him for the kind words.

Captain Cooper's next stop was to visit Bolt's campsite. When he got there, he found an abandoned site that looked like a garbage dump with empty beer bottles, broken glass, and other trash spread all over the grounds. So far his search was at a dead-end.

The captain decided to go back and start all over again and retrace River's footprints.

CHAPTER 107

Jesse tried to get some rest while the train rumbled down the tracks. He wasn't sure if he would be traveling with Shadow anymore. His guitar was in the boxcar she was riding, which was couple of cars behind the slave unit. He wondered exactly where he was. The view was spectacular, with snow on the hill sides of the tracks. The train was starting to travel into higher elevations, and the temperature was starting to drop. The benefit of being on the slave unit was that the engine kept him warm.

The young traveler had one more cigarette left to smoke and no food to snack on. All the treats were in Shadow's backpack. That would be one reason for him to stick close to her. He wasn't sure if she knew that he had made it on the train. He decided to keep an eye on the boxcar she was in and to look for any opportunity for the train to slow down and for him to jump off and go talk to her.

It was getting very cold inside the boxcar. Shadow thought about trying to close the door but decided against it because of the danger of being locked inside and not being able to get out. She had heard a story about a group of travelers who were locked inside a boxcar that traveled across the country before they were discovered and found dead from heat exhaustion. She had nightmares about that happening to her. That terrified her.

Besides her pouch of rocks, Shadow also carried with her a small medicine bag that was full of memories, like a bottle cap that was given to her for good luck by an old traveling Native American who shared with her the importance of carrying the Indian tradition with her on her journey. Shadow took the bottle cap and rubbed it several times, hoping that it would bring good luck for Jordan.

Up ahead, Shadow could hear a dinging sound. She looked outside the boxcar and saw a railroad crossing coming up. She knew that she would have to crouch down low into a dark corner so she wouldn't be spotted and hide from the idling cars that were waiting at the crossing. She was wearing dark clothes, which would make it harder for her to be seen. What she wasn't aware of was that Frank Burke had dispatched to the railroad police up ahead in Colorado and filled them in with all the details on which train and boxcar they could find a traveling street kid who had obstructed the law in New Mexico.

Jesse wasn't sure what to do when he heard the dinging sound. He felt helpless and exposed. The train started to slow down. He expected any moment to be hauled off in handcuffs. He had that experience before when he was younger and first started getting in trouble with the law. He hated and despised it.

As he crouched down, he could hear the sound of an automobile pulling up beside the train. Jesse was sure that he was going to get busted. He could hear a woman scream and a scuffle going on close to him. He crawled over to the edge of the engine room to get a peek of what was going on. Two railroad bulls were pulling a screaming and scratching Shadow out of the boxcar. She was then handcuffed and then shoved into the back seat of the SUV along with the backpacks and his guitar. Jesse crawled back into a corner of the engine room and waited for them to come find him. Lucky for him that didn't happen. The train started moving again.

Jesse was relieved but bummed that he had lost his guitar.

Shadow stared at the two bulls sitting in the front seat of the SUV. They seemed very proud of themselves with the feat that they just completed.

"Well, little lady, it looks like you will be spending some time in jail for trespassing," the bull that was driving looked back and said.

Shadow smiled back. "Yippee!" she answered back sarcastically.

Things were quiet as they drove for a few more miles. Shadow was very uncomfortable with the handcuffs clamped very tightly with her arms behind her back.

"Hey, you guys wouldn't cut me a break and loosen up the cuffs? They are starting to really hurt me."

The SUV pulled over to the side of the road. The bull riding shotgun got out of the vehicle and opened up the back seat door.

"Step out a second and lean against the car."

Shadow got out and obeyed the bull's orders. The cop unlocked the cuffs. Shadow shook both arms. "Thanks. My arms were going to sleep.

"All right, turn around, stick your arms out, and don't try any funny shit."

Shadow turned around and smiled at the bull. She raised both arms for him to put both cuffs on. This time she was allowed to have her arms in front of her.

"You boys wouldn't want to make a trade, would you?"

"What would that be, little lady?" the bull asked.

"I will spread my legs if you let me go."

"Go ahead and climb back in the back."

Shadow got back in the SUV. The bull shut the door and got back in the front seat. The SUV pulled back on the highway and drove ahead. A few miles up, the SUV turned right on to a dirt road.

CHAPTER 108

MELISSA WILKENS WAS having a rough time adjusting back into her old routine. She had no interest hanging out with her old friends. She preferred to be by herself except when her mother would drive her out to see River. Melissa appreciated the fact that her mother understood where she was coming from. Considering the options, Mary was more comfortable being a part of it than having her daughter sneaking around behind her back.

Melissa had a strange feeling inside that something bad had happened. She hoped that she was wrong. She would find out tomorrow when her mother drove her out to the camp.

She was also thankful that her father knew nothing, or so she thought, about her still keeping in touch with River. Melissa's relationship with her father continued to decline. She preferred to stay away from him. Most of the time, she was able to accomplish that, except for dinner every night at the family table.

She was beginning to see a change in him. He had a look in his eye that frightened her.

CHAPTER 109

Jordan was happy to be back with his family again. It was a tearful and joyful reunion when he first saw his mother, Rose, and Tommy. All four of them stood and hugged one another for several minutes. He really missed them.

The first thing Jimmy and Gina did was to check Jordan into a rehab center to deal with his drug addiction. Those three weeks in the hospital was one of the toughest times in Jordan's life. It was worse than starving or freezing to death outside in the cold. His dependency on heroin was extreme. The recovery was very painful, with him crying out as his muscles cramped and his nerves desired the drug in his veins.

When Jordan was released, Amaya stood back and gave Jordan plenty of room to get comfortable again with his surroundings. Jordan wasn't sure what to think about having her around. She tried her best to be understanding and approachable to Jordan. It was unnerving for Jordan to see Amaya in her police uniform. The other problem he had was that he was now used to making his own decisions, so being treated like a child again was a difficult situation for him being back living with his father. One change he did notice was that his father was trying to have a more disciplined household. He assumed that Amaya had something to do with that.

It was also good for Jordan to have his own room and a nice, soft bed to sleep in. He spent a lot of time in there by himself. He wasn't quite sure what to think about all of it. His father started the discussion about the possibility of returning to school. Jordan dreaded the idea and wasn't really committed to staying at home. He had tasted the fruits of being out on the road. Even though it was challenging, he had learned how to survive in an unconventional and dangerous world. For the first time in his life, he was proud of himself. And in his mind, he had an unfinished dream to fulfill, which was to travel across the country on a train and wind up in New York City.

Jordan wondered how his friends were doing. Was Jesse still traveling with Shadow? He hoped that they were both okay.

Rose and Tommy were fascinated listening to their brother's stories about being on the road. One night the three kids were in Jordan's bedroom, and he told them the story about his friend and mentor Bags. Tears of emotion came to his eyes when he talked about the old man. Bags was like a true father to him. Unlike Jordan's real dad, Bags really understood Jordan and didn't judge him. Jordan loved his parents, but they were complete opposites and were never on the same page.

Jordan took out the bandanna that Bags gave him and shared with his brother and sister the significance and history of the soiled rag that was hanging out of his left back pocket. He talked about the importance of having it with you when riding a train, especially when you go through a tunnel. Although he hadn't done it yet, he described in detail about soaking the rag with water and covering up your nose and mouth and to make sure that you breath out your nose and always breath slowly.

With great pride in his heart, Jordan gave the rag to his brother and sister. They smiled and gave Jordan a huge hug. Tommy mentioned how stinky the rag was. Jordan laughed and explained there were a lot of years of traveling the country tied to the smell of the bandanna that he was passing on to his family.

Amaya was standing outside the room listening to what was being discussed. She was concerned about Rose and Tommy raising Jordan up to hero status. In her mind, he was a drug addict and a runaway. She was worried about what influence Jordan would have over the younger kids, especially Rose, who had just turned eleven years old. Having Jordan around had changed the dynamics of the household. His careless attitude about his hygiene was unsettling for her. She complained to Jimmy many times about the stench that was coming out of Jordan's room. He agreed with her and promised her that he would do something about it.

A riff started between Amaya and Jimmy when she had run out of patience. The first thing she did was clean Jordan's room. The smell of stinky socks and unwashed clothes grossed her out. The other thing she did, which turned out to be the icing on the cake, was to wash the bandanna. All of Bags's history and respect was erased and lost forever when Amaya washed the bandanna in the washing machine.

In Jordan's heart, he knew that it was time for him to hit the road again. It was also the beginning of the end of Jimmy and Amaya's relationship.

CHAPTER 110

Three Months Later

IT WAS LATE September in Detroit, the mugginess was put on hiatus as the cold weather approached. After the automobile industry crashed, the American dream in Michigan had become an apocalypse. Downtown Detroit became a ghost town and a very dangerous place to live. Most downtown stores closed except for the business district, and a large majority of the people who lived in the city moved away to the suburbs, leaving the deserted buildings, streets, and broken-down cars to the gangs, homeless people, and scavengers, who would raid the closed auto plants and strip the buildings with copper wire and sell it to the Chinese. (And then the Chinese would recycle the copper and sell it back to us. Nice job, Washington.)

Jesse had just finished panhandling for the day at the Cherry Hill exit off Highway 275. He had raised enough money for dinner and a bottle of beer. He was living on the second floor of an old condemned structure downtown that used to be an insurance building that was partially destroyed by a fire. At least it was a place for Jesse to be able to have a roof over his head. The structure of the building was deteriating slowly and had no electricity, so the elevators didn't work. The corridors were always dark, so it made it difficult to move around in without a flashlight.

Several other people lived in the building, including a homeless family with two smaller kids and a cat. Jesse struck up a friendship and shared a room with an extraordinary middle-aged Caucasian man named Carl, who was balding, with thick eyebrows, and had lost both of his arms in the Vietnam war. His disability did not hamper him. It was very impressive to watch him navigate around without having any arms. He was able to use his bare feet just like a pair of hands. The soles of his feet were as tough as leather. He was very agile and could stand on one leg, and he could reach his mouth with the other foot or scratch the top of his head.

Carl was a very gentle and very quiet man. He always wore an old military Special Forces beret that had tarnished over the years. He was very proud of it but did not like talking about the war.

Because he was unusual and had his disability, most people preferred to stay away from him.

Carl suggested to Jesse that it was a good idea to migrate like the ducks before it got too cold and for them to move to a warmer climate. Carl usually liked to spend the winter in the southwest. Austin, Texas, was one of his favorite cities. Carl said that the people that lived in Austin were very accepting to travelers as long as the laws were abided by on Sixth Street, where all the bars were located downtown. Carl usually just kept to himself and let Jesse flap his mouth. He was starting to trust his young friend, and they started to rely on each other.

"Traveling to Austin was one of my favorite memories," Carl recalled. "I remember hopping off the train at the railway crossing at Fourth Street and Lamar Boulevard. I was in awe as the gleaming city of Austin's power plant sign greeted me. It was very impressive. I just had a good feeling about that town. It was a little hippie haven hidden in the vast desert of the big state of Texas. Now, mind you, the rest of the state was not as kindly to our kind."

Initially, Jesse wasn't too thrilled about the idea, but the more he listened to Carl's stories, the more intrigued he became. He enjoyed listening to Carl talk and could relate now to Jordan's relationship with Bags.

The more Jesse was around Carl, the more he opened up. He talked about his interest in reading books, which he credited for his ability to be able to have a large vocabulary. Jesse scowled at the idea of reading.

The only subject Carl still wouldn't talk about was Vietnam. He did, however, explain the reason he ended up being homeless. He talked in detail about how poorly he was treated when he came home from the war. There were no welcome arms waiting for him. Back then, being a soldier wasn't something to be proud of. No one appreciated the fact that Carl lost both of his arms defending his country. Even his own family was not comfortable being around him. But in all fairness, Carl never had a good family relationship. That was the reason he joined the service in the first place. His real father had left when he was a young boy. His mother was remarried to a man who took a strong disliking to Carl. His stepdad took his frustrations out of not being able to keep a job on Carl. He would constantly mentally abuse Carl with sarcasm about how worthless he was. Carl was disappointed that his mother never stood up for him against the abuse. That never really changed when he was discharged from the army.

Jesse was curious. "So, dude, did you every think about having artificial arms? That seems to be a pretty cool option to me."

"I looked into it when I was in the VA hospital. But I really didn't want to become the terminator. Anyway, I learned how to get along just fine without any arms." Carl reached up with his foot and scratched his head.

Jesse never stopped being amazed how nimble Carl was.

"One day, an incredible thing happened," Carl said. "I realized with the help from William, one of the therapists, that I could survive on my own."

Carl explained how William taught him that it was all in his mind. He could overcome his disability by mentally training himself. He was able to totally concentrate on using his mind to coordinate with both of his feet and to accomplish functions that he usually did with his hands. The hospital staff was amazed. They had never seen anything like that before.

After he checked out of the hospital, Carl went home to live with his family. His family was not as accepting of his physical impairment. His stepfather was embarrassed to be around him and wanted him to move out and go out on his own.

This was nothing new for Carl to adjust to. It did hurt his feelings, though, to be shrugged by his own family. Finding work was not easy either. No one was willing to give him a chance. An old bum took him in as family and taught him the ropes. And that was how he ended up being on the road.

Jesse had a decision to make. He knew that he was so close to getting to his destination of New York City. He had always heard that New York City was a great place to live. Everything was easily available. Whatever you wanted, drugs and the booze, was cheaper. Despite the perception that the people in New York were very cold and distant, Jesse was told that most people were sympathetic, especialy the Puerto Ricans, who would take you in and give you a meal.

However, Jesse trusted Carl's wisdom. Living in the New Mexico desert had schooled him on what it was like to live in freezing temperatures. He remembered cuddling up under a bridge closely to his friend Jordan to stay warm. Jesse missed his old friend. He didn't forget the pact they made to be celebrating together at Times Square for New Year's Eve.

Carl knew the train routes by heart. He was also aware of the new breed of travelers that were riding the rails for the thrill of it and for the satisfaction of beating the system. They were a group of twentysomethings who did it for kicks on the weekends. They had no respect for the bums and young travelers who were in it for the long run and rode the rails for real.

CHAPTER 111

MELISSA WILKENS'S HEART was broken after she heard the news about River missing. Not knowing what had really happened to her was very disconcerting. Her mother still drove her out to Hobo Flat every couple of days to visit Captain Cooper to find out if there were any new developments.

Captain Cooper had not given up yet. He was determined to find out what had happened to his young friend. Every morning he would sit in his old rocking chair and stare at the bathtub that he had gotten for her. He dreamed of her beautiful, tattooed white body soaking in the tub.

Mary and Melissa had developed a great friendship with Captain Cooper. He appreciated how understanding they were. Not everyone treated tramps with the respect that Mary and Melissa did. Mary trusted Captain Cooper. She knew her daughter was safe with him. She was able to drop her off for a few hours and do some shopping and then pick her up later.

Melissa had asked the captain if he would consider going to the police and getting them involved. Nathan explained to her his hesitation about involving the law and his concern about them meddling in the camp's affairs. He never shared with her the main reason for his reluctance, and that was the warrant that was lingering out there for his arrest.

"Little missy, I can handle this internally. At one time, when I was younger, I considered going into police work."

Melissa smiled. "What stopped you?"

The captain thought for a second and then answered her question.

"It's a long story. I will tell you about it sometime when you have more time. Your mom will be here shortly. Anyway, I have been doing a lot of detective work on this." The captain pulled out a list of suspects that he thought could possibly be involved.

Two of the suspects were the railroad bulls, Frank Burke and his partner, Shoog. River had told Nathan about the bulls' desire to have sex with her. Of course, Bolt and his followers were still on the list. There was a railroad worker named Timmy, who was always trying to gain favors from the female travelers. There was also that oogle kid named Marco.

Melissa didn't mention it yet, but she knew of one more person that should be on the list that the captain didn't know about. It freaked her out for even considering it. That person was her father.

She was starting to feel comfortable enough with the captain to tell him the truth one day about her father. She could see why River liked him. Even though most people would frown about such an age gap between a young girl and a man who could be her grandfather, Melissa was starting to understand that age really had nothing to do with chemistry. And if you go back and look into the archives of the world, several kings and lords had very young wives.

So what the heck! Melissa thought. Most people would judge her behavior as odd for spending time in a hobo village around a bunch of homeless vagabonds, but it was her life, and she appreciated her mother's support. Her mom was someone special, and it was a shame that she was married to such a perverted man who was unscrupulous and deceiving.

CHAPTER 112

IT WAS MIDNIGHT on September 10. Jordan had carefully and quietly prepared for his exit. He was excited and anxious to get back on the road. He had given it his best shot with living back home with his family. It was a rough adjustment for him. The constant pressure from both his parents for him to go back and finish school was unbearable. Charter school was not the answer. It was full of kids that were one step away from being institutionalized.

Trying to live in both households was unsettling. There were different rules for each place. Unlike before, his father's house was more structured now because of Amaya. Staying with his mother, Gina, was just the opposite. The household was looser, and a lot of times his mom was never home, which meant no regular meals. There was a lot of fast food, and many times she was never around, so Jordan was expected to babysit his sister and brother. Jordan knew his mom meant well and was trying to find her way.

There was also the friction between Amaya and Gina. Amaya was very jealous of Gina. She believed that Jimmy was still in love with her. There were constant conflicts and disagreements that made it very uncomfortable for the children. Amaya made it very clear in front of the children that she was disgusted with Gina's lifestyle and parenting skills.

Jordan knew this was the right decision to get back on the road. He didn't like having the responsibility to look after his brother and sister. He wanted to be free of all the pressure, and this time he had more experience and was more prepared for what was ahead down the road.

While he was home, Jordan did hook up with his old friend Tucker. He was fascinated to hear Jordan's stories. He was envious that Jordan actually went out into the world and did what they had dreamed about. But when it came down to it, Tucker didn't have the nerve or toughness to be the kind of person who could do such a thing. He was too spoiled. He had everything he wanted handed to him by his parents except one thing, and that was the love that they never had time to give him, which left him with an empty heart.

Tucker was very excited about trying out train hopping. He had no intentions of making a career out of it. He asked Jordan if he could go with him. Because Tucker had bailed on him before, Jordan was reluctant. But being the fast-talking salesman that he was, Tucker talked Jordan into letting him tag along. Jordan knew that this was a short-term kick for Tucker, and that in the long run, he wouldn't be able to count on him.

He had learned a good lesson from the last time he tried to hop a train. His addictions almost got everyone busted. And now Tucker was his handicap. At least now he was aware of it and he was not using anymore. The urge was still inside him, but it was contained for the time being.

Jordan was eager to find his road dog, Jesse. They had talked about many times before he got messed up with Shadow on what they would do if they ever got separated. Jordan had given Jesse his father's phone number to call. Jordan never heard from him. There were times he wondered if Jesse did call and that he was just never given the message. He knew for sure Amaya would have never told him if Jesse did call.

Bags had laid it out for Jordan about what parts of the country were the best to travel to during the different times of the year. The south was definitely the warmest place during the winter months. Jordan decided that would be the part of the country where he would travel to first. He had no idea if he would ever see his old friend again. He just had to trust what Bags had told him that it was common to run into old acquaintances on the road. Bags explained that it was kind like a circuit. Travelers migrated to the same places. The problem was being there at the same time.

Jordan was still very shy and didn't like to bother people, so he relied on Tucker to get the train information for him from the train yard. That was an easy task for Tucker. He had no problem approaching strangers and striking up a conversation with them. The first train they would hop on would take them to Colorado. They would then jump off and change trains in Colorado Springs and then head south.

They showed up at the jungle location with all their gear an hour early. Tucker was equipped with a brand-new backpack, ski jacket, gloves, and a Nevada Wolf Pack stocking cap. His pack was full of candy bars, peanuts, and other snacks. He was prepared for only a short joyride and had three hundred dollars cash with him to pay for a bus ride home.

Jordan, on the other hand, was prepared for the long run. He had managed to collect some travel items, including a butt flap, some cooking tools, P38, and a church key.

The train that they would be catching on the fly was scheduled to depart the yard heading eastbound at around 9:00 p.m. Most trains never departed or arrived on time. The Southern Pacific train that they were planning on riding was no different. Tucker had bribed one of the workers in the yard with fifty bucks to give him the itinerary for the best way to travel south. The hotshot priority that was leaving that night was loaded with 48s and flatbeds. The yard worker assured Tucker that the third 48 on the train had a bucket with a floor that they could ride on without being spotted.

Now all they had to do was keep out of sight and wait for the train.

CHAPTER 113

MELISSA'S MOTHER WAS losing patience. She wanted to find out what really happened to River. She kept pressuring Melissa and telling her that they needed to go to the police. Melissa explained to her the rules of the jungle and how they handled their own problems with out involving the authorities. She talked her mom into waiting until she discussed it with Captain Cooper. Her mom agreed and told her the sooner the better. Their plan was to drive out to Hobo Flat the next morning.

That night at dinner, Melissa and her mother shared with Mr. Wilkens what was going on. Melissa was curious to see her father's reaction to having the police involved in River's disappearance. There was nothing abnormal about his response to their idea. He agreed with the decision. Melissa studied her father very carefully. He didn't seem nervous about it. He was either a good actor or he was completely innocent. She was almost convinced that he had nothing to do with it. The only thing that kept him on her suspect list was his previous behavior.

Melissa wondered if the police would be savvy enough to investigate a little further into the Wilkens family's past history. Melissa was not a good liar, and a good detective would sense that.

She went to bed early and had a difficult time getting to sleep. She tossed and turned worrying about how Captain Cooper would react.

Jeff Wilkens put his jacket on and took a late walk around the neighborhood. He wasn't sure how much his daughter knew about him and his charade with the young traveler Shadow.

Wilkens was also a little on the edge about getting the police involved. Primarily because of the possibility of them nosing around too much. He had gambled before that his daughter would keep quiet. He wasn't even sure how much River had shared with Melissa about him stalking her. So for the time being, he decided to go along with their decision.

CHAPTER 114

JORDAN'S HEART WAS pounding fast as he heard the train approaching. One mistake could cost him a leg, arm, or his life. He didn't want to screw up like he did the last time. One good thing, there were no bulls around to distract him.

The train was only a hundred yards away. "Let's get going!" Jordan shouted. Tucker was right behind him as they hurried out of the bushes with their gear strapped to their backs. The train was moving faster than Jordan expected.

"Come on, Tucker, stay close behind me." It was a thrilling experience as the engine roared by. Jordan counted the first 38. The second 38 moved on by. He could see the third one just up ahead. Before he knew it, the 38 was upon them. They both tossed their gear on. Jordan grabbed the handle and swung himself onboard.

Tucker stumbled and lost his footing on the loose ground. Jordan reached back and clutched onto his arm. He hung on for dear life as Jordan pulled him onboard. They were breathing heavily. They both quickly snatched their backpacks and climbed into the bucket floor.

"Fuck yeah!" Tucker screamed. "Thanks, dude. I thought I was a goner."

"Shit!" Jordan screamed. "Now that was an adrenaline rush!"

They both cracked up laughing and gave each other a high five. It was a thrill that they both had never experienced before. For Jordan, it was an achievement that he was really proud of. He stretched out on the floor and smiled. He was back on the road again. For Tucker, it was just a thrill that he could brag to his friends about.

CHAPTER 115

JESSE AGREED TO travel to Austin, Texas. They had a big party the night before with a few other bums that lived on the block. A couple of them decided to join Carl and Jesse. One was a younger lttle girl named Peep, and the other person named Chris was a young runaway that had never been out of Detroit.

There were no problems hopping on a train when you got to the train yard. It was getting there that was dangerous. Detroit had the reputation of having the most treacherous ghettos in the country. That's why traveling in numbers was much safer.

* * *

The next day the travelers headed out for the train yard. It was very tense as they made their way through the streets. They were chastised a few times by a group of young blacks that wanted to know what they were doing in their neighborhood.

"Look at that motherfucking freak. He has no arms!" one of blacks shouted. "That is some freaky shit, man."

The travelers ignored them and picked up speed.

"That's right. You chicken shits keep moving and don't come back."

"A few more blocks to go and we'll be out of the ghetto," Carl said.

A pack of four fierce German shepherds charged out from an alley growling and barking. They were very intimidating and circled the group. The dogs sensed the fear in Peep's eyes and tried to separate her from the group.

"Everyone, stay together and keep walking!" Carl shouted. The dogs harrassed the travelers for several blocks and finally turned around and ran back up the street.

"That was nutts." Jesse breathed a sigh of relief.

Peeps was crying. "That scared the shit out of me. Why did they turn around?"

"I figure that they belonged to a drug dealer and were protecting their territory. Let's keep walking," Carl answered. There were no more problems after that. When they got to the train yard, Peep and her friend decided to catch a train and head west. They said their goodbyes and headed in different directions.

Carl and Jesse found an empty boxcar and jumped on a junk train. They snuggled up to keep warm toward the end of the boxcar away from the open door. Carl had brought along a bottle of whiskey to keep their bones warm. He shared it with Jesse and the party was on. They both passed out and were sound asleep until earlier the next morning.

The train had stopped. Jesse woke up and nudged Carl, who was snoring away. "Are we here? The train's stopped."

Carl was feeling the pain of a hangover. He got to his feet and went to the front of the boxcar to look outside. He looked around and came back and took a seat next to Jesse. "Nope! We are not there yet. We are stopped at a two-mile. Do you know what that is?"

"Uh, no."

"Do you hear that other train coming?"

"Yeah. What the fuck is up with that?

"It's no big deal. Our train has a lower priority than that one. We are just pulled over to the side until the other one passes by." Carl moaned and reached up with his left foot, removed his beret, and scratched his hair. "Man, my head is killing me. That whiskey is kicking my ass right now."

Jesse got up to have a look outside. "Man, that is a long train."

"About fifteen minutes or so, and we will be on our way. I am sure that you aren't feeling that good either. Come on, let's get some rest."

Jesse crawled back to the end of the car. "Yeah, you're right. My head's pounding too."

Twenty minutes later, their train started moving again. A frightening and dangerous moment startled the two travelers. The train jolted to a stop, and the door to their boxcar slammed shut.

"What the fuck!" Jesse screamed.

The train started moving again. Jesse got up and tried to pry the door open. He had no luck. It was locked tight. He wished that he had listened to Bags's advice and jammed the door open with a crow bar so that wouldn't happen.

"Looks like we are at the mercy of the train," Carl said. "Hopefully someone will let us out."

"Has this ever happened to you before?" Jesse asked.

"No, but I have been told about it. We haven't much food or water. We are going to have to conserve. As we get further south, it is going to get much hotter inside this car."

"Shit, dude! Being stuck in the dark freaks me out and makes me claustrophobic."

"Well, I can fix that. I have matches and candles in my backpack. Looks like we are going to have to wait it out."

"What did I get myself into?"

"It's okay. Calm down, boy. We will be all right. I have been in worse situations." Carl pulled out a candle from his backpack and lit it up.

CHAPTER 116

"WELL, YOUNG LADY, I think it is the right thing to do," Captain Cooper agreed. "Normally, I would not like the idea of the law poking around, but I agree that we need help finding out what happened to River. I have scoured the area, and there is no sign of her."

Melissa was relieved and gave Nathan a hug.

"Thanks for letting me know. I appreciate it. I will let everybody at the camp know what is going on."

Later that afternoon, Melissa and her mother filed a missing person's report with the local police. The case was assigned to Deputy Rhett Morningstar, whom they had met before. Before he met with Mary and Melissa, Rhett cleared everything with the sheriff.

Rhett took them into a private room. He was already familiar with River living with the family, and Mary explained to Deputy Morningstar about River running away. Morningstar wanted to know what the reason was for her leaving. Mary wasn't sure, and Melissa lied and said that she didn't know either. Melissa told Rhett about River's relationship with the captain. She also gave him Bolt's name as a possible suspect.

"Well, thanks for your time, Mrs. Wilkens, and you too, Melissa. We are going to search the area and see what we can come up with. These missing kid cases are hard to solve. I will give you an update in a few days."

Mary and Melissa left the sheriff's department with very discouraging looks on their faces. Mary put her arm around Melissa.

"Come on, sweetie, let's go get a chocolate sundae. That will make us feel better."

Melissa smiled back at her mom. She hugged her and thought to herself how lucky she was to have a mother like her.

Rhett could tell that he disappointed them, but he did that on purpose. He didn't want them to give anyone the heads-up that there was going to be a serious investigation. He appreciated all the information that he was given. The first person on his list to check up on was Captain Nathan Cooper. He also put out a APB with a description of Bolt across the country.

CHAPTER 117

JORDAN AND TUCKER waited for the train to slow down and jumped off before it got to the train yard in Denver. It was still daylight, but the weather was very chilly. Jordan knew that Tucker would not be able to put up with the howling, cold wind. He was fully prepared for him to say his goodbyes and take the bus back home to Reno.

Jordan looked up and saw smoke up in the air. "Come on, dude. I think that there is a camp up ahead."

"I don't know, man. Are you sure that we would be welcome being strangers and all?"

"Ah, come on. They'll tell us to hit the road if they don't want us around."

"No thanks. You know, I have had enough adventure. I think that I am just going to head into town and catch a bus back home."

"All right, dude." Jordan and Tucker said their goodbyes.

The campsite was a couple hundred yards up the road off to the left from the railroad tracks. As he got to the camp, Jordan could see five older tramps sitting around a fire. He could tell by their piercing stare that they were not happy to see him.

A scruffy old bum with shaggy gray hair and an untrimmed beard stood up and spoke first. "What do you want, boy?" he asked.

"Hi there. I, uh, just hopped off the train."

"What's a young punk like you doing such a dumb thing like that for?"

"I am a traveler trying to hook up with my friends."

"Yeah, well, you best be on your way, boy," another bum spoke up.

"I won't be any trouble. I just need a place to sleep tonight."

"Have you ever heard of the FTRA, boy?"

"Absolutely!" Jordan smiled. "You fellows ever heard of man named Nathan Cooper?"

A third old bum on the end piped in, "Nathan who?"

"Nathan Cooper," Jordan replied. "He's a member of the FTRA, right?

"So what's it to you, boy?"

"I stayed at the captain's camp in New Mexico."

"How long ago was that, boy?"

"About six months ago."

Another one of the bums spoke up, "Does Nathan still have that glowing red hair?"

"He was always wearing a cowboy hat when I was around him. All I saw was a lot of gray hair."

Jordan was getting nervous being grilled.

The first bum to talk fired off another question, "How did you get along with his dog?"

"Niko? We respected each other. I think he knew though that Captain Cooper liked me. I left him alone, and he left me alone. There was one weird thing, though. Niko took a liking to one of my lady friends."

"That's unusual. That dog never liked anybody except for old Nathan."

"The captain took a liking to that girl too."

"Shit, that dog almost chewed my leg off one time," another one of the other tramps spoke up. "Christ, I was just trying to help him hop on a train with Nathan."

"Nathan wouldn't go anywhere without that dog." The old bum coughed and hacked up some flem and spit it on the ground. "That poor son of a bitch almost got killed several times trying to get that mutt inside a moving boxcar. Must have been tough deal, the captain losing his dog."

Jordan was puzzled that they knew about the dog. "The captain was pretty devastated all right."

"You were there?"

"Yep. I helped him fight off an asshole, a purple-tattooed-face freak that was trying to take over the camp. Me and a friend of mine ambushed him with some rock throwing."

"I heard about that. Well, I'll be." The bum that was standing up started laughing. "Word is that you are nobody to mess around when the rocks start flying." The tension around the campfire started to calm down. The old bum took his seat back around the fire.

"How did you guys find out about all this?" Jordan asked.

"News travels fast in the FTRA. We keep track of what's going on with our brotherhood. Well, gents, if it's all right with you all, I think it's okay for this young man to come join us and get warm by the fire." The other men all nodded their approval.

"My name is Brick. Hey, Crackman, tell him why I am called that."

A taller, skinny-looking tramp responded to Brick's comments, "That's 'cause his fucking head is so hard and stubborn as a brick." All the bums laughed out loud and clanked their cups together.

"Yeah, well, fuck all you old farts," Brick answered. "The real reason is, over the years, I have headbutted a few of those cocksuckers like that purple-faced creep. See that scar on my face above my eyebrow?"

"Shit. That's a big one."

"Yeah, well, that scar came from a big prick who didn't respect the FTRA. I headbutted his Mexican ass right off the freight train we were riding. I told you that news travels fast on the rails. We heard about Bags too!"

"You knew Bags?" Jordan asked enthusiastically.

"Of course. He wasn't a member, but he was our friend. He was well loved on the rails. So you knew him too?"

Jordan choked up a bit. "He was a good friend. He taught me how to survive and how to ride trains."

"I always looked forward to running into him on the road. He had this cigar box full of the finest cigars that he collected from his travels. He loved opening that box and letting me pick out one of those butts to smoke. Yessir, he was a true gentleman of the rails. Word is that the purple-tattooed-face punk had something to do with Bags's death."

"Yeah, Nathan and all of my friends think so."

"Word is that he thinks that he has magic powers like a witch."

"Yeah, well, I never saw any. All I saw was that he was good at sneaking out of the bushes. He is full of shit."

"Well, I will tell you something, boy. There is nowhere he can hide. He is a target now, and his Halloween disguise will make it hard for him. He will get his just reward someday. That's a promise. We have our own kind of pony express with FTRA. We look out for each other and our brothers and sisters. All the members across the country are keeping their eye out for him."

"Here, boy, take a swig of this." Crackman handed Jordan a bottle of whiskey. "This will warm your bones."

CHAPTER 118

JESSE WAS STARTING to get paranoid. Being locked up inside a boxcar was nerve-racking. He heard a dinging sound that signaled a railroad crossing up ahead where idling cars were waiting for the train that they were on to pass by. Carl was snoring away fast asleep.

It was starting to get hot and stuffy inside the boxcar. Jesse took his shirt and coat off to cool off. The hot air was making Jesse thirsty. Carl cautioned Jesse to preserve the water and to drink in small quantities. Jesse took some extra gulps from the burlap water bag while Carl was sleeping.

Carl had told Jesse that the trip would take several hours. Jesse assumed by the change in the temperature inside the boxcar that they were somewhere in Texas. He wondered how long they would have to wait in the boxcar before someone let them out.

A half an hour had passed. Jesse and Carl were jarred awake by a loud jolting sound. The car kept moving but started to slow down. Jesse could hear the roar of the train engine in the distance moving farther ahead without them. A few minutes later their boxcar slowed to a stop.

Carl was awake but was a bit groggy.

"What the fuck, Carl. Are we there?"

"I am not sure." Carl could hear the wind blowing outside against the car. There was also a clanking sound like a piece of chain blowing in the wind and clanging against a building. Carl took a deep breath. "I had this happen to me once before. I am not quite sure, but I think we may have been disconnected and dumped somewhere."

"What the fuck do you mean?"

"One time I was dumped in the middle of nowhere in the middle of Texas."

"What now?"

"Well, let's start banging the side of the car. Hopefully, someone will hear us and let us out."

"And what if that doesn't work?"

"We just have to sit and wait it out. Sometimes the units come back and sometimes they don't."

Jesse and Carl got up and started screaming and banging the walls of the boxcar. They kept at it for ten minutes. There was no response. They went at it for another ten minutes. There was still nothing.

"Well, let's take a break and conserve our energy. I have a couple more candles to burn. How much water do we have left?"

"Half a water bag."

"Not good news. Just take some small sips."

"I have to piss and shit."

"Use one of your extra shirts and piss on it. Then squeeze one off in it and wrap it up."

"This really sucks."

"Well! Like I said before, I have been through worse times."

CHAPTER 119

A WEEK LATER, Melissa and her mother had not heard a thing about the investigation from the police. They called the sherrif's department and left several messages for Officer Morningstar, but he never returned their calls.

A few weeks later, Mary drove Melissa out to Hobo Flat to see Captain Cooper. When they drove up to the camp, things were in disarray and chaos. It was a lot different. Garbage was spread out all over the grounds. The bums around the camp made Melissa and her mother feel unwelcome. Melissa wondered where the captain was. She walked up to a group of older men.

"Excuse me, we are looking for Captain Cooper."

One of the old bums with rotting teeth and a foul smell spoke up, "Well, missy, we thought you were looking for something else!"

The old buzzard licked his lips in a very suggestive manner. The rest of the men laughed.

"Come on, Melissa, let's leave these gentlemen alone."

"Oh, you're no bother, sister. Why don't you come over here and have a seat on my lap."

One of the women travelers walked up and intervened, "Shame on you, Tom Johnson. Come on, girls, I will walk you to your car. Those old fools need to mind their manners."

As they walked out, Mary thanked the woman for her help. The woman's name was Millie. She said that she remembered seeing Melissa and her mom visiting the captain. The woman told them that Captain Cooper disappeared after the cops showed up. She wasn't sure if he was arrested or he sneaked off. She said things were just not the same without Captain Cooper around to keep people in line. They said their goodbyes and drove off back toward town.

"I hope the captain's all right," Melissa said.

"I do too, honey. Shall we go by the sherrif's department and see if he is there?"

"I would like that, Mom. Thank you. Hey, I have to go to the bathroom. Can we stop at that convenience store up ahead?"

"Sure."

They pulled up, and Melissa went inside. She asked if she could use the bathroom. The young man behind the counter smiled at Melissa and pointed at the sign on the wall that said the restrooms were for customers' use only. Melissa smiled back and grabbed a pack of gum off the shelf. In return, the clerk handed her the restroom key.

"Good timing, I just finished cleaning them," the clerk named Roy proudly announced. "Enjoy. Let me know if there are any problems."

Melissa smiled and gave him a weird look. She went into the restroom and closed the door. She looked around. The store clerk was right. The restroom had a fresh smell. The sink was clean, the floor was mopped, the toilet was scrubbed, and there was a fresh roll of toilet paper on the handle. Melissa pulled down her pants and sat on the toilet.

Mary decided to go into to the store and get something to drink. When she noticed that no one was behind the counter, she thought that was odd. She could rob the place blind. She walked over grabbed a bottle of water out of the freezer and walked up to the counter waiting for the clerk to come out of the back. "Hello! Is there anyone in the back?"

Melissa was almost finished relieving herself. She pulled some toilet paper off the roll and spread her legs to wipe herself. She heard a noise. She was nervous as she looked around the restroom. She looked closely at the wall a few feet away from her and saw a small hole lined up directly in front of the toilet.

She screamed in terror as she saw an eye staring back at her. Melissa's mom charged into the restroom.

Melissa was crying out of control. She pointed at the peek hole.

Mary was horrified and grabbed her daughter. "My god! Let's get out of here." They ran out of the store as fast as they could. They got in the car and drove off. Mary pulled out her cell phone to call Deputy Morningstar.

"Look, Mom," Melissa pointed out as they drove off. "That creepy guy is running out the back of the store."

Later that day, Rhett Morningstar telephoned the Wilkens and informed them that Roy Thorpe, the store clerk, was arrested and was put in jail. Police found several videotapes at his home of several women customers that he filmed through the peek hole. One of the women was River Walker, whom he had on film giving herself a body wash from the sink completely naked. Roy admitted that he was fascinated by River and wanted to have sex with her. He also confessed to raping and strangling her. He dropped her body into a small lake located up the road from the store.

Melissa was devastated after finding out what happened to her friend. Life would never be the same for her after that. River's death took her over the top. She was even more terrified of her father. She couldn't stand being in the same room. Her mother got her into therapy, where it finally came out about her past with her father. Dr. Markell advised Melissa that hiding her secret from her mother was an emotional problem that would not go away and only fester as the years go by. Life would not get better for her until she addressed her past, which meant finally confessing to her mother. As painful as it would be, it had to be done in order for Melissa to get well.

* * *

It was getting harder and harder to breath in the insolated boxcar. The oxygen supply was disappearing. Besides that, there were no more candles to burn, which left Jesse and Carl in the dark. Jesse was starting to hallucinate.

"You have to be strong, little brother," Carl whispered as he was gasping for air. "Don't give up yet. Someone will be here soon. I can feel it."

2 Days Later

The stench and smell of death was overwhelming for the railroad security guard who came by to check out the abandoned G train. He opened the boxcar and found Jesse and the dead body of the armless man in the back of the boxcar. It made him sick to his stomach, and he puked his guts out as soon as the rotting smell of the excrement and the dead body filled his nostrils.

Heat exhaustion and suffocation was the cause of Carl's death. The police investigation reported the temperature inside the boxcar was a hundred and twenty degrees. The medics said Jesse was lucky to be alive.

He was taken to the county hospital just outside San Antonio, Texas. His mind was traumatized, and he just lay in his bed for several weeks recuperating. He never talked to anyone. From time to time, he would wake up dripping in sweat screaming. The sedatives helped, but Jesse's nightmares were disturbing. He dearly missed his friend Carl. Besides Jordan, he was the closest friend that Jesse had ever had. Jesse was sure that he would not be alive if it wasn't for Carl's constant pep talks that things would be okay soon.

Every day they clanged the walls of the boxcar hoping someone would hear them. They didn't realize that their boxcar was dropped off at a closed-down train yard out in the middle of Texas. The boxcar was left there to load the last bit of remaining equipment at the train yard. There was no deadline on when the work was to be completed. Luckily a security guard was on his rounds and came by.

What really gave Jesse the will to keep on living was when Carl finally told him about surviving in Vietnam. Carl never liked talking about it before, but he knew the importance of giving his young friend hope. He talked about his MOS (military occupational specialty), which was a very dangerous job crawling into tunnels looking for Viet Cong. The Cong operated out of underground tunnels. That was how they survived all the aerial attacks. Carl talked about having both of his arms blown off by an explosive device that exploded when he was crawling headfirst into a tunnel. He was in shock and constant pain. A fellow tunnel rat named Sergeant Murphy pulled him out of the tunnel and stayed by his side until help arrived. Sergeant Murphy wouldn't let Carl give up. Carl said he would have given up if it weren't for Murphy's constant support.

So Jesse thought to himself, "Thank you, brother. I will never forget you."

CHAPTER 120

IN THE MONTH of March in 1998, Jordan's travels brought him to the outskirts of Austin, Texas. He had heard that Austin was a good place to land from his FTRA friends on the road.

There was a big music event called South by Southwest going on when he arrived. Several up-and-coming rock bands from all the major record labels were performing at the bars on Sixth Street. There were also stages set up at several locations on the streets where the indie bands performed for free. It was quite the party. The revelers in the streets who were enjoying the free music were a mixture of old hippies, tramps, and young college kids. Jordan was amazed how easily he fit in. Bottles of booze and joints were passed around freely in the crowd. Jordan was really enjoying himself. He had a good buzz going on. An older female hippie named Cindy, with long blond hair, huge breasts, and a nice round rump, took a liking to Jordan. After the bands quit playing, she invited him over to her house and made him a delicious home-cooked meal, which included a rib eye steak, baked potato, and vegetables. He was able to take a shower too, which he badly needed. She washed his clothes. To finish off the night, Cindy treated Jordan to an evening of the best sex that he had ever experienced. Jordan was in heaven.

Cindy smiled and teased him about how much better it was for him to be with her than to be sleeping on the ground fighting off the fire ants.

The next morning Cindy fixed him breakfast, and they went back to Sixth Street to the festival. Cindy said goodbye to Jordan and hooked up with someone else. He smiled and went his own way. He worked his way up to the front of the stage at the north end of Sixth Street. A three-piece reggae band consisting of two Jamaicans in dreadlocks and a long, dark-haired white singer were singing a ska version of "A Hard Day's Night." The crowd was grooving to the music swaying back and forth.

Jordan looked over to the right of the stage in disbelief. Standing there dancing with his arms up in the air was his friend Jesse.

He fought through the crowd, but by the time he got there, Jesse was gone. He looked around the large crowd trying to spot his road dog. He was nowhere to be found. Jordan was beginning to think that maybe he was imagening everything and had mistaken someone else for Jesse. The crowd thinned out after the band played their last song. Jordan looked over behind the stage and saw the same person he thought was Jesse helping to unload the equipment off the stage. Jordan walked up to the back of the stage and to get a closer look. The fella had his back turned to Jordan. He walked up to him and tapped him on the back. The kid turned around.

Jordan was disappointed. "Hey, dude. I am sorry. I thought you were someone that I knew." He turned and walked away. "What the fuck," He thought to himself. He walked across the street and took a seat on a bench. He was starting to get hungry and wondering where he was going to sleep for the night. His friend Cindy told him that there was a homeless shelter a few blocks down the street from her place. He decided that he would go there and see if he could have a meal and secure a bunk for the night. Thinking about having fire ants crawling all over him gave him the creeps. The shelter was full, but he was allowed to eat dinner in the soup kitchen. He hooked up with a couple of Flintstone kids who said that he could come to their camp and spend the night.

When he got there, a huge party was going on. There were a mixture of upper crusties and regular street kids, smoking dope and passing space bags around. Music was blasting from a crack box. Jordan made himself at home underneath a tree close to a stream. He cleared the area out of sagebrush, made sure that there were no fire ants, and spread his sleeping bag out. He wasn't in much of a mood to party with upper crusties. He thanked his new friends for allowing him to stay and went to sleep. It was very hard to get to sleep with all the yelling and screaming going on.

From time to time, Jordan swore that he could hear Jesse's laugh in the crowd. A couple of times he thought about getting up and checking it out. Eventually, he fell asleep after the noise died down.

Later in the evening, Jordan was startled awake by the sound of coyotes howling at the full moon. They sounded like they were very close to where he was camped. He reached in his backpack and pulled out his smiley. From then on, it was hard for him to fall back asleep. It scared the shit out of him imagening being torn apart by a pack of vicious animals. He eventually settled down and fell back asleep.

The next day, he was greeted to a beautiful Texas morning with the birds chirping and the sound of running water from the stream that was twenty-five yards away from the campsite. He got up, stretched his arms, and walked down to the stream to wash his face. As he got closer, he noticed a body lying facedown in the water. His heart was racing as he ran as fast as he could to get to the body. He pulled the body out of the water and turned him over on his back. It was Jesse.

"Oh my god!" Jordan got down on his knees and opened Jesse's mouth and performed CPR on him. He pushed hard on his chest breathed air down his throat. He wasn't sure if he was doing it right, but he kept at it. There was still no breathing. Jesse was blue in the face and stiff as a board.

"Come on, brother. Don't you fucking die on me. Your road dog's here!" Jordan yelled. He opened Jesse's mouth and breathed air into his lungs again. There was still no change. He turned him over and pounded on his back.

"Come on, Jesse! Come on, dude!"

All of a sudden, Jesse started coughing up water from his lungs.

"Fuck yeah!" Jordan screamed. He turned Jesse over on his back. He had a big shit-eating grin on his face.

It was an emotional reunion. They hugged each and didn't let go for several minutes.

"I almost fucking died, man. Son of a bitch!"

Jesse talked about how heavy he was drinking during the day. He didn't remember much after that. Jordan asked him if he was downtown listening to the music. Jesse said that he didn't recall and for sure he had no recollection of how he ended up face-first in the water.

Jordan and Jesse spent the rest of the day catching up on things. Jesse talked about his travels across the country, about his friend Carl, and about almost smothering to death being locked inside a boxcar.

"Bags warned you about that, remember?"

"Yeah, I know, and I remember him telling me that I always had to learn the hard way."

"You're a cat with nine lives and have seven left."

Jordan talked about going home and how awful that was for him. He boasted about hooking up with some of the members of the FTRA. He proudly showed off his new bandanna that all the members took turns pissing on to honor and show their respect for him.

They were thrilled to be back together again. Over the next several years, they traveled the country riding trains. They accomplished their goal of celebrating New Year's Eve on Times Square in New York City. They were just a couple of blocks away when the Twin Towers were attacked. They had learned and experienced a lot.

Jordan and Jesse were true brothers vowing to always be together. That all changed when Shadow came back in the picture. She was traveling with Bolt again. She was still pulling tricks and using hard drugs. Jordan was on a street corner in the Bronx in an Italian neighborhood panhandling when he ran into Bolt and Shadow walking across the street. Shadow was excited to see Jordan again. Jordan could see the fierce look in Bolt's eyes as he hissed at him and wasted no time pushing Shadow to move along. She nodded back with two winks, which was an old Indian prearranged sign conveying information that Shadow had taught Jordan back in New Mexico indicating that she would meet him back on that street corner at two tomorrow. Jordan scratched his left ear, signaling that he understood her message.

Bolt slapped Shadow, warning her to stay away from Jordan or he would kill him. She sneaked away early in the day when Bolt was still sleeping after a long night of heavy drinking.

Jordan was angry when he saw the bruises on Shadow's face. He hugged her and told her that she didn't have to be with that mutant ever again. Shadow felt safe in Jordan's arms.

"So you know Bolt has a target on his back. The FTRA is looking for his ass."

"He swore that he had nothing to do with Bags's death."

"He's a liar." Jesse was not happy to see Shadow again. "So where is my fucking guitar?"

"It fell off the train and broke into pieces just outside of Omaha. Sorry, dude."

He knew that was crock of shit and that she probably pawned it.

"So does that freak still have his two thugs with him?" Jordan asked.

"Rat is still with him. They kicked Blake off a train outside of Boise. He fell and cracked his head."

"What about his pit bull?"

"Savage never recovered after the fight with the captain."

"And he forgave you for hurting his dog?" Jesse asked. "I get it now. You blamed Jordan."

"That's enough. Shit happens, remember?" Jordan piped in.

Jesse knew his friendship with Jordan was already changing and would only get worse as soon as she started spreading her legs.

Jesse wasted no time. The very next day he was gone without saying a word. Jordan was upset to lose his friend, but he understood the reason he was gone.

* * *

Shadow convinced Jordan to leave town with her and head south to Tulsa, where her brother and tribe were. She was afraid that Bolt would come after her.

It had been several years since she had been back to the reservation. She was pretty sure that they would be safe there and was looking forward to seeing her brother, Charlie Little Hawk.

At first, it turned out to be a good decision. Even though he was white, Shadow's tribe was very accepting and willing to let them live on the reservation.

Jordan was impressed with the spirit and the traditions of the Indian people. The elders had not lost their respect and appreciation for the earth as it was intended to be. They still worshipped the sunrise, the birds, the water, and the moon. Shadow's generation had tarnished the strength and heritage of the old Indian ways. The infection of the undisciplined society that surrounded the reservation had poisoned the youth, who no longer supported the spiritual beliefs. Shadow's brother, Charlie Little Hawk, was not influenced by the temptation of the outside world. He believed in the old ways.

Alcohol was still the only demon of the tribe, and they liked their whiskey. Charlie Little Hawk was a different person when he was intoxicated. He was mean-spirited and was always ready for a fight. Everyone on the reservation stayed away from him when he was drinking.

However, for some reason, Jordan was able to get along with Charlie when he was mean-spirited. His jokes seemed to help calm Charlie down. The village was astonished. The elders thought it was a gift from the spirits.

Jordan and Charlie became good friends. They spent a lot of time together. They went up into the hills and slung rocks. Jordan was getting pretty good at it. His aim was still not as good as Charlie was. They enjoyed listening to music together, especially when they were drunk. Judas Priest, Black Sabbath, and the Misfits were their favorites.

Shadow was a completely different person back on the reservation. With the help from Choco, the tribe medicine man, she was able to go cold turkey and stopped using drugs. It was an amazing transformation to witness. She was isolated in a tepee that was set up in the ancient burial grounds. The first week was torture sweating the poison out of her veins. To help with the illucinations and muscle cramps, Choco gave her herbs that he had gathered from the hills. He would chant and dance around a fire praying to the spirits. Three weeks later she was completely sober, although she still had the urge to get high.

She was pleased that the tribe accepted Jordan, and she was especially happy that her brother liked him.

Jordan was able to find a job washing dishes at Andy's Restaurant in downtown Tulsa. He was a hard worker and a fast learner. The owner, Andy Rollins, took him under his wing and taught him how to cook. Jordan eventually became the head chef on the late shift. He was very proud of his accomplishment. He called his father out of the blue and told him the good news. In the past, he would call at all odd hours of the day and leave messages for his father. He was usually drunk and feeling sorry for himself. He would always apologize for being a bad son and running away.

"I am so proud of you, son. Keep up the good work, and we hope to see you soon," Jimmy Summers said.

Andy set Jordan up with an apartment at a building that he owned that was located across the street from the restaurant. He charged him half rent to live there. Jordan got himself a beautiful black cat from the humane society. It was his first animal that he owned by himself. He named her Lovely Rita. He adored her and took really good care of her.

A few months, later Shadow moved in with him. That turned out to be a bad idea. The influence of the outside world was not good for her. She started using drugs again, which caused things to spiral down for Jordan. He started drinking and using again. (And we know what happened after that.)

CHAPTER 121

Back to the Present day

JORDAN WAS NOT aware that someone was about to drive a knife into his back. He was focused on getting to the airport on time and heading home. He heard footsteps of someone running and getting close to him. He turned around just in time to see Rat attacking him from behind. Jordan could see the knife in the air. He put his arms up to protect himself.

Suddenly a rock whizzed by Jordan's head and nailed Rat right between the eyes. He dropped the knife and fell, smashing his head on the pavement. Another rock followed immediately with amazing accuracy and hit its target again.

Bolt came out from across the street screaming. "Shadow! You fucking bitch! I am going to kill you. You hear me? Do you—"

Before he could end his sentence, Bolt was batted on the back of his head with a blunt instrument. Blood spilled out of his head as he tumbled to the ground. He tried to get up as the person who attacked him grabbed him by the throat.

"That's for Bags, you freak, and this is for Jordan." The cane came down swiftly and cracked his skull. The man dragged Bolt back into the alley and laid him next to the garbage can. He walked over to Jordan.

"Hey, Captain." Jordan smiled. "Wow! Heavy shit there."

"Hey, son, it's nice to see you again. Are you okay?"

"Wow! I can't believe it!"

"You think?" Captain Cooper smiled. "I told you that we had our own ways of handling things."

"Thank you, man. I owe you."

"No, son. That's the way of the FTRA. We take care of our friends. Hey, by the way, you have your friend to thank too." He pointed to the roof on top of the apartment building.

Jordan squinted with his bad eyes. He recognized his blood brother, Charlie Little Hawk, waving at him.

Charlie Little Hawk climbed off the roof and joined the captain and Jordan.

"Wow! Brother!" Jordan hugged his friend. "How did you know?"

"It was the weirdest thing. I was walking down the street heading back to the reservation, and I ran into Captain Cooper. We started talking, and somehow your name came up. Wild, huh? He told me that he had trailed Bolt to Tulsa."

They watched Rat slither off down the street.

"Go crawl off in a gutter, you piece of shit!" Charlie screamed.

As they walked down the street, Nathan told Jordan about River.

"Shit! A lot of death in this world. River sure liked you, Captain."

"Yeah, she was special. I am glad that I got to meet her."

With great joy, Jordan hugged his friends goodbye and headed home. During his travels, he had experienced and learned a lot. He would never forget the friends he made along the way.

GLOSSARY OF TERMS

bull / railroad bull. Railroad police patrol train yards looking to bust train riders. Street kids hide and avoid the bulls at all costs. Bulls have more authority than regular police and can take street kids to jail for just walking on the tracks. You can spot them by the white SUV they drive.

boot party (boot stomp). Boot party is when a group of people decide to stomp on a helpless person with their shoes. This action can be fatal.

catch on the fly. To hop on a train while it is moving. This is extremely dangerous, especially with a dog. People lose their legs, arms, and sometimes their life.

CCR. Stands for "choo choo riders." It is a small group that consists of stuck-up street kids.

church key. A flat thin piece of metal with a sharp-curbed end. This can be used to open a bottle or make carb holes on a beer to make drinking faster and smoother.

crack box. Is a radio and tape/CD player that is battery powered.

crew change. Is a spot, a lot of times in a train yard, but sometimes not where a train stops to change crews.

butt flap. Is a cloth or leather flap that hangs from the beltline in the front or back to prevent holes from forming in pants from sitting on the ground or concrete.

dinger. A railroad crossing you pass while riding a train. The bell makes a dinging sound, which is a good warning telling you to get down and hide from the idling cars waiting at the crossing.

ditch watch. A person left behind at camp to watch over everyone's backpacks. They are rewarded with smokes and booze when everyone returns.

drop-in center. A government or privately funded center specifically for street kids in need. Most of the time, they provide food, clothing, sometimes they have packs, sleeping bags, tools, and a needle exchange. Only big cities or places that have a lot of street kids have these facilities.

dumped. The front units of your train are disconnected and you're stuck wherever you are left. Sometimes they come back and sometimes they don't.

elfting. There is a universal rule for people in the drinking circle. Never pass out with your shoes on! If that takes place, you are fair game to anyone. You can do whatever you like to someone while they are passed out. The most common thing to do is to take a marker and write on their face and body. Some kids are more twisted and imaginative. It's not out of line to sew the kid's clothing together or attach the kid to whatever they are passed out on, for example, a chair.

FTRA. Stands for "Freight Train Riders of America." It is a gang that consists of mainly older tramps. The gang is well-known for being brutal and trifling. In order to be initiated into the organization, an FTRA member or in most cases several members will take your rag, place it on a railroad track, and take turns pissing on it. Then the one being initiated must wear the piss-soaked rag until it dries.

feeding. A soup kitchen where you can get a free meal. Sometimes the food is good.

five up. Means "Stop what you're doing. The railroad bulls are coming."

Flintstone kids. Nickname the old hobos came up with for young street kids because of the striking resemblance street kids have to cave men.

freddy. Street kid knows this as a red light that blinks on the end of the train. If a train has a freddy, that means it is leaving soon.

gear/backpack. It is everything a traveler owns, including sleeping bag, cooking tools, other tools.

home bum. An older homeless person who does not travel. These people are great to ask for information about a town, feedings, good panhandle spots, or just fun to drink with, and they always know where to sleep.

home guard. Someone who has been in the same town whether or not they are from there.

hoofing it. Having to walk a long distance.

hop-out spot. A hidden place usually in a jungle where tramps can safely hop out and not be seen.

hop out catch out. To get on a train going your direction.

hotshots. High-priority trains usually loaded with 48s, 52s, and flatbeds. Hotshots usually travel long distances and are in a hurry. There aren't many cars to ride. You can ride a 48 if it has a bucket on the floor, and also flatbeds. Flatbeds are usually loaded with semi trailers. You are in plain sight, so you have to hide in between the semi trailer wheels.

hump yard. A hump yard is a place in the train yard where the railroad workers will individually disconnect the cars and send them rolling alone down a hill until it crashes very hard into a standing car. Can be very dangerous if you are inside one of the cars. You have to hold on for dear life.

jungle. Any hidden place with lots of bushes and trees.

junk train. Low-priority train usually loaded with boxcars, grainers, gondolas, and tankers. Junk trains aren't going far, but it is easy to hide from the bulls and other people on them.

kickdown. Something someone gave you for free. It could be money, food, or drugs. Travelers all love the twenty-dollar kickdown.

nodded out. To be high as hell on drugs.

oogle. Weekend street kid. They are really fresh or dumb on the street. They are usually very obnoxious. When times get tough, they run home to Mommy. Traveling kids dislike oogles.

panhandle. Begging for money. Flying a sign works the best, but in some cities you have to panhandle.

patch. On the road, you need to repair your clothes with leather or other strong material. Regular thread is too weak, ao travelers sow with dental floss.

piggybacks. Flatbeds with semi trailers on them. You must hide between the semi wheels to stay hidden. Even then, it is easy to be spotted.

P38. A very small army-issue can opener.

railroad worker. They don't work with the railroad bulls. You can walk right up to them and ask about which trains are leaving. Most of the time they are very helpful.

rag. A bandanna used for when you are riding a train and go through a tunnel. You must wet your bandanna with water and cover your nose and always breath slowly. Never hop a train without one. It also keeps you warm when you wear it on your face. Only tramps know the importance and symbolism of a rag. Hobos can tell your miles by the condition of your rag. It can distinguish your rank on the road. The longer you have traveled, the more respect you will get from other riders.

rig (works, clean, dirty, point, needle, hypo). All the different words for a hypodermic needle used for intravenous drug use.

road dog. Someone who you travel with and consider a very close friend. Most street kids would fight to the death for their road dog.

rollies. Cigarettes that you have to roll yourself.

rollie training wheels. This is an easy way to role smokes if you don't know how to. The lower corners of the papers are the hardest to learn to roll.

rubber tramping. Anyone who travels by car. The easiest way to travel.

shakes (DTs, dog sick, drying out, kicking). All the words for having withdrawal symptoms for alcohol and heroin. Both give you the shakes. *Kicking* is a word for heroin withdrawal, because when you are kicking dope, your nerves and muscles tighten up, and your legs uncontrollably and painfully kick.

side bag. It is another word for *purse*. It is a quick and easy way to store your belongings without having to dig through your backpack.

slave unit. Train engines at the very end of the train used for fully loaded trains climbing up a mountain. Conductors always leave this unit unlocked, so it is easy to ride and sit close to a nice warm engine.

smiley. It is a common weapon for a street kid. Can be made of many things. Its main design is a rope or chain with a heavy blunt object tied on the end. Most commonly a bandanna with a padlock tied on the end. Every street kid has had to use one at some point.

snipes. Cigarette butts on the ground that are big enough to smoke. Even if they have smokes, every traveling kid looks for them. (Waste not, want not.)

spike the door. When riding an open boxcar, there is a chance the train will jerk too hard, and the boxcar door will slam shut and lock you inside. So you have to spike the door with a railroad spike or anything you can jam in the sliding track. Very important unless you want to die of thirst in a locked boxcar.

squeeze one off. Since street kids live outside but are still human, they must find a very private, hidden place to go to the bathroom.

squat. abandoned building. A great place to get out of the elements.

squat candle. Homemade candle made by using chunks of wax, some paper, or cardboard melted in a tin can. Squat candles are a lot bigger and hotter than a normal candle. It produces more light and can be used for cooking.

squat key. A mini crow bar that you can snuggle in your gear. Used for breaking into abandoned buildings. Don't let the cops catch you with one.

squat mattress. Most of the time a female who is extremely easy to get into your sleeping bag. They are trouble and should be avoided.

swilly. To get drunk. Not used for drug intoxication.

tag. This is what you write on a wall or train to mark where you have been. Some riders will write down good information about train yards.

tailor-made. Factory-rolled cigarettes.

tall boys (40s, tall cans, half gallons, space bag, bum jug, snoopy special, Thunder chicken). All the different kind of things to drink on the road. Space bags is a cheap wine that comes in a big box. A bum jug is wine that comes in huge jugs. A snoopy special is half Cisco and half malt liquor. Thunder chicken is fortified wine called Thunderbird, and you add a pack of Kool-Aid to make it Thunder chicken. Gs is half gallons of hard liquor if a lot of people are drinking. It's the only way to go in a drinking circle. Swill is when you take a full swig and drink as much as you can without drinking twice and then pass it on. Ninety-five percent of traveling drunks like the same thing. It becomes quantity, not quality.

tax. When someone, most likely an enemy, takes what they want from you by force.

train cars. Boxcar, grainer, tanker, gondola, flatbed, lumber car, 48, 53, piggybacks, unit, slave unit, coal car, hazmat car.

train rider (dirty kid, street kid, squatter, gutter punk, traveling kids). Is what all street kids call each other.

tramp. They are an older street person. They are full of information and always fun to drink with.

tweaking, To be high on speed/meth/ice.

two-crew change. A pamphlet that contains written instructions and directions on how and where to hop a train. It was written by a hobo named Train Doc. A new one is made every year with updates.

two mile. A spot on the railroad tracks where lesser-priority trains stop to let higher-priority trains pass. It is a single track, and one train has to pull aside to let others through. Two miles are sets of tracks parallel with each other. This is a great place for street kids to hop out.

westbound. The direction a train or street kid is headed.

wing nut. Someone who would be considered crazy by normal people.

ABOUT THE AUTHOR

DANIEL COOK WAS born in Lovelock, a small town eighty miles out-side Reno, Nevada. He loved growing up in a small town, where you didn't have to lock the front door and you could safely play in your front yard without having your parents around. He has three kids and four grandchildren. He is a graduate from the University of Nevada. He had a thirty-six-year career in the radio broadcast business, which included being a general manager, program director, and on-air talent. He loved being on the air playing music for peo-ple. He is retired now and taking care of his granddaughter. He has always enjoyed making up stories. He dreamed one day of becoming a famous author. A while back, he was watching a feature on *CBS Sunday Morning* about successful authors. It said people his age in the seventies can be very successful writers because they have experi-enced life and can write about it. That feature inspired him to write this book.

CPSIA information can be obtained
at www.ICGtesting.com
Printed in the USA
BVHW031618300321
603710BV00002B/79